The Dragonfly Tide

S. C. MORAN

Copyright © 2022 S.C. Moran

Cover Image © 2021 Toby Adamson, used with permission.

All rights reserved.

ISBN: 9798416720735

For my brother, Michael

My dear friend Nicole,

You were here at the very beginning and here at the very end.

Thank you for everything my super talented friend!

Love always,
Steph xxx.

*"Time is for dragonflies and angels.
The former live too little and the latter live too long".*

– James Thurber

蜻蜓点水

– Chinese Proverb

Chapter One

She always knew she would die young. The day she found out she was pushing six years old with both feet and feeling old already. Her aunt opposite her pored over her palm, pushing the back of her hand up closer to her squinting eyes, her bottle-bottom glasses pushed up onto the top of her head magnifying her scalp. Jun Ching couldn't help but stare. A miniature black bamboo forest plagued by the white blanket of death – or dead skin at least. She clucked her tongue a number of times and finally, with a decisive nod, one large unique flake drifted from her head onto the girl's bare wrist. She had reached her conclusion.

"It's not good palm, girl, you will die young."

Jun Ching shook her wrist trying to dislodge the flake. She exhaled as hard as she could. It didn't budge.

"Your wealth line okay, not much but okay. Same with your fertility line, one, maybe two children, but with problems. But none of this matter because your life line, big problem, too thin." She etched out the curve of the line with a hard, grey thumbnail. "You see, it break here in middle, early, and carry on down here. This mean you have terrible accident or illness – if you don't die you may have not bad life but you probably die."

Another palm was thrust over her own.

"Can you read mine now, Auntie?" Her brother pushed himself between them. Square shoulders hid her view and replaced it with a swathe of shirt.

The aunt looked from one face to the other and dropped the little girl's palm taking up her brother's. Whilst the clucking began again, Jun Ching stared at the back of her brother, Jun Yee's, legs. Straight up and down, tanned with faint patches of pale where he hid the backs of his knees. His knees seemed almost to push backwards when he stood rigidly straight. She thought how good it was that she had noticed his knees then, because otherwise she may never have known before she died. And if she was going to die young, and she was already six, she was probably going to die soon. The thought of it landed in her stomach like an empty bucket on water at the bottom of a well. It filled up quickly until it was too heavy for her feeble arms to pull it back out again. She put four fingers into the back pocket of her brother's shorts for comfort and wondered what else she wouldn't notice before she died.

"Okay, not bad palm. Better than your sister's. You don't die too young."

But before the aunt could finish curling her first wispy prediction around her waggling fingers, he pulled his palm away.

"Actually sorry, Gwai Kam Mo. I think I would prefer the surprise."

Late that afternoon he slipped his sister past the clattering mahjong game and out of the door without anyone noticing. They walked silently to a small square with a very old and heavily laden tree in the middle - a wishing tree. It was empty, too early for the evening rush of girls on their way home in groups, giggling and twisting their double pigtails round their fingers. Jun Yee walked over to a tiny old man, emptying his pockets as he went and counted the contents out into two little piles. He handed the old man the smaller pile and took a small piece of red and pink crepe paper with a string tied to it. He fished a stubby pencil out from a pocket and started writing. Jun Ching edged round him to see what he was writing, but though she could barely read he hid it from her anyway.

When he was finished, he licked the corners and stuck them in on themselves, pressing down hard with the fleshy bottom of his fist as if the harder he pressed the less likely the secret inside would get out. He picked a stone up from the ground and wrapped the string attached to the paper around it several times in different directions, tied a knot and stood up. Walking round and round the tree, he assessed the branches – the lower ones were heavily laden with other peoples' wishes, big clumps of them bunched up together. The middle branches were more attractive with fewer burdens, but the uppermost branches were the ideal, sparsely populated but surely a wish up there would come true easier and faster. He chose a spot and weighed the stone up and down in his hand.

Jun Ching watched her brother in awe. The summer stain on his skin and twitching muscles made him look strong and restless. He threw the stone. It flew through the air with its trailing paper like a drunken bird, the corners of his wishes flapping before crashing back down to the dirt ground. It took a long time but when it finally did it catch, it was right at the top, a branch higher than everyone else's. The gods would see it first, she thought, and surely would grant it first.

As they walked away, the tiny old man's even tinier eyes followed them, a little girl with her hand in her brother's back pocket, trailing behind him.

Chapter Two

Jun Ching balanced on her haunches again, washing rice and day-dreaming. Her skin felt tacky in the heat. Everything felt slightly damp to the touch. She wondered if there were places less hot than Hong Kong, less crowded, not pushing to get in. She rubbed the hard little grains between her fingers. Rub, stir and swish. Rub, stir and swish. The water grew cloudy with starch and she let it trickle through her fingers making sure the grains didn't escape with it. The staccato sound of oil crackling in a hot wok bounced into the room. The landlady has started cooking, she thought, the Li sisters were next then it would be their turn. She hurried into the kitchen to start the rice cooking, turning inedible *mai* into delicious *faan*, the smell of it rich and musty. The landlady sucked her teeth at her as she squeezed past. An odd-looking woman, like she used to be bigger, but her bones had shrunk and not her skin, so now she was small with skin that didn't fit properly.

Back in their own little room, Jun Ching tucked her feet up under her on the bottom bunk of the bed.

"What? Bream again? We had bream last night and the night before that!"

"We did not, the night before we had crab! You do the shopping then if you so picky!"

The Li sisters' voices squeezed through the gaps in the wood panelled walls. She liked having them there it made her feel less lonely. And by the time they were quiet, Missy would be home on the other side playing her radio and they didn't have a radio. She laid down and dangled her legs over the edge till her feet touched the floor for a while. There was nothing to do until Jun Yee got home.

Jun Yee's hand hadn't left the handle to their own door when his sister almost knocked him over with excitement. She was often like this when she was left on her own all day - that was one of the reasons he missed so much school. He should take her out now, but he was tired and wary after the last time he lost her.

The last time she had stopped without a word to watch an old man stretching red paper into animal lanterns. Jun Ching was so easily distracted. The rest of the street had faded into shades of grey whilst the red paper gleamed and shone and before she knew it her hand was groping in the air for a brother who was no longer there. He was frantic, as he was every time she did this, whilst she just sat on the ground and cried loudly, confident that he would come back for her. It didn't take long to find her as he retraced their steps and soon heard her wailing. Breaking into the small human circle surrounding her, he found the lantern maker rubbing his bald head, unable to concentrate on his work and staring at the source of the wailing.

"Brother. Bro-ther. Bro-ther-er-er."

Swollen tears rolled down her cheeks, he hurried over, shook her gently by the shoulder and the wailing stopped abruptly. Not another squeak, she didn't even finish the one she was in the middle of. Having looked up to make sure it was him she dragged her sleeve across her eyes as she stood up, put two fingers in her mouth and the other fingers into his back pocket and the pair walked away, leaving a speechless crowd with ears ringing. After that, he found a long piece of string and from then on tied it round her waist and his when they went out so that it couldn't happen again. He flicked the string now hanging down from where it was tied at the end of his bunk.

He decided against going out. She was fine now that he was home. He sat down with his sketchbook turning it upside down looking for some space to draw in. He would have to start a clean page soon. This one was looking like chaos bursting to get off the page. He was careful to use every last inch. This book was a luxury, a present from Ma last birthday with a couple of pencils.

"Don't touch…", Jun Ching's eyes had crept over to the pencils. These were the only things of his she wasn't allowed to share. She clambered up to the table, her chin on one hand the other walking a grass figure across the surface murmuring a conversation under her breath.

"*Wah*, so bored you two look. Where's your ma?" Missy had appeared at their door.

"Working." Jun Yee replied.

"What a pity, working again. It's hard to make a living in Hong Kong. What are you two doing?"

"Nothing, playing. Waiting for Ma to come home."

"Did she say what time she will be back?"

"No."

"Well then," Missy paused, "Do you want to come out with me? I am going with a few friends for tea."

"No, thank you Missy, we are fine here." Jun Yee said as his sister's face lit up and fell just as quickly behind his back. Seeing Missy's eyes flick to his sister behind him he turned to see her making no effort to hide her disappointment.

"Are you sure? It's no trouble. You would be keeping me company."

"We're sure. Thank you. Say thank you, Ching Ching."

"No, thank you, Missy." Came the murmur behind him.

"Okay then, you change your mind, come and find me. In 10 minutes I go out the door." She turned and left.

Jun Yee faced his sister, or the top of her head as she looked at the ground, more despondent than a puppy with its tail between its legs and he knew already he would not be able to bear it. He sighed and she looked up at him. So, he sighed again but could not keep the smile from him lips.

"Come on then." He nudged her shoulder as he slipped past. "Let's go down to the pier. As long as you promise to do what I say!"

"Promise! Promise!" She had the string in her hand for him before she had even finished promising.

It was late in the day and the heat still baked the streets into shimmering pools of dirt and dust. The pier felt more of a risk to Jun Yee, it was further away, Jun Ching would not know her way back if she did get lost though she had never tried to find her way back even when she was one street away. She was not only tied to his waist, but he kept a fierce grip on her hand, pressing her knuckles together in a not unpleasant way. The pier was one of the less busy ones, without the grand arches of Queens Pier or the business of Kowloon. This one was tucked further along the waterfront where the *sai pan* boats bobbed from the passing traffic out in the harbour, gentle by the time the waves reached them. Here boys jumped to coat their bodies in the glistening water, to bob like the boats, to shout and to laugh, to press each other down into the water, standing on shoulders, hair plastered down in jagged teeth across their foreheads. They shouted to Jun Yee to join them so rarely did they see him here, but he shook his head, and they all knew why. The siblings sat a few feet from the edge and felt the noise of the water, the shouting, the laughter and even the gentle wooden chimes of the hulls of the boats knocking against each other in a row. A rhythm that burrowed into their skin and sat there, pulsing, waiting.

"Go in, Brother, I don't mind. I promise not to move anywhere." Jun Yee pulled his eyebrows up at her, unconvinced. "I promise! I won't even go close to the edge. You can tie me to the giant mushroom right here."

She pointed to the bollard that the boatmen tied their ropes round. She grinned up at him and it was too tempting to refuse. He secured her to the pier first then stripped down to his shorts, leaving them in a neat pile next to her to look after. She watched as he jumped in. Body stretched out, lean, slapping the water with his hands as he went in splashing it up high enough to throw salty drops over her skirt sticking the fabric to her crossed legs. His head broke the surface again. He ran his hand over his head pushing his hair out of his eyes and into awkward curling peaks on the top of his head. Then he was gone, as boy upon boy seemed to jump in on each other with him somewhere inside. Jun Ching loved to see how the boys played together, how freely they threw themselves on and off each other like they were connected, different limbs to the same body. Laughter was a different pitch here. Then, out to the side, Jun Yee popped up again. Jun Ching laughed, delighted. She could see his outline just beneath the surface pulling in long strong strokes out from under his friends, before they even noticed. A few kicks and he was out of reach. Her toes curled out of her flip flops as she shouted every sound that came into her head though they barely made sense at all. He stood out in sharp focus amongst the blur of boys. Her brother, more familiar to her than even herself in some ways. She didn't need to know herself, she was already there, but she needed to see him. He was apart, a fluid strength that flashed like liquid silver.

The light glinted lower and lower like broken pieces of glass on the tips of waves as the sun dipped. Younger children came to shout *Ma says come home*, the words fishing out a boy or two each time. A couple pulled themselves onto the closest boat and skipped across the prows till they arrived at their own. With no one to come calling them, Jun Yee and Jun Ching were in the last handful to go. Their ma never was by the water's edge to call to them back before the rice gets cold. By the time Jun Yee pulled himself out of the water the only boys left were those who nodded an understanding to each other of no home to go to that night, perhaps not much to put in their bellies, perhaps a night of being watchful not resting. And Jun Yee felt grateful to pull his sister up, tie her to him again and go back to their small, empty room.

Their ma, Sum, worked long hours as a factory seamstress from early till late and sometimes through the night. They were paid per item they finished and more for intricate patterns. So, Sum worked as long as she could and on the most complicated designs, straining her eyes till they were tired and bloodshot. One night, when her eyes were particularly tired, she laid down early to sleep. Jun Yee sat watching her. Jun Ching sat watching him, twitching her toes, crossing and uncrossing her legs, looking to her sleeping ma then to her brother then back again trying to see what he was seeing. Jun Yee got up and walked out, she followed and watched as he went to the landlady who was sitting in the main room listening to the radio and asked her if he could work in her shop downstairs.

"What would you do?"

"Anything you need me to do, I could sweep the floors or move things or polish the apples before you put them in the paper to sell."

"I don't need anything doing, I can do it myself. I'm not that old yet." She narrowed her eyes at him, lips curled into a small sneer on one side, "I'm not paying you to do something I can do myself."

"*Aiy,* ah Ma, the boy is right, you should be sitting like the big boss at the front of the shop," her son was listening from behind his newspaper. He dropped one corner, looked at Jun Ching hovering at the doorway and winked. "How much could a boy like him cost anyway? Five cents a week? Ten? It's nothing."

"What about her?" She jerked her head towards Jun Ching.

"She's staying with me." Jun Yee said without breaking gaze with Landlady.

"Tch. She'll get in the way."

"Ah Ma, women like cute children, if she sits near the front of the shop, she will attract more women to the shop and the more they come the more they buy – it will improve business. The extra money you make with her and your talent for selling will be much more than you will have to pay the boy."

"But look at her, with her pale, sallow face, people would lose their appetite just looking at her."

"I wouldn't say it like that, she might look a bit unusual but she's definitely cute. You've seen how the people around here are with her. They'll come round more if she's there. Think about it Ah Ma."

"*Aiyah,* I'll think about it then. Now go away."

Jun Yee thanked her and walked back to their room. Jun Ching stayed peeping round the door until the paper dropped; he winked at her again and chuckled to himself, wobbling his belly like tofu. When she got back to the room, Jun Yee was already up on his bunk reading his comic with his legs crossed in the air.

Their ma didn't know, they didn't tell her and neither did Tofu-belly it seemed. Jun Yee didn't tell his sister why he did it or how long he would do it for, she just followed him when he went where she sat perched on a stool at the front of the shop, smiling at passing women. In the background, Jun Yee swept the floors, threw away empty boxes or refilled shelves and, just as he promised, even polished apples until they were shiny. In the meantime, Landlady busied herself clipping packets of sweets and dried cuttlefish to clothes hangers with pegs, like tiny underwear for people to choose, picking at her toenails and examining whatever she found.

It took only a week before Landlady left five cents on the table for them without a word. That day they searched their cupboard for the biggest bowl they had and walked the lines of street hawkers, smelling the food, pushing their shoulders through crowds. Jun Ching's fingers twanged absentmindedly at the string between them and he kept his fingers wrapped tightly around the coin in his palm, the bowl wedged securely under the other armpit.

They looked up and down the street twice before they heard the sweet tofu man with his singsong '*dow fu faaa-aaa*', his bicycle and great metal vats, one in front and one behind on wooden platforms strapped down, each filled with fresh tofu. He knew Jun Yee and Jun Ching's faces though they didn't buy much from him. They were easy to remember faces, pale, odd, standing out in this crowd whereas his was so brown from the sun that his face looked like it had been marinating in soy sauce. His teeth dazzled in stark contrast when he smiled at them.

"*Wah*! Big-ear Boy – your ears seem to get bigger every time I see you! How can that be?!" He gave the left one a little tug to prove it.

"Yes, big enough so I can hear you coming nine streets away!" Jun Yee waggled his ears at him as he handed over the bowl. "Could we have a bowl of sweet tofu please?"

"Of course, and how is the little pretty one?" He winked at her. "And your ma? She's good?"

"She is good. Brother just got some money from sweeping the floors, now we're buying her sweet tofu – it's her favourite, she will be very happy tonight!"

She talked too fast and the tofu man stopped for a little moment as he skimmed tofu off the top of the vat with a metal shell-shaped scraper, the bowl was half full.

"Mmmm, well, in that case, we'd need to make sure the tofu is just right for her, do you agree? And I am not sure the tofu tastes very good today." Jun Yee's face fell. "Yes, I think there might be something wrong with this vat. You two are tofu experts... Help me taste this and tell me if you think it's bad." He handed the bowl back to them, pouring a little ginger syrup over the top, with a spoon. They tried it dubiously.

"No, there's nothing wrong, Tofu Suk, it's delicious."

"Are you sure? I'm not so sure, you'd better try a bit more." And they did.

"Go on, a little more." And they did.

"You haven't checked the stuff at the bottom yet, could be different you know?" And they did.

It wasn't till they had had the entire bowl that he was satisfied they were telling him the truth. They left him with full bellies and a full bowl trying hard not to spill any as they went back upstairs. He left them with a nod of his hatted head and an extra loud '*dow fu faaa-aaa*'.

That night it seemed the longest they had ever waited for Sum to get home. They had the bowl of tofu ready on the table with a clean spoon on the right-hand side, taking turns to sit next to it waving flies away. Finally, Jun Yee saw her from the window, and they scurried round the room not knowing what to do with themselves. She wafted in, looking like the day had worn a little more of her away. She reached for them each in turn, cupping their chins in both her hands looking into their eyes then kissed the tops of their heads. But tonight, her kisses seemed to bounce as her children were hopping from foot to foot like grasshoppers.

She had every last bit of tofu in that bowl. They refused to share any and after it was gone, they nestled in with their heads in her lap. Sum ran her fingers through Jun Ching's hair, not much lighter than her own, brown touching black but just as silky straight, it tumbled back down out of her hand. Jun Ching inhaled the faint scent of sandalwood soap on her hands as she told them about the first time she met their father – a story had Jun Ching asked for so many times that it even sounded brown and dog-eared round the edges.

The story started as it always did and Jun Ching could repeat it, nearly word for word. Sum was only young when she came to Hong Kong, 20 years old, but she was a country girl, 20 there was even younger than 20 here. Jun Ching could see her ma in her head now, younger meant smaller to her so Sum was the same, just with bigger eyes and slightly shorter. She made up 'memories' of her ma coming looking for work when her father died as there was nothing to do in her village except fish, work in the field or get married. But there was no one for Ma to marry, she had to wait to meet their father of course. Ma had eight brothers and sisters all younger, though a few had died already, and Jun Ching pictured these as withered leaves on the stalks of flowers. "We had more mouths than we had rice to fill them with...".

Empty bowls filled her head and children tapping chopsticks on the sides of them. They had all thought that if Sum came to Hong Kong she would make lots of money, that lots of people did and would send money back to the village and build big, new houses for their mothers and fathers or buy their own land to farm. But Jun Ching had no image for all this money. Money was coins counted in a palm or thin notes folded under a shelf lining paper to be pulled out once a week for Landlady.

Ma's ma, their Paw Paw, had decided Sum should come but with a warning it seemed, that she needed to be stronger, that her skin wasn't thick enough to stand up to the people she would meet, that if she didn't toughen up or couldn't find money, she would ask the local matchmaker to find a match for her. This part Jun Ching struggled to remember. She couldn't understand how skin should be thick - like the skin on your feet maybe? But who would want that all over? Her ma wasn't like that - she was smooth, and soft and everything that was not like the cracked white skin of people's feet.

She had come by boat in the dark, a little wooden boat drawn with plastic sheeting over the top for the rain to run off. Their Paw Paw had given her the money for her fare, but she was so scared the boatman would cheat her that she wouldn't give him the money until she was on the boat and in her seat. That wasn't all there was to be afraid of either and Sum was very careful about this. She was scared of the water, always had been. The boat was small, it rocked and sank lower and lower in the water with each person that got on. Sum's seat was on the very edge, she didn't want to sit that close to the water, but the boatman just laughed and turned away. Jun Ching could bring her ma's words up like a little song, a little chorus to sing again and again "Water is very dangerous you know, you must always be very careful when you are near the water, promise me that?" Sum told them she had seen, so many times, the fishermen go out and come back with one man less at night and heard the women cry so hard they could not stop, the sound of their crying would hang in her ears for days.

There was one old lady in her village who sat every day on the beach staring at the sea, every day for over 40 years. She had married a handsome fisherman when she was very young but not long after he went out in his boat alone and when she went out that night to wait for him like she always did, he did not come home. And his boat did not come either. Every night after that, she went out to watch the sea, watching for him to come back but he never came. People tried to tell her he was not coming back, that he had drowned, but she did not stop waiting. She waited until the sun dried her beauty off her face and the youth off her hands and she went on waiting – she is probably waiting still. And that's how Jun Ching learnt that the sea had no heart. No heart that was not watery and cold and willing to take anything it wanted despite what you may need.

Sum spent all night scooping handfuls of water back over the side of the boat but the more she scooped the more seemed to slosh back in until they arrived at a quiet inlet in Hong Kong among the rocks. The sky was only half-light still and there were not many people. She had come with a scrap of paper with the name and address of a family friend but when she got there it was a factory not a shop and the people there had not heard of him. So, she found a way herself, found a room to share with two other girls in a crowded flat not too different from their own and found a job, lots of jobs doing different things all to start sending money home.

Only a few months later, she met their ba. Sum's eyes would change atmosphere when she came to this bit and Jun Ching could not look away. He was the only white man on the ferry that night so everyone had seen him and were staring at him. Sum was the only one maybe that hadn't seen him as she was busy watching the men throwing the ropes off the pier, rope as thick as her neck and many times stronger. They pulled them in through the water winding them round the metal mushrooms with their leathery arms twitching and twisting just like Jun Yee would tie her to him, not that Sum knew this. He sat next to her then with no warning. She had never seen green eyes before, so she stared. They looked so strange that she could not look away but could not keep looking. They were so beautiful, not the green of jade or the green of the harbour water, they were a living green like bamboo. Sum said he opened his mouth then and words came out. She had no idea what they meant but his eyes shone their meaning at her. And she understood his smile. Each time she smiled, he smiled and that was how it started. Smiling was the only language they shared. "It did not matter though because when he smiled, I could see his heart shining through."

So it went that he would wait outside the restaurant every day for her and they would sit on the waterfront watching the lanterns on the little boats swing back and forth as people jumped from one to the next, singing songs for money in each. He learnt a scant few Cantonese words and taught her some English ones. He told her he came from very far away and it took many days on a big boat to get there, not like the little one she had come on, it was a boat so big even the waves were not strong enough to rock it. He didn't have to scoop water out of the bottom either. He was kind and asked her what she thought and who she was, and she was embarrassed that she had no story to tell him. She could hardly believe it was possible to be happy for every minute that they were together, but Sum said they were.

The pictures in Jun Ching's head became fuzzier here. The story seemed out of focus, she could not quite grasp it in her little fingers, the idea that there was nothing to think about or worry about, "If the sky had fallen down around us, we would have used it for a blanket..." One day, he said he loved her. Sum said she was the happiest she had ever been in her whole life.

The details of the story peaked or dipped depending on the mood of the day but what Jun Ching understood was that water could make people disappear and never come back or it could take you to faraway places where you have never been before or even bring a whole new person who made you happy, and for you to smile at forever. When they would ask what happened next, she would rub a little ring on the chain around her neck and say it was a story for another night but each night she told the same one again.

Jun Ching had never known her father. She only knew his face from an old photograph. He looked foreign to her, he had dark hair like they did, but his skin was pale, and his eyes seemed green, or so she assumed. The photograph had been taken on the same day he told their mother he was leaving as Jun Yee squirmed on her lap and Jun Ching squirmed in her belly. Sum was even younger then than she was now and beautiful, with tiny tea dimples on each side of her mouth. Her smile was so wide it seemed to wrap around all three in the photograph and squeeze them tight together. Jun Ching imagined her ma with her long black hair floating around her like it was waving, trying to get her attention and he wound a strand around his finger then let go, watching it slip through. She imagined that she didn't understand all of his words but just smiled as he promised to come back and to write to her every day during. Jun Ching knew that much because her ma told them about the promises and how they will still be kept. She had taken those promises and folded them away into her soul.

The letters did come, she had a small stack of them in the egg roll tin, but they were worn thin, the writing faint and in a language she couldn't read with postmarks she didn't recognise. The friend who read them to her helped her write back and send photographs after Jun Ching was born but, more often than not, she just held them in her hand, smelt them for a scent long gone and looked at the writing thinking about the hand that wrote them, the hand that held hers long ago. She had stopped working in the restaurant and found work sewing which she could do some of from home and they lived in this little room of their own. The letters got fewer and the money stopped much earlier. By the time Jun Ching was old enough to buy tofu, there was barely a letter every other month though Sum was still just as excited when they came and waved them at the children and reminded them of all the promises. Until, not long after, the last letter came. It was a short letter, just a few lines and even less emotion. And then that was it. There were no more. Not even replies to the ones she continued to send him. She kept smiling for her boy and her girl, but over her dark eyes a grey mist drew in.

Chapter Three

Ching Ming, the grave sweeping festival, came at the end of March. Each year, the little family made the journey back to a small fishing village their ma came from. This year was particularly important as their ma had been sick the previous year and missed it. She had been saving what little she could during the year for the trip but even that wasn't enough, and she worked longer and harder now to find the cash. Jun Yee explained as best he could to his sister - there would be no egg pancakes now and they mustn't make noise about it. Tofu-belly gave them an extra few cents here and there for working in the shop which Jun Yee slipped in with the rest of his ma's savings and Missy dropped round more treats than usual.

The festival was the most important in the year to Sum. Her father had died years ago, forcing her own move from the village to Hong Kong, and although she spoke to him often and his photo sat prominent on the cupboard of their room (the only one taken of him ever, which she had paid for herself), she still wanted to visit him in person, to show him how much her children had grown. And of course, there was the rest of the family. Jun Ching remembered only outlines of them all except for their Paw Paw, Ma's ma, who was more of a heavy-handed smudge in her mind. There were eight siblings originally and each were addressed by Jun Yee and Jun Ching according to the order they were born in the family. As their ma was the first born, they started with Two Uncle who was already dead, followed by Three Auntie, Four Uncle, Five Uncle then Six Auntie, Seven Uncle, there was no Eight Auntie (also dead) and Nine Auntie. Four, Five and Seven Uncle all lived in the family home, the older two had wives and jobs and the last drifted in and out seemingly not doing much but spending the little money he did earn. Three and Six Auntie were already married and to Jun Yee and Jun Ching they seemed nothing more than faint edged aunts who made occasional appearances then faded into their husbands' families. This left Nine Auntie as the only unmarried daughter left in the house, but it was believed that with a face like an overcooked bun and her disposition, she was more than likely to always remain in her father's home. Of the two dead siblings, Eight Auntie left barely a watermark, she was only a baby when she died though local gossip said this was a very bad sign – the number eight stood for prosperity and the eighth child died almost immediately, that must mean prosperity will never belong to this family. Two Uncle, Ah Choi, left more of a mark as he had grown up by the time he died. He and Sum had been close, and he often appeared in her 'when I was little' stories. He was old enough to have married before he was killed at work by a falling bag of something, she couldn't remember, and the wife he left was Gwai Kam Mo, Auntie-in-law, the palm reader, who should have been called Two Kam Mo but always insisted people used her name, Gwai, so she didn't feel she constantly came second. All those that were married had already reproduced, so a handful of cousins seemed perpetually spilt over the ground.

"Don't take too much, we are only going for six days, do you hear? If you take too much you will have to carry it yourself anyway," Jun Yee reminded his sister the morning before they left.

Ma laid out a large piece of cloth on the bed for Jun Ching and she carefully counted out the things she needed next to it: her best dress with the purple flowers, her new slip Ma had made from many scraps last week for her to sleep in, slippers and an old piece of dough (like the figurines were made out of – an emergency comfort measure to knead in her fist if Jun Yee's pocket wasn't within reach). She folded each corner into the middle and tied them, then again with each of the new corners, then once more but tied those to their opposite corner so that the little bundle was securely wrapped. This little bundle was then tied to her back with an old *mair dai,* a baby carrying cloth, a square piece of red cloth with long straps stitched into each corner. She laid the bundle in the centre carefully and Ma placed it on the middle of her back, she turned around as the straps were pulled one over each shoulder and one round each side of her waist. Jun Ching inhaled deeply the soap of her mother's hair as her nose wandered through its waves. The straps were too long for her small body, so Sum wound them round her a few times, pulling the little girl further into her then pulling away again and again. Finally, she tied the ends together in a large bow on her chest just as she did for herself years before.

"La, now it's like you're carrying your own little daughter on your back though she will be easy to look after, she won't wriggle and squirm like you did." She pulled a pigtail and kissed the top of her head.

The journey would take all day, so they had to start early in the morning. The first walk to the ferry pier was long though Jun Ching hardly noticed as her baby bundle weighed light on her shoulders and she chattered the whole way. She wasn't excited about the trip or the thought of seeing family so far away, but it was a rare treat to have her ma with them for such a long time and that was enough. After the ferry across the harbour was the walk to the main pier then another wait, for a bigger boat which was the longest part of the journey, this would take hours depending on how many people and how much luggage would need to be loaded on and off at each stop. This boat did a circular tour of the nearby islands before the longer leg across the border to Ma's village. The wait with their papers at the other end felt endless by the time they got there. When they were finally through it was one more long walk to Ma's little inlet on the far side of the island, their steps slowing and Jun Ching's baby weighing heavy on her shoulders.

The sky was dark by the time they walked past the noodle shack and cafe with their tables spilling out onto the pavements. People perched on folding stools followed them first with their gaze and then, when they were nearly out of sight, turned their heads and stared like lizards, with wet unblinking eyes. They were an unusual sight here and the little girl wilted under the attention. Being the younger, she was sandwiched between her ma and brother who always made sure she was safely between them, holding onto each of her hands. Out of the corner of her eye she saw an old woman with a black mouth and could not hold her gaze from her. She stared at the girl, eyes glinting in the dark; pulling her lips apart she revealed five stained, blunt teeth in a grimace, gathered her spit in a guttural wrench and spat to her side. Jun Ching watched the loose skin on her arm drag across her mouth as she wiped, liver spots stretching into lines, never taking her eyes off her. Without saying a word, she had sought her out and seen something that she hadn't known was there; the old woman hadn't liked the taste of it. Jun Yee felt his sister's neck craning as she stared at the old woman and letting go of her hand, he pulled her closer with his arm across her shoulders, so their legs moved in unison making them bigger, a three-legged creature striding on as he pinched her ear.

There were only a few streets in the village, it was one of the furthest areas out, so it wasn't long before the table of staring diners gave way to staring people sitting on their own front doorsteps on the side of the dirt road. People here knew Sum of course and called out to her as they walked past, she smiled and returned the appropriate greeting.

"You have come home to visit your family?" A lady called, questions asking the obvious seemed pointless, but everyone asked them. "And you've brought the children back?"

"Yes, see, these two are them. Say hello to Auntie."

"Hello Auntie." They called in unison. She wasn't a real auntie, it was just good manners to called her one. Jun Ching had no idea who she was, she assumed she had met the woman before as she knew her and knew how much she had grown in the last year, but then a lot of people in these back streets seemed to know that.

The last few hundred feet of the journey were filled with greetings, toothless grins and barefoot, grimy-faced children, gawping with fingers in their mouths. The houses here were little more than shacks made of corrugated sheets of plastic and recycled wood. Some butted heads with each other and with the road in front whilst others had marked out their own little courtyard with mismatched bricks reaching out and around like bony arms embracing nothing but the same dirt that was without. She couldn't quite remember what her grandmother's house looked like, but she was hoping it wasn't one of these – she remembered it sat above the others with several steps leading up to it, uneven crumbling concrete poured by her grandfather when he found some spare at the construction site he was working on before he died. Suddenly they turned into a narrow alley between two houses that didn't look like it would fit there, and the steps presented themselves to them. At the top sat the old house, made of wood and some bricks rather than the plastic sheets of the houses below, some new and some recycled wood with a low fence surrounding it and even a little gate which none of the other houses below had. It even had a second floor made of much newer wood and freshly painted.

Halfway up the steps was the first part of the welcome party, a frightening, skinny dog that barked continuously with a tail as rigid as the bamboo cane the children would later become familiar with and their equally frightening but far from skinny Nine Auntie who would be the one to introduce them to it.

"*Dai Jair,* Big Sister. You are back. We have been waiting for you long time." She called to Sum.

"Yes, it was a long journey." Sum looked at them, "Say hello to Nine Auntie."

"Hello Nine Auntie," Jun Ching echoed her brother's Nine Auntie from behind his shoulder.

"Ah Yee, Ah Ching." She nodded at them, she was an aunt, and they were younger so she could use their names to address them whereas they had to call her by her title, Nine Auntie. Although she was the last in their ma's long line of siblings, so despite being only a few years older than Jun Yee they still had to address her as they would the other aunts, with due respect. "I'll go and tell everyone you've arrived." She shoved the dog out of the way with her foot as she turned to go in the house shouting, "They are finally here!"

They followed her up the rest of the stairs and into the house. The front door opened straight onto the living room, the unpainted wooden walls made it dark and ominous. The incense burning in the corner stuck in Jun Ching's throat making her want to cough but not wanting to draw attention to herself, and really not wanting the first sound she made to be a cough, she pushed the incense smoke out of her mouth with a long slow sigh. The walls of the room were spotted with a few uncles sat in hard straight chairs, beside them on the floor were the cousins and a couple of wives trickled in from the back as they heard. They all stared at the trio and the trio stared back. In the middle of the room, an unsmiling stone in the middle of a dust storm, sat their Paw Paw, Ah Ho.

"Ah Ma." Sum said.

"Paw Paw." The pair chorused.

Ah Ho nodded. "You're back, are you?"

"Yes, Ma. How have you been?"

Jun Ching stopped listening to the words. Ah Ho was more herself than she remembered her, she was looking them up and down and before she said anything to her, she already felt that there was something not quite right about herself. Her single jade ring clocked against the wooden handle of her walking stick with a steady clock, clock, clock. Her hands folded over the top and from the tips thick, hard nails grew and seemed to reach for them. Her hair was grey and drawn back into a low bun at the top of her neck. Across her cheeks were light brown stains, tiny puddles that suddenly bunched together. The skin pulled up on either side of her face oddly and the little girl realised she was smiling at them.

"Ah Sum, it is good you have come home, your father will be pleased to have you look after him again." Ah Ho nodded at the black and white picture of her dead husband on the wall. "Ah Gwai, why haven't you got your dai jair a cup of tea yet? And something for the little ones too."

"Yes, Lai Lai, it's just coming."

Gwai stepped out from the shadow and went to the thermos and muttered to nobody as she poured the tea. She muttered to nobody because there was nobody to sympathise with her. This was her husband's family, her *lai lai's,* mother-in-law's, house so it was right for her to pour the tea and serve the guests. It still stuck in her chest though. Especially this guest. She thought about spitting in her tea, but it would be too visible, floating on the top above the black leaves. She'd save it for the congee in the morning. Returning, she offered the tea to Sum with both hands, eyes to the side.

"Dai Jair."

"Thank you Ah Gwai. How are you?" Sum's voice was familiar, eager even. "How have you been recently?"

"Fine Dai Jair. Looking after the house, the little ones. That's it."

Sum sat forward in her chair, keen to hear more. One hand lifted from her lap towards Gwai as though to clasp her hand in her own but Gwai had already taken a few steps backwards, head still bowed, back behind Ah Ho's chair, ending the conversation. From there she could watch each move they made without anyone noticing, so as they continued talking and the children remained without their drinks, her eyes trickled over the familiar face. Of course, she saw Sum once a year as did the rest of the family, except for last year when she had some selfish emergency and couldn't come back, but in Gwai's mind she was comparing her to the 10-year-old Sum she had known as a young girl herself when things had been very different. Pigtails in their hair tied with red string, playing hide and seek behind massive trees with armies of red ants that would march up their legs biting them until they could stand no more and come jumping out of their hiding place in a manic jig to screams of laughter from the other children.

Sum's face was darker now, she was happy to see. Darker all over and more moles had appeared to dot the expanse of that once envied skin. The lids of her eyes looked looser too. Good, she thought. And when she took the glass of tea and brushed her hand it definitely felt coarser to her and dry. Good.

"Light some incense for your father. He has been waiting." Ah Ho's voice cut through.

"Yes, Ah Ma."

Against one wall of the room was a sideboard above which a photograph of Sum's father hung. Unsmiling, his eyes fixed hard on a point within the camera or perhaps straining to see the face of the person who would look into his eyes in the photo eventually. He wore a traditional shirt with round collar and his hair combed straight back over his head, thick and all still black. The creases in his face hinted at where smiles had lived. A photograph was too serious and too expensive for smiling. Below this was another, smaller. The features within younger but drawn with the same brush. Sum lit three incense sticks, waited briefly for them to burn before blowing them out so they smouldered. Holding the ends in both hands she touched them to her forehead and bowed three times to her father before standing the incense in a small red bowl of sand.

"Ah Ba, I've come back to see you again. How are you? I have brought your grandchildren to see you too. Come, Ah Yee, Ah Ching. Come and give a bow to your grandfather. Help me watch over them, Ah Ba, give them your protection and bless them and their comings and goings safely. And you, little brother," her eyes flicked to the other picture, "Look after them." She rested a hand on each of their heads.

The next few days felt crowded to the children who were used to being at most a trio, there were relatives or neighbours everywhere. Cousins followed Jun Yee around and did everything he did, liked what he liked and said what he said for the first couple of days which he secretly enjoyed at first but quickly grew tired of and then pretended they weren't there instead. They paid little attention to Jun Ching, she was a girl, by default far less interesting and therefore usually in the way. A few times they tried to send her to her one female cousin, Dow Ling, who seemed stuck to Nine Auntie like sugar to a wet bean, forever brushing her hair for her or playing games she wanted to play. The boys called her *dow ling* or 'penny', because it wouldn't take much to get her to do something, she was cheap. Though Jun Ching thought a penny was quite a lot really, so it surely wasn't a bad thing for people to know how much you cost so you don't need to haggle. It seemed a good idea to her. She went of course, when the boys told her to, but she was bored, it didn't take long of Nine Auntie making her sit on the floor whilst she sat above on a stool telling her what games she would like to play and lose for her to go somewhere far away in her mind. Without knowing it, her eyes would drift over to the boys' corner of the room until a sharp '*wai*' rang in her ears and Nine Auntie pinched her back to attention. She was not there long though because just as the '*wai*' was a call for Jun Ching's attention, it also called Jun Yee's and within minutes he would appear above them having invented a chore for his sister or something else only she could do for him – because although Nine Auntie was higher ranked than him in the family, Jun Yee was still a boy and not only that, but he was the first-born boy of the oldest daughter and that meant something in the pecking order too. Each time he came, she knew something. That there was something inside him that made him tough, something that he didn't have to show but all the children, even Nine Auntie, could see.

Ching Ming fell on the fourth day of their visit. Sum woke her children early to take them with her to the market. The fruit and incense had all been bought days ago but Sum had placed a late order for a freshly roasted suckling pig that would only be ready that morning. It was easily the biggest expense of the trip after the travel costs, but Sum thought nothing of the money passing through her fingers, she thought only of the piglet taking the centre place of the offering in front of her father's grave.

A small row of women and children waited in line to collect from the matching rows of piglets lined up just under the tarpaulin of the shop, like a bizarre adoption ceremony except no one got to choose their adoptee, they were simply thrust one by the butcher. Each piglet was a deep red brown, sliced down the belly and laid out with its legs slightly splayed out in front of it; the piglets got gradually bigger the further back into the rows they were. As they inched closer, saliva pooled at the bottom of Jun Yee's mouth, the smell so thick he felt he was holding his head under an unmoving lake of roast pork – it pushed into his nose, his mouth and, he was sure, his ears and drenched his hair as well. At their turn, Sum said 'The Wu family', which the butcher then called out over his shoulder. As he counted the money she handed over, a boy older than Jun Yee scanned the rows trying to remember where he had seen that name before. Remembering, he came down to the front row, crouching and balancing on his heels checked the thin, pink papers that were tied to each tray. The one he plucked out was the biggest of that row, its crispy skin stood like a glistening, hard shell, slightly away from the meat. Its little tail, which Jun Ching always drew curly, stuck straight out and the tips of its ears were blackened from the open flame.

Sum carried it all the way to the cemetery but at the entrance, before they went in, she stopped and handed it to Jun Yee making sure he had careful hold of it before letting go. She rummaged in her bag for a few minutes before pulling out two small, thin pieces of metal. Crouching down so that she could look both her children directly in the eye, she held out her palm so they could see that the pieces were two tiny folding blades with hinges into their own sheaths.

"La, you see these two blades? They not used for play. They protect you. A cemetery has lots of people and lots of spirits too, especially on Ching Ming. You must be careful where you walk. Walk around the graves but if you step across someone's grave you must apologise to them. Say 'Excuse me, I am just going past, I apologise and thank you', to each person. Do you hear?" They both nodded. "These blades will just be extra. Put them in your pockets, don't play with them, don't take them out, just leave them there and if something does try to follow you, the blade will stop it. Understand?" They both nodded again. Sum gave Jun Ching hers to put in her pocket and slipped the other into Jun Yee's front pocket herself. They walked on.

"Brother?" She whispered when Sum was a few steps ahead.

"Yes?"

"What thing will try to follow us?"

"A spirit."

"A spirit?"

"One of the people whose graves we will have to go over. If they like you or if you don't respect them or if they are lonely, they might try to follow you. That's why you have to be careful. Especially if they are young people or children."

"Why them?"

"Because they went too soon."

The cemetery was teeming, and the crowd walked only as fast as its slowest member. They had a long walk as their grave was on the far side of the cemetery and it was another half an hour before they had the rest of the family in sight. The graves were packed tightly together, each one with a small portioned area in front of it like a courtyard. There were five or six between the path and Sum's father's, they were set back and forth from each other with graves above and below jutting in and pushing back. There was no room between them to walk so they were forced to walk across the little courtyards of the dead. Sum led the way, showing the children where to place their feet not to fall, and called out to the dead people not to mind them, she was just bringing her children through and sorry to disturb them. Jun Yee followed balancing and holding tight to the paper tray and its precious cargo. Jun Ching came at the end, jumping, hopping from step to step, terrified of leaving her foot anywhere too long in case lonely dead fingers reached up to steal up her ankles and make her stay for tea. She felt like someone or something was pressing on her chest and her heart beat faster as she kept up a constant stream of whispered apologies.

"Very sorry. Really sorry. I'm just going to see my ma's father, my Gung Gung. He lives just next door to you, over there. Very sorry. I'm just little. I'm no fun. Don't mind me. Excuse me…"

Some graves had small black and white photographs of the dead person at the top of the gravestone. She glanced quickly at the faces of each person as she crossed their courtyard, it seemed more respectful to know who you were talking to, but she didn't want to hold their gaze too long in case they then took a liking to her. A big sigh escaped her when they got to their grave. She looked up at the familiar photograph, the same one they had at home, and the same one at Paw Paw's, and felt a little safer.

The cousins surrounded Jun Yee immediately and squealed with pleasure at the suckling pig – unlike the squealing it had undoubtedly done itself the day before –jiggling up and down on the spot leaning in for deep breaths, tasting the pork with their noses but none daring to touch. The uncles and aunts all praised Sum for her choice and her extravagance and made space in the middle of the fruit and incense offerings. Only Ah Ho remained quiet though when she asked if the very smallest pig wasn't available Sum knew she approved and saw that she had bought the best she could afford.

The offerings were placed directly in front of the headstone. From graves further up the hill a sizzling sound snaked down to them and instinctively the children all covered their ears just in time for the loud snaps of the firecrackers to start. Their ears rang in-between the rounds which would go on all day. Singed red paper floated on wisps of smoke in the air.

"Sorry, Father, we didn't get any firecrackers for you this year - we know you don't like them that much anyway, maybe next year, okay?" Three Uncle said.

"*Aiyyy* Father's got no time for firecrackers when there's a pig this size here, right, Father? Ah, let me eat some for you now, an extra fat bit please." Seven Uncle joined in, hand out for a piece of meat. The aunts laughed, even Sum, Jun Yee and Jun Ching were a little surprised to see.

"Extra fat? You've got quite enough! You eat an orange!" An orange was tossed at him.

"How disrespectful - it's for Father, not me. As his son, this is a dutiful sacrifice on my part, right Father?" He winked at the photograph. Ah Ho reached over and clipped him on the back of the head before handing him a piece of the pig with a smile that looked awkward on her lips. He laughed loudly, throwing the orange at Gwai. "You can keep your oranges, and you'll be carrying them home too I'm sure. No one will be after them with Sum's class offering on the table! Hong Kong really does take you up a few notches, doesn't it, Big Sister?"

Sum kept quiet on the other side of the circle looking at Gwai who burned, holding the orange like a ball of shame in her hands, squeezing it and watching the tips of her fingers go white, her face flushed.

A couple of hours later, they swept the little courtyard clean again. Everyone shouted their goodbyes to their father, grandfather, husband and the entire group made their way further up the cemetery to Second Brother's grave. Gwai had already been up once today to see her husband and bring him a few fruits and meat so this was a short visit. When the party made to leave again, the remains of the pig were hoisted back onto Jun Yee - it would make a tasty soup this evening - though a few pieces of fruit were left for their Gung Gung to have later. Sum lingered. Her fingertips on the photograph.

Jun Ching was just as anxious to get back across the graves as they left and tugged at her ma's hand. Reaching into her pocket to make sure the blade was still there, she clutched it and positioned herself in the middle of the line so as not to be last. She was almost skipping into her brother's back in her hurry then there was a pause, someone in front had slipped and the line had stopped. Jun Ching found herself standing right in the middle of one of the graves' courtyards. Her heart raced again, and her whispers heightened, and she turned to see whose house she was standing in. They had not walked over this one on the way in, this was one of the lower ones that they had walked round the back of before. She saw now, the double photographs. Two children, a boy and a girl, she assumed brother and sister. Unsmiling, black button eyes and down turned mouths. The writing on the stone was fresh and there were a few fruits and sweets left from where there had been visitors earlier that day. It had not occurred to her before that there would be children on gravestones. Of course, she knew children died, Brother had even said before about children's spirits wanting to play but she just hadn't imagined their faces on a stone. She followed the lines of their faces, the shape of their noses and how the girl had her hair tucked behind her ears, short. She didn't look too different to Jun Ching herself and she wondered if she would have a grave like this. The line started to move again but she didn't hurry across anymore.

"Sorry to disturb you both. I'm just leaving. Please don't follow me, I'll be scared and I won't be able to play. I promise I'll come back and play with you when I die. Please don't follow me now. Thank you. Sorry."

Chapter Four

    The visit was due to last six long days, six days of eternity, but before the six days were even over, the children knew something was wrong. Although Sum didn't usually have many words, her sisters would bring what she did have out of her, visits before would have her sitting scrubbing vegetables over a tin basin of water perched on little plastic stools with the other women. Sitting in a little circle they would chatter without pausing for breath, giggling and wiping laughter tears as they would never do at the dinner table, so much so that the sound drew the children like moths. Draping herself across Sum's back, Jun Ching would dangle over her shoulders feeling the gentle shudders of laughter roll through Sum's body. Even when she didn't say much herself her shoulders always joined in. But this year was different, they still gathered in the same spot and the same vegetables were swished in the basin, but it was as though someone had dropped a cloth over a cage of grasshoppers, you could still hear them jumping a little inside but softer and less frequent. Sum as well seemed constantly somewhere else, saying little, hardly noticing those around her who all noticed her. Gwai noticed the most and when she wasn't noticing Sum, she would be sitting by Ah Ho's side saying quiet things that even little girls, with super hearing, could never hear.

Gwai was finding it almost impossible not to think about Sum almost constantly. The way she walked around, free to do as she pleased when she had work to do, always more work to do. It curdled her stomach and blinded her, almost literally as she stepped over the threshold into the back yard she walked straight into Sum, alone for once.

"Watch it!" She spat as Sum stepped back and aside. Gwai stepped up to her, her face less than a foot away. "You think you're better than me, don't you? Go on, say it now, no one is here and no one to hear you. It's Big Sister with all the money from Hong Kong, come to show off again."

"You know I never wanted to go, Gwai, that was your dream not mine."

"Well, you took it for your own and made it fit, didn't you? Well, I see you still. The stupid girl with no dreams, no thought of her own. Ordinary, ugly Sum, content with the scratches on her back. Content now are you with your bastard half castes?" She shoved Sum back, slamming her back into the wall behind sending a painful jolt through her shoulders. She pushed herself off the wall again, bumping into Gwai who stumbled, ankles catching on a low stool behind her before landing heavily on her bony backside. She bent to help her up but Gwai jerked her elbow away.

"No. I'm not content. Can you not see, or do you choose not to see as usual?"

"Well, I will be content, content when I watch you suffer like you deserve. You wait, it's coming. You can't steal someone else's life and not pay for it. I'll be content then." Gwai turned, walking away and rubbing her back.

Gwai swallowed hard, wincing, in an effort to get rid of the lump of bitter phlegm lodged at the top of her throat. She was half sitting and half squatting on the same stool round the side of the house. The throbbing in her tailbone preventing her from sitting properly. She was bent over a round metal bowl with a soft bamboo cage to her right that five slightly scrawny chickens were temporarily calling home. Gwai was not squeamish about killing animals so it was easy for her to do this dirty job for other people in exchange for a few extra pennies and being able to keep the blood. She reached over, lifted the lid and amongst a fluttering palaver pulled one out. Taking charge of both wings with one hand she grasped its neck with a firm grip. No one came to disturb her now, not like they normally did when Sum wasn't here, coming with questions about what was to be bought for dinner or what chores were to be done for the day. Even when she did tell them, if Sum was in the room, they would look at her for confirmation – *when she doesn't even care!* Snap. A jerk of both hands round the neck and a satisfying crack dissipated a little of her frustration. *Sum who doesn't even listen, who is just wandering through clouds in her head. When she's gone again, they will all come back to me. They can't even tell that she's barely there, that she's just desperate to get back to her grimy room in Hong Kong and wait for heaven to fall in her lap.* It never stopped occurring to her how unfair this was. Sum never wanted to go in the first place. It was her, Gwai, who had wanted to. It was her idea. But she was cheated into marrying. He promised her he was going up in the world but then he died instead and now she was stuck here. She folded the now limp neck of the chicken back on itself and tucked the head under her thumb. Picking up the small knife next to her foot, she felt the rings of cartilage through the skin then sliced cleanly in between them. She leant over the metal bowl and watched as the blood drained out and the dark red pool below grew

– there would be enough there after five chickens to mix with their rice for at least two meals. The blood slowed to a drip, drip, drip and she gave it one last squeeze and flung it to the side for plucking later. She looked at her hands, they were completely clean, not a smudge of blood. She had to leave it, she thought to herself. By the time she had finished with the chickens, their furiously plucked bodies had helped her see it would do her no good to keep thinking this way. The visit would be over soon for another year. She picked up the bodies to take them back to the families and collect her pennies.

Later that afternoon, Gwai's spirits lifted as the pennies added up in her pocket. Nothing made her smile more than the feeling of cold coins between her fingers. At the last house the door was already open, two women chattering at the threshold. Gwai had no inclination to wait her turn, holding the dead chicken aloft behind the visitor's head. The other woman took the chicken and hurried inside for the money. Gwai did not bother to make conversation with the visitor who was left with her and they stood in awkward silence for a few moments. The woman returned, handed over the coins, and as Gwai turned to leave, the conversation resumed behind her.

"- So he was old anyway, he had good luck to go like he did, in his sleep."

"It is right that way, he was always kind and good with fortunes-"

Gwai turned, cutting in again. "Who are you talking about? Who died?"

"You haven't heard? The old blind fortune teller who used to be at the temple."

Her fingers stopping jangling and her stomach fell to the bottom of her ribs. She said nothing but walked away leaving the two women muttering about how rude she was known to be. It couldn't be him... though it could only be him they meant. There was only one blind fortune teller there. Gwai had not seen him in many months now, perhaps closer to a year but every time she had she would go to him and give him her palm. And every time he would say the same thing to her, "Again it's you. Let's see if you've changed your fortune yet. It's not too late you know." And she would smile because he had been saying the same for years and because he could not see her smile. It was him she had gone to when Choi died and he sat with her in the silence that she wanted, then filled it when she needed. It was him who never stopped trying to help her understand the fluidity of fortune. Despite their infrequent meetings, he always picked up the gentle chiding thread each time, but whilst his fingertips touched the surface of many lives, hers was touched by so few that they left lasting prints. She examined these now - what did it mean? Do those marks get washed away now their maker is gone? Has *'it's not too late you know'* now turned too late because he couldn't hear her answer? The answer came itself to her. It was too late. It was all too late. She stopped then by the inlet, watching the water rush down to join the sea, imaging his spirit too in the flow in the underworld down the river to the wide expanse. The water only flows one way and she had failed to catch it despite all the warnings he gave her. When he spoke, she could feel a different Gwai, a brighter Gwai, sitting just next to her, one she could shift into when she decided to but now, that other Gwai had gone trickling through her fingers. He had taken it with him. No one would ask her again if she had changed her fortune yet and she suddenly knew beyond doubt that she couldn't.

    She hated the sight of the sea in that instant. The sea with its wide horizon, promising something else just beyond, something she used to think she could see, opportunity, excitement, just something beyond this… but she saw it now for what it was, an ending, a flat perspective for which there was no beyond - at least not for her. For some maybe, for Sum maybe, but not her. All the movement of the water in the inlet, rushing towards the sea unknowing that it is to simply join the nothing. And she was just one of them jostling in the inlet, being pushed or rushing forwards on the tide of her fortune like everyone else around her with no way of controlling where she would end up. So, he was wrong. Or at least he is wrong now. There is no way to change her fortune and probably not anyone's for that matter. But she could still try. The bitterness grew in her stomach. If her chance of change had extinguished with him then why not Sum's as well? She could force her into the eddying waters just like her, for a while at least so she could see for herself the tedium of facing the blank horizon every day. She made the resolution to herself, to the waters, then and only then did the burning climbing her throat abate. This was the only course of action left to her and she would have to take it.

    A few nights later, on the fifth evening of their visit, Jun Ching hurried up the stairs to their corner of the half floor and carelessly folded all the things she had brought. Downstairs, there was a hush as the rest of the cousins had gone outside to lie on the ground and watch the stars come out, and inside she could hear a low hum. She crept closer to the edge and held on to the bottom of two wooden railing spokes and peered through the gap. Below was Ah Ho in her polished chair and next to her Gwai, rubbing oil into her hands, with round motions on the older woman's skin, pushing and kneading as she would expensive dough.
    "You think she should go back?" Gwai whispered, "All the time she walk around like dreaming. How can she look after two children? I bet they look after themselves."

"Is it that bad? I didn't notice, she has always been quiet, and the children look okay."

"Of course they do now, but what about tomorrow, or next week, or next month? You see how they do everything for her now, it very obvious this is what they do at home too. They look after her not her look after them." She moved onto the fingers, taking one by the tip and moving it in wide circles before giving it a little snap at the end, the old knuckles easing at the pressure.

"I don't believe it is as bad as you say. She is different but maybe she is tired, she has always been soft. I always knew it would be too hard for her. I should not have let her go. I told her, big places are hard to live in and you have to be hard yourself and she isn't. And then she got herself into trouble, she can't just come back here now without a husband and with those two. People will talk. And we need the money she sends."

"You are right, Lai Lai, it would draw the eye if she just came back." She paused, pretending to think. "Ah, I know! How about if she stays longer this time, this way you could watch her for a little longer and then if you think she is fine then they can go then, at least you will be sure."

"That could be right, she can have a chance to rest properly before going back to make money. It will cost more though here, rice is expensive now and there's three of them."

"Ah, the mother needs to rest, not the children, Lai Lai. The children can help around the house and if we need to, we can send them to work to make some extra. It will be good for them to be here with family, not floating here and there in Hong Kong with no roots."

Jun Ching didn't feel like she was floating here and there in Hong Kong. It was here that didn't feel right, not really like floating but rather like being caught in a stream full of pebbles with familiar faces, constantly rushing up to her and staying there, no gaps where she could be quiet. She wanted to go home, six days was forever already, and she wanted to go home to their little world with the smell of preserved eggs wafting through the corridor. She missed hearing the sisters squabbling through the wall but most of all she missed unfolding her ma's bed every night and waiting for her to come back and get in it with a smile. But that was going to have to wait because that night before they went to sleep Sum told them that Ah Ho had asked them to stay for a few more days and that they would.

What was meant to be a few more days turned into weeks and at the end of each week was a new week. They had settled into a routine, coming down each morning to the thick rice congee, *juk*, which Penny had made with rice boiled till it broke down to mush and whatever leftovers there were to flavour it. With more people in the house but no more money, there weren't usually any leftovers; they learnt to eat it plain with just a little soy sauce and spring onions. The days here were empty, Jun Yee was not in the school and because they were still visitors, they only made them do a few things around the house like helping Penny get water or wash the rice, easy things done quickly. This left them free to wander after Sum. Sum had taken to leaving the house in the middle of the morning and going down to the beach to sit and look out on the water until supper time. In her little notebook she wrote trails of squashed characters. This was where she used to write the new English words she was so desperate to learn, but now, as the weeks knitted together, it turned more and more to Chinese and the little characters looked painfully scratched into the paper, bunched up together trying to take up as little space as they could, looking very uncomfortable.

She wasn't always writing, her children sat with her and she taught them games with pebbles, asking them to find different sizes and colours, making up rules, throwing a pebble into the air, picking up another and catching it again. Jun Ching's hands were too small and too slow, and the rough edges of the pebbles eventually put a stop to the game leaving jagged scratches across their knuckles. They built little water pools, catching mudskippers and tiny crabs, watching them and poking them until they were even more bored than they had been. After she had taught them the games, it seemed Sum had decided she had taught them enough and retreated again to behind the mist. She let the children carry on playing, smiling at them when they won or lost and turned their faces to her to make sure she was still watching. She watched less and less so that they would have to call out to her to tell her what had happened, to remind her they were still there. They grew more used to seeing the top of her head than the tip of her nose.

    Jun Ching thought a lot about what she had heard Ah Ho and Gwai saying that night, but she could see that staying here was not making Ma better. The grey mist over her eyes hadn't lifted, but had thickened to a dense fog, like the type the fisherman didn't dare go out in. Jun Yee dared to go into the fog though, to look for her. He watched her and, when she had been quiet for longer than usual, he took her hand and squeezed and squeezed some more until her eyes found him again. Then he would move her, ask her to take them somewhere or do something. Jun Ching started to understand that by making her move he could stop her from going back to that place and so that's what he did, he moved Sum constantly round her mind, never settling for too long just in case he lost sight of her figure in the mist.

    One day, after nearly four months, a large parcel arrived wrapped in faintly lined, thick green paper with Sum's name on it. Their toes wiggled with excitement, imagining all sorts of treats inside and playing a game where each of them came up with a more amazing delight. By the time Sum opened it, they had already gnawed off the corners of the parcel with impatience. She shook it and from inside came a shuffling sound, the sound of papers sliding over each other and knocking against the sides, a duller knock of something more substantial, more solid but she didn't need any further encouragement. Sum knew what was inside and now her fingers were searching the paper for a hold, a chink in the armour, to rip it off and reveal what she had been waiting for so long for.

'He's finally found us-, it must be from your-'She stopped herself, her breath catching in her throat, not daring to reach the surface. Instead, her old smile coloured her face and shimmered. Jun Ching climbed up as close as she could in relief at seeing her ma again. She knew she would come back. She knew she would. She looked to Jun Yee to join them, but his mood had also changed, he wasn't excited anymore, he was standing off to the side, eyes carefully creeping back and forth between Sum and the parcel, seeing something that she didn't. She climbed down and went to him, hooked her fingers in his back pocket and waited.

Sum kept glancing up at them, sparkling, then back to the parcel – it was the most well wrapped parcel she had ever seen, a giant papered onion, shedding layer after layer but unlike an onion, it didn't sting their eyes with little tears along the way, no, the paper onion saved it all for last, only when the last layer of skin came off did it demand all their tears come at once. In the end, it gave up their old familiar egg roll tin, the shuffling of papers were just the same old letters. Sum held it in her hands, searched the packaging for anything she may have missed, any other letters. But there was just an old egg roll tin. She shook it again next to her ear to hear the sound that made her think there were new letters, new hopes for her, she shook and shook as though she knew the exact weight and sound of the tin. She shook it one last time particularly hard in a dismal disappointment at which we heard a definite thud inside. Tears slipped down her face as she opened it. She handed Jun Yee his comic book, drawing pencils and pad from the tin then with a soft sorry handed Jun Ching two little dried dough figures of a brother and a sister. Then the two halves of what was the mother.

"*Wah*, what's all this noise for? What's this?" Ah Ho's voice startled them.

"Someone has sent a box of our things. Landlady must have thrown us out because we have been gone for so long. I must call her and send her the money for the rent so she keeps our room." Ma replied.

"No, no mistake. I called her from village last week. I told her you were not going back and to let your room out. You were just throwing your money away leaving your things there."

"But Ma, we are going back. Soon, very soon." She looked to the children for reassurance.

"No, you are not. Right at the start I told you, you had to be strong to go there, I ask you 'are you strong enough?' you say 'yes, Ma, I am strong enough' but now look. You no strong enough. Look at you. No one will want you now with these two lumps tied to your back forever. No, you will stay here now and help me. Much more useful and I can make sure there no more trouble."

"What about our other things?"

"I told her to sell them to pay for rent you owe her and send the rest. I don't know who sent you this useless tin of *lap sap*, just throw it away, it's taking up room here. What? No money? That woman cheated us. She must have made more money with your things. She even cheat an old woman. The world is changing." Ah Ho turned and left muttering to herself. Sum said nothing more.

After that the house itself seemed to drain her. Jun Yee and Jun Ching felt increasingly out of place. Gwai gave them more chores to do and sent Jun Yee out to run errands for her though they still managed to spend most of the afternoons with their ma on the beach. Tiring of the pebbles, they wandered further and further from her, glancing back occasionally to make sure she hadn't left them. They wandered up and down the beach but never ventured into the water. She was still terrified of the sea because growing up here she had seen many neighbours or friends lost to the waves whether it was because they were careless or unlucky. This meant the children were never allowed into the water because as she couldn't swim, she wouldn't be able to go after them if anything happened. They tested her, inching closer and closer. They were allowed in up to their knees but no further. She had a sixth sense when it came to them and water and no matter how far away she was or how fast her gibbering pencil was tangling itself up in her page, she would still snap her head up and shout sharply at them to get back.

    Jun Ching wondered what they were waiting for, it was clear Ma was waiting for something though she didn't dare ask. They just did everything they knew to keep her healthy so that she could keep waiting. They brought water from the house and food for the midday meal, placing them on the ground next to her so they were ready when she needed them though they were often there untouched when they returned. When the wind rose in the evening, they would tug gently at her sleeves, whispering to her, only then would she turn her smile back to them and take them home.

    Towards the end of the summer, the wind chose one day to be particularly cold and added an unusual chill to its blow. Sum sat still, her pencil motionless in her hand. She had been like this for days and the flapping pages of the notebook that had caught the girl's attention lay untouched in her lap. She wrapped her arms around her ma's shoulders and saw when she did that the skin was peeling off her lips. Jun Ching was scared. With each layer of skin she saw peeling from her went layers of kisses and tenderness which even a little girl knew were already fading. She felt the sadness that had settled in her insides push out its elbows, making more room for itself and less room for her.

"Ma, drink a little water?" She held a bottle out to her. "Just a little? Ma?"

She couldn't even hear the voice beside her; there was no reaction, no flicker in her eyes to say that she had heard. She shook the bottle in front of her face but still nothing. Perhaps she's gone blind, Jun Ching thought to herself. She placed the bottle in her hand resting on the notebook, picked up each of her fingers and wrapped them around it one by one. They were cold fingers, grey at the tips, her nails cracked and splitting down the middles. Still, she didn't grip it.

"Ma, your lips are very dry, you need to drink some water. I want you to drink some water, Ma."

She dipped a little finger in the water and dabbed a drop on her lips. Then two fingers, three. Her whole palm was soon wet and water dripping down her ma's chin and tears running down her own face. She kept going and when the bottle was half gone, her brother's hand appeared on her wrist. He took the bottle and without saying a word, he knelt beside her. Chasing strands of hair across her face and slipping them behind her ears, his touch called her back through minutes and hours, through mists and fog, calling gently until she turned her face to his and saw him. Taking some time to focus, she seemed like she hadn't seen him in years. She took the bottle and sipped at what was left.

"Our boy." She smiled.

Jun Yee felt the power he had to make her see him fade a little every day and no matter how he searched he found no way of holding onto it, no way to make that power something more, to make her move or to make her stay.

Sum only saw her daughter a few more times after that though Jun Ching saw her ma every day as she refused to leave her side. Each time she looked at her, she took longer to find her. She did not forget her way to the beach though and insisted they go every day. They stopped collecting pebbles, they stopped making shallow pools and there were no more mudskippers for them to torment or crabs to pinch their fingers even if they'd wanted to. The weather was turning as typhoon season approached changing the summer's blue skies to a dirty grey. The waters became more impatient, more violent but still they sat and watched, side by side like three figurines made of dough, one broken in half.

Jun Ching missed her ma and she knew Brother did too. Despite being with her every day, she wasn't there anymore, and she wondered who had crept into her and hollowed out her soul. She wanted it back. If only she knew who or what had taken it, she could fight it at least but she didn't and there was nothing to fight. She tried stamping and kicking to make Ma angry so she would shout at her, but she didn't. She tried crying so hard she worked herself into fits biting her own arms, but Sum didn't stop her. So, she gave up too and just sat on her feet, leaning back against her ma's shins watching the sea as she did. She laid her head down in her lap for what she knew would be the last few times. Jun Yee did the same. And she remembered and she stroked her daughter's hair, and she ran her finger along her nose, she tugged on his ears and Jun Ching could feel her brother's curls tickling the top of her head.

The following day, they went to the beach as usual and at lunchtime, brother and sister went up to the shop to find a little lunch to share as a treat. The lady who ran the shop, they soon realised, was the same one who they had called auntie the night they arrived so long ago, and she had a name. She told them to call her *Lien Yi*, Auntie Lien. The choice was so big it made their eyes dance and Lien let them wander around slowly picking things up and putting them back down again when they had changed their minds. When they had finally made their choices and paid, she gave them an extra bottle of soya milk to share though they knew it was because she felt sorry for them. The whole village was talking about them now, about Ma. Jun Ching had heard Ah Ho and Gwai talking one night as she was washing the rice just outside the back door of the kitchen. Everyone in the village was saying Ma was losing her mind, like the old lady Ma had told them about who sat by the sea for 40 years waiting for her drowned husband to come home. They had seen her sitting there day after day with her children guarding her, by her side. 'But those two can't hold her in this world', they were saying, 'she will be gone soon and then what about the little ones? What will they do with them then?' But Ma didn't have a husband to wait for, they said, so she wouldn't have the strength to last as long as the old lady did.

    They had taken much longer than normal at the shop and by the time they got back, Ma was gone. Straight away Jun Ching felt the growing sadness in her insides turn into a giant snake, curling itself round her, tightening and squeezing, she could see thee black and green pattern of its body throbbing and pulsing as she felt the sides of her throat closing in and choking her. Jun Yee had dropped the food on the pebbles and held his two hands cupped together in front of him, holding nothing, his eyes scanning the beach, the water, until his body jerked once, then twice, before his legs kicked into motion and he ran. His sister followed him as best she could, but she could barely breathe as they looked up and down the beach. They couldn't find her. What they did find round the side of some rocks in a more secluded part of the beach were her shoes, placed neatly together by the water's edge weighing down the little notebook that laid beneath them. They sat by the water's edge for three days, side by side, his pocket full of her little fingers.

Chapter Five

Three days later a fisherman, with a face etched with words no one could read, saw a dark shape floating on the sea's surface and sighed. He knew, in the early morning light, that his day was cursed, and he would return having caught nothing. He hauled the body into his boat so no one else would have the misfortune of meeting it and having their day's take ruined as well and sailed back without looking into the sightless eyes and swollen lips. The little community had been waiting for this moment; everyone knew it would not be long with these slow waters and it was likely the body would not have drifted far. It was simply a matter of who would be unlucky enough to be the one who found her. So, when the boat was early and alone on the horizon, those that saw it knew what it contained. That night, a sigh of relief rippled across the other fishermen as they returned from their day to the news that the body had been found and the bad luck was not theirs. On their way home, those who could afford to hung a fish on the unfortunate man's door as he would be unlikely to return to the water for some time until he felt the bad luck had passed.

For the children, it was still morning, the time they would have been finishing their breakfast but since Sum had disappeared they had simply sat and watched the others eating with no appetite of their own. So, when the murmurs seeped up to the house, Jun Yee was the first to sense them. Jerking his eyes to his sister's he urged her.

"You stay here, you hear? Don't follow me and I'll be back really quick."

Round eyes nodded a reply and he disappeared leaving all at the breakfast table blinking in the sunlight streaming in the open front door. He ran with feet skimming down steps to the road, past houses with open doors and peering grandmothers, past a row of shops, over stones and gravel and, as the ground gave way to sand, he could see the little crowd gathered, left behind by a fisherman, slowly pulling away his empty boat. He stopped then. He stopped when he saw the boat as though his feet knew what he was about to learn would change his life and they didn't want to bring that knowledge onto him. He forced his feet to drag one after the other across the sand leaving long unbroken trails towards the crowd. As he approached, Lien Yi saw him, her eyes jumped into protective action, turning her body to him as she strode over the sand, her steps much larger than Jun Yee would have thought possible.

"Come la, Jun Yee, let us go home," she put her arm around him angling her elbow to cradle his head and force his sight away from the crowd.

"Is it..." he twisted his head out to keep staring, his feet, now obedient, kept moving towards the crowd, forcing her to step backwards as she continued talking to him.

"Let us get home first, then talk. Come on, I walk with you home."

"What is it? Is it..." he couldn't say the words that his stomach was screaming. *Is it Ma? Is it my ma? Is it? Is it?*

"I said let's go home first then talk." Her words were firm though her tone was gentle. He pushed on.

"Is it... Is it... Is it..." he murmured again and again as he felt her grip tighten around him. She steadied herself in the sand, setting her heels in and her weight against him to keep him in place. He pushed against her and his feet continued moving, each step fell on the same spot and went nowhere. As he came to feel her arms around him, his frustration turned to disbelief. *It couldn't be Ma, Ma hated people staring at her, she wouldn't just sit there and let people surround her like that.* His head chanted the words he wanted to believe as his stomach screamed those that he could not say and finally they collided, crashing him into action, and he burst out of her arms. She didn't follow him but watched as his flailing arms and legs silently dropped his body and picked it up again until he stopped just a few feet away.

People twitched aside like hot skin burnt by ice as the silent boy pushed through, head bowed. The low hum fell away into the sand as it recognised him and said no more. He didn't break the quiet as his knees fell to the sand. Lying on her chest, her face turned towards him, he could see the faint lines of her eyelashes, her nose and lips through the knotted hair. He reached out to pull a strand away but as his finger grazed the cold, strained skin of her cheek he recoiled. This was a new side to his mother's skin he had never felt before – he didn't want this to be the way he remembered her. He sat with her, too afraid to touch her or to look in her face so he stared at one of the flowers on her dress. The blue petals were darker than usual from the water and darker still than the grey-blue her calves now were which he could see from the corner of his eye but would not look at. The flowers were a big print, only four or five across her back. He counted the flowers on all the material he could see, then the petals of the flowers, then the leaves that surrounded them. When there was nothing left to count, he strained his eyes to count the creases where there were none. Anything but to look at her or to look away.

The crowd inched further away, widening the circle around him and as they moved the low hum started once again. In time, he felt a warmth on the back of his head, cradling the base of his skull, comforting. His head felt heavy, his neck strained, he shifted the weight of it slightly back to rest in the small hand. He closed his eyes and ignored everything he could not see and focused only on what he could feel. The wind that could only reach the top of his head tossing the hair there to and fro, the sand pressing down under his knees and the warmth radiating from the little hand.

"Brother?" How long he had been like that he didn't know. He did know the voice that was calling him though some part of him didn't want to. He didn't want to know the little girl the voice belonged to, to see her face, to find words to help her understand. It was unfair that it would be him who would have to do all these things, left as she was now, as he was now, with no one else.

"Brother?" The little hand gently rubbed the base of his neck until he opened his eyes and looked up into her face. She was standing just off the side of his shoulder angled towards him, one arm hanging loose by her side but body upright and legs so purposefully straight that her knees were touching in the middle. She kept her eyes unwaveringly on his and to his surprise there were no questions in them, just a reflection of himself, a sense of belonging that smelt of home. Adult lips had no words for this.

So, she had called him back from wherever he had gone. It was far away, even though he was kneeling right in front of her and the moment he opened his eyes and looked at her, he gave her all the answers she hadn't known she needed.

She didn't look at the thing everybody else was looking at. She had seen its form when she was running here, her feet flying across the sand, silent but for the rhythmic 'gup' of her throat loosely opening and closing with her steps. She knew what the thing was meant to be, and she also knew what it wasn't. It wasn't her ma; her ma had left it behind, slithered out of it like an old skin.

He took her hand from the back of his head and pushed himself to his feet. As he stood, a voice came from behind him.

"Go home. And take your sister with you." Ah Ho's voice was flat and impenetrable, her eyes, unblinking, staring into her daughter's. How different those eyes were now from when she first opened them, nearly 30 years ago - little black beans in whites so white they were almost blue. She had pushed her little eyelids open then with a tiny yawn and curled up fists. The new mother and father had marveled at their first baby like they didn't over any that followed her. *Sum* meant heart. They named her that because that was what she was to them. Both their hearts laid bare and vulnerable in this one little one. They believed that this was the heart from which their family would grow and pulse, a strength everyday keeping them not only united but sweetening their days like a touch of pickled ginger. It didn't quite happen that way.

Those first days as a new family were the last that she really saw her husband, saw his soul. After that with each child there was less food and there were more problems, their souls stopped looking for each other and curled up in the memories instead. Of all her children, it was this one that always brought back those curled memories. The heart that was not quite strong enough. Lying there now, still and unbeating, it seemed unimaginable to have had such great expectations for something so frail. But the stillness caused a pain in her chest that dragged a sharp tear through her as she knew no more memories would be made.

Jun Yee still wavered, stuttering, looking from the old woman with her tight bun to the lifeless one on the sand. He was unwilling to even try and leave her.

"I told you to go." The words knocked past her teeth and bounced off his cheeks, but his feet wouldn't move. Her head snapped to him suddenly, her features stretched back as though the bun was twisting, tightening and pulling her face with it. "Are you deaf? Go home."

The last words slapped him across the cheek and jolted him into movement. Hand in hand they walked back to the house, each step witnessed by the eyes of the village. A neighbour's son who had watched from a distance at the edge of the beach started to follow them without knowing why, they seemed magnetic and just as he had followed them, more children joined him as they walked. By the time they turned the corner to their road, what Penny (who was waiting at the bottom of the alleyway to the house) saw was a strange giant creature, two figures as the eyes at the head with a weaving wisp of a tail, trailing behind like a ghost carp. She said nothing as the eyes went past, but the whispering tail pooled in front of her and didn't dare follow on.

Hours went by in fits and spurts, some of them they saw clearly whilst others were just a flash of greys and blues. The others saw them all with clarity and saw the ebbing withdrawal of the pair. Their silence throbbed and pulsed through the house. They had stopped speaking to each other, guiding each other with touch and glance alone.

The funeral was organised quickly, as was usual with all those who died at sea and whose bodies were already changed and distorted when they were recovered. The house had been thoroughly cleaned for the ceremony and paper money was being constantly folded in the corners of rooms. The main room where they would be receiving guests was rearranged, borrowed chairs lined up facing each other in rows on either side leaving a clear and straight path from the door to the back wall. Up against the back wall was the side table, wide and narrow and usually on the other side of the room but now was covered with a white cloth and laid with a long white unlit candle on one side and two pots of sand, one on the other side with a large incense stick smouldering and one empty in the middle. Above the table was a black and white photograph of Sum deliberately placed so that as soon as a mourner stepped over the threshold, they would be face to face with her. The photograph was recent, and she was looking directly into the camera without the faintest of smiles. The children had been cut out of the photograph and Sum's face enlarged to fill the frame so that it now was, eerily for the children who had never been to a funeral before, the same size as her face in life.

    The body was brought to the house the next day in a closed coffin and placed in the small space outside the front door, as she had died away from home her body was not to be laid out within. The coffin under other circumstances would have been open for the family and the neighbours to pay their respects but the effect of the sea water and the high summer sun on the skin would not allow it. The funeral crier who had led the coffin through the streets to them now took his place by the door to announce visitors when they came. Penny started the little fire at the side feeding the paper money in piece by piece, wailing quietly. The family took their places within the house and as they did the candle on the altar was lit.
    Jun Yee and Jun Ching, dressed in mourning white with scratchy, brown sack cloth hoods over their heads, came in first. They entered the room, hand in hand and heads down, Ah Ho led

them to the front. Just feet away from their ma's face, they knelt and on Ah Ho's count softly touched their foreheads to the ground three times. As they stood up, they were handed three sticks of incense each and with trembling fingers walked up to the empty pot of sand and stood the incense in. Jun Yee felt a tightening across his chest as he stared into his mother's eyes. He felt he hardly missed her, she had been gone from them for so many months before she died that he could hardly feel her absence now that he wasn't reminded by the shell in front of him. The sensation in his chest told him he was angry even though he tried to push it down again. But there it remained, a clenched fist above his stomach that punched him from the inside when he felt the three small fingers slip into his back pocket at that moment. His eyes twitched, narrowing, and his own voice whispered in his ears. *You coward. You've left us here, far from home, far from everything we know. What will we do?* He glanced at his sister out of the corner of his eye. *What will I do? How can I look after her? What will I do?* His voice kept whispering then shouting this question as they turned away to take their places kneeling on woven mats in front of the seats, heads bowed, eyes fixed on the ground. Ah Ho sat behind them, in black, unmoving. The rest of the family moved in a soft line in front of them bowing in turn, offering incense.

Friends and neighbours arrived through the next three days. Each person was announced by the crier who then called out the three bows they made to Sum.

"First bow. Second bow. Third bow. Family thank the offering."

Jun Ching heard these words over and over, bowing to each visitor at the end to thank them until she could barely tell if she was hearing it in her ears or in her head. The wailing in the background had grown louder as the aunts took turns by the fire replacing Penny's nervous calls with ones of appropriate anguish.

Although the sound was unsettling, Jun Ching preferred it to the silence that took over when there were no visitors to hear them. The visitors coming to pay their respects filled the seats on either side of the room, talking to the family sometimes on the more mundane, sometimes about Sum herself but always about old times, no one mentioned the last few months. Jun Ching felt constantly the gaze of lots of eyes on her back and heard the unconcealed words spoken around the room as though they simply weren't there. *What's going to happen to the children? Are they going to stay here? Where is their father? Is she going to keep them?* As people arrived, people would shift and leave to make room – it seemed to Jun Ching that the entire village was slowly trickling through the house. The flow of people wasn't constant and there were times when they were left alone that all that filled the air was the gentle crackling of the fire outside and the children were allowed then to stand, stretch their legs and have something for their stomachs.

In the mid-morning of the third day, a small lady dressed all in black came to the door. The children did not look up, her name was mentioned, *Tang Ma*, Mother Tang, but they didn't recognise it as with many of the other names that had been called through the last few days.

"First bow. Second bow. Third bow." The black slippered feet turned to face them.

"Family thank the offering." Jun Ching glanced up briefly to see who she was thanking and stopped. The woman was staring directly at her, not at Ah Ho as all the other guests had done, she was staring directly at her with eyes without irises, Jun Ching thought. Just glittering black holes, staring. She bowed her head and returned her eyes to the floor. The woman moved on. Jun Ching looked sideways to Jun Yee but there was nothing on his face, he had barely looked up and had not registered the queer eyes of the black lady.

"Jun Yee-" Whack. Ah Ho's palm met the back of her head.

"Don't speak."

Jun Yee took her hand, squeezed it but said nothing. Turning her eyes back the floor again she started counting and when she got to 49 she would allow herself to look up again, *9, 10, 11…* she shuffled her knees on the mat, *24, 25…* was she imagining it or could she feel the stare still, *37, 38…* did she even want to look at her again though, *47, 48, 49.* She found her immediately. She had chosen to sit almost directly opposite her, slightly to the right in the second row and was still staring directly at her whilst talking to one of the aunts. Her eyes were unmoving whilst her hand slowly fanned herself with a small fan tied to her wrist. She seemed not to notice that the little girl was now looking back at her. She didn't smile, she didn't nod, she showed no acknowledgement. The stare unsettled Jun Ching, it didn't feel evil, it wasn't scary, but it was bottomless – as though she couldn't see far enough into the flat blackness of her eyes to see the meaning behind it. It reminded her of a lizard.

Looking away it wasn't long before Jun Ching forgot about the woman and her eyes. The final guests were arriving, and the funeral crier called her thoughts back to her dead mother and all the people she had to thank for her. By the time midday came, she looked up and the eyes were gone.

The afternoon of the third day brought the final act. The crier came inside the house and spoke a few low words to Ah Ho who shook her head and said nothing. He moved to the front gate and called out to four men who had been sweating on the steps below. They came carrying two long bamboo canes and lengths of thick rope which they laid beside the coffin. The little courtyard had emptied now, the adults had retreated into the house and pulled little people with them. Only Jun Yee and Jun Ching stood watching. One of the men brought out a hammer and nails as he positioned the first nail on the top corner of the lid, Jun Ching moaned as she understood what was about to happen. She moaned again, low and unnatural, and made quick small steps take her to the head of the coffin, squeezing herself against the man's arm. He looked to the crier who simply nodded so he raised the hammer and brought the first tap on the nail – just lightly to hopefully shake this little girl away from the coffin. But she didn't go. She thought about her beautiful ma inside the box, trapped inside now, how can she be inside this box forever? How could they stop the light from her face forever? She could picture Sum's face, eyes closed, head resting on a pillow that would shake with each strike of the hammer, gently side to side. She wanted to touch her warm cheek again, not the cold, grey face she knew was under there. Jun Ching rested her palm on the wood above her mother's face, seeing that the girl wouldn't move, the man continued. He drove each nail in fast, halfway in with each strike because with each strike the girl jumped and moaned lightly, and he couldn't bear it. Her hand felt each jolt and her ears cowered at the sound. She pictured Sum's hands falling to her sides within the box. He had eight nails to put in but only did six before he had to move away. When there was quiet again, she turned and looked down the length of the coffin, straight through the door with her brother standing to the side, straight up the aisle between the chairs, the mats where they had knelt for three days, straight to the altar and into Sum's eyes in the photograph. The eyes said nothing to her, no comfort as fat round tears rolled down her tiny face and fell reluctantly off her jaw. Her eyes flicked back to her brother's and she drew her hand back off the lid.

The men approached again to tie the rope around the coffin and attached the bamboo poles. They worked around her, occasionally nudging her but not asking her to move. When it was finally ready the crier gathered the family and the procession to the graveyard began.

The crier led the way with Jun Yee following close behind carrying the photograph facing out with both hands. Jun Ching beside him silently walking and behind her Ah Ho, then the coffin swinging between the four men and finally the rest of the family trailing behind. The crier called loudly all the way to the graveyard to clear the spirits in the streets and threw money for the dead to distract them from this new one passing into their world. People stopped to watch the little procession go by, but the children saw only the sand and gravel under their feet. The plot they had rented was low on the hill, one of the cheapest, the ones higher up gave those that rested there a view of the sea. This one could see the sea only through the thick clumps of heart-shaped leaves of the tallow trees in front of it. The men lowered the coffin into the ground and untied the poles. There were dull thuds as the loose ends hit the coffin followed by a coarse slithering as they pulled the rope out from under it rocking it on its side before finally settling. There was nothing left but for the family to each cast a handful of dirt into the grave and turn away.

There was silence as they walked back to the house, the crier they had also left at the graveside with a red *lai see* envelope of money-good-luck, and the silence caused an emptiness in their ears after the three days of wailing. The same people that had watched the procession on its way out now turned their faces from their return wanting no part of the sadness to follow. Once back at the house the family scattered, each to their own jobs to return the rooms to normal.

The next day, the house tried to force itself back into its routine. The adults went back to work where they could, leaving a little earlier and coming back a little later to avoid the shock that had settled in the rooms and the children continued their chores with less noise than before. Jun Ching found her brother unwilling to talk or to eat the food she brought to him. He sat at the top of the steps leading up to the house where Nine Auntie had stood and greeted them the first day of this trip months ago now. He looked constantly at the sea whilst his sister sat by him unmoving. On the third day she spoke.

"I don't think she's coming back Brother."

He said nothing until he felt that he couldn't escape it any longer.

"I don't think she is either."

"Are you coming back though?"

From inside the house, Gwai watched them sitting on the step and felt a fist clench in her chest. It wasn't her fault, she kept telling herself. She had no idea when she convinced the old lady to make them stay that it would end this way. It was only meant to be for a few more days or even weeks. She wasn't supposed to send for their things and move them here. There was no need for it to end like this. She squared her shoulders. Sum was weak. It was a weak thing to do to leave behind two children like this. And selfish too. Gwai was right though, she wasn't able to look after herself and the children, she'd proven that much at least. And everyone else can see that now and that's what she wanted in the first place, for everyone to see who was better, who was in charge. But what happens now? She almost felt sorry for the two little bottoms sitting side by side in front of her.

"Penny, there is a salted egg left over, take it out to those two, it'll be a waste to throw it away." Penny's hands paused in mid-air as she was clearing away the evening's bowls. She daren't meet Gwai's eyes but she wasn't quite sure what to do. They never had extra food, even if it was uneaten at one meal it would be saved for the next, it was unheard of for it to be offered to her cousins. "What are you waiting for? I told you to go."

But Penny remained rooted to the ground, shocked. And her shock stung. Was it really that much of a surprise for Gwai to give these children an egg? Just an egg? It was true that she didn't like Sum and she knew the hostility had been noticed by others, that even the sight of her children had annoyed her but even she couldn't help herself. But as Penny stood there, her immobility an accusation of Gwai in itself, Gwai felt the fire rising in her throat and spidering up the sides of her face. It wasn't her who did this to them. They had a mother and she abandoned them. She refused to take responsibility for them, and she refused to feel guilty at the sight of them. It was not her fault.

"Well," she snatched the bowl from Penny, "If you won't take it to them, I'll eat it myself then." Before Penny could do anything, she stabbed the egg with her chopsticks and ate it. The saltiness made her mouth salivate for a second and it caught in her throat as she forced it down.

Chapter Six

Sum was the door Gwai pushed through to get into the family. Gwai had no memory of the day they met but it did twist her life, leading her here. The village was growing into a small town by then, but the two little girls lived in spheres of only a few streets around their homes, and so lived on the very periphery of each other's lives, brushing paths but never crossing. This was until the new nuns from the missionary decided to provide a free bowl of watery *juk*, in the afternoon, to help boost the children's attendance of their classes – where most of the children had no interest in learning to read or write, the opposite was true of free *juk*. Despite this, the only thing that became regular at the classes was the feel of bamboo across little palms, tellings-off punctuated by spittle rain and a desperate hope that the little bodies slumped forwards on elbows lured in by the rumble of their tummies would learn something, anything, by design or by accident whilst they waited.

After lunch one day, whilst there were a few minutes left before they returned inside for the afternoon lesson, Gwai thought about whether she would stay for the afternoon. The small group of children who were there in the morning had already almost halved in number as they often did once the food had gone. Going home would mean looking after her younger brother, the newest baby in the family, and doing whatever chores her mother hadn't done in the morning. Or she could go back into the stuffy room and hopefully manage a sly nap at the back without attracting the attention of the cane. The baby had cried through till dawn the night before and she would definitely get a better rest here than at home – she rocked from side to side from one leg to the other and back again – besides she just noticed a new face in the group, and she wanted to know who she was. Her decision was made.

The face belonged to a girl slightly taller than herself with slim features and a thin handful of slightly browning hair unlike the jet black of her own. She stood alone to the side of the group, a faint smile on her face, scanning the ground. One hand hung by her side clutching a fluttering of leaves, the other pushed a finger sideways into her teeth as she chewed.

"What are you picking up leaves for?"

She looked up and blinked.

"*Wai!* I asked you what you are picking up leaves for." Maybe she's deaf, Gwai thought, that might explain why she's on her own picking up leaves.

Sum smiled then, as though she heard her thoughts and wanted to prove her wrong, "I'm choosing leaf families – the ones that look the same are one family then, when they are together, we can make little fans or bowls or boats or lots of things. It's good fun. My name is Sum – not *sum* as in deep, but *sum* as in heart, like 'Ah, you will give me a heart attack one day'." She grabbed her chest and staggered backwards a little to the left. "That's what my ma always says. Do you want to play with me?"

Gwai liked the theatrics but not the leaf collecting. "No, I don't like leaves. Maybe when you are playing something else."

"Why don't you like leaves?"

"They make my hands dirty."

"Your hands are already dirty."

"They are not! And even if they were, they would make them even more dirty."

The nun called out the end of break and the children gathered like marbles on a slope, jostling and rolling back inside. The two girls didn't speak again but walked towards the building.

"Today is my first day here."

"That's easy to see."

"The nun doesn't seem to like children very much."

"She doesn't. You have to be careful, she likes to hit us with that bamboo cane she uses to point at things with. And it really hurts because it's so thin."

"If she doesn't like children so much why does she teach them?"

"Because her god told her to I guess."

"Her god?"

"Yeah, she has to do what he says. Like her father."

Sum slowed almost to a halt whilst she thought about this, not wanting to spend time with someone who was only there because someone else told them to be. Gwai saw her chance.

"She seems like she is in a worse mood than usual today as well. There's bound to be trouble this afternoon and that means we will all get a bit of it. I'm not going to be the meat she slaps with that cane today." She turned away from the funnel of children. "Are you coming?"

Sum was uncertain, Gwai could tell she was weighing up her options in her mind. She sighed dramatically and made to look like she was going to go without her. Sum nodded quickly.

"Come on then."

Without any warning the two girls turned and walked swiftly and purposefully off the church grounds without drawing the attention of the bamboo wielding nun.

"What shall we do now then?" Gwai turned to her new companion once they were at a safe distance.

"Go home?"

"Go home? *Wah*, you're no fun at all! I should have just left you to the nun!"

Sum panicked. "No, I don't want to go home. Where do you want to go? I don't mind."

Gwai smiled to herself. "Let's go down to the market then, I know where we can get some juice for nothing."

Sum watched the ground go by beneath her bare feet, glancing over to Gwai's. The second toe of each foot was much longer than the big toe, trying to push it out of the way almost. The big toe pushed back, causing a dent in the side of the second one though it would probably lose the fight in the end. It was a sign, the old wives used to laugh, of an unruly wife who would control her husband and give him no peace.

They wove in and out through the crowd of shoppers, it was early afternoon by now and the first of the fishermen had come in with their catch. The market was filled with busy housewives buying dinner and men having finished the early shift and resting at the tea stalls. Gwai led her round the back of one of the stalls, squatted down behind an empty table and pulled Sum down beside her. Pointing to a plain looking girl with a wide face and a long plait down her back, serving tea at the tables, Gwai spoke.

"You see her? The one with the red string in her plait? That's my sister. She's been working here for nearly two years. She'll never leave now. My ma says the best chance she'll have is if someone is willing to marry her, but her face isn't pretty, and she has no figure to help so no one's been falling over themselves for her. My ma says it had better happen soon before her hands are ruined from washing all those tea cups all day long but I think it's too late already. Her hands are already all dry so now she'll have to marry a farmer or a labourer because they don't mind rough hands. And anyway, she's been here every day for two years so all the men have already seen her and if no one has asked yet there's no one new who's going to, don't you say so?"

Sum nodded. Dry hands meant nothing to her, nor did the thoughts of men or marriage. Gwai's sister was walking towards them now with a cloth in hand. At the last minute before they were discovered, Gwai jumped up with her hands clasped behind her back, big grin across her face.

"*Aiy*! You scared me you horrid girl!" Gwai's sister pressed her hand to her chest with no smile on her lips. She glanced around her to check no one was watching and with no one tapping chopsticks on the tables calling for her attention she started to wipe down the one in front of them. "What are you doing here? Shouldn't you be at that school learning things not hanging around here waiting to frighten me to death?"

"The nun is in a bad mood today. She likes to hit when she's in a bad mood and we didn't want to be the ones she hit so we left."

Her sister's cloth paused its circular rhythm for a moment, her face didn't soften but her eyes took a step back from a scolding and then started again.

"And? So, you decided to come and scare me instead? Well, I'm busy, I don't have time for your games you can scare me later."

"Too late, I already scared you."

"Go away then."

"But Sister, we are thirsty. I beg you, do you have any juice today?"

"Ah, so that's what you want! No. No, there isn't any juice today and even if we did, I wouldn't give it to you. I can't do it all the time you know, the boss would find out and fire me then you'll be happy won't you? Now go away."

"Please Sister…" Gwai called at her sister's back. Sum turned to leave, "Where are you going? Don't give up so easily, she'll be back. Maybe not with juice but we'll get something."

And she did come back and as she leaned over to refill the metal canister of chopsticks in the middle of the table, she dropped two small stumps of sugar cane from her wide sleeves that rolled over to Gwai who scooped them up into her own.

"There's nothing else. Now go."

"Thank you! You're the best sister in the world!" Gwai whispered as she snuck away with Sum in tow. The two girls wound their way to the seafront and sat on the pebbles looking out at the water. Gwai handed her one of the fist-sized stumps and started tearing into her own. Sum did the same, crushing small chunks of the cane with her teeth to get the sweet juices out, sucking them dry before spitting out the stalk on the ground beside them.

"Your sister is very good to you."

"She's okay."

"She risked getting in trouble for you. That's being pretty good to you."

"If you say it is, it is." Sum looked at her new friend as she flicked the stalks with her fingers. "I guess you can say she is good in that way. But not in the way that matters."

"What way is that?"

"She never helps me when I argue with Ma. She is always on her side, even after Ma has left, she is still on her side. Whatever Ma says she says. It's no fun."

"Oh. What do you argue about?"

"Everything. Like yesterday, she was talking with Ma about marriage again. I mean, all she wants is to get married. That's all. She hasn't even thought past that yet. All that happens after you get married is that you have someone else's family to serve instead of your own. So, I said I thought she was being stupid and then they were both shouting at me!"

Sum had no answer for this. Her own ma often said, having a girl is just feeding someone else's daughter until she returns to them. She saw how her brothers' bowls always had more rice than hers; she saw how what little meat was on the dinner table was given first to her father then the rest to her brothers though all were younger than her. Gwai's voice continued over her own thoughts. "And another thing, who would want to marry one of the men from this village anyway? With their brown faces and smell of fish guts. You would be stuck here forever." She looked towards two men mending nets across the beach, with the corners of her mouth dragging down she sighed like a disappointed wife rather than the 10 year old she was. "This is what I mean, she has a small mind and small minds will never go big places."

"What big places are there to go?"

"Well, lots! Have you not seen the movies in the playhouse? There are lots of places much, much bigger than this where women carry umbrellas all the time and everyone goes everywhere by rickshaw. And where the ground doesn't turn to mud every time it rains but even if it did it wouldn't matter because everyone wears shoes."

"Really?"

"Definitely really! My sister's boss has a son who went to Hong Kong and he says that's what it's like there. He comes back every new year and gives big thick *lai see* packets out, you know, ones that that aren't filled with coins. When I'm bigger, I will earn money for the boat and I will go too, wouldn't that be great?"

"You have to go by boat?"

"It's across the water stupid, a boat is the only way unless you want to swim there."

Sum chewed on her lip. "No, I think I will stay here. I don't like boats and I can't swim so better that I stay here."

"You're scared!"

"Of course I'm scared. My father says the sea is dangerous and when it is hungry it can take many lives, especially of those people who play about on its waves."

"*Tch!* I'm not scared. I'll do anything to get away from here and if the sea takes me on my way there then at least I tried. You can stay here then and grow mouldy and smelly with my sister then!"

"I don't mind the smell of fish." Sum muttered.

Chapter Seven

Jun Ching looked at her hands, followed them up her arms – definitely still there. She followed her toes, her feet and up her legs until they disappeared under her dress – definitely still there. But he didn't see her, he had barely spoken a word in days. In their flat in Hong Kong she had heard one Li sister shout at the other 'did you grow up eating glass?!' when the other got in the way and they couldn't see through them. And now she knew how that felt. Transparent. And she needed not to be. She needed to be seen and spoken to.

One day, about a week after the funeral, she went to the back of the house and joined the women in the cleaning and preparations for dinner. Penny's hands stopped when she came in, dangling over the tub of warm water filled with clothes in front of her, fingertips brushing the surface. Her round brown eyes softly swallowed Jun Ching whole, a tiny smile flashed, then wordlessly she took up her scrubbing again. Jun Ching grabbed a washboard tucked into a gap between the wall and the stove and sat down next to Penny. When she turned it over, she noticed the board was covered in long brown stains seeped into the wood for years. Penny gasped when she saw it.

"Not that one! Never that one." She snatched it from her, quickly putting it back in its place, checking over her shoulders that no one had seen. She got another for Jun Ching and back at her seat she whispered this time. "It's Gwai Bak Mo's. She's had it for years and she gets furious if anyone else touches it. She never uses it but no one else is allowed to either."

"Why doesn't she just throw it anyway then?"

"Someone tried once. I think she brought it back."

Jun Ching shrugged. It was strange to prefer a dirty one, but she didn't care and reached over to the pile of clothes and took the closest thing, a vest. She trapped an air bubble briefly between it and the water as she pushed it under and rubbed it together with little intention. She pressed her small knees into the rim of the tub whilst above their heads a conversation gathered.

"A lot of people came to the funeral, didn't they?"

"Yes, I didn't think there would be so many for a suicide. Like that Wing family boy across the town, he didn't get so many. I wouldn't go to one, you don't know what kind of dirty things you might bring back with you. It would be easy for a ghost to hook onto my trouser leg and follow me home!"

"Hush! She did not kill herself. It was an accident. You heard what the old lady said. She never could swim so that's why when she was washed away, she drowned. You'd better not let her hear you say suicide, or she'll peel your skin right off!"

"What was she doing in the water at all then if she couldn't swim?!"

"Wading. It was hot."

"Tch!"

"And another thing, that Wing boy was a shameful affair, in love with his own cousin – she was practically his sister! And hanging himself too left his family no way to cover that up. No wonder people stayed away from that. You shouldn't pull Dai Jair and him into the same sentence together either."

"Nobody believes Ma anyway, she can say what she wants but everyone knows."

"That's not true. Did you see Mother Tang come? She came and she would not come if it was suicide. It would be too bad for her business, she wouldn't take that risk."

"She didn't stay long."

"Why would she? Waiting for you to help her count her toes?!"

"You'd count them before I would! I wonder why she came though, she only ever does something for a reason-"

"Enough!" Gwai spat from across the room. "No more talking. Mother Tang and everyone else came to pay their respects. That is all. No one committed suicide. Dai Jair was not careful, and she drowned. Now get back to work, your tongue's idleness is spreading to your hands!"

There was quiet for a few minutes but as soon as Gwai left the aunts began again. The girls remained quiet over their laundry until Jun Ching spoke.

"Penny, who were they talking about? Who is Mother Tang who came but didn't stay long?"

"Mother Tang was the one in all black, not tall, not short, has her hair in a bun and has little eyes like black coal splints in her face."

Jun Ching remembered the lady with the fan staring at her even after she counted to 49, still staring. "Why is it strange that she would come?"

"Because she depends on her good fortune for people to use her and people think it is bad luck to go to the house of a suicide – but there hasn't been one of those here." The second half of her sentence tumbled out on top of itself as she said it. "So, the fact that she came means there is no bad fortune here or else she would not risk it affecting her business."

"What is her business?"

"She is a matchmaker, one of the best in all the villages around here."

"What's a matchmaker?"

"She makes matches of course." Jun Ching's face remained blank. "She is the one people go to if they want to set up a marriage for their children. It is usually from the man's family and she will go and find the right girl and then negotiate the dowry and the dates for the two sides."

"Is that how Paw Paw and Gung Gung got married?"

"No, usually only rich people around here use matchmakers, people like us don't have money to give to people like her. That is why she needs to look like she carries good fortune around her like a charm – so that people trust her to find good matches that bear lots of children. And then give her a big, thick *lai see* packet full of money."

"So why was she here?"

"Just like Six Auntie says, she was just here to pay her respects. She knew Paw Paw from a long time ago. That is everything I know."

Their voices dropped into the water as they continued rubbing the clothes against the ridges of the washboard, so the murmuring of the aunts was able to find its way to them again.

"Did she say that really?"

"Yes, I heard her myself, talking to Second Sister-in-law." Jun Ching remembered seeing Ah Ho and Gwai whispering earlier that morning too. They hadn't seen her slip past them, and she hadn't listened to anything they were saying.

"What else did you hear?"

"She told the old lady it brings shame and the longer they are here the stranger it will seem to people."

"And how did she reply?"

"She didn't. What can you say to something like that? She didn't say anything wrong. It's true. People will start wondering why their father hasn't come to take them back yet. That's if they still believe that story anyway."

"Well, why wouldn't they believe it? No one's said any different, have they? You haven't had a loose mouth again and told anyone have you?"

"No! Of course not! I don't have a loose mouth! But it's obvious, anyone can guess something was wrong with the two of them when she stayed so long with the children. She always only stayed for a few days for Ching Ming festival then goes again. This time she had been here for months!"

"The old lady forced her to."

"And so what? She had hands and feet – if she wanted to, she could have gone."

"So, what is the old lady going to do with them then?"

At this, Penny stiffened then began a sudden deluge of detail on the shirt Jun Ching was washing - that is Five Uncle's shirt, he's very particular about his clothes, must make sure you get all the dirt out, especially down the front, he often dropped food down the front, like that mark, what mark is that, is it orange or is it red, something he ate at work maybe, that colour is hard to get out especially if it had tomatoes in it… But Jun Ching's ears parted the two conversations smoothly like water round a rock nodding at Penny's questions on one side still listening to the aunts on the other.

"I don't know, I don't think she even knows herself, but Second Sister-in-law said not to do anything before the return tomorrow night. If Dai Jair does come back, then she must see them here or she could become angry and want revenge."

"And after tomorrow night?"

"I think she will find a way."

Jun Ching had stopped listening. *Ma was coming back? How? Why hadn't anyone told her? Had anyone told Brother?* Her thoughts raced down to her legs, skidding from side to side, twitching with excitement as she fought the urge to run to him in case she missed anything else. Her eyes jumped up and met Penny's whose didn't reflect the same excitement back. Her brows hitched together for a second before understanding made her eyes lose their wideness and she turned her head slowly, one side then the other in an almost imperceptible shake. Jun Ching didn't see it. She just felt a dark something settle at the back of her mind when Penny didn't share her smile but she pushed it away. It was of no use to her right now. Not now that Ma was coming back.

The aunts had moved onto something new now and Jun Ching could control her legs no longer. The shirt she was pretending to wash plopped into the basin as she got up, silently but quickly so not to draw the aunts attention. Penny fished out the abandoned garment as she watched her cousin leave, her round eyes rolling back over to the pile of clothes with a sigh.

"Brother!" He hadn't moved from the top step where she had left him earlier. His head whipped round, eyes opened wide. "Brother! Bro-"

"What is it? Are you okay?" His entire body turned to face her, and he grabbed her wrists as he scanned her arms, legs, head, everywhere for any signs of hurt. It occurred to her that this was the first time in days that he had actually looked at her.

"Nothing's wrong Brother, there's nothing wrong with me. I just heard the aunts say Ma is coming back tonight! Is it true? Is Ma coming back tonight?"

Lines drew themselves across his face and he looked old and dark again, "No Sister, she won't come back."

"But they just said!"

"What they said is not true. It can't be true. Do you remember the funeral? They buried her already, there is no way she can come back now. We watched them do it, remember?"

"But they just said…"

"They are talking about the spirit. Some people believe that the spirit will come home after they have died before they go to the next world, the yin world, to wait to be born again".

"Do we believe that?"

"I don't know. I have never seen a spirit. I don't know if they are real."

"But Ma believed in them, didn't she? That's why she gave us those little blades to carry in the cemetery when we went to see Gung Gung?"

"I guess so."

"Well, if Ma believed it then I will too. Then I will get to see Ma tonight!"

"Sister, you need to listen to me." He didn't know why he was being so insistent, but he knew he had to be. "She's not really coming back. Even if what they say about her spirit coming back is true, the one that comes back isn't really her. You understand?"

She nodded silently and, in her head, thought about where she could hide the little blade this evening so it wouldn't keep her ma away.

After dinner that night, the uncles were solemn with their cigarettes wrapping them all in smoky wisps. There was a conspicuous lack of fluttering chatter as the women cleaned up after dinner at the back of the house, which usually padded out the harsh sound of bowl against bowl as they were washed. Tonight, there were only harsh noises. Even the children had been told to play outside away from the house though the sky was not even fully dark yet when Ah Ho herself told the uncles to call them into bed. Stranger still was Four Uncle going out and getting them himself - a chore left so often to Four Auntie that his own child wasn't sure what to do on seeing him. Jun Yee and Jun Ching took themselves upstairs with a good night first to Ah Ho then to Four Uncle (as he came back in), Five Uncle and Seven Uncle all of whom barely nodded. From the little balcony where they slept, overhanging the main room, they had a clear view of everything below. Jun Yee quickly undressed and covered himself with his light blanket, told his sister to do the same and rolled over to face the wall. He had his eyes pressed shut and Jun Ching tip-toed around him and quietly placed the little blade Ma had given her before into the egg roll tin with what was left of her figurines – just in case. Padding back round him, she settled herself cross-legged at the edge, pulling her loose slip over her knees and dropping her hands folded into her lap, watching everything below. She was here for the evening with no intention of sleep.

Below, Ah Ho had disappeared whilst the uncles murmured good nights to each other and moved into their rooms. Jun Ching's eyelids were slipping already as she watched Penny come out from the back and carefully sweep the floor clean. Five Auntie brought out fresh sticks of incense whilst Four Auntie laid out fruit in front of the photograph of Sum that had recently joined her father's and her brother's on the side table. Nine Auntie emerged from below the balcony clutching a bowl with both hands which she carefully placed next to the fruit. Gwai stood in the middle of the room, silently directing them all. A screen slid open, Ah Ho strode into the room and everyone stopped.

"Is everything done?"

At the sound of Ah Ho's voice, the aunts stiffened, and Jun Ching jolted up from a brief sleep she had already fallen into.

"All is ready, Lai Lai." Gwai spoke for them.

Ah Ho nodded and dismissed them with a wave and they almost backed into their respective rooms with a well-rehearsed rumble of good nights, leaving her alone in the middle of the room. She looked unexpectedly stooped. Her bun had come loose, sagging low at the bottom of her neck.

"Go to sleep." She didn't even look up but when Jun Ching didn't move, Ah Ho snapped her gaze up finding her eyes immediately. Her voice didn't break. "Go now."

Jun Ching shuffled herself back several paces on her bottom until she was out of sight before she uncrossed her legs and laid down, blinking in the shadows. She heard the old woman moving around below her.

Ah Ho walked a slow, wide circle around the room pausing to pick up a cane in one corner, stacking tea glasses in another. Her hands moved constantly from her sides to her face, rubbing her eyes, dragging her fingers from her hair down her cheeks and neck. Dry grey strands were pulled out and left hanging. Coming back round to the side table she placed both palms down and leaned in to stare at her daughter's face tracing each line with her eyes. Moving her gaze first to her son, then to her husband she asked silent questions. Her lips moved but no sound came so the child above her would not hear. Why did they go first? They shouldn't have gone before her. *Husband, why didn't you take me with you?* She didn't want to be here alone like this. Her brows crumbled into each other as she turned back to her daughter, her first, her help. None of the others were her heart like Sum was. She should have let her know that. Sum's was the heart that never hardened, not like her. It was a good photograph of her, but it caught nothing of the giggling she gave into as a toddler, and this would be how the others would eventually come to remember her as their own memories faded into this photograph. But she would remember, just as she could still bring to her ear the exact note of her husband's voice where the others could only animate the image. And her son, her first boy. Him too. The one who was in a hurry, always hurrying. Why did he have to be in a hurry to leave as well? She would remember all these things. Pressing her lips together she stopped their silent murmur and pushed herself off the table she had sunk into. Squaring her shoulders, she reached for a bowl of white powder and taking a handful she sprinkled it over the length of the threshold leaving a light white dusting, careful not to use it all. She paused. The little strength she had gathered to get across the room had gone again as she propped herself up by one hand against the doorframe and stared out into the dark.

"Ah, *Mui Jai*. Little girl. Come back la. Come back one more time."

The old woman looked down at the chalk, her shoulders jerked once before she drew herself up again and with one flick of her wrist, she hurled the remaining powder out on top of it.

Jun Ching heard the clatter of the bowl against a wooden surface where it was slung and the slow then increasingly fast whirring as it rolled on its rim until it finally lay flat. She didn't move again until she heard Ah Ho pull the screen to from her room and then counted to 43 on top of that just to be safe. When she was sure there was no one left downstairs she pushed herself up onto her knees sitting on her heels.

"Brother." She whispered but he didn't reply. She waited.

"Brother." Nothing.

Getting to her feet she padded round to see his eyes were closed. She wanted to wake him; she was scared. She knew there was no reason to be, but she still was. The back of her neck felt funny, like she wanted to keep her hands over it to protect it. She didn't know how he would react though if she did wake him. He did and said things at the moment that were strange to her, so she left him. She crept back to the banister and sat cross-legged. She grabbed the banister with both hands and pulled herself closer so she could rest her forehead on the rough wood. Ah Ho had left a candle burning which poured a small puddle of light onto the table in front of the photographs. There was a swathe of darkness from the puddle to the threshold where the moon splashed its own bluey white tint in which she could just make out the large round splat of white on the ground in the middle of the line of light dust. Then she waited. She stared at the candle and the more she stared the darker the room grew by comparison. She darted her eyes to a random spot in the blackness every time her eyes were feeling blinded by the flame to see how much she couldn't see and guess what she knew was there during the daylight. Each time her eyes flicked back the candle seemed brighter until her eyes adjusted again.

"Ah Mui, what are you sitting there doing?"

She jumped. She heard the words but not the voice. She listened again – only Ma and Brother called her *Ah Mui* and she hadn't been concentrating. The back of her neck tingled so much that it was on the verge of tickling. Whose voice was it? She sat still like a rock.

"Mui?" It was him. She let go of the breath she held to help her hear and dropped her shoulders. She thought for a moment that she was relieved. She rubbed the back of her neck.

"Nothing, Brother. I'm not doing anything. I just couldn't sleep."

He crept up beside her and shuffled so that he sat on one foot curled beneath him, the other propped up as he rested his cheek on his knee. It was too dark for him to look at her, but she could tell from the direction of his voice that he was facing her.

"You couldn't sleep?" He sounded normal again. This was not the voice he had been using in the day recently, but the old one he had before. "Why didn't you wake me?"

"I did call you, but you were sleeping so you couldn't hear." She whispered out into the dark.

"Then you should have pushed me awake." She shrugged, not thinking that he couldn't see her. He sighed. "Are you cold?"

"A little."

He rolled back until he was lying flat and at full stretch reached his blanket. Pulling it to him he sat upright again and shuffled closer to his sister wrapping the blanket around both of them. Without thinking they sank against each other.

"Brother? By the door, that white stuff on the floor, what is that?"

"It's chalk – the stuff we usually use in the kitchen to keep ants away."

"Are there a lot of ants there?"

"No, I don't think so. They put it there so in the morning they can see if anything has come in."

"But we would wake up if someone came in, wouldn't we?"

Another sigh. "It's for the spirit, sister. Sometimes you can't see spirits but if they come in, they will have to step in the chalk first and then you will see the footprints."

"For Ma's spirit?"

"I guess."

"So, when Ma comes back tonight, she won't be using her body to come back?"

"She is not going to come back."

"Oh... But *if* she comes back, she won't have a body. How will she get here then? Will she float here? If she floats, then she won't step in the chalk anyway."

"I don't know Sister. Whether they float or whether they walk it doesn't matter. I only know one thing: Ma is not coming back."

Jun Ching left it for a bit. "Brother? You know yesterday? You said that some people believe spirits come back before going to the yin world? But I don't understand why they would come back."

"They don't. We don't believe in spirits, Sister." Even he could hear how harsh his own voice sounded and sighed. "They think that after people die, they will come back to their home, sometimes the spirit is confused, they don't know what to do, or where to go, so they go home thinking they are still alive and that they belong there but once they get there they will see they don't belong anymore and leave. Or some just go home to say goodbye before they go to the yin world maybe just to see everything is okay."

"Is that why everyone went to bed early tonight?"

"Yes, spirits are meant to be scared of the yang energy of living people so they will avoid them. If everyone was still awake, the spirit won't come in."

"And the candle? Why did Paw Paw leave that lit?"

"So the spirit can see it to come home."

"How do they know it will be tonight?"

"It is supposed to be seven nights after the person died. Or something like that. That's when the spirit wanders. I don't know why but that's what they think. It won't happen though. No matter what they think." He murmured the last sentence.

"Or how much we all want her to?"

"They don't want her to."

"They do. Or Paw Paw does at least."

"And how do you know?"

"I heard her. Earlier, downstairs." A soft sound of his hair brushing against his collar let her know he was now looking down towards her. She tucked her chin in a little more so the most he could see was her forehead.

"What did you hear?"

"She was standing at the door and asked her to come back, to come back one more time. I know she was talking to Ma because she called her *mui jai* – just like Ma used to call me. She told me before, her ma used to call her the same thing."

He didn't say anything, she thought he didn't believe her.

"It's true Brother, I heard her with my own ears. She seemed sad too. Her voice was completely different. It didn't even sound like her. But then she noticed I was up here, as soon as she saw me the sad voice disappeared and the normal one came back so straight away I crept under the blanket."

He said nothing leaving silence to settle the unexpected thoughts that were rustled up by the image of a human side to his grandmother.

"So how long do you want us to sit here then, *Mui Jai*?" He shuffled a little, jostling his sister into a smile.

"I don't know. Until I fall asleep, I guess." *Until I see Ma –* she thought but she didn't want to say that. She knew he didn't think Ma was coming back and she didn't want to annoy him by talking about it more now that she had just got the normal him back. And she knew, in her tummy, that she would be able to see her ma even if no one else could.

"Okay then, until you fall asleep – that won't take long. Shall we play a game? Or shall I tell you a story? What would you like?"

"A story. About..." The pause was so long he thought she might have fallen asleep already. "Brother? What's going to happen to us?"

What was he supposed to say? He didn't know, what are brothers supposed to say to sisters at times like this? Was he supposed to be hopeful? Or prepare her for bad things? What would Ma have wanted him to say?

"I don't know, Mui Jai. I really don't know. But one thing I can promise you is that us two, we will stick together, okay? Like sugar stuck on beans. You just keep your fingers hooked into my back pocket... Go on then, hook them in." Little fingers hooked in under the blanket and he heard her smile in the dark. "*La*, there, just like that and we'll be fine. Just as long as we're together, nothing bad will happen. And even if it does, I will protect us, okay? Do you believe me?"

She nodded back against his shoulder and wriggled her fingers. "A story about a brother and sister please. A happy one with a crispy bun in it somewhere."

When he opened his eyes in the morning, Jun Ching was rolled up like a spring roll in the whole blanket an arm's length away from him, fast asleep. The weak dawn sunlight was trickling through the windows past his feet that were pressed up against the banisters. The house was still quiet, mostly. What was that sound? It was faint; *shh shh shh*. He pushed himself up on his elbows. He was cold. He groped about in his mind for the references to the night before, something had happened, something significant, what was it? Looking around him he found no clues. No Ma; Ma was still dead. It wasn't till he sat upright and saw downstairs to the outline of a woman's figure standing at the threshold to the house swaying back and forth and the faint dusting of chalk at her feet that he remembered. The floorboards crackled as he jumped up. It couldn't be. It was daylight, just. But it couldn't be. He scrambled over his sister and down the stairs towards the swaying figure cracking his knee on a banister on the way. The *shh shh* got louder as he got closer. Was she whispering to him? Hush? Quiet? Don't wake the others! Of course! *Shh shh shh*. The sound was getting shorter, sharper, more purposeful. His eyes were fixed on the dark figure in the doorway but blinded by the light behind it. He stopped dead a few feet behind the figure. His lips blurred into a faint smile. She was shorter as a spirit. He could just make out now that she had her back to him. Her hair was tied up in a small bun, how strange, Ma has so much hair and so long that she rarely wore it like that. Maybe it isn't as heavy when you're a spirit. He thought he saw the edge of her smile as her head turned slightly to the side. He wanted to reach out for her elbow, but he almost didn't want her to turn around. Something in his head whispered. *Ma*. His own smile grew a little more. She didn't look like she was swaying as much as she did from upstairs now, her body was still, it was her arms that were moving rhythmically across the front of her body. But why? What is she doing? His eyes adjusted to the light more and she came into focus, he saw the broom handle in her hand. Looking down to the other side he saw the hard bristles of the broom scraping across the ground. *Shh shh shh*.

    Gwai heard something behind her, a jagged, uneven breathing and turned to see the boy's smiling face. Her breath caught in her throat - he looked just like Sum for an instant - small, straight teeth, lips stretching, pushing cheeks back into an almost vulnerable smile. Then it fell away. Instantly she understood that he had not been seeing her. She felt the weight of his hope punch into her stomach. They stood looking at each other with no reason to continue or to break not even hearing the soft padding of bare feet coming tentatively down the stairs.

"Where's the powder gone?" Jun Ching's voice startled them both. "Brother? Where's the powder?"

"I swept it away." Gwai's voice was hard, harder that she meant it to be as she finally managed to swallow her breath again. All three looked at the small pile of chalk next to her feet.

"But… did you see… were there…?" Her little eyes trembled.

"Were there what?"

Jun Ching looked from her aunt to her brother and back then at the small white hill that seemed nothing at all and dared to say nothing else. They heard a screen door roll open behind them, Gwai's eyes flicked up over their heads as they both turned to see Ah Ho. She was a different woman to the one Jun Ching saw the night before. Her hair was scraped back again in her usual tight bun, she walked with her back straight and her hands by her sides. She was already looking directly at them, as though she was watching them even before they were in sight.

"What are you all standing here for?" She asked as she tucked the corner of a small handkerchief back up into the sleeve of her dress.

"Good morning Lai Lai. Nothing, I was just sweeping the floor."

"Good morning Paw Paw." The children said together. Jun Yee turned back then to Gwai with lowered eyes. "Good morning, Gwai Kam Mo."

"Good morning."

He looked at her once more, disbelieving his own sight, then turned and took his sister with him back upstairs. He tried to prolong each step, making them heavy, imagining each step a mountain to traverse, anything for more time.

"I didn't see anything Sister." He pre-empted her. "When I got down there, she had already swept it away. Never mind. Even if she hadn't swept there still would have been nothing. Like I told you last night, this world has no spirits in it."

She stood to the side, looking down at her fingers as she picked at the skin. He shook out the blanket they had shared and held it up in front of his face as he folded it and bit his lip.

Chapter Eight

There was no money in the egg roll tin. When Jun Yee went through all their pockets, his fingers were only filled with fluff. There was nothing in Ma's old clothes' pockets. There was nothing left. The problem with this was that he had nothing to buy his sister a birthday present. The following week she would turn eight and although he was doing his best to keep her happy, he was afraid that this first milestone would be too much for her without any distractions. He needed a plan and a secret one at that as it had to be surprise for her. She deserved a happy surprise.

Over the last few weeks Jun Ching's list of chores had grown, one slapping down on top of the other, on top of the other. She was still not as busy as Penny but was coming close. It was easy for Jun Yee to slip away one morning unnoticed whilst his sister pored over a needle and a holey shirt. He walked slowly down the dirt path, the same way they had started coming as a trio a few months before in the twilight. People still stared at him as he passed the noodle shack, but he no longer noticed them. Not far beyond this was the small clearing where many of the makeshift stall holders congregated among the more permanent stalls. In the middle were entire halves of pigs hung up on metal hooks surrounded by men with meat cleavers and women pointing at various parts that were sliced off for them. There was only the one main butcher here and he had his own sons working, the youngest one about Jun Yee's age, clumsy with his own meat cleaver. There would be no work for him there. His big ears twitched to the fishmongers shouting prices next door, their blades swift, dull thud then scrape of metal against wood across the chopping block where years had hollowed out the middle. Their wives behind them sitting on their haunches scratching the backs of fish, scales flying, and their bare calves and feet spattered with the sticky wet of guts recently evicted. He didn't know how to gut a fish. There was no work for him there either. He skirted round the fresh food to the outer circle where the dried food and tea stalls were. After an hour of being stared at, asking every stall for work and being refused each time Jun Yee gave up.

    He left the hustle of the square behind him and headed down to the beach. The path grew dry, compacted dirt, the main slope down to where the fisherman hauled their loads. His eye followed a straight line down where the path ran straight into the sea. He pulled it away from drifting to the right where the body was lying that day. He turned sharply at the edge of the beach, mindlessly walking back towards the house the long way. He was sure he would have been able to find something, just a one-off job for the afternoon maybe that would give him enough to buy a small bag of sweets or a something shiny for her hair. His fists clenched into round lumps in his pockets, but he didn't want to go back angry or without a solution. He sat himself down on a large flat rock and looked out to the sea. It was a dull day for late August; the wind was stirring somewhere far away contemplating the beginnings of a typhoon. The water was a grey-brown and the foaming waves looked cold as they sputtered up the sand. This felt like his stretch of beach. It was the same part they came to to play on in earlier years. It was the same part they came to with Ma everyday only a few months ago. It was the same part where the old lady sat waiting for her husband to come back from his days' fishing over 40 years ago. He looked up along the beach to his right and a long stretch away he could see her, sitting still, her black shape breaking up the clean line running down to the edge of the beach where the walkway dropped straight into the water. Her face turned towards the sea though he could not make out her features from here. The sight of her there was an unexpected comfort to him. He wondered if her husband had found Ma out there in the water and if they spoke to each other now, about their own people sitting on the beach and what to do with them. Without realising it his eyes drew back to the waves then back to the spot where he had knelt in front of her for the last time. He wasn't thinking of that then but just resting his eyes there, unconsciously tracing the edge of the rock with his fingers.

    Lien pushed her glasses up and peered out at the little boy. He still looked a little boy though he may not act like it. She had seen him a couple of times now since trying to hold him back on the beach that day. He had been down walking with his sister, carefully avoiding the spot. Though today he was on his own and had been looking at the spot for a while. She pottered around the shop, stacking empty boxes at the back, coming back to check if he was still there. Arranging bottles at the front of shelves and checking to see if he was still there. The third time she checked, and he had not moved, she couldn't help herself. She easily remembered Sum from when they were children, daydreaming whist sitting on similar rocks when their little shop was just a table and tarpaulin run by her parents. He reminded her of Sum as he sat there though she knew it was probably a romantic sentiment on her part as he was really nothing like his mother. She poured a glass of soya milk from an opened bottle and carried it over to him kicking a couple of pebbles along the way so not to startle him, but he was too far away in his head to be startled.

"Jun Yee?" He turned and blinked at her. "Come la, I poured a glass of soya milk for you." The glass clinked against the rock as she placed it down.

"Thank you, Lien Yi." He held the glass with both hands and sipped at it slowly. It was good; cold and slightly thick it lightly coated his tongue and the sides of his cheeks.

"What are you thinking about sitting here?"

"Nothing." He liked her and he wouldn't mind telling her what he was thinking but at that time he had no idea what he had been thinking about. He had just been drifting. He could tell she didn't believe him though. She probably thought he was thinking about Ma, but he wasn't. Not consciously anyway. He'd better say something before she thought anymore. "Next week is my sister's birthday. I wanted to do something to make her happy, take her out to play a little or buy her a little present. But I don't have any money. Today I came out to ask for any small jobs, but no one would give me anything. So, I am not sure what to do now."

Finally, a way to help – her mind ticked over quickly. "Can I try to help you?" She asked.

"Oh no Lien Yi! No, I didn't mean that."

"I know you didn't and don't mistake me, you still need to work for it."

"In your shop?"

"No, there's hardly enough for me to do, let alone you! No, not in my shop but I do have an idea. Hurry, hurry, finish your soya milk and come with me." She jumped up much more easily and lightly than he expected her to, he followed her back to the shop pouring the last dregs of the glass into his mouth. She called out to someone to look after the shop as she was going out for an hour. Jun Yee peered around the shop – he had never seen anyone else in the shop but her. It had never occurred to him even that there might be other people here, she was always alone. There was no answer though and he couldn't see anyone. She called again and from behind a newspaper covered board at the back a small head the size of a peanut poked out. An old, brown face sat sleepily on the peanut and smiled a gummy smiled when she saw him. She nodded at Lien and withdrew her head again.

"Don't fall asleep again!" She called. "And don't forget Ah May Paw!"

She walked with small, fast steps back up to the market square and through to the other side and he followed slightly behind trying hard not to jog next to her. This part of the little town was not as familiar to him, it seemed older than what he was used to. The path was the same dirt path as on his side though the buildings were mainly stone as they were in the market. A brown film of dirt and sand crept up the sides of the walls ensuring the uniform grubbiness extended out here as well. A couple of left and right turns later they came upon another small square with the temple in the middle – it now became familiar, he had been here before, but always through another route. Just around the side of the temple was the wishing tree.

Lien stopped in front of a café and told him to wait outside. Moments later she re-emerged with a fat and surprisingly ungreasy man. He looked very hot, sweating and wiping his hands across his back but smiling with darting eyes that landed on Jun Yee immediately and disappeared as he smiled even wider.

"Jun Yee, this is my big brother, Wong Bau Ming."

"Jun Yee is it? Everyone here calls me *Bau Gor*, Bun Brother, even though my name is *bau ming* as in 'understands everything' not *bau* as in 'bun' but what do you expect when you bake buns every day? It's a good name for me isn't it? Do you mind if I call you Yee Jai?"

Jun Yee shook his head, he didn't mind, it was an endearment almost, *jai*, little boy.

"How do you do, Bau Suk?" Jun Yee switched to 'uncle' not 'brother'. He was too young to call him that, Sum would say it was disrespectful.

"*Waah!* Such good manners. It's a waste for you to be here helping me! Bau Suk it is then though you make me sound old!" His eyes widened and Lien nodded on tiptoes over the top of her brother's shoulder. "But don't get too happy yet little friend! You can clean, and tidy and then we will see how quickly you pick things up. If you learn quick, then maybe I will think about teaching you how to bake."

Jun Yee couldn't stop the *wah* escaping. He thought he might get a bit of work for the afternoon and maybe enough to buy a bun or two for Jun Ching, but this was a job for longer – this was even better! His face was stuck on the same incredulous expression whilst Lien got tired of being on tip toes and walked round the side of her brother still nodding, black eyes blinking at him.

"I don't think he wants it." Bau Suk's smile dropped as he turned to face Lien.

"No, no, Bau Suk-" Jun Yee panicked.

"*Orrrr!* Just playing with you! Willing to speak now are you?!" He switched back to Jun Yee and bent down to look him in the eye, his hands resting on his knees. "Good then. You come back tomorrow, and we'll see how you do, Yee Jai."

"Thank you, Bau Suk, thank you!"

Lien and Bau Suk smiled at each other as they left. Jun Yee was quiet all the way back to the shop the tendency to skip a couple of steps every few betrayed the buzzing going on in his head making Lien grin to herself. When they got back, she called in to see if everything was okay to which the old face with the peanut head reappeared and nodded. Jun Yee tried awkwardly to thank her, but she waved him away.

"Shh, you're helping us is the truth. My brother has needed a bit of help for a long time but couldn't find anyone. So really - did you remember Ah May Paw?" She called suddenly over her shoulder. She tilted her head to listen better for a reply but there was only a soft muffle. "*Aiy*. I knew she wouldn't."

She hurried over to the soya milk and poured a large glass muttering under her breath about someone being very hungry by now. Who is May Paw, he wondered. Hurrying out of the shop Jun Yee followed a little way before stopping and watched her neat little steps take her all the way down to the old waiting lady. Lien touched her gently on the shoulder and sat down next to her. Holding May Paw's hand around the glass with her own, she helped her sip the soya milk. Halfway through the glass she remembered Jun Yee, turned smiling at him and waved him away home. Unable to stay still much longer he waved back childishly much bigger than he needed to, his whole arm levering his body from side to side then ran back to the house trying to spend some of the excitement so he could keep this new secret.

"Happy birthday!" An urgent whisper in her ear. Her face twitched. The whisper tunneled its way through her ears and tapped at the side of her brain. So, she turned over, the blanket and nightie tangled up and wrapped tight around her waist kept her from going all the way over. "*Wai*... wake up you sleepy little pig, it's your birthday!" The whisper managed to wrestle Jun Ching from her sleep, and she opened one eye to see her brother's face hovering inches away. Though what she saw first was a smile bigger than any of his she'd seen for a long time – at least since before they left home. He was whispering at her, lots and fast and she was missing all of it. She hoped it wasn't important. Screwing up her eyes she gave a huge yawn.

"*Ha?* What?"

"I said you have to get up now, quickly and make no noise. Today is your birthday, remember? We're going out to have fun today, no chores. Come on – we've got to go before everyone else wakes up!"

Jun Yee was already dressed, told his sister to hurry and meet him downstairs by the front door whilst he crept down and back to the kitchen to find something that they could take with them for breakfast. It was early and the kitchen was empty as he scanned all the surfaces and cupboards but there was only the rice porridge and nothing for him to take that in. Just as he was about to give up, he saw the wooden box in the corner where they sometimes kept leftovers. Inside were two cooked sweet potatoes – he grabbed one, they could share, it would be too obvious if he took both. Shoving it as much as he could into a pocket, he turned around to a pair of feet in between him and the door.

"Gwai Kam Mo."

"Good morning. What are you doing in here so early?"

"Nothing, Gwai Kam Mo." He kept his gaze on the floor, but the potato bulged in his pocket and the end stuck out. He clasped his hands in front of him to try and cover it.

"Stealing?" Her eyes pointed to the potato and widened in accusation.

"No, it's just breakfast. We're going to share it."

"And you are thinking of going where?"

"It's my birthday." Jun Ching said from nowhere. Gwai was irritated by the way the girl was too quiet to hear coming; she always seemed to appear with no warning.

"And so what if it's your birthday?"

Jun Yee bristled. "So, we're going out to have fun, just for one day. No one will miss us."

"She has chores."

"I'll do them for her later."

He lifted his eyes and they stared at each other for a few moments, he daring her to refuse him and she almost testing the strength of his will. She took barely half a step to the side and he dropped his eyes again as he squeezed past taking Jun Ching's wrist as he went.

"How old is she?"

"Today I'm eight!" Jun Ching whispered loudly over her shoulder. She thought she saw Gwai smile but she could easily have been wrinkling her nose to push her glasses back up. She couldn't be sure as she was being pulled along so quickly that she had to concentrate so not to fall down the steps. As they got there Jun Yee whispered to her "Run!" And they both ran towards the water as fast as they could, legs tripping out from under them, collapsing in giggling heaps by the beach and sat eating what seemed the sweetest of sweet potatoes.

After they had gone, Gwai berated herself for letting them go. She didn't give them permission to go as such, she reasoned, she just shifted her weight and moved a little and they took it as permission to go. That wasn't her fault. Jun Ching's face though when she said she was eight – she looked so pleased. She didn't have the mildly insolent look her brother often carried with him. Perhaps it was independence rather than insolence, a dormant defiance showing as a threat. And though he looked like Sum in his features, it was Jun Ching that reminded her of Sum in manner. She had the same mildness about her and lived so entirely in her own head that she was completely accepting of everything around her. This was probably because she was only just turned eight

Gwai preferred to ascribe it to a likeness to her mother. With Sum, Gwai never felt constrained into staying the person she was, she could always change, and Sum would never embarrass her by mentioning it. She appreciated this most when she was having to make amends for something which she seemed to be doing much more often than she liked. She hated being wrong and Sum would simply give her the space and chance to change whilst looking the other way. The girl was like that, she thought, she has her mother's blindness. It was early still. Gwai swept through the kitchen, her memories poking at her here and there with visual reminders of when her and Sum ruled the kitchen though it was only for a brief time. She made mental notes for her market shopping today. She would go a little later than usual today, that way she would catch the tofu man in the market. Sweet tofu, one of Sum's favourites, she was sure Jun Ching would like it as well. A small bowl for her birthday wouldn't raise any eyebrows in the house surely.

By the time they were heading home, the sun was already hanging low in the sky. For the first time in a long while, their bellies felt full with the crispy buns Bau Suk treated them to as well as a big bowl of noodles each that Jun Yee bought with his earnings that week. She grinned as she jangled the couple of sweets she had in her pocket – Lien had given both her and Jun Yee handfuls that morning when they passed her shop and she called out happy birthday to her, but Jun Yee was worried the sweets would be taken off them when they got home so only took a couple. Lien had then found a small empty jar and placed the rest of the sweets in it and put it just behind the counter – it was theirs, she'd said, they could pop in whenever they wanted some and just take them, she would keep them safe for them right there. Jun Ching immediately tested the feeling by running off and sauntering back looking casually over each shoulder as she did so. She walked up to the shop, said hello to Lien and walked right behind the counter and retrieved a sweet and popped it into her mouth. With an impish grin on her face, she ran back to Jun Yee's side and thanked Lien Yi again. He could see the sunshine beaming out of her.

Jun Ching's legs ached from walking all day though she could not remember being happier. They had spent the day together doing nothing but looking at stalls, watching old men play chess in the streets, peering round the doorway at women burning incense in the temple. It had been a few hours since their lunch and she felt a small space had opened up in her tummy, space enough for a sweet or two. Her fingers itched around the edges of one in her pocket.

"Brother, can I have another sweet now?"

"Have you got room to fit it in already?"

"I have… I found a little." She spoke softly, pointing to a spot under her ribs. "Just here."

"Then, no. I have just one more thing for you."

Slightly disappointed she followed him along their usual path home and, just before the noodle shack, he turned into a side lane and sat her down at a wobbling wooden table and went inside what just looked like a hole in the wall. There were a few other tables outside; only one was occupied by an old man who stared at her. His shirt was open at the collar and grubby, what was once blue, trousers were rolled up to just below his knees revealing brown, scarred shins. Though his body showed his age, his eyes did not. They were sharp and watched her as she swung her legs with a slight pout and one hand murmuring around the sweets in her pocket. It was the first time he had seen her as he hadn't stayed that day after he pulled her mother's body out of his boat, but she and her brother were easily recognisable. He hadn't looked at her mother's face either, he knew who she was and had seen her before as she was growing up – it was a small town. He couldn't say he saw a resemblance between them but there was something compelling about watching the daughter of a dead woman. The boy re-emerged from the hole in the wall and sat with her; he told her something that made her face jump into a smile and her hands come clapping together. The boy he had seen that day, legs flying across the sand as he looked away. He got up to leave, they looked up at him. He hadn't been back into the water yet since that day, but he supposed they hadn't either, he smiled at the fact that they had something in common.

    Strangers rarely smiled at them, and they were slow to smile back but thought nothing more of it as soon as the bowl of sweet tofu was placed in front of Jun Ching as a final treat for the day. She skimmed off layer after layer of the silky mass and savoured every mouthful as Jun Yee watched her and refused to have any himself. His pockets were now empty, he had spent everything he'd earned in the last few days with Bau Suk but he was more pleased than he thought he could have been. They walked home with her fingers hooked contentedly in his pocket.

    Gwai looked at the bowl of sweet tofu she had bought for Jun Ching sitting on the side in the kitchen. It had been there for hours now and everyone that had come in and asked who it was for had widened their eyes when Gwai told them. She felt her saliva thicken at the back of her mouth each time making it harder and harder to swallow. Where were they anyway? She wished they would just get back and eat it then it would be over with and people would stop looking at her. She refused to understand why everyone was making such a fuss of it, but it was too late to change her story and eat it herself now – she should have said it was hers from the beginning. Especially Nine Sister with her mean eyes and overstuffed cheeks making eyes behind her back. Gwai knew her character perfectly well enough to know what she was doing – all she lacked was the courage to do it to her face. She could hear her voice now from the front of the house. They must be back. Nine Sister was making fun of them, teasing Jun Ching for being Gwai's favourite, for having a special birthday treat. They came to the threshold of the kitchen and said her name in unison. She didn't turn to look at them. Just the sound of their voices made her angry, she could feel the fire of her temper rising again.

"We are late back - sorry Gwai Kam Mo." Jun Yee said.

Gwai said nothing though she turned and looked at them. The silence hung damp in the air for what felt like hours. A faint shuffling at the door behind the siblings let them know they had an audience now. Eventually, Penny squeezed out from behind them, side stepping the tense arena between Gwai and the siblings and picked up the bowl of sweet tofu with both hands. She paused in front of Gwai who flicked her gaze down at her. The lack of reprobation meant Penny was allowed to continue though without the explicit approval from Gwai her actions would be her own responsibility alone. Inching round the arena again she came to Jun Ching's side and held the bowl out in front of her.

"Look, Gwai Bak Mo bought this for you because she knows you like it and it's your birthday. What a nice thing for her to do. *La* eat now, go on, take it." Penny urged her, her eyes even wider and bulging out further than they usually did with urgency. Jun Ching took the bowl in her hands cupping the bottom. She wasn't sure what to do though. She was full. Really full, from the noodles, the sweets but mostly the other bowl of tofu she had just eaten down the road! Her brother was still staring at her aunt, so she got no direction from him and Penny just kept pushing her with her eyes, so much so she thought they were going to pop right out and land on the top of the tofu if she wasn't careful.

"But I'm really full." She whispered to Penny.

"What?" Gwai snapped. Penny's lips pressed into a tight line and she shook her head quickly and imperceptibly. She looked back down at the bowl. She didn't think she would be able to fit it all in, but she would have to try. She sat down on a low step and balanced the bowl on the tops of her knees and started eating. It still did taste really delicious, she would never get tired of that taste but it wasn't sliding down as easily as the first bowl did. She could feel the gaze of several cousins sitting heavy on the top of her head and took no notice of them. Above her something broke, Gwai turned her back on them and took up her square chopping knife and continued slicing white turnips into shreds.

"If you're too full, you don't have to finish it all." Jun Yee whispered to her. She said nothing and carried on. She didn't know exactly what was happening, but she knew that this bowl of tofu was more than a bowl of tofu. When she had finished, she washed up the bowl and spoon and placed them next to Gwai on the side.

"Thank you very much, Gwai Kam Mo. You are so kind to remember my birthday. I have been really very happy today." They left then and scurried up the stairs to their mats. Jun Yee collapsed on his though Jun Ching had to sit up for fear of the tofu reappearing. He wondered if this had ruined her day at the last minute.

"It's very lucky that I love sweet tofu isn't it?" She giggled. And so did he until they both had to clamp their hands over their mouths to stop the laughter escaping to those downstairs. His jaw throbbed with pain by the end of it.

Chapter Nine

The next morning Gwai was still simmering. The girl had forced it down she knew it. They were all laughing at her behind her back now. Snubbed by two children. Sum's half castes at that. She had spent the rest of the night silent, enduring the glances of the rest of the family except her mother-in-law. Whether she didn't know or didn't care was unknown to her but either way it wasn't mentioned. She got up early this morning and decided to go to the temple, plant some incense and maybe burn away whatever this bad luck was that was following her around. Thoughts ricocheted around her head as she walked. Every time she thought about the girl's shoulders hunched over that bowl spooning it into her mouth steadily, spoonful by spoonful, her fists clenched, and her steps turned into stomps. It wasn't supposed to be that way. It was meant to be a happy thing, just a small gesture that would make her smile, would have made her look good. But instead, it was ruined by everyone else, staring, looking, judging. What? Was she not allowed to be the good person sometimes? She could be. It was this family that turned her into the person she was now. They all think they know her so well. Did any of the new wives as they came in, one after the other even bother talking to her – they just joined the little line of sisters at the back and joined their thinking too. Not a brain between them. Fine. If they wanted to believe she was evil, she would give them proof of it – she would find a way to.

The temple was quiet this morning. It was still early, early enough that it was only the old ladies there shuffling to and fro with their hunched backs. Gwai bought her incense sticks from a stall not far from where she used to spend a lot of time years ago, a time pressed paper thin in her mind. The spot was empty now, his little table and stool gone. She still remembered his name and how the whites of his eyes were his whole eyes. Even after she stopped working, she still came back to have her fortune read by him. It was a winter morning, just months ago when she heard. She came and he wasn't there, he had been taken ill, should have been back in a few days. But it was too cold, and he was too old. He never came back. He died in his sleep with his eyes shut though it had never made much difference to him if they were open or closed. With him he took all his words he had ever said to her, drew them back slowly like a long string as much as her fingers grasped for a grip on it. Along with it that last faint hope slipped away, that the lines in her palm were not quite written, that she could bend them still. It had been tied up with his kind unseeing eyes and perhaps the only eyes that ever saw her, whose kindness never turned. It burnt now in her, leaving the bitter taste of ash in her mouth, choking her throat, the smell in her hair, the black under her nails that grew with every scratch. She had found herself here often staring at that spot, especially when she felt the path beneath her feet was not the one that she had expected. It drove her to move now, to make something happen that she never had before. She couldn't ignore it, her story was told now. It was simply playing out, but she wasn't completely powerless yet.

Entering the main room of the temple, having lit the incense and planted it directly in the middle of the communal pot outside, she felt instantly calmer. Two old ladies were kneeling on the far side of the room, prayer pots in hands shaking them rhythmically. The sound of the bamboo sticks rattling against each other pulsed along with her blood. The room felt dusky, even though it was bright sunlight outside, the large windows seemed not to let harsh light pass. The stone floors were cool and reflected the calm of the gods seated in the middle back into the rooms. There were no voices to be heard, just the shaking of the sticks in their pots and Gwai was grateful for this. She had had enough of other people's voices and opinions. She took a pot and knelt down herself looking into the half-closed eyes of the god in front of her before bowing and bringing to mind her own question, clearly as if she was speaking directly to him, then shook the pot tilting it slightly downwards. The vibration in her hands was comforting, she would easily have stayed for hours but in her trance she hadn't realised how hard she was shaking, and a single stick fell out swiftly. It was a decisive answer to her question she supposed. She picked it up and held it to her and realised that she didn't know if she actually wanted an answer or didn't want to know what the answer was at least. She wasn't even sure if she had asked the right question.

Somewhere behind the temple wall in the private hall, the sound of a single monk tapping on his hollow, wooden fish emerged through her thoughts. It was clear. Tock, tock, tock - absolute in its rhythm. A gentle but firm march. Tock, tock, tock. She wondered if the old blind man had heard it, had known how many beats he had left. did it count down like that? Did it count down for her? Tock, tock, tock. The unknowing monk chimed time away in his beat though none could hear him but souls and himself.

She returned her eyes to the stick and committed the number to memory, she could always come back later and find out the meaning of the answer if she wanted to, and slotted the stick back in. As she walked out, the translator who read the numbers on all the sticks and explained their meaning looked up at her with a question. He knew her, Gwai was often there and always used the prayer sticks, how strange that she didn't come to him this time.

A small woman dressed in black walked up to the temple and just as Gwai went past the great urn outside on her way out the small woman passed on the other side. They would easily have missed each other completely had it not been that this was Mother Tang, the matchmaker who always had one eye on the ground and the other searching around her. Peering at Gwai through the incense and joss sticks, the idea that she had been brewing since she heard of Sum's death, even before the funeral, clawed at her leg. She rounded the urn and called out to Gwai. They spoke, politely for a few minutes, Mother Tang asking after her mother-in-law, then her, the rest of the family and finally the children. During this Gwai noticed the small woman manoeuvring her towards one of the low stone benches that were dotted around the periphery of the yard. Mother Tang sat, leaving Gwai no option but to do the same and by now she knew Mother Tang had something specific she wanted to say, otherwise there would be no reason to prolong this conversation by sitting down. Gwai felt irritated again, she just wanted some time to herself and now she was having to talk about Sum again, about those two again.

A short, impatient sigh escaped quietly as she lifted her head to look at the peach tree just beyond Mother Tang's shoulder. The harvest was just over for this tree now, over for another year, she suspected the monks would have enjoyed some very sweet fruit – she remembered being given one by a young monk once when she was a little girl. The monks often gave them away as this wasn't the only peach tree here. But it would have to wait, looking plain until the spring when it would burst into its beautiful flowers again and shake off the dreary ordinary that coated its leaves for the majority of the year. Mother Tang was still talking. Gwai refocused her eyes, she hadn't missed anything important yet.

Mother Tang saw Gwai's attention return to her. She had never liked this one. Too self-centred with a mean streak down the centre of her being as well, like a branch with a rotten core hollowing it out. She was the same when she was a child – she was old enough to remember her though she didn't know her very well then. It was her own mother that told her how different Gwai was to her older sister, a sturdy girl who worked hard and knew to choose the best of the paths available to her. Not Gwai, greedy, looking for more than her share and not getting it, it seemed, had caused the mean streak to flourish. This made her a good fit to help her with her task though. Now that she had her attention, she could stop talking round the edges.

"Now, living in your home must be difficult, with two extra mouths stretching to be fed, is it?" She wasn't looking for an answer, just acknowledgement so she could carry on. "I understand, and they are too young to work, aren't they?"

"Well, no, the boy is working now. Over there actually, in that café stall, only for a week so far, I don't think it will last. They only took him on because they pity him. It was that Lien from the shop, that's her brother's place."

"Oh. That's good, and he can earn something can he?"

"We'll see, he spent all the money from his first week before Lai Lai could take any for the house. That fanned her temper's flame."

"What did he buy?"

"Nothing. That's the stupid thing. He spent it all on that sister of his! Apparently, it was her birthday." Gwai felt her own anger rise again thinking about yesterday and the embarrassment she had about it. She spat to the side. Mother Tang winced.

This was precisely what Mother Tang disliked about Gwai. She was indiscreet – she often spoke more than she should and even more offensively, she spoke about family matters, matters that should be private and not told to people outside like her. But it was this same quality that could help her in this case.

"Well, that's good. And the girl? She's not much use at the moment, is she?"

"No. No good at all. She does a few light tasks around the house but other than that she just eats."

"What a shame, such an unlucky affair. So hard for you now and to have to put up with people talking as well – you are really very strong. Very good to those children, your Lai Lai too." Gwai's wandering eyes snapped back to her.

"People are talking? What are they saying?"

"You don't know?" Of course, she knew, she just didn't know exactly what. "The good ones say what a pity, so tragic for the children. The bad ones say… well… it's not worth hearing. It will pass. After a few months people will have another family to talk about… Of course, it's harder for your family because they look so different. Every time they go out people notice them and will be reminded." Gwai looked worried. It was working. She left the silence to do its work for a few minutes. "Unless… you could send them away. People will forget faster if they see them less."

Gwai cared less about what people were saying than the fire in her belly from the night before. If anyone wanted to see them less, it was her. She hated having to look at them, to live with them. She hated that she had been weak, tricked into it by meaningless, long gone memories of Sum and now everyone was laughing at her. Being able to send them away would be one solution. But Lai Lai would be difficult to convince. They were her grandchildren after all. And where would they send them? There was no trace of their father and even if there was, none of them could read or write the stupid squiggly English that he read. There were other family members but that would just be moving the problem around between them. There was nowhere for them to go.

"Yes," she admitted. "If we could send them away that would be good but where? I for one do not know where." Done. That was all Mother Tang wanted. To plant a thought and now it was time to leave it. The mean streak in Gwai would be water enough to help it grow and she would choose her time, not long from now, to come back and tease the bud open.
"Is that so? Well, don't you worry. If it is meant to be then it will happen. An opportunity will show itself in front of your eyes."

A week later, Gwai found herself constantly thinking of where she could send them. Each time she saw them it strengthened her resolve. They don't belong here, she told herself. They are a visual reminder, poking the eye, of the shame Sum brought on the family. She built on these thoughts in her spare moments – stick by stick, propping them up against each other, ready for a flame to be set alight below. But equally building was her frustration at not finding somewhere to send them making her even more impatient than usual.

Just when she thought it wouldn't be possible to add any more to her resolve, Gwai accidentally ran into Mother Tang again. Mother Tang had been sitting waiting at a tea stall a few alleys away from the market that Gwai passed on her way. Gwai came on the same days and though not always alone, she was this time as everyone was avoiding her increasingly vile temper at home. It was definitely out of the way for Mother Tang, who Gwai knew lived on the other side of the town; she was always purposeful, every step, every word had a motive. With a strange clutching sensation in her chest that she couldn't identify, Gwai approached her when she waved.

Mother Tang spoke in slow whispers that nibbled at Gwai's ears. She didn't speak even when she had finished. This was beyond what she had thought herself, she wouldn't have been able to conceive of this. She rolled the tea cup along its bottom edge watching the tea leaves tumbling on top of each other again and again like a kaleidoscope, mirroring the thoughts in her head falling over each other, jumbling together trying to form an order. But it was a plan still. So, it didn't solve both problems, but one was a start and in the long term this one would be the harder to be rid of.

Gwai nodded and asked a few questions that Mother Tang answered without missing a beat, she had come prepared. Finally, the small woman in black said a few definite final words and got up leaving a few coins on the table and Gwai on a stool bent over a tea cup looking like someone had just dumped a sack of rice on her back. She remained there, rolling the cup back and forth for a while until the stall holder came over.

"Do you want anything else?"

"Ah, no. Nothing. I'm leaving."

The stall holder smirked showing an overbite so severe they called her the watermelon scraper. "What were you talking to Mother Tang about? Mumble, mumble, buzz, buzz between you – what, you looking for a new husband?" She cackled. Gwai stood up leaving the tea cup to clatter onto its side and walked away towards the market.

"*Wai!* I'm just joking with you." The watermelon scraper called after her. "Can't joke with you anymore?"

It was a very small town, Gwai thought. This is why things must change, people will always talk here unless you don't give them anything to talk about.

Jun Ching spent more time with Penny now that Jun Yee was working in the mornings. They had breakfast together then he went off and she followed Penny around helping her with her chores once she had finished her own, washing the breakfast bowls when they had them, storing leftovers for later, sweeping the yard outside. Penny had more difficult chores, cleaning the kitchen, washing clothes and hanging them out to dry. She helped to prepare main meals occasionally though this was usually done by the other aunts especially if it was fresh food and was being cooked for the first time as the flavours had to be just right or not only this meal would be ruined but the other meals where the leftovers would be served too.

Penny was Four Uncle's daughter, the older of his two daughters and the only surviving one. Her mother, Four Auntie, had not had the sense to give him a son and having married into the family from an even poorer one, was destined to remain obedient and quiet. She had spent the first months of her marriage balanced on her heels in the yard at the back, the sun baking brown the skin on her neck, every day chopping sticks for the fire, washing the clothes for the entire household, emptying and washing night soil pots. Nobody spoke to her except to give her orders, not even her own husband, who would call her into the bedroom when he wanted to, otherwise she would only go in when her work was done and sleep on the ground near his bed. He hadn't chosen her himself and he had no eyes for her – they had needed someone to do the heavy, dirty chores in the house after the first two daughters were married and he was the next due to take a wife, so they got him one. Once she got pregnant, they brought her in, but she still did the majority of the work and she wasn't surprised when she was returned to the yard until her next pregnancy. Therefore, she had nothing to say when her first born was a daughter and was then eventually treated the same way. It was her second child that sealed her fate. Another girl and a sickly two-year-old at that when she died last year of something no one could afford to diagnose, the house did not weep and neither did Four Auntie who tucked her memory away and cursed herself for not bearing a boy.

Of course, there was still one more daughter in the house, Nine Auntie, but she was definitely not considered useful and nothing was asked of her unless she had behaved particularly disrespectfully. By the time she came the house was too full for attention to be paid to her and no one noticed she had bloomed into ugly self-centredness and spite, as her natural tendencies dictated, without check, like a weed. By the time her mother noticed it was too late to break her without significant trouble, so she decided to hedge her bets on Nine Auntie's airs and graces, and spoilt attitude, hopefully attracting the better marriage that she obviously thought she deserved. Their family situation had got progressively better though only by small increments and this last child hadn't experienced the same intensity of hunger or fear of winter that her first few had. In the end, it was a conscious indulgence to give her last child the luxury the others hadn't got.

So, Penny spent her time between her chores waiting on Nine Auntie. Brushing her hair mostly. Nine Auntie was obsessed with having the perfect plaits in her hair. They had to be redone everyday as once she had gone to sleep at night it would be far too messy for her to bear, though she couldn't plait it herself to the standard she liked, so Penny had to do it.

Penny was only just getting used to her back being empty after her sister had gone. She had her mother's obedience and acceptance of place as well as her wide face with high strong cheekbones that their eyes tried to hide in whenever they smiled. Her eyes had only started smiling again since Jun Ching and Jun Yee arrived, only since then had she stopped dropping tears into the laundry when no one was looking. Tiny drops for her tiny sister. In Jun Ching she saw perhaps the sister that was to come, the one she would have taught things to if she had survived long enough and grown big enough. But there was no similarity between them beyond what Penny pressed on them. Jun Ching asked her for hints on what to say, how to act and when to stay out of in the house, just as she had urged her with the sweet tofu – she was a secret and willing translator for this world where she wasn't sure of the language or the words hovering just under the surface.

It was Penny who first noticed Gwai watching Jun Ching more. Gwai had been angry since Jun Ching's birthday – no one had mentioned it since, but it still hung in the air and everyone walked around it. The only person who hadn't noticed perhaps was Jun Ching herself. But things had been different over the last day or two. Gwai almost seemed relieved but also more overtly horrid. She demanded Jun Ching do more, collect buckets of water and watched whilst she did it. One day Penny heard her tell Jun Ching to scrub the floor of the sitting room which she knew Penny had just scrubbed that morning, she had walked over it, stepping on the tip of Penny's little finger herself. There was something happening that she didn't understand yet, if Gwai wanted to punish you, she would make up tasks to do, things that hadn't been done for a while but didn't need doing like beating the sleeping mats outside or clearing out the kitchen shelves to clean and then put everything back again. Not things that she knew had just been done. But then none of them had seen Gwai as angry as she was that day before. Maybe this was something completely different.

Chapter Ten

    Ah Ho rearranged herself on the stool. Her bottom, though far from large, still spilt over the sides, the wooden edges digging into her flesh. She straightened one leg then the next dangling a slipper over the water as she did. Her knees cracked each time. Her wrist went back to resting on one knee, the forefinger with a thin fishing wire wrapped around it dangled over the water, still. There hadn't been even a stirring of fish for all the hours she had been there, though it didn't matter. Not like it did when her own mother taught her how to fish in a similar spot not far away. If she didn't catch anything then there would be one less plate on the table and everyone would be a little hungrier. It was rare that she'd come home without something, that is why they always sent her. She could sit for hours waiting for the tiny tug on her wire before yanking them up and thwacking their heads swift across a rock stopping the wriggling. She could send one of her daughters-in-law now, but she still found her own thoughts more obedient when allowed to swim with those beneath.

    Her thoughts were slithering and writhing in her head. Weeks had marched steadily past since Sum's death and Ah Ho had done nothing, though she and every other adult in the family knew they could not afford to keep two extra mouths. She couldn't simply shy away and let indecision be the decision itself. She wouldn't be able to anyway. She hadn't spoken with anyone about it but strangely Gwai seemed to know something, as though a pool of still water reflecting her own worries back at her but how did she know?

Gwai was drawing black bold outlines to the faint thoughts she already had. Of the two, the more urgent worry was the girl. Any daughter, a useful one or a good for nothing, is another family's wealth. Anything invested in a daughter would only be shaken out into the palms of the family she marries into. That much was true with every girl, let alone one like this who was not even much use in the home now – they weren't even getting temporary help from her. Although there was good reason for raising a girl well, the investment; the hope of her marrying well and her worth recognised by the groom's family in the wedding gifts as part of the marriage agreement. But this one? It was unlikely that she'd fetch a good deal with her odd appearance and her mother's situation would be considered a bad omen for any respectable family to take. An uneasy sensation made her spit these thoughts out like melon seeds, refusing to let them take root.

A green, lumpy caterpillar was crawling its way up the side of her empty bucket. Its head was just one mass of black, leading the rest of it in what looked like an arduous attempt at some sort of amorous massage. The bottom appeared to be in charge, making the decisions about moving and only then could the tiny bump travel along and let the head taste around for the next direction. The tail wagging the head. It wasn't right, she thought.

Gwai had more to say. The two of them were too close. The boy was strong-willed and pushed against them, but he pushed because he had something to protect. Without her, he would blend into the family, he would bend, and temper, and his edges would soften till they no longer scratched. It was true, he did push, against Gwai especially, it hadn't gone unnoticed. Maybe it was their signs that made them clash, what were they again? Her eyes drifted again as she tried to hook the details in her head. Was Gwai a rooster? An ox? She wasn't a dragon; she wouldn't have let that enter her house. Besides, that was what the boy was. That would explain him.

The caterpillar had almost reached the top of the bucket now, it arched its back, pin-head wavering, surveying the gap between it and the handle. But it was one reach too far and she watched as the tiny legs clambered pointlessly at the air before it fell backwards, back onto the ground.

Gwai had waited and lowered her voice for her last punt. The girl, she had whispered, the girl is nearly beautiful, as she rubbed Ah Ho's hand easing out the aches that squatted in her joints. And she is different looking and that it is enough to tempt the eyes if not the hands of some as soon as she gets a little older. This is trouble our family does not need, especially if some of those eyes and hands come from within. Even Gwai was subtle enough to know not to say the words. Ah Ho's thoughts swam to her youngest son whose idleness had forced his morals to wander. But there were enough people in the house to make it difficult for him and she still held sway enough to deter him. These seeds sat spat out amongst the others.

The hairs on her left arm raised their backs and a tingling ran up the back of her elbow across her shoulder and up her neck. She turned to the little girl who had appeared standing closer than she ever had before as though the swimming thoughts had conjured her up themselves. She blinked at her for a minute, expecting her to disperse with a faint sound of lapping water. She didn't.

"What are you doing, Paw Paw?"

"Can't you see? I'm fishing."

"Fishing for what, Paw Paw?"

"Fish of course." She let the pause turn her head away from the girl. Two flies chased each other over the top of the empty bucket stopping every few seconds to rub tiny hands together. The girl didn't say much, and she wondered if it was only with her or with everyone. It occurred to her that it was odd that she didn't know this and many other things. She realised that she couldn't even bring the sound of her voice to mind, even though she had just spoken.

"Paw Paw, you look!" It was high, and excited in this instant. She was pointing to the water. "What's that?" She squinted seeing no shadow of a fish then the flickering of wings revealed it.

"It's a dragonfly. You've never seen one?"

"Never..." Her round eyes rolled over the hovering dragonfly.

"At this time of year there are lots around the water, that's because they come to life in the water and then fly out. But they don't have a lot of time to fly, they will die again soon."

"But they are so pretty."

"Yes, pretty but not for long. Do you know, when I was little, what my ma used to tell me?" Round eyes even rounder shook. "She said if a flying thing, an insect, flies to you and stays with you for a little while then it is probably someone who has died come back to see you."

"How do you know who it is?"

"You feel it yourself. For me, when I go fishing, I often see a dragonfly and I think that must be your Gung Gung, my husband, come to see me."

"How do you know he comes here?"

"Ahhh, because when we were young, before we were married, my ma would send me out here to fish for dinner and he would sneak out here to see me. Back then you couldn't walk around everywhere with a boy like now, your parents would not allow it. And he wanted to see me so much he would come here and pretend to fish a little way away, but he never caught one fish. Not even one. His ma must have thought he was the most useless boy ever born in a fishing village." She watched the dragonfly with its red-blue body flicker a fraction closer on the surface of the water. Out from under the jetty flew another and joined it.

"Wah! Another one! Who is that then Paw Paw? Could it be Ma?"

"He has always come alone before, but this is the first time he has come since… It must be your ma I guess, unless he has found a girlfriend down there." She chuckled to herself. The second dragonfly was gone as fast as it came and the first darted after it.

"Bye bye, Gung Gung." Jun Ching called as she leaned out over the water, her hand on her grandmother's forearm for balance. "When you have time, come back to see us again."

Her hand was small, not even half the length of Ah Ho's forearm, and light, and soft. Ah Ho felt something other than skin on hers, something other than warmth trickle through and tumble up through her veins, invading her body. She knew that this something would dissolve her, like hot water seeping up sugar, and she knew she had to stop it. She knew the girl had to go.

Gwai had seen enough. It was time. She had been watching Ah Ho and the plan would work. The little thoughts she had been setting in her Lai Lai's head each night had taken hold and dragged the old woman with them. She went to see Mother Tang herself once more and told her on which day to come. She couldn't risk sending her children or nieces or nephews with a message in case it looked planned on her part. Mother Tang had to look like she was coming of her own accord. Gwai just needed to lay the groundwork. They had arranged it beforehand already. Mother Tang was a regular visitor to the temple every ten days, after which she would sit down to lunch and tea at one of the stalls nearby. To keep Gwai from suspicion, they agreed that when the time was right and the preparations had been made, Gwai would pass by in front of Mother Tang three times as she ate. On the third time she would stop at the stall close by and buy water chestnuts, though never making eye contact with each other.

As the end of the eighth lunar month came to a close, Gwai found herself one morning hovering on the corner just out of Mother Tang's sight. She had just one chance to do this, she had to be sure. She called up the shame and embarrassment she felt when she thought everyone was laughing at her after they snubbed her with the tofu and set out across the market. Pretending to change her mind at different stalls, she crossed over twice and on her third time she squatted down in front of a bamboo tray of water chestnuts and asked the price running her hand across the top of them, fingers bobbling up and down over the lumpy surface. She glanced secretly over her shoulder at Mother Tang. She wasn't even looking in this direction. What if she hadn't noticed? She must do something to ensure she see her, she thought as she began her third walk back, just stop and say good morning, ask her how someone is perhaps but it had to be natural. Her left side slammed into someone she didn't see rushing by and the water chestnuts scattered on the ground around her, rolling in at least six different directions. She immediately went down to gather them and looking up to see who she had walked into she saw Jun Yee, who had been rushing on an errand for Bau Suk, standing square on as if made of stone looking back at her. By the time she finished picking them all up, he was gone again. Turning, she found Mother Tang's black blinking eyes staring directly at her with such reproach that she hurried away clutching the last few chestnuts to her.

Two days later, Gwai purposefully delayed her morning, taking longer over breakfast, so she ended up sweeping the front step much later than usual. The girls were out in the back yard doing their chores; Jun Yee was out at the café already. She paused her sweeping and worried her hands around the top on the broomstick, kneading it round and round, the bristles at the bottom sweeping a small circular whirlwind. Just as she thought it was time, she saw Mother Tang's combed, shiny head bob up the steps towards her.

Once Ah Ho and Mother Tang were seated and the tea served, Gwai stepped back from the conversation and waited behind Ah Ho's chair as they exchanged polite questions. After a few minutes, Mother Tang carefully drew the conversation round to the children, asking how they were adjusting without their mother and how the family was coping with them. Ah Ho took a long sip from her tea, placed the cup down beside her and turned her face only to Mother Tang.

"You are very kind to ask after the children. They are fine. Different. It will always be different when a child loses their mother, but it is a test most must face; it is just that they are facing it earlier than later."

"Yes, that is a true word." The two women observed each other judging their next moves, trying to guess how much the other has seen of their thoughts. "Of course, it must be even harder for them... in their... situation. And harder for you too. A constant reminder."

It was hard. Aside from not being able to feed them for much longer, there was also all the whispers and gossiping of the town. She would rather be rid of it. But there was nothing she could do. She couldn't send the children away, they had nowhere to go. At least if their father was Chinese she could try to find him and send them to him but she had no way to track down a foreigner. Even if she could, she wouldn't be able to speak or write to him. Miserable, irresponsible man. She couldn't even just wait for the gossip, the looks, to stop - they looked too distinctive. The light brown of their hair looking almost like the malnourished ones from the famine years. They would never just blend in. It was enough for her to have lost her first, even if she was a daughter, she didn't want this constant reminder. She was too tired for this.

Mother Tang sensed the gap in her thoughts.

"Of course, it will be easier for the boy, boys can work and eventually will be independent, he will move away, and people will forget. But the girl..." She clicked her tongue and shook her head. "I can tell you, in my work I see many young girls with small faults only be left unmarried at their parents' homes – a great burden for them to feed forever. And these are only small blemishes, not like... well, so visible."

She left those last words to sink in and find their way to the seeds Gwai had already been planting over the past few weeks to make Ah Ho think these were thoughts of her own that had been troubling her. Ah Ho took another sip of her tea and looked around her. Gwai took her cue to refill the cups.

"Gwai, the tea pot is nearly empty. Refill it, what's left is cold."

"Yes, Lai Lai." Dismissed, Gwai left the room without looking up. At the kitchen threshold she found the other aunts eavesdropping though they scurried like cockroaches into the corners as she came. With her audience disbanded, Ah Ho turned back to Mother Tang.

"I have no choice. Where would I send them? Who would take them?"

"It would be difficult for anyone to take the two together. But for one there may still be hope."

"Which one?"

"The girl."

Ah Ho held the silence for a while. The next words she spoke she knew would change something. So, she waited in the familiar for a moment longer.

"Mother Tang, we are polite people and I trust your well-known discretion as a matchmaker. Are you saying that you can help us? And if you are, how?"

"Mrs. Wu, I have always admired your honesty and your words that do not turn this way and that. Yes, I have heard of something, a family, that might be of help to you. And you to them too." Ah Ho said nothing, staring at a spot on the ground a few feet in front of Mother Tang's tiny feet. "They are a good family. They have been poor before, but they worked hard and now have some land of their own, built more rooms to their house and even have servants. The eldest son married a good woman and she gave him several sons, few daughters. Now, one of their sons needs a wife."

Ah Ho turned this over and around in her head and it still didn't make sense. "Why would a family with money and good fortune want a little beggar girl like mine for a wife? She is useless, like dragonflies on water, nothing she does leaves a mark."

"You are world-wise, Mrs Wu. They need a girl with no airs. One who will be able to help in whatever work needs to be done, not one who will need servants herself. And most importantly, one they can trust as well. You see, something that not a lot of people know." She lowered her voice. "One of the sons cannot look after himself. He is not right. He behaves as a child. And as a child clings to his mother so he clings to the servant woman who looked after him as a baby and it is no longer appropriate for this to continue."

"Why is it not appropriate? He will grow out of it one day."

"They had hoped he would, but he didn't. He is unlikely to now."

"How old is this boy?"

"This year, 12." Ah Ho's hand stopped mid-air for a moment as her chin twitched to the side though she said nothing.

"And it is this son they are looking for a wife for?" Mother Tang nodded. silence hung for a while before she spoke again.

"It is a good match, Mrs. Wu. The girl they take in as daughter-in-law needs only look after the boy. There is little other work expected for her." Ah Ho still did not speak. Mother Tang gave her a few minutes more, in case she had questions, but the silence was unfilled. She sipped at her tea and coughed, bringing Ah Ho's attention back to her.

"I do not know. It is a hard fate, even for one like this girl, to be looking after a man who will be a child for the rest of his life."

Mother Tang knew this tactic and nodded as she rose to leave. At the threshold she turned. "They of course, would compensate you more than fairly for this."

Ah Ho raised her chin slightly though her eyes didn't flicker. Mother Tang left. Ah Ho remembered then the weight of the small hand on her forearm and how that weight made her feel exposed to the world. The decision was still not easy, but it was made.

Ah Ho summoned Gwai to her. She was surprised by the words she heard as it had been weeks since Mother Tang had last been there and Gwai had settled into a strained equilibrium of disappointment and relief.

"Tomorrow, the child leaves. You will take her. To the village where my niece lives with her family. They are richer than we are and need a servant. They will teach her the many things she doesn't know how to do yet to prepare her for her marriage."

Gwai had no words to place carefully in front of her, she fumbled in her mind for something. "Yes… Yes Lai Lai. Do you need me to send for Mother Tang?"

"No. It is all decided. Do not tell the girl. You will set off after the boy has gone out and you can tell her along the way if she asks. My niece will look after her. She will not be there for long. Only until she learns, so the faster she learns, the sooner she can come back. There is no reason to tell her about the marriage as yet. Do you understand?"

She nodded. And she did understand. She understood too well, the part she had played in this.

Jun Ching waved to her brother from the bottom of the steps until he turned the corner and couldn't see her any longer – just as he did every morning. She let her arm drop and let her eyes drift out of focus for a moment before returning to the house. Just inside the door Gwai was waiting with the same small bundle that she had brought with her on the first day.

"Take it." She said, thrusting it towards her. "We are going out."

"Where?" She asked as she took it from her but Gwai didn't answer and she knew better than to ask again. She saw Penny's eyes peeping round the side of the kitchen door. They wobbled with tears. She stepped towards her with a question and as she did Penny took an equal step back. One big, fat drop escaped running down her face hesitating briefly on the side of her cheek before plunging to the ground. She didn't go any further for Penny's sake if nothing else. She followed Gwai out into the courtyard where the aunts had seemed to congregate with mismatched and disorderly chores. It wasn't right. It was as though someone had taken all the right ingredients but messed up the order they were supposed to be in. Even Ah Ho stood here watering her plants that she didn't usually do till the afternoon. The aunts stole glances at her as she walked past but said nothing. There were no clues to be eaten.

"Be good." Ah Ho almost bit the end off the word. Jun Ching faced her but couldn't see her eyes to find and answer in them either.

"Where am I going?"

"You will not be gone long."

"Will you tell Brother where I'm gone?" Ah Ho nodded. She paused before going on. "Say hello to Gung Gung for me when you see him next time."

Gwai said no words all the way along the waterfront and down to the pier. Jun Ching peered into Lien's shop as she tottered past behind Gwai's faster footfalls but only caught the side of her face in the shadows and could say nothing. They had arrived just in time to see the last few carts remaining loading up fish to take to the next village to market. Gwai spoke with a few of the men before settling with one and with a drop of coins into grubby hard-nailed hands she seated them both on the back edge of his cart when he set off.

Jun Ching pegged each passing sight to a point in her mind so she could tell everything to Jun Yee so he could find her. But quickly, the cart left the village entirely, and she wasn't able to find her bearings again. The buildings were gone now and to each side of her were empty fields as they moved away from the sea.

She spoke without looking at Gwai or her empty hands folded in her lap.

"Where are we going?"

"To Paw Paw's niece's in the next village."

"Are you going to leave me there?"

"Yes."

"Why?"

Reasons ran over and under each other in Gwai's head, scattering like fish when a pebble drops into their world. She watched what had seemed like real, valid reasons flick their tails at her before disappearing in the distance and grabbed the lame one that could not get away.

"Because you are useless. You don't do anything that helps the house so you will go there to learn." It flapped feebly in her hand as she stared down at it.

"Will I come back when I have learnt useful things?"

"Yes. If you learn them well." Even the lame one seemed to die in shame from the lying and lay still.

The village Ah Ho's niece lived in was verging on a town. It sat at a crossroads where both fishermen and farmers had met for years from all directions to trade. Gwai and Jun Ching hopped off the cart just outside the market where Gwai arranged to meet the man again in a few hours for the ride back. They walked swiftly through the market. Gwai knew her way and dodged easily between people and stalls, through streets and down alleys where Jun Ching had to trot once again to keep up. Not daring to lose sight of her for fear of losing her completely, Jun Ching saw nothing of her surroundings and the route they had taken. They came finally to a small two-storey building of grey brick and stopped. A small boy hiding in a colourless shirt and no shorts stared at them both. His chin popped suddenly out from the collar, he quickly tucked it back in again and turned to scurry away but not before they got a glimpse of little buttocks wobbling.

Gwai's knock was sharp and unanswered. She pushed the door as she stepped in and called out, announcing herself. The room was brighter than Ah Ho's. The walls painted white reflected the light from the windows and back door. Deep red wood furniture told you where to sit and where to stand. As Gwai called a second time a voice answered her from outside followed by a fast-slippered shuffle. The woman who came in wore a smile and her shoulders up around her ears. She reminded Jun Ching of a terrapin she saw in the market once. This was the niece.

"You have arrived? That's really good, I was worrying. You must be Gwai. Sit. Sit. I will pour you tea, you'd like tea?" Without waiting for an answer, the Terrapin hurried out again. Gwai perched on a corner of red wood. "You must be tired. Are you tired? How did you get here? Did you walk? No? You got one of the market carts then. Yes? Yes. They are just the same uncomfortable. All that bumping. And the smell of fish – well, at least it not too hot at the moment, not so bad then."

Gwai had no need to talk and simply held the glass of hot tea. Her fingertips tapped as each got too hot and moved to the next. The rising steam from the tea fogged her glasses for a moment. She waited for a pause.

"This is Sum's daughter, Jun Ching." She paused, turned her head by a fraction towards Jun Ching with her eyes on the ground indicating for her to come forwards. Jun Ching stepped out from the shadow just inside the door, clutching her bundle. The Terrapin's entire head and shoulders turned towards her and swept up and down. "Don't be fooled by her skinny skinniness, she is strong and can work. She just doesn't know how to do it properly yet. You don't need to hold back with her, just treat her like you would your own... your own girl." The Terrapin's eyes glinted for a moment.

"Oh, okay, okay. We won't treat her bad but we will teach her like you want. By the time we send her back to you she be able to run your whole household!"

She was surprised but there was nothing left to say. Gwai looked around at what she was leaving the girl in. She could ask to see the rest of the house, where she would be sleeping but she didn't want to be able to picture it once she was home. She made her excuses to leave, handing the half full glass of tea to Jun Ching as she did. At the last moment, Jun Ching's hand slipped into hers.

"Gwai Kam Mo? I don't want to stay. Please?" She looked up at her.

"That is not relevant." She left.

"What are you just standing there for? You're not stupid, are you?" Jun Ching shook her head. The smile had dropped like someone had pulled a string releasing the mask from her face as soon as she closed the door behind Gwai. "Dumb then? We don't have to fear a non-stopping mouth then."

"N-no, auntie, I can speak." Her voice stumbled to get out and she coughed. She raised the glass to her lips, but the Terrapin snatched the glass from her hands before she had any.

"Well, there must be something wrong with you, that old aunt of mine would never be so good unless there was something in it for her. There are no plump chickens just jumping about in the street you know, if you want chicken you have to pay for it. There, learn something. I will teach you smart before you go back. Now get upstairs, you will be sleeping at the top of the house, go up two floors to the attic. Don't go wandering around the rooms either. I know what's in each room and I'll know if you steal things." She waved her hand towards the stairs and turned her back on Jun Ching as she adjusted the chair Gwai had sat in. "They think I don't know what happened over there, what happened to her ma. I know. Something like that doesn't need a fish cart to get here. The shame on the family. Lucky she is on my mother's side, still shameful but at least it is not my family now. How bad this looks. And two that look like this!" She forced out a sigh. "Wah! You still here! What are you doing just standing? I told you to go! Fast. You just standing waiting for your luck to change? You can wait forever. A girl like you, your luck will never change."

Once upstairs, Jun Ching sat in the middle of a half empty landing. Half a dozen or so dried fish hung from one beam to the side, underneath them stacked hessian bags full of what she wasn't sure. She could not remember a time when she faced being without Jun Yee for any length of time. She kneaded her fingers. "It's okay, it won't be long, Brother will come very quickly then everything will be okay again. He never takes long to find me" she whispered to herself, pressing her fingers to warm them like they would be in his pocket. "It's okay."

The house was silent when Jun Yee got home. His sister had not been waiting at the top of the steps as she was most days. Round the back of the house was only Penny's ma, Four Auntie, crouched on her haunches at the far end alone with the striking of her knife along wood. The kitchen was empty. He had seen the two other aunts in the market much later than usual. He was sure they had seen him but had avoided him. Back in the main room he found Nine Auntie perched on a stool with the square patch of sunlight creeping reluctantly up to her fat toes. Penny stood behind her pulling her hair into one big plait down her back. They both had their backs to him and neither turned when he came in.

"I saw you come in." Nine Auntie stated.

"Where's my sister?" Jun Yee asked and turned to peer up the stairs to the railings where they slept.

"How would I know?"

"Penny? Do you know where Ching Ching's gone?"

"Don't ask her. She's doesn't know anything, do you Penny?" Penny's hand jerked accidentally. "Ow! Don't pull so hard are you trying to rip my hair out?"

Jun Yee left them to go upstairs. She would never be helpful, and Penny was just as useless when she was around her. She's probably just gone down to Lien or gone to sit by the old lady by the water and forgotten the time. He'll go and fetch her before she gets into trouble for being late. He looked around. Jun Ching's blanket and pillow were not sitting neatly nestling against his as usual. He opened the cupboard to see if they were in there. Nothing. Even her clothes were gone. Panic rose in his throat as his stomach pulled up into his chest. Had she run away? She wouldn't go without him. He hadn't paid as much attention to her recently as he had before, maybe she felt he had abandoned her now that he was working at the bakery? He grabbed the egg roll tin, fingers scrabbling for grip around the edge prying it open. But the figurines were still there. She wouldn't have left them, her fingers needed them. But her square cloth she travelled with was gone. The details contradicted each other in his head pointing at each other and confusing him. Slamming shut the cupboard again he threw himself against the banisters folding almost double at the waist.

"Where is she?" He shouted down to Nine Auntie and Penny making her jump and clutch the half-finished plait to her chest, pulling a scream out of Nine Auntie as her head went with her. Nine Auntie ignored him, greasy fingers stuffing broken biscuits into her mouth though Penny jumped and turned her goldfish eyes to him wide with silence.

He ran down the stairs and out through the kitchen into the back yard calling her name, checking the laundry line where the lack of her blanket or clothes made the fear rise faster. He called down the side alley to the street but nothing. Running back to the house he shouted again from the door. "Where did she go?"

"Shut up! Do you need to be so loud? Who do you think you are?" Nine Auntie shouted back.

Jun Yee lodged himself between her and the window. Her fat cheeks pushed up towards her eyes as they had nowhere else to grow making them even smaller than they were already.

"Where is my sister?" His voice rumbled low and angry. Penny shrank behind Nine Auntie's head.

"I don't know where she's gone but she's gone!" Crumbs from the recently devoured almond biscuit were still swimming in small pools of sticky saliva in the corners of her mouth. They jumped at him as she spat her words. "This morning they took her somewhere with her little bundle of things. And that's good. One less mongrel to sit here panting for food and making our eyes sore!"

Jun Yee felt his knees and elbows lock and his fingers curl into his palms. "You think we want to be here? We would be happier starving, begging on the streets at home than be here!" He spat back.

"How dare you speak to me like that." She rose out up off the stool pulling Penny with her. "I am still older than you. I am still your Nine Auntie. You just remember that. You dare speak to me like this? So, go then. We don't want you here. You just everyday remind us of the black cloud over this family, the shame! Poke eye, poke nose – that's what you do, remind us every day! The longer you stay here, the more we suffer!"

They stood toe to toe, equal in height, panting in each other's faces.

"Enough!" Ah Ho's voice sliced the two of them apart. "Enough. You two, go outside." Penny picked up the stool and allowed Nine Auntie to lead her outside as she kept a tight hold on the half-finished plait. Where Nine Auntie's eyes dug at Jun Yee as she went, Penny's quivered at him. Both made him angrier.

"Come here." Ah Ho sat in her chair and he came to stand directly in front of her, where he stood the first night they arrived with Ma, where Jun Ching had stood half behind him and where he now had neither of them. He felt naked in the space around him and missed the feel of her fingers in his pocket. "I have sent your sister to my distant niece. There she will learn to manage a house. She was not learning here, and my niece needs help. Understand?"

"No. I don't understand! Why didn't you tell us?"

"You are too stubborn, too hard. You would have made trouble and that would make it even harder for her to go and she had to go. It is better this way"

"But why did she have to go? I could have taught her. I could have taken her with me to the bakery and she could work there."

"You? What could you teach her of women's work? She doesn't need to work in a bakery. She needs to learn how to be a woman so she can be a wife one day. She needs to learn how to look after a baby and we don't have any here. You cannot teach her these things."

"She's just a little girl." Jun Yee whispered to his feet.

"What? What did you say?"

"She's just a little girl, Paw Paw. She is too young to be someone's wife. She doesn't need to learn now, does she?" His words surprised her. She wasn't expecting him to have understood. She had expected this from one of her sons or even in a look from one of the wives but there hadn't been a word until now. From a boy.

"She will not be young for long, she is already eight. When I was eight, I was fishing every day for my family. I could cook and help my mother with the house. She must learn now before she gets stubborn like you. You think she can stay with you forever? She cannot."

"When will I see her?"

"When she has learnt then she can come back and see you."

"When?"

"That depends on how fast she learns. I think, slowly." She didn't move as she spoke, both wrinkled hands rested on the rounded top of her walking stick standing between her legs. "Enough now. You know enough. You can go now."

"Where is your niece's, Paw Paw?"

"I said you know enough. Now go."

Jun Yee turned to leave and came face to face with Gwai just arriving back, hovering in the doorway. She forced herself to look at him though her gaze sank to the ground like old tea leaves in hot water. He knew then the part she had played and that he was now completely alone here. He said nothing as he stamped on her foot and pushed past.

Chapter Eleven

"So, guess where I went today?"

"How would I know?"

"That's why I said guess." Gwai said as she lowered her eyes quickly then raised them again, fluttering her short lashes at a passing stranger.

"The market?"

"No." Her head snapped back to face Sum now the man had gone. "Guess again."

"The tea stall?"

"No, it's my day off! Guess again."

"I don't know." Gwai widened her eyes at her. Sum hated guessing, just say or don't say but don't make her guess. She just didn't care enough. "Errr, the temple?"

"Yes! And what did I do there?"

"Just tell me, you know I'm not as good as you at guessing."

"That's true, waiting for you will take so long even the mosquitoes will fall asleep." Gwai hopped up onto the low wall next to Sum whose legs had sprouted out long beneath her next to which Gwai's now dangled, like two pairs of trousers on a washing line, one cut off mid-calf. Gwai swung her long single plait over her shoulder and twisted the loose end round her middle finger. "You should wear your hair in a single plait you know, you're too old for two now. No one will look at you, they'll think you're just a little girl."

"What do I want people to look at me for?" She threw her own two plaits back over her shoulders and leaned forward on her arms, elbows locked the plaits out of sight. "So, what did you do at the temple?"

Gwai sighed. "They'll never marry you out like this. Anyway, you know the old fortune teller?"

"The blind one or the bony one?"

"The blind one."

"I know him."

"Well, I've been watching him for weeks because I thought he couldn't see me so what's the harm and you know I am interested in these things. But today, after one of the ladies he read had left he turned right at me with his eyes shut like always and said, 'What are you still lurking for after so many weeks, I already know you're there, come, sit down'. I was so surprised I couldn't say anything. I opened my mouth, but it was just a hole!" Gwai made a large round hole with her mouth, eyes wide. "So, I went and sat opposite him and he asked me if I was interested in palm reading and I said yes then he asked me if that was why I was hanging around because I wanted to learn how to do it and I said yes."

"He wasn't angry with you for eavesdropping for all this time?"

"Just a little, he said I shouldn't have been but then said if I was really interested then if I promised to help him do little things here and there like make his tea, he would let me listen properly.

Then he said that he would even teach me some of the really basic things to read." She paused to give Sum time for the appropriate reaction.

"Wah! You must be happy, you've been hoping for someone to teach you for ages."

"Exactly! But there's more! He told me to give him my palm to read so I gave it to him, and he felt it, ran his fingers all over it, feeling for the lines. It felt a bit strange because I thought he would be rough, but his fingers were really soft." More pausing, Sum knew she was stretching out the story, pulling it long like the noodle puller in the market. And she also knew she wouldn't carry on without encouragement to grease the way.

"And? Well, what did he say then?"

"He said a few things. He said that my lifeline is strong so I will live a long time. He said I will marry and that the man will have a job, you know so he won't be a labourer or a fisherman, he will do a job and someone else will pay him for it and that is how I will become rich!"

"He said you'll be rich one day?"

"Well, no, but he said my husband will bring me better fortune than I have now."

"Tch! That could mean anything, you have practically nothing now!" Sum laughed.

"Think what you want but I choose to believe good things." She said with her nose in the air.

"Did he say anything else? Where are you going to meet this saviour husband?"

"He says I probably know him already! Isn't that strange? I can't imagine anyone I know already being rich or having fine hands from working a proper job. All the boys around here are just like their fathers before them and will do all the same things. He did just say probably though. So, I think maybe I will meet him soon. I still think he is in Hong Kong – I mean there are so many rich men in Hong Kong the chances are it's one of them."

"Did he see Hong Kong in your palm?"

"Well, I did ask him, but he said he couldn't tell that much detail from my palm. He said he could from my birth hour and date but I'm not sure what they are, so I'll have to ask Ah Ma and tell him when I go back."

"Well, that good then, you got what you wanted, you've got someone to teach you how to read palms – it's the perfect job for a person as nosey as you, *bak gwa por!*" Sum leapt off the wall she was perched on as Gwai's hand shot out to slap her.

"I am not a *bak gwa por*! I simply like to help people. Besides, if I get good at this it could earn me money one day and that would be better than working at the tea stall." She glanced at Sum who was savouring the end of her laugh. "You'd better be good to me, if not, when I am rich with my good-looking husband and big house on the hill, I won't give you anything."

"He didn't say he was going to be good-looking!"

"He must be with all that money! Have you ever seen an ugly rich man?"

"No, but then I haven't seen any rich men in the flesh at all."

"There you go. When you have money to buy nice clothes and get good shaves and haircuts, even an average man can be a good-looking man."

Sum said no more. Gwai was starting to get annoyed as Sum wasn't excited enough and was pointing out the gaps in the fortune teller's words. It was just another story, Gwai's story, and it didn't affect her future or even change her chores for the day.

It was only days before Gwai was back at the temple with her birth numbers running over and over in her head. But he didn't ask for them. She made tea, poured it for him and his customers, she even emptied the disgusting spittle can he kept by his stool. He didn't spit on the ground like the other fortune teller. He said it was disrespectful to spit where one made one's living, especially so close to the temple, and it wasn't nice for people to come to see you and be surrounded by your spit. Of course, that was good enough for him to say, Gwai thought, but she was the one who had to empty the can. He may be blind, but she wasn't, and she could see it and had to clean it out. Still, she made only silent faces at the can and only behind his back, just in case.

The numbers ran in her head unused for weeks but Gwai didn't quite have the courage to bring up his promise to the old man. There was something about his constantly closed, wrinkled eyes and the way he didn't move or respond to her presence at all that made her feel thin in existence, ghost-like. She knew he couldn't see her, but it made her feel as though she wasn't actually there, and she was afraid to break that.

Finally, as the numbers threatened to slip out and run away from her completely, one day she found a quiet moment.

"Yuen Suk?" She spoke softly but his hearing was good, and she was surprised he didn't hear her.

He remained unmoving, one elbow on the table in front of him holding his pipe and the other hand under the table clutching a string of prayer beads on his knee. His fingers didn't move the beads along, he said no words in his head. He simply liked the feel of the small polished wood, kneading them between his fingertips.

"Yuen Suk?"

"I can hear you. My eyes are blind, but my ears still work for now."

"Yes, Yuen Suk. Yuen Suk, I was thinking. Do you remember when I first came to see you?"

"You are talking about the first time you came to hide behind that pillar and eavesdrop on me?" Gwai blushed at this and took half a shuffle back, head bowed.

"Errr, no Yuen Suk, I mean when you read my palm. Do you remember you said if I brought you my birth hour and date then when you had time you could have a look at them for me?"

"I remember. But you never brought them. I even thought you forgot too."

"No, Yuen Suk, no, I didn't. I just didn't want to impose on you that's all. I… I have them now."

"Now?" The old man lifted his face to the sky, smelling the dampness in the air mixed with the scent of cooked rice seeping over the temple walls. "Even the little monks are eating their lunch now, so I suppose it's time. I think people won't come this afternoon anyway, there is rain on the way." He lowered his face and was still for a moment. Then he tilted his head suddenly, chin pointing at her. "Tell me the numbers then get my lunch ready, I will tell you everything when you come back."

Gwai hurried. She would have run if that wouldn't have drawn attention to her but there were very few girls running in a temple at the best of times, so she didn't. She walked as naturally quickly as she could to the courtyard at the back where the incense seller, the path sweeper and other fortune teller gathered to eat, away from the worshippers outside. Yuen Suk often ate here with them when the sun burnt down into the temple and he needed the chance to cool his feet which he would never do in front of potential customers. But summer was a way off yet, the air was still light and tinged with the scent of peach blossoms so he remained in his place to catch any extra custom that he could. The little square was empty now and Gwai went over to the back to fetch fresh water from the little well there and returned to Yuen Suk. He kept his lunch in a little bundle on a table behind them.

She unwrapped the small bowl, a pair of chopsticks and a metal canister full of whatever his niece had leftover from the night before for him. She used the chopsticks to slide the rice and fish across into the bowl, almost in one movement to keep the rice on the bottom, he didn't like it being all mixed up, then stabbed at the rice, twisting the chopsticks to break it up where it had stuck together in the carrying. Dumping the canister and the cloth in the corner again, she stepped quickly, small steps, knees together like a geisha, and both hands clasped around the bowl.

"You are sure you want to know then?" He asked as she placed his bowl in front of him.

"I'm sure, Yuen Suk."

"Because one of the most important things to learn is if someone does not ask you, you must not tell them their fortune. You hear me?"

"I hear, Yuen Suk."

"And even if they come to you, you must ask them if they are sure. Not everyone can take it. If it is bad, you must be extra careful of what you say and how you say it because if you say too much you can ruin people's lives. If they hear a bad reading, some people can completely give up. They might do something they would not have otherwise as they think there is no other path. Even if the reading is not bad, it can affect some people badly, it can make them think their life is blessed and they don't need to work anymore. But this is not true, human being must always work on their lives, they can change fortunes by what they do every day." The old man wished he could see the child in front of him, to see if she was indeed listening, if she would remember and ultimately if he would be right to teach her how to read. But for now, all he could hear was a faint but constant rustling of cotton as she fidgeted. He paused. "Fortune telling comes with responsibility."

"I hear, Yuen Suk, one must be careful when telling fortunes."

He doubted she heard at all but there was nothing else he could do. He had planted the seed in her head and there would be time enough for him to make sure it grew. He picked up his chopsticks and she pushed his bowl of dried fish and rice into his hands. He wouldn't tell her everything that he read in her numbers though, only what she asked.

"So, what do you want to know?"

"Tell me everything. Tell me about what kind of life I am going to have."

"You have quite a good fortune. At the moment it is not good and not bad. You are too young for it to be set as yet, it can still change easily. You were born with a hard life though, so you need to be hard too to get through it. Surround yourself with strong people if you can. You can draw from their strength."

"How will I know who is strong and who isn't?"

"You will know if you watch and see."

"What about the people I can't choose? Like my family?"

"Then you have to choose to stay or choose to go depending on what you see. You cannot choose them but if they are not strong enough, they might suffer from your life."

"Oh." She sounded despondent.

"Don't fret just yet. Like I said, this might be where you are starting from, but it can change. And here is a good thing, you have a lucky person in your life. Someone who brings you a good luck and if you take it and appreciate it then you will have a good fortune."

She brightened. "How will I know this person? And how much luck will they bring? And what kind?"

"Tsk, greedy already. You have to be careful of this, girl, this will be your challenge."

"It's not greed, Yuen Suk! It's ambition! It's true, I just want a better life for me and my family."

"It's greed, girl. From your dates and your palm, it's greed. A better life your lucky person will bring you and your children will have more food than you have had to eat but what you want is for people to do as you say. You like to tell people what to do, don't you? Even now." She didn't say anything. "You don't make a sound, that means yes then. Just be careful. That status is not for you in this life. If you take it, you are borrowing this power from someone else and that could have bad consequences for you and those around you.

"As for children, you should be prepared for some to die, probably girls, because of how hard you are, your energy, your spirit will be too hard for them to survive. But not all will die. You will have some for your funeral procession." Gwai didn't mind this so much, she was never bothered about children and even then, almost everyone had some who died, it was normal.

"What about my husband? You said before I will have one. Is he my lucky person? You said he would have money?"

"I said he will have a comfortable job, that he won't have to carry things or labour for a living."

"But that means he will have money then, doesn't it? And power? Anyone who can earn a living while they sit must be rich!"

"Do I look rich to you, little girl?" The old man tapped his stool with his chopsticks. "Whether your stool is warm or cool has little to do with money. A man with no job can warm his stool all day and have no money but a busy tailor sitting on his stool sewing all day will have money to pour over his family. Yes, this man will have some money but remember that, little girl, money is the same as water. It is easily spilt from your fingers and if it's not poured into something worthwhile. Then it will be gone forever." Gwai nodded and although he couldn't see, he carried on. "So, you have a strong body thanks to your hard life, you have a marriage that could bring you prosperity and you have children for your funeral procession. That is good fortune, no? Are you satisfied?"

Gwai hesitated. It sounded like little more than average to her. The kind that her sister would have been happy with if she hadn't already married one of the fishermen in the village. Was this it then? She didn't want to be ungrateful, but she felt disappointment scrape down her throat like she had swallowed a handful of gravel.

"Thank you, Yuen Suk, that is good fortune. But just one more thing, will I go anywhere? I mean, I have always wanted to see what's beyond this village, maybe go to Hong Kong even, will I go?"

The old man brought the bowl to his mouth and scooped the last pieces in chewing slowly to savour the saltiness of the fish. Truthfully, he didn't know, and he debated what he should say to her. He had known people to go and never come back and of those that did some had good fortune and some had bad. His own nephew had gone to Hong Kong and came back not long before a year had passed and told stories of the other side of Hong Kong. The side where there was no work, food was short, and people slept on streets that smelt of rotting flesh. But he couldn't see how it lay for this girl. He put down his chopsticks across the top of the bowl.

"Whether you get to Hong Kong or not, I don't know, I cannot see it. What I can see is that you could go and that is a path you can make for yourself. Everything else we talked about will be connected to this somehow, and link by link you will put this chain together yourself. But you must always remember one thing: this fortune that I have read today is true of today. You can alter the course of it by your choices and your actions. If you choose to help people and do good deeds, you can make your fortune better, if you choose badly, it could get worse. Think of it like a stream, it will run in its own direction, but you can change its exact course."

He opened his eyes then to show her the white milkiness in place of his irises in the hope that she would remember his words in this moment and remember that the course of her own stream was in her own hands.

Chapter Twelve

She turned over, sighing over the hard wood digging into her hip. It was time to get up anyway. She opened her eyes and turned onto her back. The sky was still dusky through the window. At least she was not late yet, not today anyway. Just to be sure she shuffled over to a bare floorboard and pressed her ear against one of the bigger cracks. Snoring, rhythmic but shallow. She laid flat on her back again for a while longer allowing the dreams from the night one last flutter across her mind. Here in the half world between sleep and reality, she stole back through the fuzziness to their room in Hong Kong. The wooden floor beneath her faded into the cold stone of their floor. She could almost see the bunk bed to her left, almost feel the little cupboard beyond her feet but most of all she could smell the market below wafting through the open window. Taking a deep breath, she filled herself with the memories, turning in her head to the image of Jun Yee on the upper bunk, the soles of his feet swinging back and forth, pale compared to the tops.

She rubbed her own feet together, sole over top over sole over top, urging blood and warmth back into them. The skin on her heels was getting harder. One particular bit dragged across the top of the other foot in a long scratch. The floor was too hard to curl up into a ball on again. It was time to get up, to get working, she knew it but even the memory of home was hard to leave. Later, she told herself like she did every morning, she could come back later. She sat up pulling the empty rice sacks covering her up around her shoulders as she waited for sleep to clear from her head. The sacks scratched across the back of her neck as she yawned. Shuffling them on top of each other into a little pile in the corner she pulled on cloth shoes, crouching to avoid the slanted roof. Since she was already wearing everything she owned she was fully dressed and ready to start the day.

    She crept down the first flight of stairs in the dark, past the room directly below hers where the snoring continued and then past a second, completely quiet except for the youngest child, the boy, that still talked in his sleep. Creeping down another flight she straightened her back and was able to walk normally to the kitchen and to the firewood just outside the back door. Splinters on the branches stuck easily into her hands and the cold made each scratch hurt more than it should. It had taken her weeks to learn how to get the fire started properly and quickly but now she did it without thinking. On tiptoes she peeped into the clay pot. There was enough water just for the tea and *juk* for breakfast. She should have gone to the well yesterday for more water, but she had forgotten in the midst of looking after the boy who was sickly again. She hurried, pouring half of the water into the thick *juk*, thinning it to enough for the whole family. The rest of the water she left ready to boil when the family was on their way so that breakfast would be served as soon as they came downstairs, distracting them from checking how much water was left.

    A floorboard creaked above. She cocked her head to hear where exactly it had come from. Another creak. It was the snoring room, definitely, though the creaks meant the snoring had stopped. She sprang off the wooden shelf and shuffled up next to the stove and sped up the stairs without a sound waiting just a few steps away from the first floor watching the door. The door opened. A green, ceramic chamber pot with a wooden stopper slid out pushed by a white, bony foot. The foot retreated and the door shut again. She carried the pot down to the back yard in both arms with the weight of it, her face pulling back as far from it as she could. The contents slopped from side to side, she could feel the vibration of it against her chest. The stopper was loose when she pulled it off at the back of the yard and poured it down the ditch. It was warm still and stank, dark yellow. Her throat closed. This was the worst bit of her day. She didn't see why they needed a chamber pot, she didn't herself and she was only a child. It made her feel sick. It was always worse when he was here as well.

    The Terrapin's husband was often away, doing business. What the business was Jun Ching didn't know. He didn't carry anything with him when he came back or when he left. All she knew was that he was often away for weeks at a time. She also knew that when he was back everyone was less happy. He was going again today, that would be why he was up earlier than usual. By the time she had returned the empty pot outside the door and made the tea, she could hear footsteps coming down. Heavy footfalls. That was him and not long after were more, this time the Terrapin.
    "Girl! Where's my *juk*? I'm in a rush." She already had the bowl in her hands but was just half a beat too slow. The Terrapin cuffed her across the back of the head when the bowl was safely deposited. "Get the children up." Jun Ching hurried upstairs. She was barely out of earshot when he opened his mouth for the first time that morning.

"That girl is no use. Why is she here?"

"Yes, she is no use for now, but she will be. It is good to have someone do the dirty chores and not your daughters, don't you think?"

"It's another one to feed. It's not worth it."

"She doesn't eat much, and we can give her less if you want. How about just morning and night?"

"A little better. I still don't think we need her here, you are too lazy to work yourself, don't think I don't know. I didn't marry you so you could do nothing you know. I don't want my daughters growing up to be lazy like you either."

"Of course not, Husband, of course not. You won't even notice her soon and think how this looks to the neighbours that you have a servant in your house now. That you have money for one – must mean life is good in this house. It's not that your daughters *can't* work, it's that they don't have to. Now that is a luxury." He straightened up in his chair a little at this. His left thumb and finger went absently to rub a protruding mole on his jaw. This was a good place to leave him, thought the Terrapin, and said nothing more.

"I'm not in the business of charity." He said and walked out.

Upstairs the two girls were up and dressed already. "Good morning, Miss Flower, Miss Blossom." Jun Ching repeated as the Terrapin had taught her. They both stopped and stared at her. They were still unused to her and spent most of the time when she was in the room watching her do all the things that they had to do only a few weeks ago. Flower had even tried to push Jun Ching aside when she was washing up the first time before she was reprimanded by her mother and lost her only use in the house. Now she just stood with one shoe on, the other in her hand staring. Blossom gave her a faint smile and carried on. She tugged on her sister's elbow breaking her gaze, so the other shoe found its way onto her foot.

"Are you hungry this morning?" Jun Ching tried again to no reply. They didn't even acknowledge her this time. At first, she wondered if they couldn't understand her. If she wasn't speaking clearly but the Terrapin understood her so that couldn't be it. The two girls squeezed their backs up against the door as they went past her keeping as much space between them and Jun Ching as possible. Both pairs of eyes bound to hers as she turned and watched them go by. "I've put your *juk* on the table already, Miss."

As soon as they were past, they scampered down the stairs. Jun Ching frowned, she wanted them to speak to her. She wanted to find out if they would be a Penny or a Nine Auntie, someone she could talk to or someone to avoid. It was hard that the only words in her ears now were biting ones from the Terrapin. She hadn't been there long, but she already felt the empty nothing that was trailing around next to her. The nothing that the girls won't feel because they had each other. She envied the girls their elbow squeezes and again thought how much she missed the back of Jun Yee's knees or even anything familiar.

Flower was the elder of the two. The Terrapin named her Spring Flower as she was born in the spring but found herself devoid of further inspiration when the second came also in the spring just 13 months later. So, she named her Spring Blossom and that's exactly what happened, one blossomed and the other remained a bud. They were twins who should have been born together but Flower had to wait a lonely 13 months for Blossom, crying constantly until they were reunited then tucked away her voice completely. She had everything she needed. She barely spoke at all so her sister often translated her silences for everyone else. To each other they spoke through their eyes, through the faint elbow squeezes and at times urgent sounds that only they understood. They were two halves of one peanut. They barely even noticed the existence of their baby brother and that seemed fair since once he had arrived, no one seemed to notice the two of them at all. The two flowers had been left to wilt.

After having two daughters in quick succession, the Terrapin was desperately chasing a son to stop her husband even thinking about taking another wife, though it was his empty pockets that stopped him more than anything else. It wasn't until years later that the Little 'Pin stuck his head out, blinking his little black eyes. Jun Ching had taken to calling him the Little 'Pin as he was very similar to his mother in many ways, and even more like a terrapin in his own right since the cold weather had come and now he was wrapped up in so many layers his head barely poked out amongst them. That morning his chubby fingers were grasping and warm as she pulled them through his sleeves. It took time to guide him down the steps as he still went down only on his right foot each time. By the time they got downstairs the bowls were empty, the tea drunk and the husband gone. The Terrapin looked more relaxed already.

"I put what was left of the *juk* in a bowl for my son. What he doesn't eat you can finish." She got up to leave. "Don't think I didn't notice you didn't bother fetching water yesterday you lazy thing. Make sure you get enough for a wash for all the children tonight or you'll have my cane for dinner. I'll be back later."

On her third trip back to the well, her mind turned over the thought of her brother's visit again and again, kneading it like soft dough. She was sure he would come soon though. The first nights alone stretched as long as the night seemed dark to her. All her nights before had been padded by the soft sound of breathing around her helping minutes and hours on their way to dawn. Alone she didn't know how to make them go faster or the dark more friendly. The scratching of the rats against the sacks in the corners was unfamiliar and frightening, scratching out her whimpers and tears. A few days later she came across Lien in a doorway so busy sneaking surreptitious peeks around her own shoulders that she hadn't noticed Jun Ching until little arms were thrown around her waist. She had big smiles for her and brought promises from Jun Yee that he would come himself as soon as he could. It was lucky that that was enough for Jun Ching because Lien could do no more, her own heart heavy with impotency as she left the little girl.

After a few weeks the nightly tears gave way to sleep and a few weeks more they stopped coming completely and sleep came alone. The scratching didn't stop though it did edge closer and closer until one night she jumped at a nip on her foot stamping on the rat at the same time.

Little 'Pin coughed on her back. She craned her head round to try and get a look at him. "Don't be sick Little 'Pin, or I'll have trouble." She patted his bottom a couple of times and rubbed the little legs that stuck out on either side of her. He rubbed his forehead on her shoulder blade in reply. He's tired, she thought to herself, brushing past her own surprise at how well she read him already. He'll sleep on her back, he always woke if she tried to put him down so she hoped he wouldn't sleep too long. She was tired already.

Just one more trip should be enough, she thought to herself as she bent her knees, gently lowering the two buckets on each end of the bamboo pole across her back to the ground, careful not to bump the baby's head on her back. It wasn't worth not going one day and having to carry so much more the next, better to spread the work next time. The queue at the well was gone now, no one else had as much water to collect as she did and she took her time pulling the water up, hand over hand, putting off the final walk back as long as she could as the weight across her back was starting to make her knees buckle. She thought of the tap in the street back at home, she'd never realised how easy it was to get water there. Tofu-belly, the landlady's son, flashed across her mind. She had forgotten how he'd often appear and carry her water upstairs for her, always a wink and a shush, don't tell anyone. She even missed him, she realised. So many people and things to miss. She wondered if they had given someone else their room, if someone else was happy lying in her bed pressing their feet against the underside of the bunk above. She hoped not. Without any thought of how they would or could ever go back, it was a comforting thought to think their place was still there, waiting for them to slip back into. Her next breath sighed out slow and long.

When her two buckets were full, she crouched under the bamboo holding on with both hands on either side to steady it. She had learnt quickly, the first day she carried anything she hurt her back trying to lift it from the waist. This time she pushed up with her knees as she had learnt watching an old man with his load of bricks do. It was slow walking back to the house but from a distance she saw a figure by the door that wasn't there before and a small crowd of three or four children standing just a few feet in front staring directly up at him. Her feet shuffled faster to get to him since she couldn't run, and her knees did buckle a couple of times with the extra effort. He was steadfastly keeping his eyes off the children in front of him, staring in the opposite direction from her. The children saw her approaching and started to move away though as with Lien, she didn't call out to him until she was only steps away with the water still softly lapping against the sides of the two buckets across her shoulders. He said nothing as he took them from her, and they walked through the house together leaving the children peering round the door until it was closed on them. Only then did they speak.

She felt her voice return as though it had been hiding, quivering in a secret pocket of her throat but with Jun Yee it came bounding out, excited and stumbling on its weakened legs. She had been walking behind him from the street but now she passed him to lead him through to the kitchen and only then did he notice the boy tied to her back. He helped her hoist the buckets and empty them into the big tub in the back yard and pull a heavy wooden board across the top again. She didn't pause and immediately went into the kitchen checking the flame under the stove was still smouldering. He followed her in.

"Let's stop and rest a bit."

"No Brother. I can't. Before the Terrapin comes back I have a lot to do. If it's not finished, she gets angry."

"So what if she's angry? Then we can chat. And you need a rest anyway."

"No matter, I can work and chat at the same time. With you here to chat with me, I will be done very quickly. Here, you sit here Brother and keep talking." She pulled out two little stools, one for him and the other she sat on herself next to a large tub. Plunging in up to her elbows she fished out several shirts, hanging them over the side and started scrubbing the first. The back and forth motions made Little 'Pin's head swing from side to side, pivoting on his chin. His small black eyes blinked piggishly at Jun Yee. It made him angry, his finger urged to poke them and hear his cry. His chest clenched with the sight of how dirty her own clothes were compared to the ones she was washing now.

Her hands didn't stop with her chores, she did them without a thought, with him there the simple sphere of protection had returned. She didn't feel the icy water or the sting of the chilli in a cut from the morning. Shaking off the awe, Jun Yee took up the little axe and started on replenishing the firewood stack whilst she chirped on. When everything was finally done, she looked around the kitchen with her hands on her hips like a small young old woman.

"Where do you sleep then? Do you have to sleep in the kitchen?"

"No. Up at the top, I have my own floor, would you like to see?"

The house was empty except for the silent baby and Jun Yee took in as many details as he could as they walked though. His sister was not giving him a wholehearted tour. They certainly seemed richer than their Paw Paw. They had good, polished furniture. Seemingly more furniture than they needed for such a small family. They lived alone as well, no other family, that didn't necessarily mean they were rich, but it still made them better off in his eyes than the crowds at Ah Ho's. There were a set of very new-looking thermoses on a side table with a row of upturned glasses in front. Recently bought he presumed since there was now someone whose job it could be to keep them constantly filled up with hot water. He followed her up the stairs looking at the rounded bulging bottom of the baby hanging heavy in the sling. He was almost half her size.

"You can't put him down? He looks heavy."

"Not heavy. I put him down he cries then I have to put him back and tie the sling all over again from the beginning. Might as well save the trouble."

"You carry him all day every day?"

"Not usually. When the Terrapin gets back, she will take him. Or his father will. Then I'm free!"

Immediately round the corner where it couldn't be seen from downstairs, the atmosphere changed. The walls were marked and unwashed unlike the white clay of the downstairs. The wooden floorboards creaked, and the doors were thin. Jun Ching called out the rooms as they went past. There were three on this floor, the children's room, one empty room and the Terrapin's room with her husband then up the stairs again she skipped. His heart fell. Up the next flight the atmosphere dived again. The walls were not only unfinished but the clay that once was on was now crumbling. The planks for the floor didn't even creak like the ones below as the gaps between them were regular and wide.

"This is my room." She stood to the side by the wall so he could get a full view of the space. "Isn't it big? Like I told you." He walked slowly round, peering behind boxes stacked in the corners. "What are you looking for Brother?"

"Your bed, you sleep where?"

"Oh! That's easy. I do this!" She bounded in front of him and by his feet between two boxes she pulled out five empty rice sacks all rolled up together. Holding onto one end she flung it out unfurling them across the floor. "See! I can sleep on different layers depending on how cold it is. Right now, it is getting colder so I lie on top of two and sleep under two, so I am in the middle. When it gets even colder, I can sleep on one and under three. It's quite good, isn't it? The fifth one is for my head."

She was kneeling on the floor looking up at him, needing him to tell her it was good. To agree with her and make her little paper castle stronger. He sat next to her and felt the draught come through the floorboards and chill his bottom.

"It is good, Sister. Good enough for now but one day you will have better. Much better." He squeezed her hand.

After he had gone, Jun Ching admired the sweets from Lien and the crispy buns from Bau Suk again before wrapping them in several bags to hide them and rolled up in her rice sacks. There were three buns, two fit comfortably in the roll so she had been forced to eat the odd one out with Jun Yee still there though she refused to have any at all if he didn't share it. It tasted better that way she insisted. She sat cross-legged on the floor of the kitchen and watched the flames in the stove beating each other around the base of the pot. The front door closed and there was a soft slither of slippers across the floor.

"Girl? Girl! Where have you crawled off to?"

Jun Ching scrambled to her feet, trampling the warm memories she'd been curling round her fingers. She ran into the living room, tiny steps taking her to an abrupt stop in front of the Terrapin. But not too close.

"There you are. Stop running around. You'll break something. And then what have you got to pay for it? Nothing. Who was here today?"

"No one. No one came today Auntie."

"Liar." She spat, spraying Jun Ching's face. Her hand twitched to wipe it with a sleeve but that would be a mistake. She controlled it. "Lying little beggar! Who was here? I know someone was. Look at the floor." Across the floor was a trail of dust from Jun Yee's shoes. "Unless all this was you? Well, was it? Are you that stupid to do it again? Was the beating I gave you last time not enough?" Jun Ching didn't say a word but, in her head, she shouted at herself for forgetting to wipe the floors. She should have known better. "Right. You've got nothing to say? That means it was you then!"

The Terrapin leapt up, startling the toddler as she did. She whipped out a feather duster from behind the side table. It was about three feet long, half covered in feathers, the other half a bare, thin cane. Holding onto the feathered end she brought the cane down hard across the small of Jun Ching's back. A pained howl broke out immediately. They both turned, surprised, to look at the toddler standing, holding onto the seat of a chair with one hand and his wide eyes pouring tears down his chubby cheeks. He was as surprised as they were and his howl stopped as suddenly as it had started as he stared back at them. The Terrapin hesitated only a moment longer before bringing the cane down again, this time squarely across her buttocks. She tensed her whole body, willing herself not to move.

"Well? Do you still want to lie? Go on. Lie then!" The howling started again. "I know your filthy, mongrel brother was here. Everyone in the street saw him, saw the two of you together. And he carried the water for you, didn't he? You lazy pig." The cane came down a third time, somewhere between the first two strikes. "What else did he do? What other chores?" The fourth time the cane came down Jun Ching couldn't keep still any longer and jumped.

"I'm sorry, Auntie. I didn't know he was coming. He only carried the water once. I carried it the other times. Please Auntie. Please."

Satisfied by the cowering child, the Terrapin stopped. The howl trailed into a whimper. "Get out. If you don't want another taste of the cane, do not appear in front of my eyes again tonight.

The Terrapin took the children out that night for noodles. Only after they left did Jun Ching creep down the stairs again. She swept the floors, calmed the flames in the kitchen and placed the empty, clean chamber pots under the beds. Up in her room alone she knelt on the floor, sitting on her heels, her bottom and back too painful to take the pressure still. She tried to reason with her stomach that drummed with hunger. There were only two buns left. The longer she held onto them, the longer it seemed Brother was with her. But they would go stale, and quickly, her stomach beat back. She unraveled the rice sacks to make up her bed and the buns toppled out, conspiring with the drums. She squeezed one of them slightly, the sweet topping crackled and crumbled a little. They were going stale already. She licked the crumbs off her palm. She sniffed it and took a massive bite. Even she herself didn't know she could open her mouth so wide.

She kept out of the Terrapin's way for the next few days and the Terrapin mostly left her alone, gaping her sharp little mouth only when the breakfast was not on the table when she came downstairs or if it was too cold when she came down later than usual and it had been there too long. Her temper was turned low, set at simmering only but even Jun Ching had already learnt this would not last long. Her husband would be back in the morning and when he did it would turn up to a boil. Little 'Pin would stop toddling, staying still in whichever corner he was placed in. Flower would be absolutely silent. Jun Ching watched fascinated. Just the threat of his presence seeped into the corners of each room like a creeping black cloud. She ran through all the men she had known or did know, the uncles, Bau Suk or even Tofu Belly back home. Their faces floated past her and none could even threaten a similar power to cow an entire household. She had few references for marriage, perhaps this was how it was to be when people were married but if that was the case, it jarred that anyone like Gwai would ever endure this. She wouldn't be cowed, Jun Ching was sure of that at least.

He arrived in the afternoon of the next day. A few weeks since the last beating, on the day he went away. The girls were playing outside and came in suddenly and quietly when they saw him through the crowd at the end of the street. A blanket fell over the house, muffling the sounds of life within. He didn't call out when he opened the door though the girls, in unison, gave their 'hello father's even before he was entirely in. Inside he collapsed in a sweaty heap, one leg draped across two chairs calling for tea and rice wine. Jun Ching brought the tea quickly, placing it on the table next to him. He grabbed her wrist, rolled his head towards her like a corpse on a slope and looked at her for a moment too long.

She pulled back but he held on. Her eyebrows hurried together to shield her eyes from his face, but she could still feel the glisten of sweat on cold skin.

"*La la la*, rice wine, Husband. You must be tired, have some and relax. How was business this time? Was it good? I am sure it was with your ta-"

"Shut your mouth! You're annoying me already." He dropped Jun Ching's wrist his hand moving swiftly over slapping the Terrapin across the face as she bent over pouring the wine. She barely flinched. The stream of wine jerked forwards and back. Only one drop on the table.

"Sorry Husband, I've missed you and was excited to talk to you." She shuffled backwards towards the kitchen door. Jun Ching made sure she had slipped out before her. Little 'Pin shuffled himself on his bottom further back into the corner of the room. Nobody remembered to pick him up.

Their father's presence made the girls scatter in front of him each time he came near like a jar of mung beans dropped on the floor. They played out in the street, leaving the house to him and taking their brother with them when they could. The older girl struggled to carry him now, he was over half her size and she had to stick her hips so unnaturally far out to balance him on that she looked like two halves of a ghost walking side by side. After dinner and the washing were done, Jun Ching sat outside the front of the house watching the girls playing with the children with bulging eyes from down the street. They had a collection of stones, one big and round, a little jagged, and several smaller ones. They took turns, throwing the larger one in the air and scooping up one small one before catching the big one again. They did it repeatedly until they missed, and it was then someone else's go. The person with the most small stones at the end won. The sisters were good at the game and often won. Whereas the children they were playing with had fresh cuts and old bruises on the backs of their hands where the big stone had hit them several times.

Mostly though, their father would pull Little 'Pin to him, making him face him on his knee, throwing him about to repeated chants of "My son, my heir", muttering how rich he would be one day and powerful with lots of people to tell what to do. Little 'Pin would keep quiet, afraid to move until his father tired of him and, satisfied with his reproduction of himself, thrust him aside on his feet and gave him a little push to walk away, with little regard for the fact that he hadn't learnt to walk yet. Little 'Pin would fall forwards on his face with no whimper. He would be picked up by a sister and taken outside where he'd stay very still perched on his sister's hip with his head resting on her shoulder looking away from the games, unmoving until he saw Jun Ching. Then he wriggled and pushed himself away with fat fists. He dropped softly to the ground and she kept a halfhearted hold of him which he wriggled free of with skill. He crawled straight to Jun Ching and pushed his head into her lap, bottom sticking out and was quiet again.

All four of them avoided going back in for as long as possible each night. Even the Terrapin came to the door and stood for a while on the periphery of the gloom within. A shout soon came from inside throwing itself around them, drawing them together and pulling them back. The girls hurried upstairs, and Jun Ching gathered the softly whimpering Little 'Pin. The first night he was home, the Terrapin shuddered a sigh as Jun Ching squeezed past her. She trailed her fingers over the boy's downy hair.

"Put him in bed. Then you get upstairs." Her eyes didn't meet Jun Ching's and she didn't want them to. Her voice was lower and unfamiliar. She didn't want to know this voice.

Even the house was affected by him. Some nights it groaned and moaned a bit more, sounds like branches knocking on the walls came in intervals like the trees themselves objected to him being there. In the mornings, the Terrapin was always bleary eyed. Jun Ching guessed she didn't sleep much when he was back. He snored loudly, she even heard him herself through the floorboards in her room. But it was then that Jun Ching realised she had many voices. Other than the high-pitched bark she had for Jun Ching and the girls, she had an equally high pigeon coo for Little 'Pin and now, she discovered, she also had a low smooth tone which she must have kept at the very back of her throat for her husband only. This one was spread thickly when he could hear it, to Little 'Pin, the girls and even some overspill on Jun Ching on occasion, but it lasted only as long as he did and that was rarely more than a few days.

Chapter Thirteen

Jun Ching woke to a strange noise. She lay still for a while listening. It was regular. Was it the wind? The sleep in her head muddled the sound. A branch knocking against the wall? No, it was close. A sticky fist squeezed her heart and her fingers reached out for her brother's pocket that wasn't there. She pulled it back in and squeezed it till the joints in her fingers hurt to take her mind off it. The bumping continued. It seemed to be getting harder. It wasn't moving. It wasn't getting any nearer, that means it probably wasn't after her. Was it an animal? A dog or something that was thumping its tail? But they didn't have a dog. Forcing her courage into her elbows she propped herself up and cocked her head. It was coming from below. She shuffled under the sacks, the floorboards creaked but the sound didn't pause. It couldn't hear her, but she could definitely hear it. Soft candlelight was shining through the cracks in the boards. Pressing her eye against the biggest crack she peered down into the room below.

The candlelight outlined a heaving mass of blanket with two heads. It throbbed and pulsed with a violent motion that frightened her. The two heads faced each other, one looking down into the bed, driving the motion. The other turned her face to the ceiling though Jun Ching had never seen her face like that before. She looked like Penny did when Nine Auntie pinched her hard then twisted the flesh in her fingers – a face scrunched up in pain and lips bitten together. But Penny's face was passing. It would appear suddenly then be gone but this, the Terrapin's face, got worse with every thud. He was on top of her. She didn't understand. The bed was big enough for them to sleep side by side. He knew that, that's how they normally slept. Was he dreaming? Is that why? She had heard of people walking in their sleep. In fact, sometimes Jun Yee said she talked in her sleep. Was this the same thing? He might crush her if he was. Why didn't she push him off if he was asleep? It didn't seem right, and it looked like it hurt. Thud. Thud. Thud. It was getting louder, more frequent. She couldn't stop looking at the Terrapin's face. It was turned towards the candle by the side of the bed that threw varying bright streaks across her face as it flickered. From the deep folds of skin where her eyes were during the day, Jun Ching saw drops of water run away into her hair. Her mouth bitten closed before now cracked open and a short shriek jumped from her gut. The thudding stopped immediately. A hand appeared from beneath the blanket, grabbed her hair and yanked it back.

"Shut up." He spat at her.

The violent motion started again but there was no noise now as her head was held back in his grip of her hair and could no longer smack against the wall behind them. It looked unnatural. Her eyes were pulled open and her head remained eerily still despite the motion all around her, like her neck was broken. The only sound left was his ragged panting filling in the rhythm in the spaces the thudding left.

She wanted to move. She didn't want to see the Terrapin's broken face. She felt like she was crouching on his back and watching, and she didn't want to be part of this. Shame curdled in her stomach.

With a final vicious pull of her hair, he collapsed. He pushed himself up with one palm on her bare breast. She winced again. He pushed her out from under him, looking at the tangle of hair he had ripped out between his fingers clicked his tongue in disgust shaking them off on her face before rolling over giving her his back.

"Blow out the candle. I don't want to see your face."

The Terrapin clasped the torn strands in her hand holding it to her chest, curled up in the opposite direction, and blew the candle out. The two heads now like repelling magnets as far away from each other in the same bed as possible.

The next morning, he left early for another trip. The Terrapin was unusually late coming down for breakfast. The girls were outside playing already, Jun Ching had given Little 'Pin his *juk* and he was happily chasing a small spider around the back of the cupboard. She couldn't leave him alone to fetch the water before the Terrapin came down, so she loitered. She crept up to the bedroom more than once worried that the Terrapin was still curled up like a beaten dog on the edge of the bed, but she heard nothing on the other side. It was an image she couldn't push from her mind. She ran through all the women she knew in her head, Ma, Ah Ho, Gwai… she could see none of them curled like that, taking up so little space. Terrapin felt so familiar to Gwai but her above the others, Jun Ching could not equate to this. What would Gwai have done? Jun Ching had never met her uncle, Gwai's husband, but she was beyond doubt that Gwai would have bared her teeth and bitten back ten times more and harder than what she had received. She could see that image clear as spring water. There was something fundamentally different then between them, that if you knocked on the two of them Gwai would be solid and the Terrapin would give you a hollow echo, that if you scratched at them, Gwai would be Gwai all the way through but the Terrapin was a hard shell with little underneath to support it.

She finally appeared just as Jun Ching was putting the bowl away.

"What you doing? You think you have no mistress?" She slapped her hard across the cheek. It had come out of nowhere. Jun Ching stared, shocked, up at her slightly swollen eyes. They were flat, pupil-less. "You dare look at me? What behaviour is this? While you here in this house you are mine. My servant. How I want to treat you I will treat you."

Jun Ching's own eyes stuttered, failing to look away. "There's... There's nothing wrong with you, is there?"

"Me? What could be wrong with me? I tell you what wrong with me. I have lazy and nosy servant girl, that what wrong with me! You understand? I see you too stupid to understand. I beat you until you understand!" Her tiny terrapin feet blurred over to the cane, stepping over the toddler. She flicked it a few times through the air warming up her wrist. The whipping spattered across Jun Ching's still raw back like hot oil on new skin. She cried out and tried to wriggle away but the Terrapin had her claw wrapped tight around her upper arm and seemed not to hear her at all. Little 'Pin wailed in the corner. The spider forgotten.

The Terrapin left not long after for her mother's. Energy spent from the whipping she went without any further words. She had to go now when her husband could not see, he stopped her if he could. He hated the idea of them scheming behind his back, the women together kneading and smoothing, whatever it was they were doing, always seemed to be more happening that was not for him. Something only the women could see. It was better to keep them split up, divided and obedient – they were less trouble that way. For the Terrapin, that was exactly why she wanted to go. She could sit with her mother for hours bent over sewing or washing, chores she wouldn't touch in her own house now that she had a servant of her own. Their words and silences would travel over the everyday - the children, the money, the coming festivals and their preparations – and the more important with the ease of grains of uncooked rice pouring softly over each other. She had taught her how to run a household in this way, how to teach her children and the things a wife must turn her hand to and her face from and pretend she hadn't seen. The Terrapin always returned soothed and that morning, after the whipping she gave Jun Ching relieved none of her wounds, she went to her mother. For the first time she returned home in the evening still swollen with rage.

She had hesitated. She counted 16 rows of 12 perfectly wrapped wontons in front of them both and she still hadn't said anything. She watched her mother's fingers gently holding the fine rice pastry across her fingers. A chopstick-ful of filling, spring onions, prawns, chopped to make them go further, and winter greens to bulk it out. Then the pastry folded round it into a little parcel, pinching closed the lip and sealing with beaten egg. She took her time. This was her pride. The wontons the Terrapin made were obvious, uglier, carelessly put together, edges uneven, some full to bursting whilst others were limp and empty. The older woman shook her head. They would have wontons for supper that night; they would have to, she couldn't sell those. The filling was running out. Here was a saving grace. The Terrapin noticed at the same time and put down the piece of pastry she was holding. Taking handfuls of the vegetables, prawns and onions she chopped them roughly. The aimless strikes of the meat cleaver were more suited to her talents than the precise folding of the wontons. And the sound was so comforting the filling ended up more finely chopped than it needed to be. The chopsticks squelched into the mixture and both women were relieved at the temporary reprieve the wontons had from her hands.

Between two square sheets of pastry, she found a little courage to hint at what had been happening in the nights to her mother. Her mother's hands paused mid-fold just long enough for her to see – she stared hard at one still brown liver spot on the ageing skin then it moved - her mother carried on. The silence drummed her ears. Then they moved on. Wasn't she going to say anything. Did she not hear?

"The new year is coming in only a few weeks, preparations must be made. You must buy the children new clothes if you can." The Terrapin heard her mother's voice brittle like glass and nodded her reply. She must say something. *I am her daughter. Her daughter.* She repeated to herself. "The girls should have red."

Screaming shook the inside of the Terrapin's head, screaming for help, pounding on the walls of her mind. After a pause a while later, her ma spoke again.

"As a woman, once you are married, you are his - there is no changing that. Every man has his faults. It is better to swallow than to choke."

The screaming died away. The Terrapin accepted not for the first time then that it was not her place to change her husband. She came seeking support to change something and got nothing and could not stand alone. Less than a handful of wontons later she left. A small clump of hair was left behind on the stool she had been sitting on. Her mother brushed it off quickly for the wind to blow into the grass.

Jun Ching kept a wall between herself and the Terrapin when she got home. Her temper still burnt inside her, and Jun Ching didn't want to risk another beating. Wherever the Terrapin sat that night, Jun Ching was right next door, making enough noise so there was no doubt she was working but close enough to be there fast if summoned. Little 'Pin was a problem. It was impossible to tell in these moods if the Terrapin wanted anything to do with him or not. If she picked him up when the Terrapin wanted to there could be trouble. If she waited for her to pick him up and he cried there could be trouble too. The end of the afternoon approached, when being far from sleep and close to hunger would confuse him and make him whimper. Jun Ching found more chores around the doorway. She watched the Terrapin who watched nothing. Little 'Pin tested his voice checking he was still there. He crawled to his mother's feet and pulled himself up by her trouser leg. Her face didn't change, her eyes didn't flick to him. If she felt his slapping at her knees, she chose to ignore it. His face changed instead. His eyes narrowed by a fraction and he opened his mouth, still undecided if he would go through with it. He tried once more on her knees but nothing. He shouted, an abrupt blast. Then he started a whimper. Jun Ching allowed it to test but the Terrapin didn't move. The whimper rose to a wail and she rushed over just as some consciousness twitched between the Terrapin's eyebrows. She swept him up and back into the kitchen with her. Happy with the attention, Little 'Pin turned his wail into a chuckle and chewed her pigtails. She bounced him a few times on her hip singing a song she couldn't remember before putting him on the ground again placing a long wooden board in front of him, penning him in, away from the open flame of the stove.

The next day Jun Yee found the smell of fish coaxing itself up his nostrils and tickling his brain. Looking over at them he was surprised. He expected to see curling tendrils snaking towards him. But there was nothing but mounds of fish in separate cages. The bottom layers slid over each other, the top layer stuck, scale to scale, to the layer below as the sun was still strong enough to dry out the lubricating water between them. The smell didn't bother him now, the summer was the worst when the smell would punch through his nose and into his chest. A dry, gaping mouth stuck out at him wedged between the reed strands of its cage. With the bumps of the cart, it had jumped closer and was now kissing the edge of his precious cargo. He shuffled round, swinging his legs over the back ledge of the cart so he was travelling backwards watching the road he had come by with the fishy mouth kissing his bottom instead. The thought made him chuckle.

His precious cargo sat in a roll covered in his lap. It was wrapped up tight and so felt harder than it did when he got it. Lien had wrapped it in a borrowed sheet overnight but still he was protective over it. He could already see his sister's mouth growing wider and wider as she got more and more excited and how she would jump tiny jumps clapping her hands together as he rolled it out in front of her. He pulled the package in closer and dropped his elbows on top. The road beneath him seemed to be stretching, repeating itself, making sure he went nowhere quickly. Even the sun was stuck above, unmoving, refusing to let time pass.

By the time he arrived, the sun had finally moved high into the sky, looking down directly on him. It was bright but too weak to burn off the outer coats people were wearing to ward off the winds. He waited as he did the last time, behind one of two pillars on a shop front, diagonally opposite the house. The package stuck out to one side. He pulled it in, but it made him push his shoulders out of the other side of the pillar. After shimmying back and forth for a while trying to fit them both in, he saw her, bent almost double under the weight of the full water buckets, coming back down the street, water splashing over the sides onto her bare ankles. Adults and children lazily followed her with their eyes as she went past and then dropped her to follow something else. No one helped. When she stopped in the doorway, he ran over to her.

"Ching Ching!"

"Brother! You're here!" Her smile was almost too big for her face, showing all the teeth she hadn't grown into yet.

"Yes, I've come to see you! Are there people in the house?"

"No, no one. You can come in."

She hurried as much as she could with the water and passed straight through the house to the yard. It was her last load for the day and her legs trembled as she placed it down. Jun Yee had followed her into the kitchen and seemed to be struggling with something behind his back. He kept dodging from side to side like he was balancing.

"You go upstairs first, Brother. The Terrapin will be back soon. She must see me working down here when she is back, or she will come looking for me and see you too then we will have trouble."

He backed out of the kitchen and ran up to her room still hiding the package. He was bouncing on his knees when he heard the Terrapin come back and stopped mid-spring. He heard her go again and heard his sister pad swiftly back up to him. By the time she came up the stairs he was bouncing again and jumped to his feet immediately. It was unlike him to be so twitchy, like there were ants biting at his bottom, she thought but it made her happy. She wondered why but before she could ask, he ushered her to sit.

"Ching Ching, I have a present for you. *La!*" He whipped off the top sack from a small mound and beneath was the package, wrapped in Lien's white sheet.

"*Wah!* Thank you, Brother, thank you!" Her hands flew together with little claps as he placed it in front of her. She touched it carefully. It was soft. She pressed a bit harder and it gave to her. She laid her head down on it and sighed. "It is so soft Brother, thank you."

"*Ha?* Open it you silly girl! You don't even know what it is yet! Open it!"

"*Ha?!* There's something inside? I thought it was a big pillow! I thought this was it!" Her small fingers struggled with the knot Lien had tied underneath to keep it all together. The cold had numbed her fingertips so much that they fumbled uselessly, picking and grasping but not loosening.

"Let me do it." With a few short moves he peeled back the white sheet to reveal a bright sky blue, soft cotton. Her mouth grew wide. "Look, look, look!"

Jun Yee stepped back and with one flick of the wrist threw the entire spread of the blanket out over her head. For a moment she was gone, just a peak in a blue mountain. He pulled it down and she popped into view again, hair ruffled, pulled over her head, and a massive zero for a mouth like the end of a horn with no sound. She stared at it, her eyes wandered over the endless reams of cloth. Her fingers rubbed the hem between them.

"Ching Ching? You like it?"

She nodded and fell face first into it. Muffled giggling gushed out and Jun Yee felt his chest explode as he too fell face first into it. The giggling took over their bodies and they turned over and over until they were a tightly wrapped spring roll with feet at both ends.

It was a bigger blanket than either of them had had before, big enough for two people at once. The edges were slightly frayed from use and the outside edges a bit bluer than the middle, but it was clean, Lien had made sure of that and patched up a few small threadbare squares that wanted to turn into holes, but above all it was soft, very soft.

"Where did you get it from Brother?" She asked, eyes swimming in a vision of blue; the crowns of their heads pushing against each other.

"The nuns. They gave it to me. The fat fish boy in the market told me they give things away sometimes, so I went, I had to go a few times, but they gave it to me in the end." His tongue pressed back the words he had to use to beg for it, to explain where his sister was and what had happened to her, having to convince them he really needed it. "It was easy really. But we have to believe in their god now and have to go to their heaven after we die. I promised."

"What about Ma?"

"They said she might be there too. If she isn't, we'll just leave, okay? And go to find her in the underworld. The nuns won't be able to do anything to us then."

"We won't need the blanket then anyway, we can give it back."

"Exactly."

But for now, the blanket was amazingly soft. Jun Ching shimmied, flapping her spring roll bound arms inside it feeling the soft material rubbing against her skin like a million tiny kisses. He flicked the blanket open and wrapped it round her shoulders.

"This is your safety blanket, okay? Whenever you are unhappy, you come up here and wrap yourself up in this and remember what it was like to be a double ended spring roll today, okay?" She nodded. "I will protect you and when I am not here, the blanket is like a magic cloak, you wrap it around yourself and nothing can get through, no one, and you will be alright, okay?" She nodded again pulling the blanket a little closer around her.

"Brother? What if we don't die together? How will I know where to go without you? Or where to wait?"

"Don't worry sister, I won't let you go without me." She looked away, unsatisfied. He smiled harder in the hope that she wouldn't see through the holes in his logic. She tucked his words up in her head to examine later but for now all she wanted was to be a spring roll again, just like they did back in their room in Hong Kong.

"Roll me up, Brother! One more time!" She demanded as she threw herself on the floor.

And he did, tucking her up tighter and tighter until she wriggled to get free. She slid out of the bottom, the material pulling her shirt up her back. Before she could pull it down again, Jun Yee saw the criss cross of red, angry lines. She saw his face and pulled her shirt down as fast as she could but in her hurry it dragged hard against her skin. She gasped.

"What's wrong with your back?" He was behind her in an instant, pulling her shirt back up. She struggled against him, ashamed. "Let me see!" He was stronger and pushed her more roughly than he meant to onto her hands in front of him. Right in the middle of her back was one line, blistering with repeated strikes. It seemed to grow in his sight. Pulsing till he saw nothing else but the puckered red outline and the bulging liquid bound in skin in the middle.

"I'm sorry Brother. I tried to hide them from you. I'm sorry. I'm so sorry."

She twisted round and sat cross-legged, head hanging so low, her chin on her chest. He stared at the line of scalp running down the middle of her head dividing the two plaits just behind her ears. He couldn't see but he knew they were tied with thin red string at the bottoms that Ma had bought her. Red, lucky, for the new year. He would buy her new ones, blue ones, to go with the blanket.

In the same moment that the blue string trailed through his head something broke, and out of that something seeped a thick burning, gathering ground. This was not alright. No. No! This couldn't be happening. He was on his feet suddenly scanning the room for something to punch, to kick but his sister had nothing.

There was only the wall where his knuckles now rammed themselves again and again. Why didn't it hurt more? It should, it must, hurt more. So harder he punched.

Jun Ching had never seen him like this. He could be angry or upset but it was usually a quiet type of angry where you're watching for where it might spill over but not this. This fury was loud, and it didn't know or didn't care who was watching. She felt every punch in her throat until they forced her to sob. He stopped then, fists still raised, knuckles red, a splinter he couldn't see sharpened his senses again. For a moment she thought he might be done but in two long strides he was behind her lifting the back of her shirt to see the scars once more. She twisted away from him, crying, scared now.

"Up! Get up. Get your things. We are leaving. Now!" The words burst out of him that she didn't dare question. Together they threw her spare clothes into the middle of the blanket then that into the middle of Lien's sheet and wrapped it up. Jun Yee threw it all over his shoulder and grabbed her by the wrist pulling her down the stairs and out into the fresh air of the street outside.

He pulled her directly into the first side street they came to. He had no idea which direction the Terrapin would be coming from or when, so they had to move quickly. No doubt they were easily tracked by bored gazes lining the streets so he had to put as much distance between them and the Terrapin as fast as he could. That was their only chance of getting away. He sped along, Jun Ching running to keep up. He could barely remember the path he took to get there from the market where the cart had dropped him off but it would be too dangerous to go that way anyway. The streets were unfamiliar and he wasn't sure he wasn't leading them in circles, all he knew was that he had to keep them moving. Standing still meant going back, and he could not let Jun Ching go back there. The blistering lines on her back flashed in his eyes and he stumbled nearly dropping the bundle. He needed to stop and think. They darted down an alley way so narrow his outstretched arms could touch the walls on either side. At the other end was a doorway, the exit of the picture house, but nothing was showing right now, there was no reason for anyone to come this way. Halfway down the alley was a small pile of woven baskets and mats, left by a market stall holder who hadn't come that day most likely. They hurried up to it and crouched between them, pulling the mats in front of their feet just to be safe.

Their breath rasped and reprimanded as it bounced back at them off the opposite wall. Jun Yee let go of Jun Ching's wrist finally, dropping his head between his knees grateful for the dark on his eyes. Blood throbbed in his ears demanding a plan, an answer to what they were going to do. He didn't know. He always knew. How was he in this place? How were they both in this place? What had he done? He squeezed his knees together until his temples felt like they were touching in the middle, but the questions remained. He threw his head back against the stone wall. His skull bounced. That one really hurt, he thought, as he stared up at the sky. He had not one single answer for what to do.

Jun Ching's hand slipped behind and rubbed his head. She was feeling for blood but decided to keep rubbing anyway. She liked the motion and the feel of the slippery strands of hair. It was a surprise though that her brother wasn't bleeding from somewhere though, either fist, his head. He was battering himself today. The dash from the Terrapin's house had run out any apprehension that might have nibbled at her ankles. As the realisation tickled over her, she squeezed the back of his neck until he looked sidelong at her.

"Brother, I'm so happy." She squeaked, her eyes jumping in a way he hadn't seen since before they left home.

His shoulders just fell away and he laughed, sputtering at first, like the communal tap below their building in Hong Kong, a gulp of a laugh. Then it came, from the belly, gushing. And she laughed. And they both laughed loudly, uncaring who heard them as they rolled on the ground between the baskets, jaws aching, tears escaping. When it eased away, the smiles remained, and Jun Yee pulled Jun Ching to him in a rare hug and held her close. He would make sure she was okay. He would do anything to make sure.

They slept under the mats that night, sharing the blanket. The next morning Jun Yee scouted out the crowded market at the busiest time using the people as cover, expecting to bump into the Terrapin at any time. But he had never seen her, he had only heard her so he wouldn't know who she was until it was too late, until she recognised him, which it was much easier for her to do. They couldn't stay there he knew. He emptied the coins in his pocket into the scrubbed hands of an old man in exchange for all the *bays* he could spare and smuggled themselves onto the back of a half empty cart heading back towards the sea.

By the time the sky was turning down its colours, the sea had crept into the air and into their noses without their noticing. They slipped off the cart at one of the turns to their village and Jun Yee led them, skirting around the outside, to the shore. In the twilight they settled between the legs of the trees a little way from the water, close enough to hear the rhythm of the waves. They lay still and in silence until their blood rushed in unison.

The next few days, Jun Yee eked out the buns he had bought, avoiding the village for as long as he could, but in their hands, days seemed to multiply, their stomachs bulging with the time spent together. Jun Yee's pockets were light to begin with but now were filled only with Jun Ching's fingers as they sat unspeaking and smiling. He wasn't going to think about it until he had to. Tomorrow, he'd worry tomorrow.

"Brother, do you remember how the Li sisters used to argue all the time? And we used to pretend to be them through the wall?" Jun Ching giggled.

"What? Like this?" Jun Yee put on his most nasal, annoying squawk, "'*Why do you always put your chopsticks at that angle? It's so annoying.' 'Because I like to and I know it annoys you.' 'You're so annoying.' 'Yeah, well you smell of fish!'*" Jun Ching folded over into her knees laughing, wrenching air in with every breath and nodding furiously. Jun Yee carried on. "'*No, you smell of fish, of rotting fish in fact.' 'You LOOK like a rotting fish!'*"

"No more, Brother, stop!" She was on her side now laughing almost unwillingly. The laughter having been denied exit so long was refusing to be tamed. Jun Yee laid down next to her. Very slowly, it spent itself out. They stared up at the stars and carried on, there was Missy too of course, and the landlady who led to the tofu-belly who led to the tofu man and soon they were walking back down their street, smelling the roasting chestnuts and fish balls, the thwack of blades stripping sugar cane in their ears. Jun Ching curled down, pulling the blanket up under her chin just the feel the softness of it on her skin.

"Do you think we're ever going to see those people again, Brother?"

"You want to?"

"Yes."

"Okay then, yes." Jun Ching chuckled again.

"Ha! So easy?"

"Yes, for my little sister, what she wants I get."

"You already did, Brother. We're already here." She paused and as though she had considered it to be the best sound for the moment, she sighed, with a smile. "We can't stay long. But I am so happy we're here. So happy that I can't stop my feet rubbing."

They agreed and lay making up stories to the stars until her feet finally fell asleep.

The tomorrow that came was one with no stale buns left at all. Jun Yee knew he could manage but, watching Jun Ching's ribs rise and fall as she lay on her side next to him, he knew she couldn't. The Terrapin had made sure of that. He scuttled back and forth in his mind but thought of nothing except taking the risk and going into the village. He went early leaving Jun Ching dozing under the blanket. She slept a lot more than he expected her to and more comfortably too. He thought she would fret more but she seemed utterly content smiling from minute to minute and not once asked what they would do next. At this hour, the streets jangled with just a handful of people. Jun Yee sat in the branches of a tree far away from the road into town watching, fearful, his mouth dry and his chest pounding to explode. Anyone could see him. If he crossed this road, he risked everything. He thought of Bau Suk, the sounds of the wooden shutters to the bakery opening, the smell of the first buns rising in the air. He thought of the springy feel as he gently pressed the top of the buns to check they were ready. But with that was the prickling across his neck, they would know he would go there first. The dark, creeping presence of Ah Ho threw a cold shadow over the warmth of Bau Suk's presence. He couldn't risk it. He slid down again and crept back through the trees.

His hands were empty of anything but shame when he came back to find Jun Ching was walking back and forth along the shore. Her body angular, like the back of a chair. All straight lines waving at him when she saw him before running back. Her legs should have snapped on impact with the stones with each step she ran. But instead, she folded them carefully under her with a compactness of movement that flashed Sum before his eyes. The wind paused then, everything hung in mid-air and in that half beat in which only Jun Yee moved, Jun Ching's face shifted sideways into Sum's in a way he could not unsee. Her hair had come loose in her sleep, long strands racing across her face, trailing down her neck just as Sum's used to in the mornings. The wind stopped it from tickling and without anyone to scold her for it, she had no mind for her appearance. The memory of Sum's wet outline, face down on the beach punched him in the chest, jarring him back a step. He ran then. Ran down the beach, past Jun Ching who was running towards him, he threw off his shirt, kicked off his shoes and splashed out way into the water till it was deep enough to jump in.

"Come on *la*!" Came the single gurgled shout as his head bobbed out for an instant and a shriek of delight and Jun Ching followed. Her legs trying awkwardly to hurdle over the waves until she too plunged her head in safe in the knowledge that Jun Yee was nearby. It should have been too cold, but they didn't feel it. The next few hours they spent in the water, in the shallows with Jun Yee showing her how to move her arms and legs, how to stay still and float on the surface, how to hold onto him and not to struggle. She did it all, imitating, laughing, finding strength in her arms but not the fear that she always thought the water would bring and of course, oblivious to how Jun Yee was pushing Sum further and further away from his head with every stroke.

Exhausted, they hauled themselves back onto the beach. The noon sun high now, the wind flapping at their clothes to dry them. Side by side, toes under the blanket, quiet now with their own voices ringing in their heads. Jun Ching slowly realised she could feel her face. Her eyebrows weren't trying to meet each other in the middle and somewhere at the back of her teeth the knot had disappeared. She smiled and slipped her fingers in his pocket. It was a happiness that didn't begin, it just was, and so she knew it could not end either. She let that drift down inside, tiny ripples quivering out to the edges of her and perhaps beyond.

"Thank you, Brother." She wriggled her fingers. "These have been the best days ever ever ever."

"Really?"

"Ever really ever. And the best thing is that now that we've had them, they are ours to have again and again in our heads whenever we want to."

Jun Yee chuckled softly. Jun Ching watched him in the silence that settled. "I'm not afraid to die, you know." She pulled her palm out of his pocket, tracing the broken lifeline with her finger.

"Ching Ching, don't talk like that. That fortune stuff is rubbish. Everyone in the world has two palms, they can't all be different. And all the ones that are the same can't have exactly the same lives. It's rubbish."

"I'm just saying. If it is true. I'm not afraid. I am happy you see. You made me so happy. And so, to die is no loss, I am already happy. You should remember that."

He turned and smiled at her with one corner of his mouth. Out of the corner of his eye, he saw a movement, coming closer. They had run out of food anyway, he thought to himself, he had tried, and he had failed. There was no point in trying to run He turned his face back to the sea and sighed. He pulled her close into the crook of his arm. With her head resting on his shoulder, she heard Five Uncle's voice behind them.

Five Uncle was one of the fatter ones, and he needed to be too. Jun Yee was thrown over his shoulder like a sack of rice with much less care, kicking and punching while Jun Ching quietly wrapped their things into the blanket and walked alongside. She asked after every member of the family, even Nine Auntie, which took them all the way back round the outside of the village. By the time they rounded back up the beach towards the house, Jun Yee had run out of shouting though Five Uncle didn't risk putting him down, and Jun Ching had got to telling him about how they had spent the last few days. In her mind it had been a holiday, each day was a pleasant curiosity, the lack of food just an inconvenience.

Jun Yee landed on his feet with a jarring of the knees in the middle of the room with his back to Ah Ho. He found his voice again before he turned to her but didn't see her face for the slap that knocked his head back.

"Don't you dare disrespect me again." Ah Ho rarely raised her voice, the edge in it enough to cut through steel, but this time the volume was a slap in itself. He reeled, cheek hot and stinging. Jun Ching couldn't even hear what he was shouting over Ah Ho's voice as well, but he wasn't stopping. The whole family had gathered around the outside, skirting the room, bottlenecking doorways.

Ah Ho raised her cane and brought it hard against the back of Jun Yee's legs bringing silence at last as he stumbled back, stunned. She raised the cane again, high, but this time it was Jun Ching who ran between them and caught it on her forearm. The impact shuddered her back an inch, but she remained standing, holding Ah Ho's eyes as her hand twisted to grip the cane.

"I will go back myself, Paw Paw. You don't need to hit anyone else."

Ah Ho jerked her cane out of her hand. "You will go *now*."

She nodded her head towards Gwai who stepped immediately to the open door picking up Jun Ching's little bundle from the floor. Jun Ching squeezed her brother tightly on her way past and whispered in his ear.

"Thank you, Brother, for such a happy few days. I was so happy, and I am still. Come and see me soon. And don't let them get you too angry." Another brief squeeze and she was gone again.

He watched her go. Her feet stepping carefully over the raised wooden threshold and out into the sunshine of the courtyard from the shadows of the house. There was a small wave back at him before she was out of sight down the steps behind Gwai. He didn't wave back. He had tried. He had tried to protect her, to take her away but it wasn't enough. He had failed her. His feet felt strangled and rooted to the floor of this wooden shack, tied and bound to it, unable to run after her and he wished the shame that burned would take the whole place. Every last one of them gawping at him now from seen and unseen corners, all to go with him into those flames. Did Ma feel these roots curling around her ankles? Did she wish for the flames as well? He looked to her photograph, her faint smile in black and white, benign and suddenly so stupid. And the flames rose higher in him. That barely there smile, that barely there voice. The barely there mother who now left them so definitely here. Had she also been careful to step over the threshold when she left for Hong Kong on her day? If she had tripped, would it have turned out any different? Did she turn and wave at her brother? Did her brother feel the same way he did now? He didn't think so. His uncle's sloping shoulders and hooded eyes spoke of no anger.

Sum's steps had taken her a certain way that Jun Yee promised to himself he would wipe from Jun Ching's path. No footprints for her to follow he thought to himself. That could not be her way. He looked back to Ah Ho, sitting now, one hand on the top of her cane. Unmoving as though already dead. The others returned to their places in the house, parting smoothly around her like the rock that she was. Water and stone, water and stone, he thought. But surely there is more than one rock in a stream. He just needed to find it. He turned his back on her and walked away.

Chapter Fourteen

A few weeks after Jun Ching was returned, the Lunar New Year approached, children felt the anticipation in the increased bustle around them. Extra chores and stocking up crept in – whether children helped with the first or second of these depending entirely on the weight of their mothers' purses. Every family made its own preparations, even the ones with nothing had made some savings for this time.

Blossom particularly knew what this meant and whispered even more with eyes wide and pointing all over her own body. She was well prepared and ready by the morning when the Terrapin called them and Jun Ching to get ready to go out together. Jun Ching was ready of course, still wearing multiple layers everyday meant there was nothing else for her to put on, so she added an extra quilted jacket to Little 'Pin instead and stood waiting and curious at the door. She felt Little 'Pin's chubby hand on the top of her thigh, pulling round the back, round the other thigh, across the front and round again as he practised walking in a continuous circle around her legs. She looked back in her head and could think of no other time when she had been asked to go out with them. She had only been out with the Terrapin a handful of times in all the months she had been there. But since the brief taste of freedom, the Terrapin either took her with them or locked her in the house, not trusting that she wouldn't try it again just in case the thrashing she had got when she got back wasn't enough of a deterrent. Little 'Pin stumbled briefly right in front of her over his own feet, slightly surprised at the size of them and the space they needed. At the same moment the Terrapin came down the stairs, saw the stumble and frowned at Jun Ching.

They walked through the streets like a small lizard, the girls the thick middle, Jun Ching alone trailing a couple of steps behind and the Terrapin, slithering head at the front holding onto Little 'Pin's hand walking himself as he had started to do more of outside. The streets were busier than usual. Rattan trays filled the street sides, on the ground or stood up on crates, piled up high with pyramids of food. Jun Ching recognised her favourites from the shops in Hong Kong, short fingers of pale green dried winter melon, sweet enough to make your teeth chill if you had too many. Sugared nuts and melon seeds, both black and red. An image of Sum stole into her head, sitting with her feet up on the bed, a bowl of empty husks and a bag of red seeds on her lap and Penny's radio seeping through the wooden panels. One seed at a time at her lips, cracked between her front teeth, turned sideways her teeth pushed back either side of the husk, pinched out the soft inner seed and chewing, dropped the husk into the little bowl as her fingers reached for the next. There was a rhythm that Jun Ching liked to watch, though it seemed a lot of effort for one tiny seed to eat. Sum floated away on her bed in Jun Ching's head as she fingered the red string on her plaits and swallowed the nothing that was in her throat.

They had stopped in front of a stall draped with bright fabrics and ready-made clothes. Reds, some yellow golds and blues, spreading to the bolts of cloth stacked like fat greasy fingers on top of each other. There was one other woman there forcing a frustrated looking boy to hold out his arms for her as she measured a pale green jacket across his back. In one hand he held a white floured bun with one small hole where a bite had once been. He stared at it, willing it closer despite his rigid arm. When he felt the release of the grip on his shoulders a much larger chunk disappeared into his mouth, and just in time before he was told to hold his arms out again for the next size up. He chewed slowly, from behind Flower Jun Ching could see the red bean paste bulging. And so had Little 'Pin too, who had started to walk towards it with one hand outstretched. The Terrapin caught him quickly but not before the mother of the boy flicked her eyes up, catching sight of them. Her mouth twitched down at the sides and she poked her boy in a shuffle round until they were facing the other way.

"Come little son, be good," the Terrapin said, a little too loudly, "After we've bought you and *both* your sisters some new year's clothes, I'll buy you the biggest bun in the whole market. Okay? You want to do that? Little 'Pin nodded, and the woman snorted. The Terrapin snatched the first material to her hand, a pink silk embroidered tunic. "Blossom, this one looks perfect for you, come here." She held it up across the back of Blossom's shoulders. Flower tugged at her sleeve with an urgency then pointed at the other woman who was now handing coin after coin to the shopkeeper. The Terrapin jerked her arm away, ignoring the obvious sense of her oldest and picked another, red tunic. "Stop being so impatient, Flower, of course we won't leave you out. Your father said to make sure you all have new clothes."

The woman had finally finished paying and laughed with the shopkeeper. "How quaint. Flower, Blossom – what fitting names for country people. Perhaps the boy is called Plough?" They laughed again as she pushed through them to leave. When she was out of sight the Terrapin dropped the tunics in her hands.

"No, the material is too rough for my children's skin. The silk is no good and the stitching, my blind great aunt could stitch better than that. Let's go find a better shop, children." The shopkeeper smirked as they left. Jun Ching turned round to see her dusting off the clothes they had touched, inspecting them for dirt or damage.

But the Terrapin didn't look for more stalls. Her eyes narrowed almost whiteless trained on a spot only she could see in her head that twisted round corners and through crowds leading them straight back home where she could wait for this cloud of shame to dissipate before showing her face again. The girls kept pace with her quick tiny steps – one disappointed, one relieved. But little 'Pin, stumbling and struggling to stay upright at this speed, and oblivious to the invisible string tugging his mother, pushing her past people but more importantly past trays of sweet, sticky buns, of spun sugar sweets, of desiccated fruits, strained his little arm towards each of them and reaching none, slowed down even further to accommodate his wails. She turned without breaking step, sweeping him up into her arms. His face turned a mottled red, his lips parted into a perfect pink ring, displayed an almost complete set of baby teeth. His screaming was not loud amongst the hustle of the market, it found companions in other children somewhere in the crowd crying and with the voices of a hundred women bartering and stall keepers shouting their deals. No one noticed them but the noise in the Terrapin's head was too much. She turned and thrust Little 'Pin at Flower, having forgotten Jun Ching who was shorter and out of sight right behind them, and marched on.

By the time they turned back into their dusty street, it was obvious they weren't stopping for anything. Not even for the small group which clustered a few feet from the doorway of a house scruffier than theirs, several doors down at the bottom of the street. Jun Ching noticed them early, a group on this street were rarely silent. The only sound from the group was a shout every now and then. She heard it once as they were approaching but as she passed them, she heard it again and realised it came from inside the doorway. It was dark, she could see no more than a foot inside, beyond that the sunlight refused to fall. The shout she heard had turned to a dull moan with words that blurred and blended into each other as they squeezed out. A small boy sat outside the door, ignored by the women peering in. He was the same dirty faced boy with no trousers Jun Ching had seen the day she arrived and often hung about the shoulders of an older boy who played the stones game with Flower and Blossom in the street in the evenings. The little one was wearing trousers now, grey-once-blue materials with what looked like fresh stains down the front. He sat like an old man, staring at the ground with his hands in his lap, coughing. Jun Ching was the only one who watched him as they sped past, straining round to keep her eyes on him for as long as she could but he didn't look up.

Inside, the Terrapin flung down her purse, still bulging with the savings she had been so careful to make over the last few months and so excited to spend when they had left only an hour or so before.

The next morning the drawn-out moan they had heard previously jumped suddenly up to a wail, screams between teeth. The Terrapin, unseeing the day before went out to find the cause of the wailing but the children stayed indoors not daring to move. She was back quickly.

"You are not to go outside, especially to play with those dirty urchins down the road I've told you about before." She spoke to the girls and turned to Jun Ching. "And you, keep my son inside. If anything happens to him, I will look to you for answers." Three sets of eyes blinked at her, nodding, as she pulled the front shutters to, shutting half their faces in shadow.

A few weeks later, in the morning, Jun Ching found Little 'Pin lying on his back in the Terrapin's bed where she often took him when her husband was away. He fussed listlessly when she came to pick him up. His skin hot to the touch.

"*Wah*, Little 'Pin. What's the matter with you? So hot. Summer nowhere near here yet, why are you so warm?" She murmured to the top of his head. His thin hair was sweaty and flattened against his skin in small circular patches. He rubbed his face in her shoulder and released a whimper only.

Something stirred in the deep of her stomach. And that something was not right. She dressed him in clean clothes, rubbing his hair with the discarded shirt till the strands stood up waving alone. Downstairs there was no one. The girls were still in their room, she heard them chattering as she passed, and the Terrapin had left early that morning. She sat down, placing him on her lap though he was almost too big for it now, and lifted a spoonful of congee to his lips. He turned away dragging a trail of congee across his face. Was it too hot? She blew on it gently and tasted it. Definitely not. But he wouldn't take it, any of it. Not even the fried dough sticks they dipped in it till they were soft that he usually grasped and sucked until his little chubby fingers were greasy and slippery. This time he pushed it away. This was definitely not right. Even when she woke him early from a deep sleep, he would be smiling by now and eating. Instead, he rubbed and rubbed his head against her, his face red and damp.

"Okay, we will do it your way and try again later." She kissed the top of his head and tied him to her back so she could free her hands for her chores though all the way through them she could feel the gentle push and rub of his head between her shoulder blades. She tried every hour for the rest of the day and still he would take nearly nothing. He was quiet too. Tied to her back for the most part of a day he would kick his legs about by the afternoon, itching to get down and practise his new walking abilities. But nothing today as he channeled all his little energy to head rubbing.

The Terrapin came back in the early evening taking little notice of the sleeping Little 'Pin and Jun Ching didn't bother her. She looked like she had drowned her face in a dark cloud – it would be a fool who would incite the thunder that could come from there at this time.

The following day he was no better. He had sweated through the night again and watched as he was picked up and taken downstairs. When he refused to eat again, Jun Ching had to tell the Terrapin.

She pushed her forehead onto his and held it for a few seconds. Jun Ching recognised the action from her own mother but stripped of the tenderness.

"He's got a fever." She snapped. "I told you to look after him. What have you been doing?"

"Nothing Mistress, the same as every day. Nothing different. He was the same yesterday. Wouldn't eat, just hot."

"What? Yesterday he was like this and you didn't tell me? Evil girl." A sharp slap across her face stung. "You trying to kill him?!"

"No Mistress. No."

"You better not. You hope he get better fast. You get nothing to eat until he better." She swiped at the half bowl of congee Jun Ching had barely touched knocking it over and spilling it across the counter. The bowl rolled on its side. "Don't break that." She hissed as she walked away with Little 'Pin on her hip.

By the evening his temperature had come down. The Terrapin handed him back to Jun Ching with a sneer and a threat to look after him properly this time. He still didn't move much on her hip. He burrowed his head into her neck and stayed there. He wouldn't go down to sleep, so she kept him tied to her back for the evening as she cleaned, craning her head backwards to check how he was. He mostly dozed but it was impossible to tell without looking at him as his little legs hung limp at either side of her.

The sky had closed in with darkness and the rest of the household quiet in their rooms by the time Jun Ching went to lie him in his cot. He fussed a little but went down staring at her. Big, black eyes in the dim light. They blinked at her with something her stomach could read but her mind could not. She patted his chest lightly humming a low sound, not a song, that meant nothing but comfort in her head but, even when he finally closed his eyes, she couldn't leave the room. Eventually, she fell asleep kneeling by his bed.

Early morning light fingered its way under her eyelids. Her knees creaked a complaint. It took a look at the sweaty headed Little 'Pin for her to remember why she was there. She placed a palm on his forehead and it came away wet, the sheet beneath him damp. Something was not right. She picked him up and immediately put him back down again. He felt lighter. That wasn't right, he couldn't. He only gets heavier. She picked him up again and he did really feel lighter. Noticeably lighter. The Terrapin will be able to tell. She'd blame her for sure, but the fear in her chest forced her to the Terrapin's door with Little 'Pin in her arms. She could feel the heat coming off him as she called through the door.

The Terrapin took him with an irritated jerk. "Useless mutt", she spat at Jun Ching as she pushed past her and down the stairs. She watched her try to feed him, but again he took very little. His two sisters looked at each other, he was even less likely to eat with their mother thrusting spoonfuls in his face than with Jun Ching's coaxing. Frustrated, the Terrapin pushed him back into her arms.

"Keep him cool, don't put him down even for a second. I will speak to the healer on my way back from the market today." She left without further instructions.

Breakfast was still underway when the Terrapin burst back into the house. The girls spilt their spoonfuls with a jump whilst Jun Ching's hand jerked, knocking the ceramic spoon into the two new teeth Little 'Pin had been growing. He didn't make a sound. The Terrapin flew to him snatching him into her arms, her own hands now feverishly pushing back the damp strands of hair holding his forehead to hers. He coughed in her face.

"No, no. Can't be. Won't be." She muttered to herself. "Not possible. Not so unlucky."

Rarely was such fervent contact seen in the Terrapin as she rocked him, clasping him to her. Flower felt a small green bud grown in her chest wishing it was her who was sick with the sticky head, being suffocated in her mother's arms. For the rest of the day, the Terrapin didn't let go of him, watching him almost like prey. Little 'Pin burned through the hours. By evening he started to cry. Soft cries that wouldn't be lessened by any shushing or singing from his ma. Jun Ching couldn't keep herself away from the room but each time he saw her he reached his little arms out, his little face, thinner than a few days earlier, squeezing tiny tears out. Even this the Terrapin didn't notice, and Jun Ching tried to stay out of his sight. She tried to understand his cries, but they weren't ones she had heard before. They sounded similar to his hungry cry but a little sharper, and similar to his tired cry but slower. She had not seen him sick before and wondered if this is what a sick or painful cry sounded like.

The Terrapin took him with her to bed that night leaving Jun Ching with an unexpected amount of spare time. She sat on the doorstep, the uncomfortably silent house behind her though the street was quiet too, as though an invisible fog had descended to deaden all sound. She thought back to the little boy with the stains down his shirt a few days ago, coughing like an old man on a step. In her mind he couldn't stop coughing and coughing until blood came out in small bursts and dribbled down his shirts – that's what the stains were. Was that true though, she wondered, was that really what the stains were. She hadn't seen it. Probably just her mind, she always saw things in her head very clearly, sometime clearer than in real life. She knew one thing though. She hadn't seen the old man boy since that day.

That tiny ache that had taken root grew now. It curled around Jun Ching's heart and she dropped her head to her knees. With nothing to do, no chores to perform she was left to feel. And she felt the weight of little 'Pin in her arms. And she felt the touch of his forehead on hers when he leaned in smiling so like the feel of her ma's forehead when she used to do the same. Her gentle presence when Jun Ching was ill, , her hand resting on her head as Jun Ching curled towards her. The memory took her to all the places she didn't even know she wasn't allowing herself to go to since Sum had died. The tears that had stayed away for so long came now, falling free. Her shoulders shook. A lump was in her throat that she could neither swallow nor choke on. Why did it have to be that Sum died? Why are her and Jun Yee left here like this? She wasn't angry with Sum. She just wanted her back. Her softness and tenderness, the feel of her skin when her arms were wrapped around her. It had been so long. Little things that she didn't even realise were there, but they were, flavouring each day just right. This house had no affection. Only Little 'Pin and now he was sick. He was dying. She knew then that she wouldn't be able to carry on living if Little 'Pin didn't. He was her little lifeline. Somehow, they were tied up together, entwined. She just knew she was tired of being sad, of being alone, of being untouched. Her fingertips pulsed at the memory of touch. She spread out her favourite scenes in front of her and they were all from home, the call of the sweet tofu man, the smell of the coal roasted chestnuts, the splash of water as Jun Yee dived in the harbour. The sweetness in that moment was so foreign now, almost imaginary, that she understood that those memories and that time had passed into dreams for good. She thought of Jun Yee then knowing that he would be fine when she was gone. She thought of him telling people that he had had a sister once. She wondered what he would say about her. The thought of Jun Yee had focused her again and dried the tears. She was relieved to turn away from the face of the fire telling her how much she had lost. She would know in the morning how Little 'Pin was and therefore how she would be. She could wait till then.

  One morning, after nearly a week of watching, Jun Ching did something she had never dared and crept her head round the door of the Terrapin's bedroom whilst she was still sleeping. She had been in before to clean but never when she was still in there. It was strangely tidy. It was usually strewn with clothes, logically in a path from the door to the mirror to the drawers to the bed, as the Terrapin came in and dropped her clothes on her way to her brush, her bed clothes and then to sleep itself. After so many nights Jun Ching had expected it to be messy, like a pig pen she had heard Gwai say before, but it wasn't. She must have stayed in the same clothes all week. None of them had noticed. The Terrapin laid in all her street clothes on top of the bed, curled up like the dried shrimps she saw piled up in buckets at the market. So she even sleeps curled up like that when he's not here, Jun Ching thought. It somehow made her feel more sad, seeing her close up like this. Little 'Pin was lying on his stomach facing away from his mother, his back rising softly, his head sweaty again. He opened his eyes, saw her and whimpered. She could see his eyes whereas before his chubby cheeks, pushed against the mattress and upwards, meant he had to lift his head before you could see them properly. He had lost a lot of his cheeks now. He looked like someone had let the air out of him.

    Jun Ching crept into him. Through the cracks in the boards, she had been listening to the Terrapin pacing for several nights now, murmuring the same little refrain about luck, that it couldn't happen. Whatever it was she was worried about happening, it seemed to Jun Ching was happening now as the Terrapin just held him to her and did nothing. She would let her sleep for now.

    Downstairs, the sisters were already up and sitting on the floor with their bowls of congee. Sitting up on Jun Ching's knee, Little 'Pin looked odd. He certainly looked different to a few weeks ago but something had changed since yesterday.

    "He must be getting better." Blossom said. "You look, his buddha belly is coming back."

    And it was. That was it. For days his clothes had been hanging straight down past his belly but today, sitting up, it was pushing out again like before. Just a little but it was just the same. But how? He hadn't eaten in days. She gave it a rub and it felt tight. Not soft as it used to but like a ball, filled tight with air. She lifted his shirt and flowered across his belly were pale pink spots. Jun Ching did the only thing she knew her own ma would do – she licked her thumb and rubbed at the spots. They didn't even fade. She did it again until she could barely see the spots because the skin around them had got so red from the rubbing. But then they reappeared again slowly. She didn't like this. This was wrong, she could feel it in her chest.

She hugged him tight then, tighter than she had ever though he didn't chuckle or drop his head to her as he had before. He was the only one here who cared about her, who defended her with his wailing when she was beaten, feeling every stroke like it was his to own. It was this fat little man who left the Terrapin's side, sticking his little head out to Jun Ching, and gaped silent-mouthed at her until she picked him up and folded him into her heart. But now, something was wrong, she had not seen him sick since she had arrived, but she knew this was not an ordinary illness. The spots, the hard belly, the silent staring. The little old man boy down the street and his stained shirt kept coughing into her thoughts. The Terrapin was sleeping, but even if she was awake what use would she be? For over a week now she's been getting worse herself. At first, she kept him with her, trying to feed him herself, getting frustrated when he ate very little. As she watched him grow silent in her arms she took to talking to her ancestors. She had paid little attention to them before, not like Sum who used to speak to her own father's photograph every day as though he was sitting beside her. But now, she spoke directly to them, standing in front of the wooden plaques asking for their help to make him better. It hadn't worked though, had it?

The last tight hug pressed her lips into a firm line. She needed someone who would come and pick up Little 'Pin and tell them what was wrong and how to mend him. The best person she could think of was Paw Paw. She would know how to make him better, but would it be too late by the time she got here? Jun Ching would have to go herself to get her and then come back with her. Would she even come? Jun Ching had never heard Ah Ho mention the Terrapin before the day that she was sent here. Maybe she wouldn't come and help her. She didn't want to leave little 'Pin either. Maybe she could take little 'Pin to Paw Paw? No, she didn't even dare think of how the Terrapin would react when she found them gone. Jun Ching didn't have the money anyway. She felt her thoughts turning and twisting round like they were stuck at the tip of a bull's horn unable to find a way out.

"How about *our* Paw Paw? We can get her quickly." She must have been whispering her thoughts aloud as Flower's voice sliced through. She was standing, ready to go.

Of course! The Terrapin's mother – Paw Paw's sister. They must be something alike. She could help. Flower was gone, faster than even Blossom had seen her move before.

"Bring him to me." The old woman demanded before she even sat down. Flower ran to take Little 'Pin from Jun Ching and brought him close. She stared with no expression at Jun Ching then turned her attention to the boy. After only a few seconds she spoke again. "Flower, go for the healer. We need him. If this is what I think it is then your little brother will die. And soon. Blossom, where is your mother? Get her."

The two girls gone, Jun Ching was left alone with this new woman. Ah Ho's face flitted in and out of her cheeks and jaw. She wondered who was older? Who had seniority? She guessed Paw Paw must be younger since she was now working in her niece's house. If only she remembered. The Terrapin crept down the stairs, dishevelled, behind Blossom.

Words poured out from the old lady's mouth so fast Jun Ching couldn't catch them if she tried with both hands. The Terrapin almost wound her head into her neck it was bent so low.

Jun Ching never seen her like this, not even with her husband. Her husband!

"What are you doing just lying upstairs while your son dies down here? You only have one, you know that don't you? What will you do if he dies? You didn't have the brain to have more than one and you know your husband, what do you think he will do if his only son dies?" She stepped forward and drilled her finger into the Terrapin's temple. "Find another woman who will give him more sons – that's what! So, go on then. Lie down in your bed and do nothing because when your son dies you won't have that bed to sleep in anymore. And don't think you can come back to our house, it will be a disgrace!"

"Die? He won't die, will he Ma? It's not that serious, he's just a little ill." She stepped sideways, tentatively, away from the finger.

"A little? Look at him." She thrust Little 'Pin towards her as she stepped back again. He lingered there, held out in between them for a moment, little legs not kicking. Jun Ching jumped forward to take him before they dropped him on the ground. "Look at the spots, the belly. Feel the fever. Don't you know what that is?"

"It's the same as what the little boy had down the road. He's dead now." Jun Ching whispered. The Terrapin slapped her hard across the face. She knew before she was slapped she shouldn't have said that. Both women stared at her.

"You stupid girl. It's typhoid. You knew someone close had it and did nothing for so long? You deserve for him to die."

The Terrapin crumpled to the ground with no words to prop her up. Broken, choking coughs bubbled up to her quivering surface but nobody touched her to help her up.

"What can I do?" She cried again and again.

"Pray. Pray to the ancestors and beg for their help." And she did. Incoherent begging on her knees, making all sorts of promises. She looked more like a terrapin than ever crouched on the floor in front of the ancestors' incense bowl. Despite the seriousness of the situation, Jun Ching couldn't help but think how this looked just like one of the comics Jun Yee used to read. It didn't look real and how could it be, when this crying and begging was not making Little 'Pin feel better at all. It was all so stupid.

Flower tumbled back through the door. Words going faster than her legs. "He won't come. The healer won't come. Too many sick this way. He say bring little brother to him."

"I take him myself." The old lady took Little 'Pin into her arms and headed out the door, both Flower and Blossom following on her heels. Over her shoulder she threw to the Terrapin, "You better stay on your knees and keep begging."

Jun Ching watched as long as she dared. The Terrapin stayed exactly as she was told, on her knees, eyes cast up to the ancestors, sometimes sat back on her heels, but mostly silent now, hands clasped together shaking like the women in the temple shaking for fortune sticks. Jun Ching went back to the kitchen but came back to check on her whilst pretending to clean or dust in the room. By the time they brought Little 'Pin back the Terrapin's knees ached from the hard ground, but still she sprang up.

"What did the healer say?"

"As I said, he has big chance of dying. It's typhoid."

The old lady didn't pause, sweeping past her daughter to take him straight upstairs. It was as though her own anguished cry struck the Terrapin back down onto her knees in front of the ancestors, and she started her begging afresh. The Terrapin was running out of promises, getting increasingly desperate when she found one at the back of her throat that Jun Ching hadn't heard before.

"If you protect him through this and make him better, I promise I will never have a full bowl of rice again!"

Jun Ching coughed in surprise. It sounded so out of place, such a silly thing to promise in such a grave time. Surely, she couldn't do it anyway. The Terrapin loved rice, she had at least two bowls every day! She carried on scrubbing the table in wide circular motions when a sharp yank on her plait snapped her head back. The Terrapin's blotched face was inches from her own and looked upside down from here making her eyes even smaller and more unnatural.

"Are you laughing? What are you laughing at? It's worth laughing at my son dying?"

"No Mistress, no."

"Then what?! What you laughing at?" She yanked again, so hard on her plait that Jun Ching's head snapped back again. She lost her balance falling backwards onto the floor. The small of her back jammed into the edge of a little footstool on landing but the Terrapin didn't let go, twisting Jun Ching's head in the opposite direction to her body as she tried to shuffle away. She twisted the plait round her hand for a better grip and yanked again. Now her face had come round upright again, Jun Ching could see the spit jumping from the corners of her mouth like hot oil in a wok. "It was you, wasn't it? You filthy, diseased mongrel. You got him sick. It's your fault. If he dies it will be your fault."

She punctuated each word with a pull on the handful of hair as Jun Ching tried to follow her, holding onto the plait herself now to try to stay the pain. She didn't dare say anything to defend herself. She knew it would be useless whilst the Terrapin raged.

"Enough. Let go." A new voice. A loud one. The grip was gone. Not new to the Terrapin then. She knew exactly what the voice meant. They both turned to see the old lady standing at the stairs. "What are you doing? She is still my older sister's granddaughter. She is not a cat for you to drag by the tail."

Jun Ching scrambled to her feet, her head throbbing, and backed away from the two women staring at each other. She thought how different her own ma was to these people. To all the women they had met since they had been here, even Lien. And as if she had opened her hand in front of her and seen what she knew was there, she understood that Sum had had to leave here and leave them behind. In a way, she was glad she did.

The old lady stayed for a week, maybe longer, it was hard to tell during that time as the days merged into each other. Jun Ching was barely allowed near Little 'Pin. It almost broke her. The only source of affection taken away. But instead, she poured her hugs and silent kisses into the clay pot with the dried flowers and herbs the old lady brought back from the healer and she brewed it like the magic potion she hoped it would be for him. And it was. It was barely noticeable at first, but the red spots faded and as he became less clammy, his head stopped burning. Within a few more weeks, his little Buddha belly retracted until it was soft again though Jun Ching couldn't get near enough to poke it and find out for sure.

The Terrapin kept her last promise as well and at each meal ate only half a bowl of rice though it grew a little every day, so it became a big half, and a little bigger still so more like three quarters but it always stopped short of the rim of the bowl and she certainly wasn't able to have the second bowl she used to do. Jun Ching would catch her sometimes when her first bowl went too quickly, her chopsticks still clicking in the air and her lips worked up into one corner considering that second bowl. Then she'd glance to the ancestors' plaque and set her bowl and chopsticks down with a sigh.

She said nothing more to Jun Ching though, who also stayed out of her way. Whilst the old lady was there Jun Ching felt she was drinking out of a very thin glass, one that could shatter at any moment, cutting her again. She didn't want the old lady to go even though she had barely said a sentence to her directly. But the husband would be returning soon, and the old lady decided to leave before he arrived.

Jun Ching gladly took Little 'Pin back onto her hip when the old lady left. She was resisting tying him onto her back so soon so she could see him even though it only left her one hand to work. She didn't mind in order to see his face, despite the slightly deflated look of his cheeks still. A few weeks later, whilst she was clearing the table after dinner, she felt a prickling sensation across her neck and shoulders. The Terrapin was sat at the table still and seemed to be watching her. Jun Ching tucked her plait inside her collar in a defensive move. As she took the Terrapin's bowl, the woman stood up suddenly, sliding her elbow into the back of Jun Ching's hand. She lost her grip on the bowl that went rolling towards the edge of the table and though Jun Ching tried to catch it again she only grasped uselessly at the air whereas the Terrapin who could have reached it didn't move at all. The bowl smashed on the floor. The Terrapin clipped her on the back of the head hard, her hand only just missing Little 'Pin himself.

"Stupid girl. If you had any wages, I would take the price of a new bowl out of it!"

"I'm sorry Mistress. I will go out and buy you a new one straight away."

"Don't need you. I'll go myself since I have to go out today anyway. If you went you would probably break more things and I will have to pay. Useless." And she left.

That evening, Jun Ching found a new bowl in the kitchen. A big one. Almost twice the size of any of the other bowls they had. She laughed out loud and clapped her hands. She hoped she had made enough rice for this new bowl.

Chapter Fifteen

Short, hard raps on the door called Gwai to it. Mother Tang stood on the threshold. Not a hair out of place, not a hint of sweat on her skin despite the sun gaining strength with every day now inching into summer, her lips pursed into a smile too serene for her face. Once inside she whispered to Gwai. "The time has come." It was too soon, wasn't it, she thought. The boy-groom was young, she thought it would be a couple of years in the preparation at least.

"Good." Ah Ho said from behind them. "Let's get this done with."

"So fast?" Gwai asked no one.

"The young master is growing and his health not improving. They need someone to look after him faster than they thought. This is not a problem, is it?" Mother Tang looked at Ah Ho.

"No, the sooner it is done the better.

"It so easy to do things properly with you, Mrs. Wu. Now, I help you negotiate with the family. We talk wedding gifts for the girl. What are you thinking of wanting?"

Ah Ho looked at Mother Tang and for the first time saw the silver tumbling behind her eyes, the feel of the cold coin clasped in her fingers. The clink, clink, clink in her hands. Her tongue felt suddenly thick in her mouth. Her top lip pulled into a frown and her eyes turned away. There are too many mouths around this table as it is. Too many eyes and chattering neighbours still following her house. Something had to change, had to shift. She needed rid of them, one of them at least. It wasn't about the money, she wasn't selling her. But she was being asked for a price, a price for the girl, the daughter of her daughter. This sticky little woman was asking for a price. She forced her eyes back to her. She hadn't thought about it. What was reasonable for a half-caste girl with no future and no one to argue for her?

"What would you advise Mother Tang?" She could take whatever the woman said and double it. This was a game, one she was good at, and she was going to win.

"*Wah*, it hard to say. This is different to the usual cases I help with." She paused, waiting for Ah Ho to jump in. Silence. She left the longest one she could. "Well, you know the situation is not good. Don't blame me for saying Ah Ho, but the whole village and the next, know what has happened here... What I mean to say is this will affect things..."

"That is not advice Mother Tang. What would you advise?"

"Times are hard for everyone now. The family have connections with cloth-makers, I think several bolts of cloth would be a good arrangement. Something useful, could serve your family for long time, you never need buy cloth again. For at least a few years."

"My family cannot eat cloth. I want coin."

"*Wah*, Mrs. Wu, you think what is happening out there now, there is no money. If I go back and say coin, they will send me back right away! Cloth is good, just like coin, *flowing coin*, when you save on buying it for your family. It the same as making coin."

"Cloth and I have bad luck together. I want no cloth."

"Okay, okay. If not cloth, then grain? Rice? The family have connections there too. Rice enough for six months for your house."

"The girl is young. Unspoiled. They will have a faithful server for many years. I want coin, 20 pieces. And rice."

"The girl is half-caste. This affects things. We are lucky to find people willing to overlook this."

"The boy is feeble-minded. They are buying a servant, not a wife. She will have to do everything for him. People willing to put their daughters into this are not jumping around in the streets like chickens." The women stared at each other.

"Very well, I will go back to them and tell them. But they will not accept this. You risk the deal, Mrs. Wu." She said shaking her head. "Where is the girl? Let me look at her so I can at least sell her strength, or face. I need something for my case."

"She is not here. I sent her to my sister's daughter, to learn the ways of a home, to learn to look after a baby as I understand her husband is to be." Her gaze didn't flicker from Mother Tang's, although something pointed her towards the door. She rose to leave.

"How long has she been there?"

"The big half of the year. Nearly 10 months by the time she comes back."

"At least that is something. They won't need to train her as long. Let's hope that helps our case." She sighed. "I will be back when I have news."

She left Gwai and Ah Ho in silence. Gwai daren't move. Her feet felt as though they were sinking through wet sand, too close to the water. A wave of memory broke over her ankles before she could get away. A picture of Sum drawing a comb dead centre down the back of a three-year-old Jun Ching's little head for a plait on either side. The edges of her feet and toes tingled as the sand trickled away beneath her.

"Go fetch the girl. She should be ready to go as soon as the deal is done. Don't want to give them time to change their minds." Ah Ho turned her face back to stone.

Gwai couldn't believe it was her who had to bring her back again. She walked through the town towards the house she had left Jun Ching in nearly ten months previously. She wanted to spend as little time with her as possible. Didn't want to see her face, didn't want to answer any questions. The girl's brother could have come but no, the old woman had asked her. It was as though she knew. But how could she? Gwai had been there every time the old woman spoke with Mother Tang and never was there even a hint of their understanding. No mention of their own conversation under the peach blossoms. No, the old woman couldn't know. And so what if she did? She was the one who did it. She bartered the price.

The town had changed since she saw it, or she imagined it had. It looked more grubby. Dirty in the corners. The fat rich people were still fat, but the skinny people looked skinnier, gaunt and yellow, like half-plucked chickens. Children lingered in small packs with cheeks sucked in. She stopped at a market stall for a mung bean sweet before turning down the road she needed. Like the rest of the town, the street felt different, but even more so, this was where the pebble dropped, and the change rippled out from here. Bare bottomed children that played in the dust were gone, as were the older ones who had called names and laughed. The women who had sat chattering in bunches in door frames or between houses had thinned out to just a few here and there looking over their shoulders at her now as she went past, unblinking, taking her small smile giving nothing in return. Aside from the women the street was empty. At the other end three or four houses were boarded up. The house she wanted was halfway down, the door was shut tight. She could hear angry shouts from inside. She knocked again and a small girl opened the door. Must be one of the daughters, Gwai thought. She didn't pause for long before walking straight in. The room was unchanged, cleaner it seemed and neater. The toddler boy sat crying to one side looking stretched – taller and thinner than last time she saw him. The girl who opened the door stood behind her. In the middle of the room the Terrapin stood with her back to Gwai. She held Jun Ching by the wrist in the air, her arm pulled unnaturally high dangling the rest of her body. Her toes skimmed and kicked at the floor. In the Terrapin's other hand was a bamboo cane that she brought repeatedly down, punctuating her words. Each thwack on Jun Ching's back wrenched a cry from the stretched boy.

"What? Not one sound out of you. I don't hit you hard enough? Had plenty to say before, though didn't you?"

Jun Ching refused to make a sound. She screwed her eyes shut, bit her lip, head lowered away from the Terrapin. Her shirt was riding up and the cane came down on bare skin. The Terrapin was angry luckily and her aim poor, so the cane didn't catch the same position too many times. She could feel the tingle under her skin of specks of blood rising to the surface just before it breaks through.

"Hit enough yet?" Gwai's voice was sharp, clipping the Terrapin across the back of the head. Jun Ching knew the voice instantly and twisted round with bone-dry eyes not to meet her gaze but to witness the challenge between the two women. The Gwai that stood there was the same but different. She was absolute in her stillness. She looked like you could crack bowls on her, beat her with bamboo till they split, and she would still remain.

"No. Not enough yet. How I teach my servant girl is not your business."

"She's not yours to teach anymore. I've come to take her back." Even her voice seemed to come from somewhere unmoving. The Terrapin gaped at her for a moment, opening and closing her mouth, tasting the air. "And she is not a servant girl, she is still family." Jun Ching heard 'family' and little else.

"You cannot. I say no."

"It is not your say. Let her go."

Jun Ching could not look away. She had not seen Gwai or anyone else like this before. She almost glowed with an unspoken strength. Her eyes never left Terrapin, with a look that contained as much fury but cold, much colder than how Terrapin's husband looked at her. Even the girls could see the challenge in it that promised to thrust Terrapin to the ground herself if she defied her. But Gwai - of all the people Jun Ching would not expect to be standing up for her. She saw the mirrored images of the women and saw the water's blurring of the Terrapin, an unstable reflection of Gwai's hard edges, a cheap copy.

Jun Ching felt the Terrapin come to the same tumbling realisation. She hesitated then tightened her grip on her wrist and brought the cane down with all her strength one more time, dropping her wrist so the cane slanted upwards cutting across several long thin red stripes across her back. Where they crossed over several spots of blood leapt forward immediately just straining at the skin as they were for release. Jun Ching cried out this time, from surprise not expecting this last blow. The Terrapin smiled and threw her wrist away from her pushing Jun Ching off balance and onto her knees.

"Get up. Get your things."

Jun Ching scrambled, staring up at Gwai from her feet, up to her own. For once Jun Ching felt what it was like to be on the right side of Gwai's anger, felt the shelter of this unexpected protector albeit briefly. She expected her to be taller, wider in the shoulders, when she stood up next to her, but she wasn't. She was even a little smaller than she remembered since only one of them had been growing in the time apart. She stood between the two short women, neither flinching for several moments, the silence respected even by Little 'Pin, until the unyielding stiffness of Gwai imperceptibly pushed the Terrapin back and down without her moving at all. The Terrapin would have felt it, Gwai would have expected it but Jun Ching was the only one who truly saw it. Only then did she run up the stairs to pack.

Gwai had imagined this trip going differently on her way here. She had thought she and the Terrapin would sit together with a cup of tea, not chatting necessarily but talking, agreeing what a nuisance Jun Ching was, how useless. She hadn't expected this. Nor this feeling of what? Of sympathy? Not exactly. Perhaps annoyance, like someone was trespassing on what was hers to hate. It was easy to turn upon the Terrapin, enjoyable even, no one to witness what she said, she didn't have to check herself and as she stood staring at her still, chest-fuls of restrained temper heaved at the seams to burst onto the woman. But she didn't let it. The Terrapin was already shrinking, a few steps taken back and almost half the size. Gwai recognised in the Terrapin one with no foundations, the one who had plenty of noise but no filling. She was exactly the type of person that drew contempt from Gwai, one who would cower to her husband, take whatever she was given and do nothing. The inertia of one who had never tried to get anything for themselves unlike Gwai who had tried everything and failed. But at least she had tried. Gwai was the typhoon that was desperate for the chance to lay waste to all in front of it whilst Terrapin's blustered and dwindled like swirling leaves and dust on the floor, lacking the purpose and conviction that Gwai had always clutched within her to justify her every action. Gwai felt disappointed in her.

The boy was whimpering now and the girl who opened the door had gone to sit behind him wrapping her legs round the outside of his and her arms around his belly. Jun Ching appeared again with the same red cloth bundle she carried when Gwai left her here at the beginning and a large blue blanket rolled up and tied with string twice around.

"What's that? Ma! That's pretty! It must be ours, she must have stolen it!" Gwai hadn't noticed the other girl until she shouted out and darted across the room grabbing at the blanket. A tug started between the two girls each with one end of the blanket roll.

"I didn't steal it! My brother gave it to me! Let go!" Jun Ching found her voice and used it. The two women said nothing, watching.

"Your brother? Filthy little peasant, where would he get it from?"

Without thinking, Jun Ching let go with one hand and punched her in the mouth. The girl fell to the floor stunned. The Terrapin went to grab Jun Ching again but one step forward from Gwai was all that was needed to stop her.

"Th- thank you," Jun Ching stuttered, surprised at her own reflex then bowed to the Terrapin, "For teaching me so much for the last months, Mistress, and thank you for feeding me and giving me somewhere to sleep."

Then she turned to Little 'Pin. She wanted to pick him up once more. His fingers grasped for her, opening and closing in the air outstretched. But Gwai was waiting, watching and she could only squeeze them gently and go. "See you again, Little 'Pin. I'll think of you every day."

She heard him howl as the door closed behind her.

Gwai said nothing to her all the way back, not as they waited for the cart, not for hours bumping over the dried, rutted soil with their legs dangling off the end. Jun Ching gave up saying sorry each time she jostled into her over a particularly violent hump. She held on instead to the side of the cart with such grip that her fingers stiffened around the wood. Gwai felt ants crawling under her skin, prickling. She flung her arm out, shaking it but the ants carried on. Completely without reason, she felt like she wanted to be the one who had punched the girl. Or perhaps, she should have punched the Terrapin when she first came in and saw her dangling her girl in front of her like the butcher did with a pig flank on market day. No, not her girl. This was Sum's girl, never her own. She wondered what it would have felt like to punch the other girl. There were so many people Gwai had wanted to hit over the years, particularly when she was younger. Her own sister who was content with everything… her mother who dreamt of nothing… Ah Ho… Sum… perhaps most of all, Choi. But she hadn't. Her arm pulsed, she shook it again. She had hit the children plenty of times, her nieces and nephews. That Penny always gave her plenty of reason with how slow she was at everything. Didn't feel the same though. It was a different fire that flared when she saw Jun Ching fighting for herself. She had wanted to join her, step in and fight. Her hand twitched in her lap. Something had expanded in her chest when Jun Ching had punched that girl, something that made her happy, something that made her stand a little straighter and want to tower above the crawling Terrapin. What was that? That wasn't a feeling for her to have. Not her, who was even now, playing one of the biggest roles in this girl's 'marriage' to a feeble-minded boy who will never look after himself.

Perhaps not though. Perhaps not the biggest role. Surely Ah Ho had the biggest role, she was the one bartering for bags of rice or bolts of cloth or whatever it was she had agreed on. It was her granddaughter, her blood that flowed in them both, not Gwai's, hers was different blood. Or even Mother Tang, surely a matchmaker had some responsibility towards the people they matched, especially when they are so young, she is the only one who had met both families, she was the only one with all the information. She was the one who was selling this little piglet down the river. No, Gwai only introduced the two of them. It wasn't even her idea. Mother Tang would have found another way to Ah Ho even if she wasn't the one. And if she was to think about it, the biggest responsibility was with Sum. Stupid girl to leave her two brats to fend for themselves. To walk off into the water like that when everyone knew she couldn't swim. Yes, she had done it to herself even if no one dared to say it. Gwai knew it. Maybe she was the one who knew Sum best after all. She always thought she was a bit feeble minded herself. Just payback then that her own daughter will be stuck with a feeble-minded one for the rest of her days. Somewhere inside a chuckle tried to surface. It died in her throat. She coughed and spat it out.

The sky was murky by the time their village came into view. Jun Ching had been watching the sea get closer in a shimmering line for the last half an hour until now it finally had some depth. She held up her fingers to the horizon, two fingers deep it was. She sucked in the salty air, deep until it felt like it was stretching the skin on the soles of her feet. That's what was missing from the air in town. That's why she couldn't bite it and chew it. That's why it tasted so foreign.

Shuffling back round to dangle her legs over the back of the cart again, her bottom numb against the wooden slats, the lines of the boards probably permanently dug into the cheeks. It hurt a tiny bit, but she quite enjoyed it. Relief and pain at the same time, like the sweet and spicy chicken Brother used to like so much from the corner stall back home. If only she could surprise him with some now, just suddenly appear with one of his favourites, that would make him happy, really happy.

"Gwai Kam Mo? Does Brother know I am coming home?" Surprised that neither of them had thought of this for so long, Gwai had to admit the truth.

"I don't know. I only found out this morning when Lai Lai sent me. I don't know if she told your brother before he went to work."

They fell back to silence as the houses started to gather closer together. They drew up parallel to the sea front now, Jun Ching turning to watch the water slip by, sparkling shards of broken glass on the crests of waves, scattered further out towards the horizon. Somewhere out there was what Ma was looking for when she walked in, hidden amongst the broken glass. Did she ever find it? Or has she found it now? Thoughts of her ma had rarely slipped across her mind in the last few months, but the sea reminded her. She felt an odd suffocating sensation on her throat and pushed it away. She had simply had too much to do looking after Little 'Pin and everything else in the house there to think about Ma. It wasn't that she hadn't wanted to. She could bring up Ma's face immediately in her mind if she wanted to… couldn't she? The odd suffocating grip on her throat tightened. She couldn't. She couldn't bring up Ma's face. She saw her hair, her lips and nose, her chin and neck but where were her eyes? She couldn't make her eyes appear or her lips smile. Jun Yee. Jun Yee would know, would make it happen. His face appeared in front of her, superimposed on her mother's but the eyes still weren't right, and the image scared her as it too started to fade further away into the sea.

"I want to see Brother." She said it louder than she thought.

"We're going now already."

"No. I want to see Brother now." Without thinking about it she pushed herself off the back of the cart with both hands. The blanket fell from her lap into the road, she scooped it up before she turned round to see Gwai unmoved on the cart, drawing away from her. She looked neither angry nor surprised. She moved as if to say something but looked away instead. She knew her own way home. She had brought her back this far and it had been hard enough to sit for hours next to her in silence. Several times she had felt the urge to ask about her time with the Terrapin. What for though? To find out if she was ready for her husband? She didn't even know about her husband. What did it matter whether she was ready or not. It wouldn't change anything. It was nothing to her anyway. Soon they would all be rid of her, Gwai knew they would all be grateful once she was gone but no one dared say anything. Then there would just be the boy, harder to get rid of him but once he was gone too everything could go back to how it was. Before Sum came back and disgraced them all. Before she came back and wasted everything, all the years of living out there, of stealing other people's dreams, of years spent hating her. Yes, she'd brought the girl this far, she could make her own way home, like a stray dog with that stray brother of hers.

Jun Ching patted the dust from the blanket roll. Luckily here by the sea the road wasn't as dusty as the town she'd just left and just a few vigorous throws and catches were enough. She looked once more at the disappearing cart then turned heading off at a sprint down a side street leading straight into town and to the bakery.

Dark grey metal trays lined the bakery window filled with buns of every sort. The majority of the buns had already been sold by this time of the afternoon but those left behind still bulged at each other's sides, stuck to each other, as they would have when jostling for room to grow in the oven this morning. A low wall of noise from inside stood here punctuated by a sudden shout of 'I don't believe it – *mm sun!*'. She peered round the windows. It was a long narrow room, folding brown tables lined each wall all the way down. Every table was full with varying degrees of outstretched limbs. The bright red of a tall shrine and incense stand stood out from the grey-blue walls where it was wedged, at the very back of the room with a hot tea urn, an open doorway in between and a beaded curtain to either keep flies in or out, it wasn't immediately clear. Jun Ching took a few steps inside, clinging to the threshold, the noise grew more distinct, fading into several different conversations, peaking at punchlines. No one noticed her. Through the beaded curtain came a pair of hands with two plates, a bun on each, and a glass of hot tea, followed by a full, round-bellied, white vest just below it and finally the man who owned it all. Unluckily for him, the table he was trying to get to was right at the front of the shop, so he forced his way down the middle of the tables, his tummy grazing shoulders and bumping off people's backs no matter which way he turned. He brushed hard past one man jerking his hand splashing tea down his chin.

"*Wah... Bau Gor*, no need for extra oil *la*... Oil's for the *bau*, not my back!"

"You should be so lucky!" He deposited the spring onion bun in front of the man then grabbed his belly and jiggled it up and down, "This is pure Mak family blend, very rare and not for just anyone!"

The room cackled like a crash of mahjong tiles falling on top of each other at the end of a game. He smacked his belly again as he turned round before rubbing it with downcast eyes when he thought no one could see. A smile sprang back to his lips when he saw Jun Ching almost hiding behind her blue blanket by the door. He needed no guesses for who this was. The light brown hair matched her brother's, as did the high nose but the high cheekbones, standing more prominently with the lack of the usual children's chubby cheeks, were all her own. Well, he thought to himself, her own and her mother's. He remembered Sum's cheekbones well. A rather small sigh. Little muscles stood out too prominently on her bony arms and her elbows pointed at awkwardly sharp corners. Her body was skinny enough to be completely obscured by the roll of blanket. Right at the bottom her toes wriggled nervously, sticking out of the front of her slippers. The rest of her remained completely still.

"I bet I know who you are little lady. *Lei... lei...*" he ushered her to a little table and stool by the till, "You sit here and I bet I can bring you something you'd like!" And he forced his way back down the room shouting "Move, move, oil tub coming...Big tub of hot Mak oil coming... move if you don't want some..."

A moment later, Jun Yee came rushing out through the beads, head faster than his body looking like he was about to topple over at every step. Weaving easily and with familiarity through the tables he was with her in seconds. Jumping off her stool they hugged each other hard, squishing the blanket between them.

"*Aiyah*. It's not like you've never seen each other before. Sit down *la*." Bau Suk was right behind them, hands full again whilst hooking one foot round another stool and kicking it towards them.

"*Chor la!* Sit!"

"But Bau Suk, I haven't finished working."

"Yes, you have. In fact, you did overtime today. Don't say I don't pay you overtime." He set down two plates filled with little buns in front of them – roast pork buns, egg buns, sugar buns and of course, a sweet crispy bun – all flanked by two tall glasses of creamy soya milk, drops of condensation oozing at the sides. Jun Ching stroked the top of a couple, the heat from the oven kissed her fingertips and ran up her arms. From across the room Bau Suk watched them, chatting like a band of chickens couldn't peck them apart. No one else noticed them in the corner there, both swinging their legs under the table, in time, back and forth, never colliding, slowing and speeding, mirroring the flow of their words. He wished not for the first time then there was some way he could take them both away. Scoop them up over his shoulders and carry them off somewhere to start a new life. But he couldn't. Everything he had was tied up in this shop, the shop his own father had left him, the one he was to take over and pass down, that was the way of his family and he could not dishonour that. He had given them everything he could, and he hoped that was enough. He turned away as the buns cooled between them.

More buns came, the plates were magically refilling themselves and each time with different flavours, always two of each and they picked through them. Jun Yee telling her exactly what was in each one, how they were made or testing her, making her guess what the flavours were. She clasped the glass of milk in both hands in front of her face, shifting it this way and that, peering over the top and round the sides, pulling the same faces she used to in their little room above the market in Hong Kong when Ma came back with little surprises. When the variety of buns ran out, they started appearing from the beginning again until they cried out with bursting bellies to Bau Suk to stop and only then did they see the sky was quite dark outside and the bakery empty but for a few stragglers right at the back.

"Thanks for eating up those leftovers for me then." Bau Suk said as they stood up to leave. "I didn't just want to throw them out to the birds. What a waste. But then, you're not much more than a little bird yourself, are you?" He poked Jun Ching softly in the ribs. "You can come and eat the leftovers anytime. Any time of day, you hear?"

"They weren't leftovers!" Jun Ching shouted and threw her arms around his fat stomach as far as they could go. "*Dor jair* Bau Suk! Thank you! And thank you for looking after my big brother too." The extra squeeze she gave him almost squeezed out a tear.

They walked the long way home that night, by the waterfront, passing Lien's little shop and jumping up at the windows making her come running out to squash Jun Ching's thin face in her hands. They couldn't get away without taking another bottle of soy milk each despite telling her that her brother had filled them up to the chest already with *baus*. They opened one, saving the other for later. Soon they saw the old lady waiting for her husband to come in from the sea and sat with her for a little while, giving her their other bottle. No need for words, her face expectant that perhaps, just maybe, after all these years, today will be the day he comes striding up the beach to her, now an old woman. For no reason at all in Jun Ching's head, Sum was down there, hair wafting suspended slowly in water, holding his hand, holding him back from walking out of the water to his love. He was young even, younger than Sum, and he wouldn't go – he was waiting too, waiting for her to come to him.

By the time they reached home, dinner was finished and cleared, and the uncles sat in the front yard smoking. They looked up at them as they came up the steps, Seven Uncle was the only one who spoke.

"You're late. Be careful." He leaned back against the wall, taking a deep drag from his cigarette. The other two smirked.

Inside it smelt of rice and steamed pork mince – a special occasion dinner for them – so that's what they had done wrong already. From beyond the kitchen came the sounds of water and bowls. Jun Ching itched to run straight through to Penny, the only one it could be washing up for everyone and see her round face light up for her. But before that was Paw Paw, sat in her wooden throne like a Buddha – impassive and impassable. Jun Yee pushed his sister towards her.

She seemed oddly alien to her now. Not the same old woman she went fishing and watching dragonflies with. She could see now, the trace of her in the Terrapin's face where before she saw her own mother's face there in the shadows. Instinctively she moved close enough to be just out of arm's reach.

"Paw Paw, I have returned." She bowed slightly as the old woman examined her.

"Well, they haven't given one grain of rice more than they needed to. Did you learn anything?"

"Yes, Paw Paw. I learnt lots of things. I can cook now – breakfast, lunch and dinner - all the meals. I can clean too. And I am strong. I can carry water. I can look after a baby too."

"Don't boast. A girl must always know her place. So, you can help Penny in the kitchen more now. There are leftovers for you two." She turned away, dismissing them both.

That night, they had the sweetest sleep they remembered, kicking up the sky blue blanket big enough for both of them before falling asleep on top of it since it was too hot for under it. Even this felt like home to Jun Ching and she smiled.

Chapter Sixteen

She flung her slipper off as hard as she could. It landed upside down, several feet in front, on the pebbles below. Closing one eye she kicked off the other and just missed the other by inches. She jumped off the low stone wall and wriggled them back on. From the corner of her eye she saw them, heads bent towards each other, whispering, nudging shoulders. Sum jumped back up on the wall and aimed her foot again. She was a talisman against gossip, that was all. She flicked both feet as hard as she could. Both slippers went flying up but still not far.

"I'm going." She said.

"Oh don't." Gwai barely looked up.

"I've got to go home and help with the dinner." They both looked at her now and she turned to Choi, her brother. "Are you coming?"

"Come *la*, Big Sister, stay just a little while longer."

"Ma will shout. I don't want to be the one receiving that. It's up to you what you do. Bye Gwai." As she walked away, she heard them scramble goodbyes to each other before hurried steps caught up with her.

"Wah, that Gwai really is, well, so, *aiy*, I don't even know how to say it!"

"If you don't know then don't say anything."

"She's just different from most other girls around here. She wants to go away from this village and see other places. Maybe Hong Kong you know?"

"Yes, I know *la*. Hong Kong this, Hong Kong that. Hong Kong is all I've heard about for years now."

"Well, soon you will hear all about Hong Kong from me too. I'm going to go myself and take Gwai with me!"

"Well good then, then I don't have to listen to either of you talk about it anymore. The sooner you two go the better!" They walked quietly for a few minutes, Choi meandering along the streets of Hong Kong in his head, hand in hand with Gwai, buying her spun sugar sweets. "Ah Choi? You know you can't just both go off together like that, right? People will talk."

"And so? Let people talk then. I couldn't care about them."

"You might not care, Choi, but Ma and Ba would. And Gwai's ma and ba."

"We'll find a way, Big Sister. We're getting out of this place and no one's going to get in our way."

"You sound just like Gwai."

"I sound like her? She sounds just like me more like!" He threw her a wink and raced up the steps.

They ran together, laughing through the courtyard tumbling into the sitting room. Their father was home already, early, sitting next to Ma on the wooden bench.

"How old are you two running around in the street like that?" Ma snapped.

"Sorry Ma." In unison.

"Choi, your father is home early to speak to you. Sum, go and help with the dinner."

As Sum passed her father, he caught her gaze and twinkled a smile at her quickly before anyone else saw. In the kitchen, her younger brothers and sisters were elbowing each other around the curtain in the doorway, peeking through gaps though as careful not to touch it as they would a hot griddle. She pushed them aside though a couple of stubborn ones stayed as well as the youngest, the ninth, just a baby and strapped to the back of an older sister with no choice but to watch.

Even on the other side of the kitchen, Sum could hear her parents' voices. It was about Choi and Gwai. There wasn't much rice left in the bucket, she took half and a ladle of water to wash it. Slowly swirling the rice round, listening as the clouds seeped out of the rice colouring the water. *You must not keep going about together like you are, stuck together at the head. People are talking.* She poured out the water into a different bowl. A new ladle of water. *It's inappropriate. It doesn't matter that Sum is with you, everyone with eyes can see what is going on. It's not right. Especially not for Gwai, she's a young unmarried girl.* The water had turned cloudy again. One more round. *That's the end of it. I don't want to hear more. It must stop. You are not still young children playing hide and seek in the streets. You're both old enough to behave in the proper way now.*

Choi walked through the kitchen like a bullied cat, sulking with his bruised ego as she poured the last of the water into the bowl. He paced outside the back door until his shoulders unhunched and his back stretched straight again.

A week later, Sum paused and waited outside Gwai's house. They were shouting inside. She heard it as she got closer and already decided she wasn't going in. It was Gwai of course.

She shouted words that punched through the air smashing her mother's shrill complaints.

"I don't care what you think."

"It's not what I think. It's what he is. He's lazy. He doesn't work."

"He's not! There is just nothing for him to do here."

"*Ha?!* He's too good to help his own father, is he? Look at him Gwai, look how a man treats his parents and you see how he will treat his wife. With him you will have no good life."

"What do you know of a good life, old woman?" Sum winced. "You rot here in this stinky little backwater your whole life and you think you know a good life? You think you know anything?"

"You dare speak to me like this?" Her voice juddered. She must be thumping her chest with her hand again. She did that a lot.

"Everything you have is from your father and I. Even your life was given by me to you!"

"If I could give it back to you I would! It's no life living here! I'm going to marry him and we're leaving this place." Gwai slammed out the door, striding off leaving her mother yapping her name after her to come back.

Weeks later, they were done. Sum sat watching as Choi hung a pair of her trousers over their front door frame. When he went out later to collect his bride, he would have to walk under them. If he didn't, he would be climbing over his older sister to marry. It was disrespectful and out of the proper order as the second of the children to marry first and they didn't want the gods to overlook Sum's need to marry in the future. Ma sat to the side, staring but not watching. She hadn't touched the food preparation that morning, just as she hadn't said a word when the boys brought in planks of wood and sectioned off an extra little room from the back courtyard for a new bedroom. It showed as well. Both jobs seemed to be done by a line of drunken ants bumping into each other. But still Ma didn't move. She wouldn't have moved at all from her very first objection if it wasn't for their father. He was the one who Choi wore down, who Gwai flattered, who eventually gave in. And Ma was a traditionalist still and did what her husband wanted. Though she didn't have to be happy about it.

The hour of good fortune had been read for the early afternoon and Choi in a new shirt, left his home to bring back his new wife. Children ran around in front and behind him on his way there shouting and laughing, pulling his spirits up higher, in their heads, their chances of a few coins at the end even higher still.

Gwai's house was quiet. It was one of her younger sisters who opened the door when he knocked. No games, no bartering for his wife, no laughing on the threshold. He saw Gwai immediately, sitting on the edge of a chair alone, hands folded in her lap on a new red dress, eyes fixed directly ahead. Her parents weren't to be seen, leaving her sister to shut the door softly behind her. Choi didn't have anyone with him himself to see this wedding, soundless like it was underwater. On a table to the side of her was a pot and four small cups with no handles. She filled two then instructed him to do the same and arranged them in two rows and left. Side by side they walked back together, not touching, not speaking. Halfway back, he snatched her hand and she let him.

As they came up the steps to her new home, Gwai was grateful to see someone had at least hung a few red ribbons around the doorway and windows. On each side of the door were stuck two long red strips of paper with blessings written for their new life. At least this looked more like a wedding, she thought, they may have made a fuss at first, but they've made some show. They hadn't even done the tea ceremony with her parents. She thought about the four little cups of tea sitting on the table and wondered if they were cold yet. Did it mean they weren't really married if her parents refused to drink them? It didn't matter, she thought, her mother would cave and drink them, even if she had to when her father wasn't looking. Sum opened the door to them here with a smile and inside were sounds of children shouting. The younger ones toddled into view, giggled and toddled out again.

    The rest blurred in all their memories. Everyone but Gwai had more food in their bellies than they could remember for a long time whilst Gwai assumed they hadn't bothered to get more food than usual as a sign of displeasure. That made sure that dinner the next day was a shock to her. She had always known they didn't have much, but she hadn't expected to have to go to bed with only the small half of her stomach full every night. Still, it was short term only, she told the big half of her stomach, before they knew it, they would be out of there. She counted her coins when nobody was watching from a secret pocket in her shirt. Counting for the boat fare.

    Months later, when she counted again and the boat fare was there in her hand, twice, she waited for Choi in their tiny bedroom bolted onto the back of the house. She looked around her, the wooden boarded walls shoved up against corrugated metal sheet on the outside. It was raining and she listened to the drumming of the drops, with her eyes closed it was the same sound as warming oil softly popping up from the bottom of a wok. They had already lived through the heat of one summer when the sun was so hot it even made her black hair boiling hot to touch but being in this room was unbearable. The metal sheets amplified the heat. She felt trapped but not for much longer she kept telling herself. She was jangling the coins in her cupped hands when Choi walked in.

"Husband look! Look, we have saved enough money! We can go now!" Choi looked at the coins and back at her.

"Later. We go later."

"What? Why?" The coins stopped moving.

"I said later, so later!"

"Not later! You tell me why."

There was something in his manner she didn't like. The same something that she had had to grind with her heel to get him to understand marriage was the only way. She hadn't thought it would reappear, she thought she had ground it away entirely. He emptied his pockets and still said nothing.

"It's not your family again, is it? What have they got to say this time? Your mother? Or your father? It must be your mother, always meddling."

"Don't you speak about my mother like that. You should know your elders." He was quiet, still.

"So, what then? What did your precious mother say this time?"

"Just later, okay?" He paused, knowing he wouldn't be allowed to leave it at that. "I'm going to help in the shop. Learn the trade and then take over from father. The boss will give me his job when I'm ready and then we can save some real money to go with. It will be better that way."

"What? No. No, that means we will never go!" She threw the coins on the floor scattering them violently. "I will not rot here in this fishing hole. If that's what I wanted, I could have done that with someone richer than you!" He was hurt. His face looked like a scar. The scar blinked.

"Really? I didn't know there was a queue of men waiting to take you on." Pause. "I didn't know there was anyone else as stupid as me to have believed you could love."

"There wasn't." She lifted her chin. "And I never said anything about love."

They let the last words hang there, a curtain between them. Choi changed his clothes as she crouched on her haunches picking up the coins. He was leaving the room when she spoke again.

"You promised me we'd leave this place. That's why I married you. You have to deliver on that promise." The rain beat harder above them, the oil was boiling.

The following day, Gwai sat in the backyard scrubbing clothes on a rough wooden washboard. She had thought married life would be just like life before, but without her mother nagging. She thought she would spend her days chatting with Sum as before and the evenings with Choi until the time came to bounce right off away from here. But from the very first day after the wedding, her new Lai Lai gave her a list of things she was to do each day. Washing clothes like now was just one of them. Her fingers were wrinkly. A house of eight children, and then parents and herself made for a lot of washing. And, since none of them had many clothes, they had to be washed frequently to keep everyone dressed. She thought how she used to complain at home and slip out of the house coming back only when she knew her mother would have lost patience and done the washing herself. She scraped her knuckles across the raised rungs of wood on the board and winced in pain. Her temper flashed in her chest with the pain, the annoyance of doing such petty, boring chores. She was meant to leave all this. She was meant for exciting things. She threw the shirt she was clutching into the bucket drenching herself. Even the water is against me, she thought. Just bear it a while longer. She just had to outlast Choi. She hadn't spoken to him or let him touch her once since they spoke the other night. He was feeling the strain, she knew it. She could tell by the way he slept scrunched to the side at night like he was having to keep himself away from her. His hands had wandered over to her the first night and he pressed himself into her back, but she had slapped him back hard. The next night only his hands wandered searching for her breasts to cup before being slapped again until over the following nights they gave up completely. He wouldn't be able to stand it much longer and he would make a stand for them. Just as well, she was the first daughter-in-law here and that meant servant. That meant doing all the things Lai Lai didn't want to anymore. That meant looking after the baby whose peeking around legs and loud giggles which were amusing at first turned out to be just the first in a string of ways to demand attention, quickly escalating to shouting and hair pulling if Gwai or whoever else she was targeting did not respond immediately. Despite being the youngest in ninth place in the family, she was noisier than her position or her size should have afforded her.

 Gwai woke during the night, sitting up she felt the empty bed beside her, cold. It had been empty for a while. Not unusual, since she stopped speaking to him or letting him touch her, Choi had taken to sleeping outside in the heat – their time holed up together in newly-wed privacy had been shorter than most. But she rarely woke during the night, she only ever noticed he was gone in the morning. Something must have woken her. The room had not cooled yet and the dark she could see through the window was thick so it couldn't have been long since she fell asleep. She didn't even remember him getting into bed. A flicker of annoyance danced in her chest, he even had to disturb her sleep, he can't even do this right. She sat, eyes adjusting to the dark, considering going outside and shouting at him. But that would mean breaking her silence and he'd think she wanted him inside with her. Not worth it. Perhaps it was the toddler crying, pity she still slept with her parents or she would go and stop that herself, a good slap should do it, she wasn't slapped enough that was the problem, she thought. She laid back down and turned over, stretching one leg out into the space.

Just as she drifted again into the half sleep, she heard a strained, quiet whisper. Her eyes sprung open. Her calves twitched. Something interesting must be happening, to who though? There was more than one voice whispering, seeping in from outside. She lifted the blanket gingerly, bare feet skimming the floor creeping to the window, crouching below the sill.

The dark was thick, but the moon dusted the outlines of the two figures. She squinted and was surprised at how easily she could make out the shoulders of her husband. Choi stood facing his father's back and from here Gwai could look over both of their shoulders into the black of the trees beyond. They said nothing for some time, and she was ready to turn back to bed when it was broken.

"It will be better for all of us, Father. Once we are there, we can earn money to send back to you and Ma for the others. We can help properly then and... We all know it's not working now... No one is happy..."

"So, this is your final decision? You will leave your family, your responsibility?"

"Not leave, Father, I fulfil my responsibility from there."

"Despite knowing my wishes."

"It is for the best. You will see."

Another silence before the low scraping gravel of his father's voice again. "I see nothing. I see no son of mine here."

She looked back to Choi for his answer. Surely, he couldn't leave it at that. It was not fair. There were so many things he could come back with. He can't just say things like that. What was the point of being the son in a family so short-sighted anyway that they couldn't see the opportunity? She stared her words into the back of

Choi's head but none of them went through or, if they did, he brushed them aside before they reached his own mouth.

Choi left then without another word leaving his father standing alone in the dark. As soon as he heard the door close behind him, the old man turned to look at it as though there may be some mark, some instruction as to how to fix this. He lowered himself on the wooden bench by the table next to him and although he was in profile now to Gwai she couldn't make out his expression in the dark so she filled it in with what she thought it should be, a mixture of pain and regret. A murmur in her chest told her to turn away, she was intruding here. His back curved forwards, forcing his head out and down. He seemed a lot older than he was. His trousers hung from his bent legs and she noticed for the first time how thin his bare ankles were. Even his knees looked sharp through the material. He looked limp, like someone had taken all the strings of a puppet and all the wooden limbs now tumbled helplessly over each other. *Don't feel sorry for him,* she said in her head, *that's where the danger is, you'll never get out of here then.* A shiver shrugged her shoulders then.

He turned and looked directly into her window. Her breath caught in her throat. She couldn't see his eyes, could he see her? Was there enough light to? She dare not move in case it revealed her. He raised his hand to his chest and looked away. She exhaled and took a step back. Too close, she thought, time to get back into bed, the show was over anyway. She toyed with going out into the house to look for Choi, he deserved some praise for standing up for them, but she hadn't even moved to the door yet before she changed her mind again. Best not to reward until she saw something definite. Don't give in too soon. She nodded slightly to herself. Sitting back down on the side of the bed she smiled - it had been a satisfactory evening, her plan was working and she was that bit closer to leaving.

She glanced back up through the window briefly. The old man was still sitting in the same position, not facing her now but still with his hand held up to his chest. It didn't look right. He should have moved by now. There was a strange feeling in her stomach, and it was trying to climb up through her throat. She swallowed and she stood up, closer to the window. He looked rigid now, heels lifted off the ground, knees higher. She still couldn't see his front properly, but she was sure his hand would not be clenched into a fist and elbows locked in. What was happening? Her closing throat told her it was something and something bad. She fought the urge to go out there. Why should she, that would really be intruding then. He was fine, she repeated, lips moving. As she watched, his body seemed to release, relax. He leant forward and his hand dropped to his lap. She exhaled too. He leant further forward till he tipped and tumbled like that stringless puppet to the ground. She jumped back into the bed and pulled the blanket over her head screwing her eyes shut. It had nothing to do with her, whatever it was. She hadn't seen anything, that's exactly what she would say.

The clatter of the bench hitting the ground as it slid out from under him must have called Choi back from wherever he had gone. The next thing she heard was his voice repeating 'Father' again and again, then shouting for Sum, for his mother, but not for her. Footsteps beat down the stairs and she had cover now, she could get up without suspicion. Back at the window she silently watched her husband clutching his father in his arms, Sum came stumbling through the back door stopping dead at the sight. Choi staring helplessly at her and finally their ma pushing Sum out of the way, flying to her husband almost violently, like a moth covering him with huge wings.

It was too late of course. Choi was sent for the healer but by the time he arrived it was too late. It had been a heart attack.

His father before him had died of one and the doctor said the years of hard labour before would have weakened his heart already. It was young but not unheard of for a man in his 40s. A week later he was buried. Gwai clutched the secret of having witnessed it all, the last moments, to herself. There were no questions of if he would have survived if they had reacted quicker. They all knew that it was unlikely and even if he had, he may well have been paralysed and that would have been even worse, they couldn't afford it, though nobody mentioned that either. So Gwai was spared torturing herself with the responsibility of his death. She didn't need to hide her story but something still poked shame at her about it. That was Choi's fault too, she thought. He beat himself each day with the thought that it was his words, his defiance, that had blocked his father's heart that night and so Gwai was guilty by association.

Days after the burial, in the middle of the night when everyone had hidden in their rooms, Choi moved silently around the house alone. He placed Gwai's wooden washboard in front of the newly framed photograph of his father, rolled up his trousers and knelt down. Ah Ho was first to find him there the next morning. She said nothing and one by one the family found him kneeling still when they woke, his mother sat behind him facing away without a word. Gwai was the only one who dared approach with water or food, but he ignored her. The younger children were terrified into a constant whisper. This was a punishment they knew. Some had even done it before themselves but only for a couple of minutes. It was painful, so painful, those ridges were made to scrape clothes over. Just minutes on it left deep red gutters in their knees that they'd rub for hours after to make the pain go away. Gwai remembered the pain when she caught her knuckles on them a few weeks earlier, when she was angry with Choi. The anger wasn't anywhere to be found as she watched him, straight backed, kneeling, unflinching.

Towards evening of the next day, spots of blood appeared on the board where the ridges had finally broken the skin, but he didn't move. When Ah Ho finally left her seat to sleep, both Gwai and Sum pleaded with him, urging him to stop but he ignored them still shrugging Gwai off when she tugged at his arm. Still no words. The next morning the same. Ah Ho came down and sat behind him all day not looking at him. Turning only occasionally as he shifted his weight on his knees only tore the skin more and allowed more blood to seep. It didn't gush but by the second evening, the troughs between the peaks were stained with tiny rivulets of dark red. Still, he ate nothing, although he took sips of tea at Sum's urging. Gwai came back secretly to sit with him through the second night after everyone else had gone to bed. His face was a scar again and he grimaced with only the light of the oil lamp, hoping the shadows would cover this shame. She placed her fingers on the back of his neck and he dropped his head, taking his eyes off those of his father for the first time. One, then two tears fell onto the board below and she whispered his name looking for other words that she had either lost a long time ago or had never learnt at all, tender words, soft words. She found none and he lifted his head again to meet his father's gaze. She sat with him till dawn when she heard Ah Ho moving upstairs and went back to their room. The women orbiting around each other each careful not to show too much care.

Ah Ho came downstairs on the fourth morning and placed her hand on Choi's shoulder.

"Enough." She said. "Enough."

She helped him to his feet though he could not straighten his legs and his knees could take little weight. Wedging her shoulder under his she carried him back to his room where Gwai looked as though she was just emerging for the morning. Gwai stepped aside and Ah Ho laid him on the bed. He curled up on his side his body choking with sobs.

Choi got up after three days in bed and another three days after that old Chan Lo Ban, his father's boss, came to offer him his what had been his father's job. Choi took it without a word to Gwai who equally had no words when she heard. She heard along with the rest of the family that evening at the dinner table. He looked at his mother, not her, as he made the announcement. The question about their leaving stuck in her throat like a fish bone. It grew until it was so big it was painful, and her eyes actually watered as she tried to swallow but even she knew that this wasn't something she could bring up here. She'd have to wait until they were alone later. She placed her chopsticks over her half-eaten bowl of rice. There was no way she could get that down now. The small, unsure hand of Chung, the seventh son, reached for it. She looked sharply at him and felt instantly sorry at the look on his face. He was hungry. They hadn't had fresh food in days. There had been no money since the death and what little savings there were in money and in rice were running out. She knew more than the children did, she was the one putting the rice on to cook each night. Soon she was going to have to scrape for the grains hiding in cracks of the wooden bucket. She thought about her own brothers and sisters and although they were poor, they had never come this close to an empty rice bucket before. They had never had to eat just rice and oil and nothing else for dinner as they were doing now. They never heard the jangling of chopsticks against half empty bowls at the beginning of a meal like they did now. Gwai pushed her bowl to Chung flicking her eyes to his sisters on either side of him. He grabbed the bowl and shared out what was left between the three of them. Gwai had to look away when she saw it was barely a mouthful each.

The first thing she saw when she opened the door to their room that night was the washboard. It was propped up on the set of drawers leaning against the wall facing their bed where they could see it from every angle in the room. The blood had now dried into dark brown lines in the troughs where it had pooled and seeped into the wood. They were ugly lines, ugly reminders. Choi didn't look up at her. He sat on the edge of the bed unbuttoning his shirt, folding it carefully and placing it at the end of the bed. The bone in her throat was back, throbbing, but didn't want to move.

"Choi-" she started.

"Chan Suk gave me a bit of money today." He pushed in. "A bit of my salary ahead of time. I gave it to Ma. Go to her tomorrow for the food money."

Gwai nodded. He placed his shoes now under the bed, wincing as he bent down, his knees unforgiving. She took a step closer and instinctively reached towards him, but he equally instinctively moved away. A thought flashed in her mind of all the caresses, the kisses, the slightest touches she had been holding back from him to force him about their leaving and now it was visited back upon her – was it intentional? A punishment? Was he giving that much thought to it? Or was he just recoiling from her now? She hadn't felt the touch of his skin since those first few nights in the dark. He slept so far to the side of the bed now that they wouldn't even brush skin by accident though she had thought about waiting till he was asleep just to put an arm around him.

"Choi-"

He pushed in again, standing up abruptly, lowering his trousers carefully over his knees, careful not to scrape them with the material. They were covered in long thin scabs. Red and brown, puckering the skin in rows surrounded by pools of blue and green bruises like a paddy field of pain. She felt suddenly angry at the sight of them, angry as he rubbed the sides of them, angry at what would grow there.

"I don't want this here."

She grabbed the washboard, fingers pressing hard onto the ridges and understood for just a second what it must have felt like for a grown man to have his full weight kneeling on them. She pushed that thought down and swallowed it. It joined the bone choking her.

"That is not relevant." He yanked it out of her hands and replaced it.

"Aren't those ugly scars reminder enough?" She spat at him.

"No." He got into bed turning his back to her. "But you are."

Choi's knees either wouldn't or couldn't recover. Each week, he straightened them more and grew a bit stronger until one week they just stopped. There was no reason for it. He went to see the healer who could find no reason either. But they stubbornly remained, an inch away from full recovery. Each morning he hobbled across the yard, around the house, until they loosened up enough for him to hide it. The place he couldn't hide it though was at Chan Lo Ban's, Boss Chan, where his father worked his way up from carrying heavy bags of rice, sometimes two at a time, where he was known for his strength, where whispers and sniggers now dogged Choi himself, how the great ox gave a lame calf. Though Chan Lo Ban saw early and moved him onto shop work where he could sit most of the time, it didn't help, the lame calf had already made a home in Choi's head.

It turned out that the calf was not only lame in the knees but also in the head. Once it realised this, it gave up on both. Choi stopped on his way to work for tea as he had done before but this time when the time came to leave, he didn't. He simply sat there and stayed well into the morning, drinking pot after pot. Around the time when chopsticks were coming out for noodles and the sun was high in the sky, Chan Lo Ban found him and brought him back to the shop. After a few handfuls of times (and he knew how many as his wife reminded him that she was running out of fingers and toes to count on), Chan Lo Ban came to Ah Ho and explained he could only pay the hours that Choi actually worked though he was happy to keep his stool for him whenever he did come. Somewhere in Gwai's head a memory murmured. The voice of the fortune teller muttered something about a stool.

Sum had finally found something she enjoyed doing. The seamstress in the village was a distant cousin of her father's who had swapped a few kind words with Sum at the funeral. Sum dropped in to see her a few weeks later and again not long after, and soon found herself little jobs around the shop. The seamstress, Limp-legged Ling, had her leg run over by a cart when she was a girl, chasing after rolling white turnips that had been knocked out of her hands as a man ran past shouting with a knife. The turnips tumbled to the ground, she knelt in the dust kicked up by the feet of the paused crowd stopped to watch what the man did next. The boy with the cart, like everyone else, was watching the knife disappear not the path in front of him, not the girl crouched on the ground. The legs around her parted just as she started to get up and the wheel went onto her left calf. A dark blue canvas was tied tightly over the bolts of cloth in the cart protecting them. Despite the dry, compacted ground, its wheels dug into the ground leaving tracks along its slow progress. She felt the crunch in her bone. The boy had yelped until he was sure his cargo was unharmed. Her calf healed the best it could but ended up a little shorter than the right one with an odd bend in it. It earned her the new nickname too and a new job, though each time she couldn't reach a bolt on a high shelf she heard someone behind her whisper why.

The range of colours in the bolts both captivated and jarred Sum. They were arranged by colour, but once with their little family, they were disorganised, jumbled like sandpaper on her eyes. With each customer, Sum replaced the bolts according to shade, and over a few weeks a subtle wave swam over the displays to reveal a fading in of the lightest purple, darker, darker until a tinge of red then faded through to pink, orange, yellow, green and blue.

Once the customers left and the shop was quiet, Sum watched Limp-legged Ling weave her needle in and out, the point of the needle poking it's head up and out, until it danced a flower out on the cloth. Her gaze was so unblinking that Limp-legged Ling drew her in one day with a scrap piece of silk and asked her what she could do. Sum's fingers spoke easily through the simple stitches her ma had shown her, the ones she used to patch up the natural tears and holes that came from being the eldest of nine brothers and sisters. All of them functional, none of them beautiful but each slipped from her needle perfectly taut without scrunching up the fabric, even and tidy. It took little for Ling to teach her how to make them dance for her as well, dance into simple leaves. Sum sewed and unpicked her thread over and over again until each design was perfected. Within weeks she was catching scraps of work the seamstress was throwing from her own crowded table in exchange for which she slipped Sum a few coins and a more difficult challenge every now and then for a bit of flavour. For Sum though it was magic. As she took up her needle the cloth almost fell around her blocking out all thoughts and sounds, leaving her to bob along the waves of fabric, following the water snake until it became beautiful.

One evening Sum stepped over the threshold into the house, one hand in her bag fingering the tail of a phoenix she had just finished. Her hand brushed against the cold coins jostling at the bottom of her bag, the most she had ever earned in one week. She went straight to her ma and slowly dropped the coins into her open palm. She nodded whilst a pair of sisters stared in surprise. Sum was proud of herself and felt strangely full as she walked away. From behind her she heard Ah Ho.

"That's enough for your boat fare."

"Boat fare?"

"You are going to Hong Kong. Next week. I have discussed it with Ling and she said your sewing is good enough. You can get a job there and earn good money for your brothers and sisters."

Someone dropped a rock into water very close to Sum's head with hollow liquid thump.

"I don't want to go to Hong Kong." She whispered.

"The next boat leaves in four days. The deposit for your place on it has been paid."

"But… Ah Choi and Ah Gwai-"

"Are staying here. The deposit has been paid."

There was nothing left to say.

Alone in her room later, Ah Ho placed her hand out onto her husband's side of the bed, as if daring the emptiness to show her how deeply it could cut her. Perhaps that was what she was doing with sending Sum away. She couldn't see a clear path to their survival as a family. Choi would work, but he was lamed deep in himself now and could only go so far as his scars allowed. Did she have to send Sum? This was a moment that she would look back on. Ah Ho made her choice. She would send her heart away from herself. She would raise and keep this family, what was left to her yet, together, to defy hunger and empty pockets at whatever cost it came. And only here, on her bed, alone at night, would she ever allow herself to look deep into her own grief and allow herself tenderness.

"No! Why? What reason you and not us?!" She shouted at Sum when she told her.
"I don't want to go either. I never did."
"You say that now. Now it is done! How do I know you not scheming all this time?" She threw the broom she was holding to the ground, fists throbbing at her sides as her dream that she had almost, but not wholly, given up on now sailed away with Sum. Her face pasted over with Sum's, Sum's eyes glittering with the lights of Hong Kong, Sum walking the streets laughing, clothes bright, smile wide. She saw it all in her head vividly, saw Sum snatching it all from her. "You take it all then? And what's left for me? Dirt and sand and rotting here?"
"I don't want-" Gwai slapped Sum hard across the face, chest heaving, eyes hard.
"Don't ever speak to me again."

The spring onions were chopped to a paste that night. Gwai slammed the meat cleaver into them at every chance. She had expected Choi to say or do something, but he didn't even look at her. The mark on Sum's face faded quickly and no one questioned it. She equally had nothing to say to Sum in the time she had left. She should have refused to go. It was her dream, her place to go. Sum had taken it for herself. Gwai just knew Sum was secretly savouring the glee of taking this from her, knowing for so many years that's exactly what she wanted. She had pretended she didn't want to go but evidently this was her plan all along. Sum never had an original idea of her own, she would have to steal Gwai's. What was left of Gwai then? She would have to steal away from her marriage if she still wanted to go. Spend the rest of her days hiding, never coming back. She had too much pride for that. With one tacit acceptance of her Lai Lai's word, Sum had condemned Gwai to a life in a bolt-on wooden shack at the back of a pauper's crumbling house. She would not let that lie, Gwai promised herself. She would take back ten-fold what Sum had taken from her. There must be a way. She tucked the promise into herself, willing it to take root, to grow and poison itself into something she could not even conceive of yet.

Sum left late in the night, four days later, with a small bag that looked like an apologetic cat. The little ones hung about her knees and cried. Ah Ho reminded her to thicken her skin or she'd never last. Choi wobbled his goodbye at her with jelly-eyes not knowing it was the last time he would see her. He was killed the following year as the floorboards gave way under several bags of rice above his head in the office. He was the only one killed, the others ran out of the way fast enough, but his knees kept him in his seat. Gwai didn't need to know that she would be a widow in just over a year to be angry, but it helped the poison inside to rankle and rot even deeper. As Sum reached out for her hand to say goodbye, she said not one word, hands by her side. She stared straight ahead determined to remain betrayed.

Chapter Seventeen

In the weeks that came after Jun Ching's return, Ah Ho seemed to test her. Different flavours of *juk* every morning, different dishes every evening but not once did she feel the sharp rap of chopsticks across her knuckles if it wasn't quite right. Just orders given, 'less salt', 'boil it for longer', 'add more water to make it go further'. The lack of pain was a tenderness in itself to Jun Ching. So, she watched Penny and soon learnt more tricks. Jun Ching thought no deeper than it being a test, just to see if she had spent her time well whilst she was away.

Ah Ho was shocked though at the condition the girl was returned to her in. She was skinnier than any of her children had been at the worst depths of their poverty, skinnier than the urchin beggars in the street. She made Jun Ching wash in front of her in the courtyard the day after she got back when she saw how thin her arms were so she could see exactly how bad it had got. The protruding ribs down her front were bad but she could understand, food was scarce for many, perhaps it was worse than she knew of for her niece but when she turned and Ah Ho saw the bulging red lines across her back, criss-crossing dull brown healed lines beneath, her breath caught in her throat. Even she had never hit anyone like this let alone a child. Jun Ching winced no matter how gently Penny poured the flask of water over her shoulders and a bubble of bile burnt in the old woman. It didn't even occur to her that she might be treated even worse by the family she was to be sold to. She would have to put off the wedding date by some weeks though, to give her time to put some meat back on her bones and for the sores to heal or else they might send her back or only pay a lower price.

Nowhere in Ah Ho's mind was there a thought of hiding the arrangement from anyone let alone Jun Yee and Jun Ching themselves. But since nobody asked, she didn't see the need to say anything either and chose, for convenience's sake, to meet next with Mother Tang at one of the tea stalls rather than at home. It would, after all, be easier if it continued for nobody to ask.

Mother Tang's features screwed up into the middle of her face with displeasure. A good date had been picked and the preparations had already been made all of which would have to be redone. This would cost them. Ah Ho, with nothing to hide, explained the rows of bones she saw in the girl and even Mother Tang agreed this was more damaging, more likely to result in a refusal to accept the goods. It was whilst Mother Tang was talking that she noticed Jun Yee across the dirt alley watching her. He had barely stopped, on an errand for the bakery no doubt, as he continued walking round, he caught a side profile of Mother Tang. She didn't think he knew who she was, it didn't matter anyway; there was nothing he could do. In her other ear Mother Tang continued a monologue of how long she could buy her, *six weeks, two months at the most then they must complete the deal.* The boy had gone and there was no time to waste wondering over what he thought. *There is no saying whether they will try to find someone else in the meantime, it's possible but she'll try her best not to let them get away.*

That evening Penny and Jun Ching were shocked to find Ah Ho herself in the kitchen with a fatty cut of pork she slapped down in front of them asking them how best they would cook it. Neither girl knew, it was an expensive cut – one they had rarely seen above a couple of times a year on their table let alone been allowed to cook themselves for risk of spoiling it. Penny was quickly sent to do the usual washing of the rice, the vegetables, the preparation whilst Jun Ching carefully watched the marinating, the tenderising, the slicing of the pork. Ah Ho remembered for a moment the hour they spent together watching dragonflies on the pier. Jun Ching thought how wasteful they seemed to be being with two whole spoonfuls of soy sauce and sugar going in the marinade – the Terrapin would never have allowed that. Her back twitched at the thought.

Seven Uncle was the only one who asked what the special occasion was that night at dinner. He got no reply and was offered no pork either. Only the oil that had oozed out of it to flavour his rice – the same as what the children got. All except Jun Ching into whose bowl Ah Ho dropped four or five pieces of the meat. The entire table fell silent. It was odd enough that Ah Ho had made the girl sit next to her at the table when they were usually dismissed to eat outside on the steps. She must be regretting sending her away, they thought, her heart was softening. There was no mistaking how badly treated she had been. They could all see that. Gwai alone kept her eyes in her rice bowl and chopsticks gripped, the sight and smell of the pork filled her mouth with saliva just as it did right before she vomited. Her stomach turned.

It didn't stop there. First two, then three times a week there would be meat at the table, or a whole fish, white eyes and all, and each time, Ah Ho would have supervised the cooking of it herself, watching over Jun Ching and then making sure she ate a good proportion of it at the table. By the third time when Jun Ching got an entire preserved duck egg all to herself the others had lost interest. Only Nine Auntie's fat lips kept pouting with their emptiness.

Jun Ching accepted it as she did any piece of luck good or bad that blew across her path, but it niggled at Jun Yee. Something didn't fit. Something itched under his shirt telling him something. But what was it? Ten days after Jun Ching's return, he was sweeping the back courtyard when Ah Ho thrust into his hand a small glass pot.

"What is it?"

"Rub it into your sister's back."

"What is it?" He repeated and opened it. Inside was an orange-brown paste, oily that smelt of something halfway between paraffin and edible. The warm day had melted it and he could swirl the top layer of oil around the brim.

"Don't play with it. Just rub it on her back. Anywhere there are sores or scars. Two, three times a day if you can." For a moment he looked doubtful. "It's not going to harm her. It will make them heal better. And faster." She snapped and was gone into the house again.

Across the courtyard, Four Auntie looked up at him from the half shadows where she was silently scraping twigs and small branches smooth adding them to a pile beside her. She never spoke to him, he had barely realised she was there, and he jumped at the sound of her voice. It was softer and kinder than he knew to expect.

"Be careful, little man." He moved closer to her, but she moved silently away.

Something was wrong. He watched Ah Ho but understood nothing. Ah Ho changed no further than she already had. He watched for some clue, anything to help him see what was happening. He felt it too. They were being watched as well but he couldn't see the eyes on their backs.

It was Gwai that watched them. From behind curtains and over the top of a rice bowl. She saw in Jun Yee how he said even less than he did before, trusting no one with his words or thoughts, perhaps not even his sister. How he kept her close by him, how he kept them separate from everyone he could except the stupid girl Penny. She recognised in him the drive with no cause, the feeling that he had to do something, in this case, he had to protect his sister, himself, but from what he could no longer be quite sure and that made him unpredictable and suspicious. She had felt the same herself after Choi died, the flames of anger and disappointment, of a drive having lost its direction but not its force, needed somewhere to go and leaked onto everyone around her until she found it a new home in Sum. It occurred to her now that it had happened again when Sum died. The flames rage in fury, the drive does not die for her, it burns her own self until she redirects it, looking for the next closest thing to ensure its survival, her own survival. She didn't know about other people but perhaps it was this rage that kept her alive. This time the flames latched quickly onto the ones closest to Sum, but she felt the heat as well. She was standing too close to the flames this time and she could not afford to get burnt. They cannot know her part in this, she thought to herself.

She chose a quiet afternoon to start the first time. Only a few of the children were in the house including Penny and Jun Ching, Four Sister crouched out in the yard as usual and Ah Ho was out fishing or staring at the water at least. She could test it here she thought before pressing out a short sigh. Both girls looked at her.

"*Aiy*... I don't know where the money goes. This week's food money is already gone. It's like someone is stealing it away like that." The girls turned back to their chores deaf to the undertone. How much further to go this first time, she wondered and waited.

"Was it you two? One of you stolen into my room, took the money, ah?"

"No, Gwai Kam Mo." Jun Ching was quick to answer, used to having to cover her back by now probably. "Us two would not dare."

Gwai snorted. "There's a ghost then. Maybe your dead mother. And we will all be forced to lick our fingers by the end of the week for flavour."

The girls thought nothing more of it. It slipped from their minds amongst their washing and cleaning and chatting with shoulders pressed together. But for Gwai, she had started. An easy start but one that she would build on quickly - she mentioned it again the following day to the aunts as something peculiar. This had never happened to her before and they all agreed that she was so good with money, given how greedy she was they thought but dare not say. The third time she mentioned it was a week later, the second time the money had apparently gone missing and this time she made sure she had more of an audience. It was early evening, before dinner, the children gathered in the yard playing out of the way of the final dinner preparations which the aunts were in charge of. Ah Ho had come in to dictate what she wanted bought for the following nights.

"*Hai,* Lai Lai - I do my best. It just that the food money seem to disappear. It's the second time this month that it's just gone. Last week too, I don't know if because we have more mouths to fill now." Gwai threw a glance outside to where they knew Jun Yee and Jun Ching were with the others in the yard then hesitated, unsure of this last bit. "Like someone's just taken it."

Ah Ho screwed her eyes on her, raising her jaw at the same time considering. She was doing something here. Waving at smoke she couldn't see through, yet. "Just gone, ha? Then you should be more careful. And use your own personal savings to make up for your carelessness."

Ah Ho left and Gwai turned to see Jun Yee standing in the door frame looking at her, silent as usual. She left it there for the night.

The next day it was time to put some foundations under her actions. Gwai loitered, clumsy this morning, dropping things and having to clear them up and whilst she was doing that she may as well sweep and clean other parts of the house, taking her well past the time she would normally leave for the market. With the house empty now, she clutched at the coins zipped into the inner pocket of her shirt. She slipped upstairs, wincing at the creaking floorboards with no one to hear them. Along the landing where Jun Ching and Jun Yee still slept, as they did on those first few nights with Sum. She opened the small sideboard against the wall where they neatly folded and placed their mats and blankets each morning. She pushed them aside, it was dark up here, the windows small and far apart hiding the sun from the corners of the shelf and she had to plunge her hands in, groping to the back, to find what she was looking for. Her fingers came across cloth and cloth, all rough cotton, impossible to tell if it was the same piece again and again. Then, to the right, at the very back there, was the feel of cold metal and a faint tick, tick, tick, as her nails brushed up against the old egg roll tin. She pulled it out, watching which way round it came so she could replace it exactly the same way. She crouched down to the floor, feeling suddenly exposed. Second, third and fourth thoughts running through her head - was it really necessary to do this? She hadn't spoken to Mother Tang about it, or Ah Ho, but Jun Yee couldn't know, the family couldn't know, how she had brought Mother Tang into their nest in the first place. If they did, she could lose the standing she had worked so hard to maintain here, even after Choi had gone, such as it was. This place was all she had left. Looking over the edge of the landing, making sure no one was down there, and no one was, just the photos of the dead staring into nothing and seeing nothing now. She prised the tin open, her nails hard as a screwdriver. She was surprised to find it almost empty. They must have removed the letters that were left or thrown them away - she could see Jun Yee doing it. Not Jun Ching, she would hold onto them she thought, waiting and waiting till she could read. Just like her ma. The figurines had disintegrated now and covered the inside with a layer of coloured dust. It hadn't been opened in a long while it seemed, forgotten. She unzipped her pocket and pulled out all the coins, counting them again, pausing for barely half a beat before placing them softly into the tin and replacing the lid. The sound of them as they scraped along the bottom of the tin, scraped against her ears, almost painful making her neck shrink into her shoulders like a terrapin. No, she straightened. Not like that Terrapin. I am nothing like her, she said to herself. Pushing the tin to the back with a definitive thud to prove that she was not ashamed though no one was there but her and she already knew she was lying.

Over the next few days Jun Yee began to understand what Gwai was implying. Her looks grew more pointed at them, her suggestions were repeated that the only thing that had changed in the household was more mouths to fill. So, this is what it was. The food money wasn't lasting because of Jun Ching to feed as well and with Paw Paw demanding slightly better food, Gwai was angry, jealous even, and it was apparently Jun Ching's fault. He earned only a little from Bau Suk, but Jun Ching was his responsibility, and he wasn't going to have her feeling bad that she was back after everything she had had to live through whilst away. They had not asked for any of this, he thought as his own annoyance bubbled up in his throat. He decided he would give Gwai, from his weekly earnings, a small amount for Jun Ching. That would put a silence on her about it and perhaps this feeling of something wrong would shake off and away then.

But when he got home that night there were raised voices being carried down the steps. He raced up to find Nine Auntie at the door watching, an indiscreet smile on her lips, enjoying every moment.

"What's happened?"

"Ah, you're back at the right time - it's your sister. Looks like she didn't just learn to cook whilst she was away. She learnt to steal too!" The words dripped off her tongue with relish.

Jun Yee pushed past and in the main room there was Gwai, shouting accusations at Jun Ching, standing a few feet in front of her. Jun Ching's eyes were swimming in her face - or was it Jun Yee who couldn't see properly - they seemed huge, twice the size of normal and pleading.

"I didn't Gwai Kam Mo - I didn't take anything." She kept repeating.

"This is the third time in four weeks now that the money is short - someone is stealing it and I know it's you! Who else would it be?"

"It wasn't me, Gwai Kam Mo! Truly it wasn't."

"So that means you say it is one of your cousins then? Or your brother? It started when you came back so it must be you - no one else is that stupid!" Gwai saw Jun Yee now, it was time. She took a step forwards reaching for her. "If you don't admit it, I'll beat you till you do!"

Jun Yee crashed between them throwing his arm out the way exactly as Gwai had hoped. She couldn't hit the girl, she knew, her back was healing, and Ah Ho would not have anything set that back. But the boy. He was an open target.

"Stop! It wasn't her! She didn't take anything." He shouted.

Gwai raised her hand to strike him. He caught her wrist. He was unexpectedly strong. Her wrist was immobile, caught in a vice. She struggled with it, pulling it back, forth, to each side, jerked it down to break the grip but nothing worked. She brought her other hand swift and hard across his face. A loud slap of skin on skin with the sharp snap of his head to one side then back again came with a cry from his sister but nothing more. Nothing else changed, he still held on and stared at her.

"She did not steal your money." He threw her wrist away from him.

"Prove it." She spat back.

"How?"

She didn't answer him. She turned and marched up the stairs before any protest could be made. Everyone remained stunned, rooted to the floor below. She knew exactly where to look, but pretended to rummage, to pull out everything they had and shake it all, checking pockets from which nothing fell. Something in her heart creaked on seeing how pitifully small the pile was, how very little they had, but it was too late to stop now. She finally came to the tin, shaking it as it came out and allowed a triumphant grin to dash across her face.

"*La!* I said, didn't I?!" She opened it, walking to the edge of the landing, and tipped the contents over the wooden railing to the floor below. Jun Yee raced up the stairs. The figurines. Jun Ching loved them. Even though she had not played with them since she was sent away, he had kept them safe for her in there. They would be smashed if they fell from that height. But Gwai's planted coins clattered in a rain of coloured dust and silence before he could stop her.

For a moment, nothing happened and Gwai thought with exasperation that she would have to do more. Why did she have to do everything? Then, below, a child coughed on the dust, breaking the silence. She couldn't tell which child. Her body then continued as though she had been stopped in mid-movement. It took no more than a few steps to reach Jun Yee.

"Nothing to say now, *ha?*"

"She didn't do -." He repeated, but she struck him before he finished.

Standing at the top of the stairs, the unexpected blow forced him to take a step back to nothing and he fell, his body collapsing and rolling backwards and down the stairs. His head hit the wooden hand-rail two, three times before he managed to grasp one of them breaking the momentum and slowing his fall. Only he saw the split second of the widened eyes on Gwai's face - the slip of a mask he didn't know she was wearing but it was gone so quickly he would forget it was ever there.

Gwai pulled it back. It was lucky it was him, she hadn't meant for that to happen - if it had been the girl it would have all backfired. Her trembling hands gripped the railing, searching her mind for where she was in the lie, where to pick up and carry on from, before it was all ruined. Jun Yee was standing now below her, he was not badly hurt. She was surprised at her own relief, though she trampled it down inside to find the words she needed next.

"You wait until Lai Lai hears about this." Walking down the stairs, she dropped her voice as she reached him, whispering loudly into his face. "She will give you two what you deserve."

Jun Yee watched, expecting something else. The fall on the stairs had shaken him. For the first time he felt his entire body coiled, tense and constantly looking around him. He felt something else as well. A surging sense of something unfamiliar, building inside him, urging him to an edge over which all could be lost or won, and he didn't know which yet, but he would never know without going over.

The money had been taken back. He didn't want it. He didn't care either that it got into their tin, only how it had, and by whom - without that knowledge he couldn't trust anyone. Ah Ho was told what had happened but had no reaction and that was even worse. It unsettled him like dropping a stone in water with no ripples. Ah Ho had stared at Gwai saying nothing for several minutes. Jun Yee imagined them talking at a different frequency, one that didn't require moving their mouths, talking with their minds maybe, until finally Ah Ho said to the air between them,

"Gwai, you have had your justice. There will be no more."

He strained to hear it or feel it. The fact that he couldn't unfocussed the rest of his thoughts, until he could think of nothing else. He threw away the old egg roll tin and with it the last physical connection they had with Sum. The final fragments of a happier life already severed snapped back to sting his fingers as he did it.

Six weeks passed and the sun had started its earliest climbs of the year, blanketing the village in a heat that slowed everyone's pace and caused little beads of sweat to sprout on the upper lips of old ladies by mid-morning. Those weeks had been pulled taut by Jun Yee's hooded concentration on Gwai, the easiness of Jun Ching's initial return scattered as easily as the petals of the peach blossom trees. It was with some surprise that Jun Ching realised that the photograph of Sum which she regularly dusted around on the sideboard was nearly a year old. Her face was still familiar, though Jun Ching couldn't make it move anymore. When she called her ma's face to her mind, she only saw this picture, static and flat. She could turn it in her head from side to side, tilting it, pushing it far away, pulling it right up close to her nose and even stretch her faint smile into a bigger one but that was all it was. Just the same photograph. Although the photograph was there, no one spoke to Sum either, pretending she wasn't there when they spoke to the photograph of her father right next to her all the time as though he was in the room, asking his opinion, asking for his help. And so, Jun Ching muttered to him as well to look after her ma under the water please, at least until she could come and do it herself.

Days later, mid-morning, there was a knock at the open door. An unfamiliar voice called into the house with a delivery. Nine bags of rice were piled in the courtyard whilst Gwai was told to count each as they were carried up by two bone-and-muscle men, sweat pouring off their brown skin, leaving faint patches of dark on each bag where they had carried them up the stone steps on their neck and shoulders. Not a grain less, she was told to count. Following the last bag was Mother Tang who nodded at Gwai and went straight in to Ah Ho turning on an excited bluster as she stepped over the threshold.

"Ah, the wedding presents are here – good la! Good la! Are you satisfied? You must be happy Mrs. Wu. The coin I will bring back once they have inspected the girl on arrival but for now here is the last part." She handed Ah Ho from inside her wide sleeve a package wrapped in red cloth. Ah Ho sneered.

"What's this? Are we really pretending this far?" She unwrapped the cloth and laid on her lap the traditional gifts from the groom's parents to the bride – a needle and thread, ruler, scissors, comb, mirror and some red string for her hair.

"Mrs. Wu, if you put on a play you have to put it on till the end. You cannot act half and not act half. And besides who says this is not a real wedding – this is a happy occasion. Look at how much rice you have. You can feed your whole family for months, a year if you are really careful! If you don't celebrate that I don't know what you would!"

Ah Ho folded the cloth back over and put it to one side. Seeing her enthusiasm wasn't getting the reaction she was hoping for, Mother Tang pursed her lips and left a silence in the air for a short time until Gwai came in to report that everything was as it should be, all bags accounted for.

"I'll tell them they can leave then. And don't forget, the date cannot be moved again." Mother Tang rose to leave herself, looking around the room as she did, stopping at the photograph of Sum. "Truly fast, isn't it? How time goes? A year to the day since Sum died, that this marriage will happen. I can't believe it."

"Really? I hadn't noticed." Ah Ho replied. Her tone flat, eyes pointed.

"Well, that's good then. From this year on you will remember it as this lucky occasion of the marriage to a good family. Not the *accident* that everyone in the village still remembers it being now." She left.

By the time Jun Yee got home that evening, the rice had been put away and the red cloth package hidden, but the children were still murmuring about it with expectations of overflowing mounds of rice that evening, only to be disappointed by the usual amount for each one followed by the familiar sound of chopsticks scraping at the bottom of empty bowls. Jun Yee waited till the end of the evening, when some of the children had laid out their mats to sleep in the slight breeze of the front courtyard under the stars and the smoke from the uncles' pipes, before they padded away to their own rooms. He found Four Auntie squatting on her heels in the double dark of shadows at night stripping what looked like the same thin branches as before. He got up close and squatted beside her before whispering.

"Four Auntie, everyone has been talking, not just here, I heard it in the street as well, there has been a big gift of rice today. Is it true?" She was silent. He pressed her. "Something's wrong isn't it? I don't know what it is, but I can feel it. It's about Jun Ching. Isn't it? Do you know what it is?" Still, she carried on, he would get there himself, she thought. "Paw Paw is treating her better. Is she making up for sending her away – is it that simple?"

"There was a lot, much, much more than your Paw Paw can afford to buy…"

"They are saying it's a wedding gift, that it has to be when it is that much. That can't be true, can it? Who would be getting married?"

"*Ach!* Don't be so blind boy!" She spat suddenly. "Open your eyes! Which piglet is being fattened?"

"What? You mean Ching Ching? It can't be. She is only a child."

"Believe it or not, up to you. I have only ever seen a poor girl treated well for one reason." He waited for her to finish and moved even closer as she dropped her voice. "To make her valuable for marriage, like fattening a pig for sale. It happened to me before I came here. But my ma had the heart to cry as she did it and gave me all my favourite foods. Those dishes were both delicious and choking at the same time." She paused a while, her tongue rubbing against the roof of her mouth, tasting each dish again. "You don't fatten a pig, or a piglet, for a pet. You fatten them up for slaughter."

The next morning, Four Auntie's words still sat on the surface of his mind as he poured the thick, yellow and slightly sticky oil into his palm. Rubbing them together, it loosened as the cooler early morning air still hung about them. The salt blew in on the wind from the sea, cool enough to make the first fishermen heading out put on their sleeves, an extra layer for now. Jun Ching sat crossed legged in front of him with her top pulled up to her shoulders revealing the raised lines across her back, some fading into brown, a couple still holding onto hints of red. Those were the ones that had been piled on top of others before they had healed, burn on top of burn. They were getting better though. Ah Ho had given him this oil days ago and told him to rub it into her back as many times a day as he could remember. At first, she had winced and pulled away, but each day he could rub a little harder, trying to rub away the old pain. He was the one left wincing now. He was glad to do it, though. It meant he could see day by day if she was getting better. Even after these short weeks of being back, the ribs in her back seemed less pronounced. The tops of her arms were growing slowly thicker than her forearms, her elbows looking less like tree knots in the middle. He just didn't want to think about what it meant – for her to put on weight so quickly once back, what did that say about what she had when she was away. Every time he thought of it, he would bring her back something extra, either from the bakery, from Lien's shop, sweet tofu or anything else he could think of. Jun Ching was having to create an additional mealtime for herself to fit it all in, not eating whilst he was away so her tummy wasn't always full. Without realising it, he was working with Ah Ho, making her task easier.

  Downstairs, a voice called Jun Ching into the kitchen whilst he was summoned out to the front courtyard where Ah Ho sat alone.

  "How are her scars? Is the oil working?"

"I think so Paw Paw, it looks like they are fading. And they don't seem as painful to her anymore. I think she's even been slept a bit on her back. She hasn't done that in a long time."

"She looks better too – not so much like those chickens people pay us to pluck for them." The boy nodded like an old man, thinking about whether or not to voice his next thoughts.

"Paw Paw... everyone is talking, about all the rice we received yesterday, that they are gifts, wedding gifts..." He didn't want to ask, didn't want to know. Since Jun Ching got back their mutual concern for her had drawn an invisible peace between them. Even if it came from different reasons, he didn't want it broken. He swallowed. Her face a rock. She gave nothing away, barely registered him standing there. "Who is getting married, Paw Paw?"

She didn't care about telling him. She had thought he knew already anyway. What could he do? She was the head of this family - the decision was hers alone. She was tired of doing this alone, irritated from having to do it herself. Even having to see the look on his face. Of anger? Hurt? Accusation? Whatever it was, she was too tired for this.

"Your little sister."

"She can't."

"She is."

"No."

"You think it's your place to decide?"

"I'm her big brother!" He shouted, startling himself. His fists curled at his sides.

"And I am her Paw Paw." They left it to hang, waving in the air for a while. Her hand was higher than his. From inside a sudden burst of laughter came from Penny and Jun Ching in the kitchen. "And we need the rice. Everyone's got a gaping, open mouth and empty stomach. We cannot afford to keep the mouths that we do have let alone add more."

"So, you are selling her? For rice?"

"No. For survival."

He had no more words. He shouldn't have been surprised, he was almost sure before he asked that this would be the answer but still he didn't know what to say. He just stared at the side of her head, swaying slightly from foot to foot, feeling heavier in his jaw with each second, felt like it would crack when it next moved, fracturing into tiny pieces.

"Please don't do it."

"It's done." She turned her heavy-lidded eyes at him finally. He saw the woman who had slapped him as he knelt by his mother's body.

"Since we are talking about it now, you might as well go and get your sister so I can tell her too. She should know, the date is set. Tomorrow."

"Tomorrow?" His voice ran away from him now shouting again but once it was out it set forth a year's worth of everything he had not said.

He heard the gathering footsteps of the others behind him, but he saw only the old woman in front. No need to get Jun Ching now, she would be there, at the front of the pack. He spat on the ground between them. Several gasps were gasped off stage. She slapped him, hard, across the side of the head. Then they both stared at each other. Both as shocked at the other, pulling in directions opposite to each other, Jun Yee testing, testing his strength against the power of the old woman, the pull of tradition. Did he imagine it, or could he feel it creak? Between the wrinkles and the liver spots on her cheeks, could he see the gap? Could she? Where he could creep in and change something? Something small but big enough for them, for him and his sister to get through and out forever.

An expectation hung in the air for Ah Ho to end this, to crush the defiance daring to stand in front of her for the first time but the next words did not belong to her. The boy dragged his anger with everything he had back to words, controlling it, harnessing it.

"Tomorrow?" He said again. "She's just a child."

Ah Ho brought her stick up and swiftly down again, cracking across the side of his left knee. He buckled but did not fall, wavering momentarily as the crowd watched on. Straightening he spat once more, further in front. Specks landed on the gnarled and thickened skin on her foot, skin she could not feel anymore. He backed away for a few steps. She raised her stick again, but he was just out of reach. He turned his back on her.

The spectators moved not half a foot. The world had just shifted beneath them and they felt it. The meeting of thunder and lightning in one horrifying clap, the awareness of the shift between them and that they would also somehow be changed by each ripple that now spread from it. Jun Yee, the low rumble, gathering strength, ominous, a promise of more to come. Ah Ho, the slaps of light, more obvious, but somehow now seeming more fleeting and unpredictable. *You had better hide when you hear thunder* they were all told as disobedient children and they all imagined cowering between the legs of a worn, wooden table somewhere waiting for their thunderous fates. Finally, it felt as though they were understanding why.

Jun Ching just blinked and nodded when Ah Ho told her after Jun Yee had gone. The family was three or four villages along the coast. Only a little further than the Terrapin's but they will treat her better if she treats their son well. Their son was young, though a few years older than Jun Ching and her job will be to look after him. This will not change. He will not grow up even when his body grows his mind will not. She will be his wife and carer. The date was set – tomorrow, an auspicious date, they will come to take her to her new home. *Questions?* She shook her head. Ah Ho was surprised – she expected some kind of scene, some reaction after her brother's. But she just stood there staring at her, saying things she could not hear, hands clasped. It occurred to her that none of her own remaining children had the gall, the will that these two had. It was a shame. Perhaps it would have been better to send off one of her own. She wiped the thought away along with sight of Jun Ching in front of her and the lingering feeling of Sum gazing out at her from her daughter's eyes.

Jun Yee joined them then and they walked down the steps to the street side by side, conscious Ah Ho's eyes would be following them until they got to the bottom and dipped out of sight. By the time they reached the water, they still hadn't said anything. Just one question ran circles round in Jun Yee's mind, *what are we going to do*, and he couldn't seem to catch its tail, no matter how hard he tried, couldn't move the thought onto solutions, just the same question round and round, blurring.

"Nothing." Jun Ching broke the circle, catching its tail feather with one swoop. "We don't have to do anything, brother. I don't mind looking after children and I'm good at it. Little 'Pin was the only good thing about the other place. Leave it. I will be fine. I don't mind. Really."

She let go and the thought limped away from Jun Yee. He'd never felt more useless.

But he couldn't leave it. That would be impossible. He thought back to her face as she turned to wave at him in the sunshine following Gwai back to the Terrapin - the day he failed

Jun Ching the first time. How much she looked like Sum. How her once energetic bounding had been cowed into the measured steps that he now recognised were their Ma's. Was that the first time though he had to ask himself? Or was there more before then? How many times had he failed her? He couldn't let her leave his sight again, rounding those steps into a world he could not even see. Something else too was flicking at the edges of his mind, bothering him, a persistent tickle. How when it came to it, when he stood alone in front of Ah Ho and said whatever he wanted, did whatever he wanted, no one came forward to stop him. There was no supporting voice behind her to pull him down, to hold him in the allotted space he was supposed to stand in. It was just him, a boy, facing an old woman, an old woman who for whatever reason could not even reach to beat him when he stepped away. But he could stand, he thought. He could stand and walk, run and jump, or slither even, if he needed to, out of grasp and he could do it all with his sister in tow. He straightened his knee a few times where she had struck him, barely registering any pain. There was a gap there - he had seen it, where he had spat, and no one had stopped him. He practically spat on her. The question was, just how far did he dare to go?

    The answer came into focus as the waves of the morning calmed in his mind and he could gradually see straight through the water. With the number of times that they had asked Sum to tell them the story of how she did it, it surprised him that it took so long for him to think of it himself. There was only one way in or out of this place he could see it now. The same way Sum had got out all those years ago, the same way she brought them in - the only way out for them. In addition to the boats that had brought them here with Sum over a year ago in daylight, there were still those that left in the dead of night, those like the one Sum had taken the first time she left this place. It was a merry-go-round with one exit that he could see rushing by in a blur as he went round and round - he had to jump off at exactly the right time. Could he time it right? They had to get as far away as possible before anyone realised they were gone, they could have people waiting for them when they docked at the other side if not. If reported as missing they would be sent straight back no matter what they said, trapped again in the spinning circle that Sum could not break from in the end. The one that spun her into the sea and kept her there. No, they had to get back to Hong Kong and disappear among its streets, sink beneath the surface froth of a bubbling crowd so that they could never be found again.

He had some money, not lots but he had been working for as long as Jun Ching had been away now, and he had never given all he earned to Ah Ho, barely half if at all. She had no idea just how generous Bau Suk was. Other than buying treats for Jun Ching when he visited her, he had spent nothing, and he had kept none of it in the egg roll tin. Still, the price of anonymity and safe passage to Hong Kong was likely to be beyond his savings, but he had to try, his problem was time, he had even less of that. He knew where to go though, and he went now, passing the stools and benches that even this early were gradually filling up with men with alcohol to drink and wives to not return home to. He knew who he was looking for, a man he had seen before, always sitting in the same position at the same stall with an empty looking face shimmering in and out of different shades of yellow and brown. If he wasn't sitting drinking with one foot propped up on the bench almost tucked up underneath him, he was creeping slowly there, on his way. Jun Yee didn't know his real name, he had overheard him referred to as 'Find-a-way'. He seemed to be the one who could find a way to do things, to solve problems if people couldn't do it themselves. He certainly seemed to do nothing else but move from sitting place to sitting place, so that he was easily found and equally easily paid.

Jun Yee skulked around the stalls on the opposite side of the street to the shop. Find-a-way as he usually was, was waiting. Jun Yee didn't want to be seen talking to him there, he was too recognisable and if anyone saw them and told Ah Ho she would know he was planning something. It wasn't the first time he cursed his light brown hair pointing him out in every crowd. He dipped both hands in a bucket of water by a stall, scooping a little out and running it through his hair, darkening it fractionally, making no real difference, except to make him feel ever so fractionally better.

Find-a-way came creeping down the road, Jun Yee saw him from a distance and walked immediately to the other side of the street, circling back up behind him to meet him. He caught him at least half a street away from his usual place, giving them plenty of time to talk. Find-a-way didn't seem surprised at this random and unknown voice that spoke to him suddenly, didn't slow his creeping pace or turn to face Jun Yee. He just took a sidelong glance at him as he dragged on a cigarette, ostensibly only turning his face from the trail of smoke.

They spoke in fast mutters, far faster than Find-a-way walked. He didn't do that sort of thing, he said. He can get him stuff but not take him places. He didn't like to move himself. But he could tell him where to go.

"One of the fishermen, one of the early ones, he is the one to talk to – he goes out early and comes back early and so is often sitting outside his house before the streets fill with people. Easier to talk then. He is the one to talk to. Don't ask him his name though. Everyone knows his name anyway, it's such a small village, but he doesn't like to say his own name, especially when talking about things like this. Just call him fisherman." Find-a-way chuckled. Jun Yee tried to pay him for his help and got waved away. "Come back to me one day when you need something. I'll just charge you double then."

Jun Yee walked by the address of the fisherman straight afterwards, expecting disappointment as the day had already crept just past noon. The house, on a dusty side road, was a quiet one and the houses opened right onto the road with only a small sectioned off courtyard in the front for drying nets. But he had to linger, had to risk it, tomorrow would be too late. He didn't dare approach the door but just paced back and forth in front of the windows and quickly drew the fisherman out like the man had probably done himself that morning, drawing fish to the surface with shadows. He came out without looking at Jun Yee and sat on his doorstep in the patchy shade of his nets, bony knees poking up like tent poles in his trouser legs, level with his shoulders. He had the same wiry, burnt faced look as most of the men along the coast, hidden muscle, long and sinewy, the kind you'd have to boil in soup for days and still need to spit out as gristle in the end. Plenty of flavour though probably, Jun Yee thought.

"Did you catch anything today, Uncle?" Jun Yee asked.

"Of course, but the wife dries them out the back, not out here for everyone to steal." His words glinted like a sharp blade, Jun Yee was unsure how or if to continue. He drew breath before he was cut off. "Don't bark at me from over there boy, if you want to speak come here and sit down. We are not dogs."

As open an invitation as he knew he was going to get, Jun Yee squatted next to him and asked all the same questions Ah Ho must have asked years ago.

The fisherman did not make the trip too frequently. His boat had to be compact to pass as a working fishing boat and could carry only a handful of people hidden under the canopy of night on each trip. He was well known for it, even amongst the authorities but with a little sweetener of his own, they left him to it. The villages along this coast glowed green with resentment towards Hong Kong. It was a greedy place, full of opportunities and money to be made but selfishly keeping it all to itself. It wasn't that different. It too started as a fishing village. Just lucky to fall on the right side of a randomly drawn line. Adopted by a richer family, it had all the prospects whilst those left behind rotted in the sun. How was that to treat your own people, some thought. The same people thought it was just luck, good fortune that meant Hong Kong was carved off the China coast and given away. Arbitrary, and all good Chinese families knew that if one prospers so should they share it with their family. And Hong Kong, and its people, didn't. So why shouldn't they seize the chance for themselves – there were success stories of people who had done it already.

The borders were closed but perforated and although anyone caught trying to sneak across were sent back, the waterways were harder to police and once in it wasn't hard to get documents that allowed you to stay. The fisherman gave no guarantees or refunds. If you get caught on the other side and get sent back then you'll just have to pay again if you want another chance, no matter how long you have to save. There were some who had made the trip a couple of times and although he laughed to himself each time they came back to him, he took their money all the same. It wasn't his problem if they wanted to throw their money into the salty water. He muttered all this without knowing there was only one chance for these two.

He was only making the trip every few months, but the boy must have good luck, there was one tonight, after that there would be a long wait. The date was chosen as they would arrive tomorrow - an auspicious day - the same day chosen for the marriage- a lucky time to go. Perhaps they won't get caught. For the first time in his life, Jun Yee felt the hand of luck in his favour. There was no margin for error but then Jun Ching had no margin at all now. But it was a chance at a new life, priceless life said the fisherman and it would cost them.

Jun Yee returned to the bakery and his neglected rectangular trays. The baking was done for the day, all that was left to do was to sell out of everything they had as the afternoon ticked by. They almost always did. Bau Suk believed it was better to run out and leave people feeling they've missed out than have just enough, or too much, and leave people satisfied. Jun Yee, frustrated, elbowed the trays out of his way, sending them clattering to the ground. He didn't have enough money. That was it then. The fisherman's eyes glinted at him, telling him he was lucky, there was one boat leaving that very night, he never let people on so late, but he could see he needed it. But he had a price, and that price was more than Jun Yee had ever held in his fingers. Throwing his fists into the tub in front of him, he covered himself in slightly oily water, making him even angrier burying his fists now in his hair, pulling for pain.

"Tsk tsk tsk... you see..." Bau Suk's voice behind him, "now you're angry and wet. Wasn't it better just being angry?"

"You wouldn't understand."

"No?"

"No! Not doing everything, trying everything and still getting nowhere, being no one!"

Bau Suk sighed. "*Lei la*, come on boy, no one is no one unless they let themselves be. So, let's choose not to be." He pulled Jun Yee by the shoulders to him. Jun Yee felt tears escape down his cheeks, turning to shame, dropping heavy to the floor. "Tell me now. I could see it this morning on your face. Do you need help? You're a man now, and a man knows that you cannot pull a cart alone, sometimes you have to ask for help... Sometimes, anyway." He winked.

They sat, heads together, leaving the customers barely tended and feeling neglected. Jun Yee emptied his head for the first time. He told Bau Suk everything, the deal Ah Ho had made, how they argued, how he spat, how he found Find-a-way and the fisherman and how in the end he remained trapped for the sake of money. Bau Suk leaned back and saw with curiosity that the boy in front of him had become a man but he just hadn't realised it himself yet.

"You know what my old dead ma used to say to me? 'If it is a problem that can be solved with money, then it is no real problem at all'." The boy looked unconvinced still. "Everyone has a price, boy, we just have to find it."

And he showed him, it was late in the day before a trip. If the fisherman was willing to consider them, then what did that mean, boy? That there was still space. What do they do at the very end of the day if there are still buns left that would be no good tomorrow? Reduce the price, he replied. Yes. Of course they did. And selling buns is less risky than people smuggling, no? You would want the maximum you could get. So Jun Yee understood, there was more power in the jangling coins in his pocket than the empty seats on the fisherman's boat. A few coins short were better than no coins at all. Then he saw the patience in the fisherman's eyes, this was a man who knew to leave his line long and to wait before reeling in. Jun Yee had to mirror him, do the same and carefully play the power he had in his own hands.

So, he waited until the sun was fading and heat was turning to a gentle stroke on the skin in the early evening. With every step it came down, Jun Yee imagined that exit spinning nearer. He returned to the old man, still sitting outside, enjoying it now, pushing something round and round in his mouth, never swallowing, sucking, chewing.

"You back, boy? You found some money?"

"Uncle, hear me please..." He started deferentially, "I have a sister and she-"

"I don't want to know your story." He cut him off. "The less I know the better. And don't uncle me. I cannot eat nice words."

Jun Yee squared his shoulders and stood up from the position he had crouched into. He filled his chest with the breath that he knew might change everything for him, for Jun Ching.

"Uncle, your boat leaves in hours. You still have space on your boat, or you would not even risk talking to me now. There is no one else who will come to you so late and those seats will remain empty if you do not take us." The fisherman looked up at him. A wriggler, he thought. "Empty seats are wasted money, Uncle, wasted risk. Why not take what we have and reduce that waste. No one will know, we want to disappear so we will speak to no one. If not tonight, for us it will be never." Jun Yee held his expelled breath now. He wanted to say more, he could have begged even but he had to hold. Let the silence do its work, let the carefully cast words rise in the fisherman's mind before he tried anything else. A minute passed before the fisherman looked up at him again, maybe two, stretching, elastic.

"You know the time. Be there. The boat will not wait for anyone."

Jun Yee almost forgot to thank him before he turned and ran, ran back to Jun Ching, ran for pure elation and to run out the excitement that he knew he must conceal when he got home. He ran fast enough not to see Bau Suk, smiling from the shadows.

And so, it was done. By the time he finally slowed, Jun Yee decided not to tell Jun Ching. The less she knew the better. A heavy stone cradled in the pit of his stomach told him, the sister that came back was different to the one who went away last year.

And this one might try to stop him. This one who he didn't know a year ago - this one that Sum didn't know at all. He had so often tried to block out the memory of Sum's death that it slapped him in the face suddenly to realise it was tomorrow. Tomorrow to the day that he stood next to her body face down in the sand. Was it possible, he thought to himself, that the date that brought them such misfortune last year could bring good this year? And was it really only a year? That small hand on the back of his neck that called to him from far away, called him back. That call was fading, retreating behind the same fog he had seen in Sum's eyes that he never dared follow before, but this time had to be different. Sum was gone, out of sight before he understood but Jun Ching he could grasp, and he had to grasp. He had failed to see the beginning when they sent her to the Terrapin, but he could see it now, as she backed further into the fog with her silent acceptance of this new fate. And just as she had called him back, he knew now he would go after her, into the fog, retrieve her from Sum. He would not allow for this circle to close around him again.

Chapter Eighteen

The night before the wedding all the women were gathered in the main room and all the men banished to the courtyard. The married aunts were invited back to join their voices to the laughter, to make it extra loud so all the neighbours and passersby could hear – if a show was to be played then it must be a complete show, Ah Ho reminded herself. The men in the courtyard took long drags of their pipes, exchanging what could only be described as a slightly ashamed glance when their eyes should accidentally catch. Even the boys played quietly in the middle of them, all the boys, except Jun Yee.

The warm glow of yellow electricity from a single bulb lit up the laughing mouths and serious eyes supported by several candles around the room. Full bellies made for louder laughs and this evening everyone had had enough to eat – it had been a feast, in Jun Ching's honour, overflowing bowls of rice, fish, steamed whole chicken, eggs, soup and now there was even dessert to come. In the kitchen, Penny hacked a fist-sized chunk of yellow rock sugar with the heavy meat cleaver into small pieces and tossed them into boiling water, then with the same cleaver, delicately sliced several slivers of fresh ginger, slipping them off the blade straight in with the sugar and the few salty tears she had let roll down her wide face. Jun Yee came in then from the back courtyard rubbing his hands on the back of his trousers. She wiped her nose with a sniff on her sleeve still clutching the meat cleaver whose blade obscured her face for a moment. He felt a little anger subside looking at Penny, but it came rearing back up as a shout came from the other room.

"Penny! Where are those *tong yuen*?"

"*Lei la*! Coming!"

Making sure the sugar had completely melted in the boiling ginger water, she rolled little white balls of dough off the side of a plate with gentle hands. The little balls were filled with sweet ground sesame seeds, black and grainy. They needed only a few minutes rolling around in the water to soften up their glutinous jackets before she fished them out with a little netted spoon. Each one caught, nowhere to hide or run to, even the last one trying to make a break for it dancing around with the bubbles. Three each in each of the rice bowls with the sugar water, a tray laid full. Penny brought them out to another chorus of raised voices and cheering. Everyone was included in this round, even her own mother who for once was not left working in the dark outside. Four Auntie remembered these *tong yuen*, they stuck in her throat last time, all night until she went to sleep and had to sleep with her mouth stretched wide open, trying to clear it before her new husband came to get her the next morning. She'd had no such treat since then and often thought how much better it would have been if she had choked on them, for them to find her dead in the morning.

Concentrating hard on Jun Ching, who she could just see in the middle of the room, she willed her to splutter and choke too. That would be preferable for her, but she didn't. She carried on looking up at the false smiles around her, her eyes bright, laughing with them.

From the middle of the crowd of women, Jun Ching heard and saw nothing beyond their immediate circle. She didn't see Jun Yee creep round the edge of the room and join the men outside, she didn't see Four Auntie hunched in the corner of the room on a small folding stool, she didn't even see Penny darting in and out with bowls sloshing sweets. It was almost as if there was an unspoken rule that at least three women had to be speaking over each other at any one time and those voices came together to weave an atmosphere both hot and loud in her ears. It hurt slightly but she liked it, particularly as early on, Nine Auntie was told to keep her mouth shut and her jagged comments inside of her where the only thing they could cut was her own stomach. That made Jun Ching smile. Nine Auntie had sulked for a little while until more food was put in her chubby, piggy hands and she soon forgot herself.

"It's you *la*, Six Sister! You have had the best fortune! Look at you and your rich husband." Someone shouted.

"Us? We have no money, you know that!"

"You have more than the rest of us!"

"*Tch!* And you? We may have more money, but you have sons – two as well! I haven't got a son!"

"Yet!" Another aunt screeched from somewhere. "You have to try harder. Or at least more often!" They cackled between them and pretended to argue on until someone shouted above them.

"*Wai wai!* We're forgetting about Gwai! What about her *la*?"

"Ha! Second Sister?! Married to our dead, old lame donkey Second Brother? Rest in peace Second Brother - hope you're having a good rest!" A burst of laughter cut short when they suddenly realised they had gone too far. Gwai ignored them turning away. She wanted no part of this now. It seemed vulgar. Her own voice, once the loudest of them all, now refused to join the chorus, a chorus that the fish wives talking up their catches in the market for their customers would have been proud of. But this sale was already done, she thought then pushed it out of her head before she could admit again her role in this play. Ah Ho hammered her walking stick on the floor.

"Enough! Have some respect."

She was astonished at times at how stupid her own daughters had turned out to be. They had no sense of what was happening in front of them. She had, of course, kept the details to herself intentionally but were they so unaware that they didn't notice the full rice bucket, the new clothes, the slightly fuller bellies all that happened at the same time as this wedding. Irritation climbed up her spine. For a moment, she remembered when they were all little, when Sum and Choi led the pack and now they were both dead. Jun Ching was watching her. Sum glinted at her from her eyes and Ah Ho looked away. There was nothing she could do now. The rice was cooked, time to eat it, even if they refused it would just rot. There can be no regrets now. There had to be this happy show. All her life, that's what she had hated the most - the show. "Third Daughter – you do it."

They tittered still whilst the red clothed package was brought out again, unwrapped and laid on the table. Three Auntie withdrew the red comb and stood behind Jun Ching taking her plaits out of her hair, shaking them loose so that her silky dark brown hair flowed down past her elbows. As she did this, Ah Ho took out each item in the package holding it up to her.

"These gifts are from your new family, from your husband's family and you must use them to look after your new husband. This needle and thread are for you to mend his clothes when they are worn and have holes in them. This ruler and these scissors are for you to measure cloth and help to make new clothes for him when you can no longer mend the old ones. These represent the duties of the wife amongst others and you must do as they tell you." She paused, waiting for some sign of understanding from Jun Ching who took a moment before remembering to nod.

"The comb and the mirror are for this evening, hold the mirror and look at yourself, see who you are and who you must become. Start now."

Jun Ching watched in the little mirror as Three Auntie took section after section of her hair and started combing. The teeth of the comb scraping gently across her scalp flashed a picture of Sum brushing her hair every night on a plastic fold-away bed with the sound of the street below. Tears leapt down her cheeks before she could stop them. The women around her laughed at her drowning out the street sounds and she laughed too. What a thing to remember at that moment. She had given no real thought to her new family or even to what would happen past this wedding. It couldn't be any worse than the Terrapin, she thought, and she couldn't change it, so why worry. She tried to pin down where that gap was where the worry should have been. Right now, she felt a blank space for these women and that wasn't anywhere in her body. In her head she felt grateful to her grandmother for making sure she would never miss her or them. She felt for Penny, she would be sorry to leave her. Sum she could take with her when she went, though she thought less and less of her as the seasons faded into each other. It was Jun Yee. There it was, in the very top of her stomach, a stretched sensation like someone pulling taut an elastic band. How would she see him? He always made it to the Terrapin's, but this was different, permanent. Once she was married, she would belong to her new family, not his responsibility anymore. Maybe he would stop coming. The elastic band pulled taut and that would grow until tomorrow, when they finally came to get her. Only then would she know what it feels like when the band was let go. The anticipation was the worst part, in some ways she wished she could just go now.

Having combed out the kinks in her hair, Three Auntie started the wedding preparation rhyme in a calm and rhythmical tone. Somewhere someone lit some incense. Tiny swirls of smoke curled round the room. The comb, starting at the very front of her hair line, pulled slowly through in one long motion as she spoke, then a second time and finally a third.

"One comb, combs to the very end. Two combs, combs till children and grandchildren fill the floor. Three combs, combs till white hair comes together at the end."

Three Auntie tied the red string in her hair for luck. The women cheered when she finished, the clapping travelling out to the men outside who threw glances at Jun Yee sitting on the top step with his back to them all, made of stone.

Hours later, the house was silent. Snoring seeped through the gaps in wooden planks and waving curtains assuring Jun Yee that it was safe to move.

"Ching Ching." He whispered, shaking her shoulder. "Ching Ching. Wake up. We've got to go." She slept face down so all he saw was a mass of hair before she turned her face towards him. A small trail of drool fled from the corner of her mouth and several red lines overlapped each other on her cheek where she had slept on the crumpled blanket. "It's time to wake up."

Thinking she was late for her morning chores, she got up. No faster than usual but having forgotten that if it had been morning it would have been her wedding day and she would have no chores anyway. But it wasn't morning. The sky outside was still inky black and the house covered in the muffled silence of stale sleeping breath. She turned to ask him what was going on but finger to his lips she knew to say nothing and follow him. He guided her down the stairs, pointing for her to place her feet on the same places he did at the edge of the steps to avoid any creaks. The wood was cool under her bare feet, she could feel the splits in the planks where the sea's humidity had made them expand and contract like wooden lungs.

Downstairs, he pointed to the front door then held up his palms, asking her to wait there. He disappeared through the curtain to the kitchen and out the back. He tiptoed over the sleeping bodies of cousins who had not woken earlier and stumbled in to sleep. They will wake in the morning slightly damp from the morning air, shivering to crawl into their mothers' beds like babies. He thought to himself and smiled despite that it made this bit a little more difficult. He looked up and with a stab of panic realised the low tree where he had hidden their packs, where Four Auntie usually crouched, was in direct line of sight of the sleeping cousins. He thought it would be a safe place to hide them since no one ever went near her, but he hadn't counted on her being included in the celebrations that night, leaving her tree empty. If any of the cousins had seen them, they could have moved them, or worse, they could have told someone and if Ah Ho knew… He couldn't think of that possibility now. He needed those packs, it had all their things in it, all the money he had been saving, without it they would get nowhere, they might as well go back upstairs and wait for the wedding sale. He leapt over the remaining inert limbs and as silently as he could bounded over, frantically scanning the branches. They weren't there. It wasn't even a matter of looking thoroughly. They simply weren't there. He cursed himself. Of course, they saw them, Jun Ching's pack is red, they would see that. But they never sleep out in the back courtyard, they always sleep in the front where the breeze is stronger. They weren't supposed to be here. He smacked his head hard with the heel of his hand again and again. What was he going to do? Staying is not an option. He swore. He swore it to himself.

Jun Yee sank to his heels, his entire body curled into a solid stone, his hands buried in his hair, clutching at clumps, pulling them out. He rocked back and forth between his toes and heels, his throat tensed, seconds from wrenching a howl from his stomach when, as he raised his face to the sky, a bird called out. Quietly, gently and just the once. But it came from the side, in the dark by the wall. It couldn't be, there were no night birds here. He squinted into the darkness and crept a step closer, a scratch of a foot across dirt urged him closer still. In the darkness he made out Four Auntie's crouched outline. She stood up, at full height still shorter than him, at the very edge of the shadow. Their hands met between them. He looked down, his skin painted pale blue in the moonlight, hers a dark grey with the line of the shadow drawn across the packs as she handed them over. The red cloth shone bright now in a field of monochrome. She didn't dare cross over the boundary of the shadow, nor did he dare to go into that darkness, a darkness he wasn't sure if he would be able to leave again. Somewhere behind him he knew his sister would be started to wander, waiting for him and below her in the streets their chance of escape was also moving on. He had to catch it, he felt it ticking away in his chest. There was no time or space to change anything for Four Auntie now. He knew what she risked being out here, taking that extra step that wasn't asked of her. In the silence he grasped her hands and squeezed their gratitude into them until she pushed them away gently, urging him to go.

He turned and skipped over the uneven ground. His pack was slightly heavier, fuller it seemed. He paused to pull aside one corner of the cloth and saw stuffed inside a handful of small, white steamed buns wrapped in leaves. They must have been meant for breakfast in the morning. He looked back to thank her again. Her back would pay for this in the morning under Ah Ho's stick compounded by the anger of discovering they had gone. Or would they simply forget about the buns in the mayhem? There was no way to know. Four Auntie had stepped out a little now, half in moonlight, half in shadow. He wavered to go back to her, but she motioned for him to go. He gave her a low bow, his head close to his knees. He felt the strength of his straight back returning as it did when he used to dive off piers and slip into the harbour waters. The familiarity warmed him then he turned and was gone.

Jun Ching had started to wander back through the house looking for her brother. He found her by the kitchen curtain, grabbed her wrist and dragged her out through the house without a backward glance. Down the concrete front steps and into the street he suddenly stopped, whispered to her to wait. Don't move. Not even an inch. Hold the packs. He flew back up to the house, three, four steps at a time and was back gliding down the steps with the fluidity of a stream over rocks, barely a bump, with the picture of Sum from the sitting room sideboard in his hand, in its frame. He slowed down as they started moving again, his body in communion with the dark now, dancing with no effort, speeding and pausing in perfect unity. Down the street he guided them, whispering still as the neighbours, like them, like everyone in the village, slept with their doors open to entice a breeze in the summer.

The streets were large with emptiness, no lights and only a very occasional oil burner or bare bulb threw a weak glow from someone's window. In the sky, there was no sign of dawn, no pale grey tinge to the edges of the sky to give away the sun's approach. Jun Ching could see now that it was deep into the night, not even touching dawn. This was the sky she saw and wept with at the Terrapin's house when she had given her a meal of cane on pig flesh as her Mistress used to say. Jun Ching always the pig. They skirted the main part of the village where occasionally a low hum, a shout or laugh, came tripping towards them where men were still drinking.

They were heading for the water – this was the same way Jun Yee had run when they found Sum. But this time he was taking their ma with them, clamped under his arm now her stilled eyes peeping over his arm at Jun Ching. At the corner of the next road, the water shimmering in the background, a couple of figures sat, outlined by the moonlight. They skidded to a stop almost tripping over their own feet. They couldn't see their faces, could be anyone, drunk men who had forgotten the way home or people who would recognise them, raise an alarm. They could go around, take a few minutes longer but the only way to the jetty lay behind them, they would have to circle back round anyway. Jun Yee's gut twisted. He had to make it to the pier, the tiny boat with the blinking yellow light wouldn't wait. The fisherman had made that clear. No waiting and no refunds. They were high visibility and high risk enough as it was. Jun Ching could actually see it from here, the light bobbing up and down gently on the waves at the end of the makeshift wooden pier.

They had to go ahead. There was no hiding that they weren't meant to be out of doors and no hiding in shadows or the doorways of others either. He glanced back the way they came. Nothing yet, but he couldn't be sure they hadn't been discovered. Any uncle could be running them down right now. Jun Yee straightened his back, drawing himself up as tall as possible and strode forwards. He felt Jun Ching slip her fingers into his back pocket. It cleaved his chest in two. It was the first time she had done it since she had been back, and he hadn't even noticed how much he had missed it. He grabbed her head and squeezed it to him.

"Don't worry, everything's fine." He whispered into her hair. And stepped forward again.

A million thoughts ran through his mind. He checked, the alleyway on his left would be the easiest to dart down if needed. He wasn't sure where it ended though, they might miss their boat. Then what? They could try walking to the next village, but it was too easy for Ah Ho to pick them up there. They couldn't blend in – anywhere they went they would be watched, and Ah Ho could trace them. Each step took them closer to having to make a choice. They would have to hide. Find somewhere deserted until the next boat but that was months. Or find someone they could trust. There was no one. They walked as far to the other side of the road as they could, hugging the dark. He hoped at most only he was visible, that he was covering Jun Ching. If the figures made one move towards them, they would run, straight for the boat. They could probably make it. It wasn't too far, and Jun Ching was stronger now, legs longer. He was running out of time to think. Suddenly one of them laughed, loud and unselfconsciously. Not the laugh of anyone who could see past their immediate surroundings, not one looking to catch anything at all except for more alcohol perhaps.

They relaxed and hurried on, less cautious now, eager to be away. Their feet reached the jetty which bobbed up and down this evening, the waters unsettled. They wobbled their way down looking slightly drunk. At the end, the fisherman perched on his heels at the very tip of his boat moving with the waves, secure only as a bird gripped on with its claws. The single yellow bulb flickered and swung behind him, pale under the canopy, covering half the boat and throwing shadows over bare boards and huddled faces. Somewhere below them a generator whirred.

They felt the pier move more violently, the slapping sound of flip flops on wood, as another passenger hurried onto the boat behind them dropping a flip flop into the water with a plop. He snatched it from the surface and looked up directly at Jun Ching for a moment. The bones in his cheeks and jaw stood out cutting into the night, his head too big, protruded from his clothes like a very old turtle. The fisherman was up now, pulling in the rope, hand over hand. He sucked his teeth at them and jerked his head towards the boat.

Jun Yee jumped onto the boat, his feet landed in an inch of cold water. He turned, holding his hand out to help Jun Ching over but she had already jumped herself and was standing with him. The fisherman moved to the rear of the boat and with a long pole steered it round in a wide circle. They shifted to the other side. Jun Yee noticed for the first time then how low the boat sat in the water. How the bigger waves already lapped high and slipped over the sides. Sum's words came back to him telling them how scared she was, how she spent the journey scooping out water from the bottom of the boat and that fear leached into him. The boat rocked as people shifted to find their seats. It became clear there wasn't actually enough room for everyone on the boat. Every word Sum ever said about how frightening the sea was, how heartless, how powerful, made him want to drag Jun Ching right back out onto the jetty. What was he doing? What was the right decision? He had in his mind a bigger boat he supposed, a drier boat, a scary journey but not one that rode the very line between swimming and sailing. Was he taking Jun Ching away from or to the end of her story? There was no time to answer any of these questions but the realisation that he hadn't thought of any of this scraped his chest hollow. He felt suddenly stupid, stupidly young and naive. The tension he forced into his legs to keep them still paralysed him, and he sat coiled in the dark clutching her to him. They had pushed away from the jetty before he could let go.

The entire boat sat in silence listening to the prow cut through the water, each enveloped by thoughts of danger, of security left behind. Then a shout rang out. A single shout, like a single firecracker gone off by accident. Everyone on the boat looked back rocking it even more and more water slopped over the sides. Running to the pier were two outlines, one fat, one thin, the thin one way out in front. They were too far from shore to hear what they shouted but they shouted again. They were on the far end of the jetty now. Jun Yee grabbed Jun Ching's hand and squeezed. He looked back up to the fisherman for a sign, a clue as to what he was going to do. Turn around? Turn them in?

"Don't stop." Jun Yee whispered in a firm voice. It was his decision to make. "Keep going. We are gone."

The fisherman's face said nothing as he watched the two figures then he leaned over and flicked off the gas lamp, plunging them into moonlit darkness and continued his rhythmic work of the oar.

On the jetty, the fat uncle caught up with the thin one. Heavy breaths filled the air between them. Their voices would be wasted cast out there now catching nothing. They could not see the fisherman's face before the lamp died off but they both knew who he was with the equal certainty that they knew they would never say his name. They sat down feeling the sway of the jetty beneath them, allowing the silence to form the story they would tell and retell for the rest of their lives. Shimmering and blurring in their old age - was it the children or was it Sum they watched sailing away until it eventually didn't matter anymore as no one listened or no one remembered who they were talking about. What they did remember always was the shift that took place here, the pebble that felt like a rock dropped in water and its ripples that meant everyone suddenly doubted the inevitability of their path. That from here on in, everyone under Ah Ho, whether they took the chance or not, wondered 'what if' for a different reason. They were the first to be caught up in the effect so that they were able to return and lie that they weren't sure if they saw them, didn't know who the fisherman was, that there was nothing more to be done. They were the first ripple.

Once the boat was facing the open water, the fisherman left his oar and came round to collect the rest of the fares from the few who hadn't managed to pay in full in advance, like Jun Yee. He had it now, but it would clear his pockets completely. He had no thought as to what they would do when they arrived, he would have to find work straight away but at least they had their papers so they wouldn't be sent back. But the fisherman stepped over them, passing them by. He stood up, his money clutched in his hand. The boards creaked beneath him.

"Excuse me Uncle, you didn't see us. We still need to pay."
"Pay? Bau Suk paid already."
"What? He couldn't have, I have the money here." He showed him the scrunched-up notes in his palm. He looked down at them before pushing them aside with his forearm.
"You think I don't want to take it? But no, I'm sure. Bau Suk paid this afternoon."

Jun Yee and Jun Ching both looked back towards the shore, to Bau Suk, to the bakery, to where Sum had come from and led them, but the dark had pulled the land back into itself with only a few pinpricks of light here and there still blinking. Their eyes found nothing now. The first of the bigger waves on open water hit them. The boat creaked, a voice of its own, old and weak, exactly as Jun Yee had heard it in Sum's story. He heard it as that, the repeated striking chord of his ma's journey playing to him now. He prayed that they weren't singing the same song.

Jun Ching found a space they could squeeze in on one of the benches running along each side of the boat facing each other. They were near the front and from here the breeze made their hair dance and blew away the stagnant heat of the shore. It felt fresh like the water itself splashing her face, running over her skin, washing away the sweat and tears. Jun Yee gulped lung-fulls greedily with his eyes closed whilst Jun Ching took in the other passengers. Eleven others there were, including them, that's thirteen and the fisherman is fourteen, *sup sei* – sounds like death, definite death, that's not a good sign she thought to herself. A bone-faced man sat opposite, the same breeze cooling them shook his bones against his skin. Best not to think about it, she told her thoughts and rubbed her thumbs in her palms without thinking. She wondered what was happening on the shore, what would the uncles say when they got back. Who would Ah Ho be angry with? With her and Jun Yee of course, but she would need someone present to shout at, to actually beat. Or was that the Terrapin who did that? It was all starting to bleed into itself and each other in her mind. She started trying to sift through but suddenly realised she didn't need to anymore. It didn't matter. There was no point in worrying, there was only one way to go now, following the tide, and like the shoreline itself, all the rest was far behind her and getting further with the crest of every wave they climbed. Besides, in this moment she was happier than she had been in a long time. If this was her last moment that would be okay as well. Her face crept into a smile.

"What are you smiling at?" Jun Yee asked, watchful.

"Nothing. I'm just happy. I'm lucky. I was thinking, if I die here now, I'd still be happy." He clicked his tongue at her in irritation and she changed tack. He didn't want to hear these things, but she was. With no threat of a cane, no shouting, no insults, all there was to do was sit with him. She couldn't ask for more. Or perhaps, just one thing more, Sum, and the smell of her sandalwood soap. "And what are you thinking about, Brother?"

"Not much. That we don't need to do anything for lots of hours now. We can just float and float on the waves for a while." He paused before looking at her. "Are you tired? You can sleep for a bit if you like. Shuffle down here and you can lean on my legs."

She nodded and slid onto the floor of the boat and rested her head on the side of his knees. A growing puddle of sea water seeped into a cold damp patch across her bottom, but she didn't move or care. The breeze of the open sea swept across her face and in doing so swept away something else too. She didn't know what, a shadow, a dust. Just something and she felt fresh again. She just closed her eyes and let the heavy warm hand of content fall onto her chest.

When she woke the hand was gone. A different hand gripped her heart, a cold and a mean one. Eleven pairs of black eyes darted from one to the other, agitated. Something was wrong. The boat lurched up and down as the waves tossed it up and caught it back down again. How had she not woken before now, she thought. The damp patch on her bottom had spread down her thighs and up her back. She put her hand down to push herself up and found it in inches of water. The puddle now washing back and forth over her toes that now felt like loosely packed soaked prunes. Jun Yee was still there.

"How long have I been asleep?"

"A long time, I'm surprised you slept that long. I think we're very nearly there." He stretched his legs, rubbing his knee that she had just freed.

"What's that sound?" The sound of frying fish in a giant wok surrounded them.

"It's raining. It's just a little storm. Nothing to worry about."

She thought he should tell the others that. They looked worried. They were murmuring to each other, casting furrowed brows out past the prow of the boat into more and more sea. She looked up to see the sky had turned a murky grey, clouds and dawn. She could make out the horizon in front now.

Jun Yee saw her face searching for something to latch onto and that the only thing she had was him and that stupidly, she had believed everything he said. He felt he had run out of lies for her now, he was jangling an empty bucket in which only his own heart thumped against the sides in fear. They were going to drown. How had he not seen this? Their path so far had been a stony, poorly-trodden and a lonely one, and he had made it even worse by veering them off into an vastness they had no knowledge of. There was nothing to hold onto around them in mind or body. The boat was heaving up and down maniacally and holding onto the sides made no difference. And he felt the same. He had made a choice, a poor choice that dragged his sister behind him and now it was revealed to him how groundless this choice was, that he had taken her where there was nothing to hold onto, nothing to save them and his voice alone would cost her the very breath she smiled with every day. These felt like his final moments. There could be nothing after this and he understood himself that he was defeated. There was nothing else left he could do but be swept away and surrender to the paths that they were placed on, alone. His head sank trying to block out each of these thundering blows to his chest.

The man sat opposite them was shaking his head, arms wrapped tight around himself, rocking at odds with the boat and everyone else in it. Jun Ching hadn't noticed him before. He was muttering something again and again, the same few words, but the two people next to him were either ignoring or couldn't hear him as the murmuring rose, straining at the edges. The rain pushed now harder in waves. They were surrounded by waves, being thrown up then pushed back down again by sheer mountains of water. The man shot up out of his seat pointing at the horizon.

"The shore! I can see it. Faster. Now. We're saved!" His weight unbalanced the creaking boat even further. A violent wave slapped the prow at that moment throwing everyone back and to the side. He fell, body still rigid and arm pointing, over the side. Several men lunged towards him to catch anything, an arm, a shirt, hair even, to be able to pull him back with the fisherman shouting in the background. The combined momentum rolled the boat and Jun Ching felt herself flipped surprisingly gently in the air then over, crashing into the waves.

Water smacked her in the chest. She expected it to be freezing but it wasn't. It was cold but not freezing. She couldn't take a breath. Something somewhere in her chest felt stuck and no matter how hard she tried to heave it out it would not come. Sound had stopped. Water pressed on her ears; thicker than usual, like she should be able to walk on it, but she couldn't. Her arms kicked and her legs flailed for moments. She felt her flip flops fall off her feet, her toes trying to grip onto them and failing. Jun Yee's words came staccato back to her now: *float your body, kick this way, your arms - move them like this,* the words were forever drenched in the warm sunlight of an afternoon long ago trying to teach her to swim. But the words were no use to her now other than to calm the panic in her chest, that she was finally in the water that she had been told to be so frightened of her whole short life. She didn't need flip flops now. Down here, under the water, everything was three beats slower, ordinary movements turned graceful. Perhaps ordinary thoughts turned graceful too. And that grace turned to peace. Her body quieted and for a few seconds she enjoyed the strange tickling sensation of the air bubbles in each of her nostrils. Then in the distance in front of her, she saw something move. She squinted, it was too dark to make out properly. It was a figure, she thought, long black hair suspended in mid-breeze in the water. She couldn't see the face. A woman. Jun Ching watched her, stretched one hand out towards her. A little laugh slipped out and the air bubbles in her nostrils chased each other out and up to the surface.

A hard sensation was building in her chest, every breath she had ever taken trying to burst out. Her lungs choked quietly now, her stomach buckled, spasms slowly climbing her throat. She reached out her hand, brown from the sun towards the pale, almost translucent one. She felt her mind unclench and wander, picturing her life like the water that surrounded her, slipping, dripping through long fingers. It felt good. It felt easy and comfortable. She coughed and dragged in her first mouthful of cold, salty water. Her body shocked at water not air, tried again, snorting water burning through her nose. She drifted closer to the figure with every mouthful she swallowed. Another mouthful. The face still obscured. And another. The dark around her brightened, colours grew more vibrant even as she watched, greens, blues, greys. Everything in view was tingling. Something swam out of the corner of her vision. Her fingertips brushed against a cheek. Jun Ching felt the relief seep through her. A sigh and another mouthful. She smiled faintly for no one to see.

But it was wrong somehow. The cheek should have been cold. It wasn't. It was warm. The gentleness gone, unwelcoming. The fingers were clutching at, not reaching towards her. It was as though the breeze that blew away the dust on her last few months had cleared her vision now. If that was Sum, she did not want to go with her. She was not her, didn't want to become her. She could feel and see, whilst Sum saw nothing, not even her, her own daughter. She wouldn't go. She would not leave Jun Yee. She had watched for so long to see how things would be, how they would end. She couldn't just watch and see her own end. She felt the pain of an air bubble in her chest, hard and uncompromising. This was not her end. She had to do something to change it, otherwise, it was always Jun Yee. Always Jun Yee who fought, who protected, who was the hero in her story. But who would protect him? Who would see the soft parts of the backs of his knees? Who would know to pull him back from the punishing places he goes in his head? But was it too late now? The pain grew in her chest. Her nose stung. The hand appeared again now. It all swam in front of her, confusing, it was different again. Everything was so slow. The hand, outstretched in front of her. Whose hand? She couldn't see. Her eyes dimmed further. She had to reach for it, she would trust, believe and hold onto the warm fingers.

His search was silent and urgent. She wasn't on the surface. Jun Yee could see that easily. But that meant at best she was drowning right in this moment, at worst that she was already gone. Drowning. Drowning, the one thing they had been avoiding their whole lives, was happening to her right now because he had led her here. It was him who did it. A ragged breath and he dove down again. He was surprised how much he could see down here. To his left side, the bone-faced man was swimming after a sinking bag, legs kicking weak like a child. He turned again, eyes scanning back and forth over every inch of murkiness. Nothing. His body moved as it always had in the water, easily, with little worry. All the terror in his chest now was for her. He saw nothing at first then all of a sudden, he saw her below, frighteningly still except for one hand outstretched in front of her. Towards what? There was nothing there. Why wasn't she…? What? Swimming? Fighting? Anything? She was perfectly calm, just hanging there. There was something below her too, sinking, a shadow he couldn't make out and couldn't waste time thinking about. Then there it was. A kick. A buckle of the body and thump of her fist on her chest. He was so nearly there. He twisted round in front of her and stretched his body full length, as far as he could towards her, one hand in front of her but still could not quite reach her to pull her to him. He saw her eyes unseeing and heard a roar inside his head. If she was gone, if she was dead, he would make himself live and punish himself every day for what his choice had done to her. It could not be true, that reality that threatened in his head could not be, he could not allow it. He screamed to her silently under the water again and had to believe that she could hear him. Then her hand raised to his and reached for his fingers. He found one more kick, propelling himself closer, grabbing her fingers. He had her.

The fingers had grabbed hers. Something else had grasped her collar at the back of her neck and yanked what she guessed to be upwards, she couldn't tell. Her mind was out of focus. The figure before gone. Her arms and legs responded without command, snapping into action, pushing through the water again for what seemed like longer than she could survive. Then a pop, sound returned with a hundred buckets of water crashing down, then thud and pain as she smacked the top of her head onto something hard above the surface of the water. It was black, her eyes were open but returned nothing. She threw up, gushing water, her stomach forcing what she swallowed back out of her. Then panting that echoed. Other noises echoed back, drips onto water, sloshes of waves both inside and out. A bigger wave bobbed her up with more force and something hit her head again. Reaching up her hand met wood, a long piece but thin, a shelf. She held on, giving her legs a chance to rest. Another splash and she felt something pop through the water next to her.

"Ah Mui, are you okay?"

Jun Yee pressed his cheek hard to hers, his hand on the back of her neck. She nodded, coughing and sniffing at the same time. "The boat turned. That man screaming tipped it. We're under it now. The other people are everywhere, swimming for the shore.

I don't even think they are all swimming in the same direction. We're okay here for a few minutes, catch your breath, but we can't stay for long. The boat is too easy to see. Are you sure you're okay? You didn't drink in any water or choke or anything, did you?"

She didn't think she should mention she drank mouthfuls of sea water, almost greedily. Or anything else she saw down there for that matter. It seemed unfair and hurtful somehow. "No, Brother. I'm fine."

"Good, when you've caught your breath we've got to go okay? Ready? Now." A deep breath and they dove together, Jun Yee leading the way under the edge of the boat and back up the other side. Everything felt loud. A fractured shriek bobbed in and out of the water.

"Broth-" She gasped, before salt water rushed down her throat. Spluttering, coughing. "Brother!"

"I've got you. Kick your legs. Slowly. And try to keep your bottom up and float on the surface more if you can."

He guided her away from the boat. She looked back and in the weak dawn light the upturned boat looked to her like an empty tortoise shell floating on the surface. She could see from here the broken hull, splintered wood bleeding from it in pieces. Jun Yee wedged one of these under Jun Ching's arms to help keep her head out of the water and give her a rest when she needed it. The waves seemed to have calmed now it had claimed the boat. The rain turned down to a drizzle. She tried kicking.

"That's it Ching Ching, follow me. Swim as much as you can, like I taught you before, remember? When you're tired, you just hold onto me, okay?" She nodded. "No, Mui, you have to talk to me. I can't see you in this light especially if we are swimming. I'll be in front so I can't see you. You must talk to me if anything is wrong, understand?"

"Understand."

"I don't know how far it is we have to swim but it's going to feel like a long time. Are you ready?"

"Ready."

And they set off on a journey they were already on.

There were a few men from the boat swimming in one direction in front of them, so they followed them. It wasn't until they passed the body of the panicked man that Jun Ching noticed that the shrieking had stopped. His face was still scared, stuck in that moment, never reaching the peaceful slipping away to the underworld. Dragged there instead.

They swam, slowly, supported by the water. The waves that had slapped their little boat into submission seemed sated and calmed, and now they simply floated on the top like froth. The other men who were swimming disappeared from sight ahead of them and still they kicked. Talking only occasionally. A reassuring squeeze of a hand every now and then and some very wet smiles.

It had felt like hours. But both of them had little energy to start with from months of minimal food. Although the time with the Terrapin had made her muscles more capable, stronger, it had also battered her stamina, stripped her of reserves that Ah Ho had not had time to replenish whilst she fattened her up. Jun Ching was grateful for the wood beneath her chest. It buoyed her more than she wanted to admit to Jun Yee. She was shifting her weight onto to it more and more, pulling herself further up so her body was simply draped over it. It dipped under her, sinking, jolting her eyes open with a splash of water down her throat. The weight of the water was becoming unbearable. Her legs were slowing, unresponsive, hanging in the water behind her as she leaned more heavily on the plank dipping further still. A sharp edge wedged so far into the underside of her arms that it hurt more to release it than to leave it. Her legs were going numb. She could barely feel them to kick anymore. She slowed further and Jun Yee got smaller and smaller ahead of her.

"Ching Ching!" Her eyes must have slipped shut again for a second. Jun Yee was growing large again in front. "Ching Ching, you can't go to sleep, you understand? Come *la*, put your hand in my back pocket like always and I'll pull you with me. Don't let go, that's all you have to do."

How long they went like that for she wasn't sure. She drifted in and out of unconsciousness chanting to herself *'don't let go of the plank, don't let go, that really would be it then, don't let go'*. Each time she opened her eyes, she saw the back of Jun Yee's head bobbing in front of her, felt the wet cloth of his pocket twisted in her fingers until finally when the sky was spitting its first rays of sunshine through the clouds turning it from murky grey to blue, she opened her eyes to Jun Yee rubbing her cheek.

"Ah Mui, little sister, wake up. Look how close it is. We're there. We're home!" He pointed out ahead of them. She could see a lumpy shoreline, rocks, lots of big ones. She could just make out a tiny figure clawing up one, crouched low then scuttling to a patch of scrubby looking bushes. Must have been one of the men ahead of them. But Jun Yee was breathing hard. His chin and mouth dipping deeper with each bob, struggling to keep above the water. His skin was pale even in this light. His eyes black and fixed on her. "You have to swim now, okay? Take your hand out of my pocket and swim properly like I taught you. You can do it now, you've had a little rest. Straight to the rocks ahead, you hear?"

She nodded and peeled her arms off the wood under her arm pits. It stung a little, the skin there strangely dry from the compression. She readjusted it under her chest.

"Good girl. Now listen to me, when you get there, if we get separated, you have to hide, okay? Don't let anyone see you. See how that man crawled away like a beetle? You have to do that."

"But we won't get separated, Brother, will we? We'll be okay. I'll find you."

"But if you can't straight away, you need to get away from here. Find your way back to the old flat. I will find you around there. If you get too scared, see if Missy is still there. She will help."

His words were heavy, sinking in her ears. Somewhere she knew what they meant but not here and not now. She refused them.

"Okay, but you stick with me too. Don't think I can do it without you."

He turned and they moved forwards again, together side by side but unattached. The rocks drew closer and behind them to the side they could make out a small stretch of sandy beach which would have been easier to climb but far too exposed. A stray dog ambled across it looking for scraps. The sea-bed dropped away steeply under the water level so there was still some way to go before their toes could grope for it beneath them.

A sensation blew over Jun Yee as they approached. It wasn't relief. He knew they weren't safe yet. They weren't even on dry land yet. His legs were hollow now, his shoulders solid from the tension. He was slowing down, his sister's head pulling further and further away. Even his fingers were tired. His arms barely made an effort and he found his legs treading water, with each kick moving only a fraction forward. The water lapped higher up his neck, his chin, his mouth as he bobbed up and down. His eyelids mimicked the motion drooping down, down a bit more. Stinging water up his nose startled him for a moment. He was going under, down where he didn't want to go. It was okay, wasn't it, he had her away from them, brought her home. She'd be okay now. But no!

No! Not good enough, he had to make sure! He flung his arms and legs with all the strength he had left but it was useless. They were useless, they had nothing left. The water closed above his head. He could still feel the slight chill of air on his hands above the water and the warm creeping water climbing his forearms. He threw his feet out from under him with a force that felt it would pull them from his hips, ripping them from sockets but he only inched up a little before the water sucked him further down again. He imagined a giant hand, pressing down on his head, on the water, pushing him down. There was nothing he could do, no strength left. He thought if he had done enough. If there was more that he could have done or if he should have done it sooner. His thoughts blurred. He hated water. It was a bully. Pushing its way into his body, into his head now. It separated them from home. It took their Ma. As it takes him now. It will leave his sister floating with no one else left. It grew heavier and thicker all around him. Despite the heavy clambering of his thoughts, he could hear the quiet down here, pressing on his ears. Frantic, he thrashed his whole body again but nothing. Just a slow, steady pull down.

    Jun Ching turned every few minutes to make sure her brother was right behind her, just over her shoulder. He had slipped back a little, but he was still there. Until he wasn't. He just disappeared. There was no swirling spot to give away where he had been just the ever-swaying waters, unbroken. She shouted for him but nothing. She turned back. Her arms clawed throughout the water. Her legs scissored below hoping to feel something. She stopped moving finally, feeling every minute that had dripped through her grasp. Her eyes raking the shadows. And there several feet below her was a particularly dark, unmoving shadow, sinking slowly.

"No! Jun Yee no!" She shouted down at him. She thrust the plank away from her now but even as she dove down to him, fingers outstretched, she knew he was further than he had ever been.

Jun Ching refused now to let him go. She understood now that whilst she saw little of herself, she had always seen him. Her brother, she knew, went to darker places in his head, places she didn't know but that she could draw him back from. Her brother, she knew, would go where he needed to keep her safe. She understood that she knew the back of his shoulders, his outline more than she did his face and equally saw that it was time for her to be the one to lead him back firmly and permanently. For herself she was barely interested, she was happy to explore the path that was open to her but for her brother, that wasn't good enough. She forced her way through the water, down and down to his side. As she went down, she remembered standing behind his kneeling form next to Sum's body on the sand. She had brought him back then, but he had been willing to come. Would he be this time? Would she have the strength to bring him if it was just down to her? She hadn't even looked at Sum's body then, and she didn't see her now. Sum was gone, a fading idea, a shell she was willing to break to free her brother.

He wasn't far below the surface. She reached him easily though pulled and dragged with nothing to push against, not lifting him at all. He was heavy and still fighting himself. The only way to help him was to fight with him. Using his body, she pulled herself further down, below him and pushed as hard as she could, pushing him back up to the surface whilst the effort pushed her equally down. One last push, with every shred of strength both of them had combined, Jun Yee shattered the binds holding them in the invisible pattern they had felt for so long. Jun Yee broke the surface. Jun Ching repelled an extra foot further down and unexpectedly her feet hit something solid. She kicked off it and shot upwards to Jun Yee who was thrashing, choking, spluttering. He felt her rise beneath him and grabbed for her dragging her too to the surface. They clung together, flailing, dipping beneath the water, then slowly calmed. Drifting together on the surface, entwined.

The other passengers already at the shore paused, crouched at the rocks, frozen by the sight of the still children floating. They didn't see the struggle, they had just appeared. Must have drowned and their bodies for some reason risen to the surface. They should fish them out. Hide them perhaps. Make sure they stay in each others' arms. Murmuring to each other, they stood waiting for the waves to lap them gently to the rocks, securing each other, one man reached down and grabbed the nearest scrap of clothing, Jun Yee's. He was heavy, heavier than he expected the body of a child to be. The girl's body he couldn't see anymore, perhaps floated away as their grip on each other loosened in death. He pulled hard, he guessed he would be heavier with the water he had drank, the water in his clothes. But as he pulled Jun Yee's limp body clear of the water, he found it continued, a hand clasped around his forearm, his hand clasped around another forearm. The grip unyielding. They emerged finally like a child's paper chain of people, joined at the arms, holding on still. The men pulled them clear of the rocks to a patch of scrubby grass behind and left them tumbled on top of each other not knowing what to do. Until in the silence Jun Yee coughed, rose bent over to his knees, water gushing out of him. And he dragged his sister with him, not letting go of her arm, still holding on.

Jun Ching opened her eyes, everything strangely clear now without the sting of the salt water. Jun Yee hovered above her, turning her over, rubbing her back as she threw up the water that she thought she had welcomed. He pulled her into his arms then and both of them coughing still with spluttering mouthfuls of water with lungs bursting with pain.

"We did it." He said.

"You did it."

"No, we did it." He repeated.

His voice was different. An edge, hard enough to bruise on, had taken root that would never leave it. He had left in the water every doubt, every wonder and every thought that questioned how he strode along his path. And now he knew his path was his. And his sister's path was hers to walk as she wanted. And he would help her. Amongst the splintered wood of the boat lay also broken Sum's circle that he had felt unable to break free from for every one of his days, treading in her footsteps, round and round, each step was hers for him to repeat. But now he had brought them to new ground. Away from the sand, where no footprints could be made or followed where every step was their own to choose. He propped himself up on his arms, still hunched in the shadows but drawing deep, full breaths again. He stared at the pool of water he had expelled from his lungs expecting to see the images of the last year, of before that, something to say goodbye to but there was nothing, only sand. The water out of him now made him light, the incredible strength he felt now that he only had the weight of himself and his sister and not of everything that had gone before him, the weight of a whole family of tradition and unfulfilled dreams. There was only them now and he knew that they were enough.

The women from the boat appeared from the surrounding bushes and pulled them both in out of sight. They faded together with them into the shadows, the young man and his sister folded into their arms.

Epilogue

It's incredible how even the sensation of something so profound as drowning can eventually leave you. How in those few minutes your thoughts rush at you like the water down your throat. Do you want to go or do you want to stay. How many thoughts you can wade through in such a short time. How in the end, it's instinct and maybe some kind of fate that decides. And how, fifty years later, you can no longer remember what those exact thoughts were. I guess they were coughed and spluttered out at the same time I came back to the surface. Useless to me now as any such thoughts to someone who's just come back from the edge of the underworld. They say to reach the underworld, the world of the dead, you have to cross a river. I had already had enough water at that point and decided not to. I was angry when I realised I was drowning. That after all the effort I had made that I was going to go like that. No, I had thought to myself. This was no one's choice but mine, not even Ching Ching's. Mine. That's all I remember.

I guess that's when she came for me. Like she had done before, a light hand on the back of my neck to bring me back. A slight pull on my back pocket to remind me she was still there. What I thought then was she needed me. But what I hadn't realised was I had it the wrong way round. She gave me purpose whilst I was still in the shadows of my early life. Only that time in the water, her usual gentle touch wasn't enough and for the first time I felt the urgency yanking on me trying to pull me up, then an arm around my neck choking me to the surface. Then finally, the full force of her strength behind and below me, pushing me back up to the surface, hands under my armpits pulling me past her, around my waist pulling then pushing me up. With each push, she herself sinking lower as I got higher. One last shove with both hands on my backside, upwards until I flew through the skin of the water, a new being in a different world. A world where I could no longer hear the ticking beetle of fate in my ears. Or I heard it and told it to find someone else. Not us, not anymore.

Reaching the shore was a blur. A handful of us from the boat got there at the same time. I remember huge, smooth rocks to climb when I thought I had nothing left in my arms and legs and a man's face and hands that hauled me up over them. And I remember the surprise on his face at how heavy I was. How he called for help when he saw as he pulled on my one arm, I emerged from the water, my other arm followed, attached to it another arm, another body, limp and soft. The end of me. Thinking back on it now, it is like someone has erased the picture, leaving only the sound; coughing, spluttering, moaning. I cannot see Jun Ching's child face as they turned her over. Sometimes my mind tries to force Ma's face on her, when we found her on the sand, but I beat it back. It cannot be and I know it wasn't but sometimes it still laps at my dreams. At those times my gentle wife with her almond eyes and calloused hands shakes me awake, brushes away the drops of sweat and reminds me of the life we have built for ourselves - our shop, our children, our grandchildren, our decades of love.

I don't remember how or when we left those rocks or even how we found our way back. I do remember her coughing and vomiting water as I held her in my arms. I knew then as she dragged her first breaths again that we were leaving everything behind on those rocks, in that sea, that everything was different now. The busy streets, the smells, the press of people - all were in vivid colour as we wove our way back to our own street, winding up an old thread erasing our path. I licked the air, and an old familiarity tickled my tongue opening a long-forgotten box of favourite things. I laughed at how stupid it seemed that it was all waiting here unchanged. I wept at how much my sister had had to suffer whilst this was all here waiting here unchanged. I didn't know what to do then. Everything I had saved was gone. Our world was small before, I hadn't realised how small, until I tried to find us somewhere to stay where we wouldn't be recognised. I had no plan. I had thought no further than getting us back home perhaps assuming that our old life would be here for us to slip back into but of course it wasn't. I avoided anyone who would recognise us but sleeping on the streets made us an easy target.

But I also had this new sense though that the places we were going, although familiar were fresh, clear. For the first time we walked without the cloak of Ma on our shoulders. I did not think if she had done this before us, what did she think because I knew she hadn't. We had broken the thread that kept her running around the outside of her circle and were free to go beyond her rutted path.

It was nearly a year before I felt I could write to Bau Suk. It pained me to wait because I knew the fate of our boat, the fisherman and all the passengers would be news in the village. But it was news on only one side of a black hole. Bau Suk, and consequently Lien, were the only ones who knew beyond doubt we were on it. Even the uncles on the jetty couldn't be sure. To leave them thinking that we had drowned was nearly impossible but equally, I knew then that when I did write, it had to be definitive. We had to be safe. It could not be an extension of concern. So, we took those new roads, finding a Hong Kong that was undiscovered to us as children but held no apprehension for me then. Everything seemed to have taken on a different shade - I felt no fear going to shop after factory after market after trader to ask for work and something told me that each no was one step closer to a yes. That was the way it had to be. Eventually I found work, I found it in the middle of a *bau* - impressing with a recipe of Bau Suk's the baker had never heard before. It earned me a job and us both a shelter at the back of the bakery away from typhoons in the late summer and biting sea winds in the winter. When I finally spoke to Bau Suk again, I was compelled to tell him I had traded in his recipe, betrayed a secret to secure ourselves, and he laughed his belly laugh and told me that knowledge, that or any other, was all my own and mine to do with as I pleased. It was only then that I truly understood I had flipped our fortunes for good. To this day, the smell of freshly baked *baus* makes me take the deepest breath I can settling a warm hand of comfort across my chest.

It was through writing to Bau Suk that we learnt of the aftermath of our leaving. Ah Ho was furious. She was left with a marriage arrangement and no one to fulfil it. Penny's mother hid her up the fire tree at the very back of the garden taking beating after beating but never slipping one word or glance whilst Penny's tears rained above. Her daughter would not repeat her own life. If they had shared any of the work with Four Auntie over the years, they might have known their own garden better and found Penny but they didn't and Four Auntie turned her prison into her daughter's escape. After putting it off for as long as she could, Ah Ho could avoid it no more. She had to produce a girl from somewhere for the bargain, since the rice was already half gone, and she had no option other than her own. After the screaming, the spitting, the fighting were wiled out of her with the same bamboo cane, Nine Auntie was the one who filled the red carriage with red eyes and a red lined back, taking with her her bitterness, her venomous tongue and her precious pigtails. We heard nothing more of her though from time to time it makes me smile to think of her wiping the backside of her child husband. To this day, hopefully, if there's any fairness in the world.

Penny we very occasionally hear from. She stayed in the tree for a week after Nine Auntie had gone I think, Four Auntie squirrelling her scraps to eat when she could, before she snuck down - she said she was half monkey by this point. Four Auntie's act of defiance, Penny told us, would never had been possible without our first one that showed the fissures in Ah Ho's power. Penny left the village not long after, travelling as far as the fish carts would take her then working hard until she was finally rewarded with a husband who she chose for herself and daughters of her own. Her mother she wasn't able to take with her. She came back years later to demand her mother, to take her with her to her new life but she was broken to find that Four Auntie had already died after a particularly savage beating under the same fire tree. The most savage thing to me is how some people who can show us how to change the fate of our worlds, cannot or do not see that they can do it for themselves as well and remain on the same path of fate they thought they had to tread. Four Auntie will forever remain for me in the moonlit shadows.

The rest of them are unknown to us, behind a thin veil we have no interest in lifting. We know Gwai stayed in the family, servant to Ah Ho to the end. Paying her penance for a role she chose poorly. We know the venom Ah Ho funnelled into Gwai and poured on her at every opportunity twisted them into burnt, blackened trees, entwined, suffocating and propping each other up. And Gwai for her part still strong, taking it all, providing the other half of the pain that had to be to sustain the torture. We know the animosity that grew between the two women and can imagine how they poured it into each day, locking each other into unending days of jaundiced bitterness. Two women unknowingly fighting to control a matriarchal destiny that was never in their hands, stretching time taut and hard and binding them together whilst everyone gradually left around them until in the end it consumed them both.

Ah Ho lived until recently. She was over a hundred when she died. They found her sat in her chair one morning, one hand on her cane, eyes open, facing the photographs of her husband and son, her daughter stolen forever. There were no photographs of us.

As for us, I asked Jun Ching to stay with me as her body was draped across those rocks. I held her hand and squeezed my plea. And she responded. She came back to me and guided me and together we found a new way, our way, away from lines pre-drawn for us. We had good years, numerous years where she became again the girl who was curious about everything tugging at my pockets, so I never missed the beauty or laughter of a moment though she had a new focus that kept her from wandering as she used to. She saw the man I had become in the water and made sure I would never turn back though that would never have been possible and I saw in her core the little girl that did not change and that was the biggest victory of all. Her tread was ever gentle though, that flickering presence of a dragonfly, hovering, forever skimming the surface, too graceful to break it.

She stayed long enough to find me a new home, a girl with almond eyes and a gentle heart, steering me into safe waters. Then she left me again, still young though forever slightly stooped, through an illness she should have survived. She squeezed my hand in return as she laid dying, asking me to let her go and I did. I think she just chose to go this time leaving my pockets empty.

So, in the end Gwai was right. Jun Ching did die young. In some ways she died many times before she finally left me. In another way, we both drowned that night in the sea and were reborn free of the shackles of fortune they pressed on us. My life has come to be a series of delicate pages rattling past my ears reminding me of a wish I once scratched down and tied to a stone to throw up a tree. I don't know if I got my wish. I do know that Jun Ching has flicked forward, pages ahead of me, impatient for the next life and eventually I'll catch up and find her there.

ABOUT THE AUTHOR

Stephanie Moran was born and brought up in Hong Kong during British colonial rule before moving to the UK in 1997 after the handover of the territory to China.

She is fascinated by the duality of identity, particularly in shifting cultures, having experienced this throughout her childhood.

She believes that as the boundaries of the world we live in shrink, and ever more people are forced into increasingly unbearable situations, we will see more than ever the playing out of what people are willing to do to survive. And that in a few of these many heartbreaking and desperate moments, occasionally some of the most beautiful tensions and loyalties can also be witnessed.

Stephanie now works in the international development sector and lives in London with her husband and two young sons.

With thanks

To Kate Leys, whose kind words and professional guidance gave me the confidence to keep going and to keep believing in the story - thank you, it would not be here without you.

To Gaia Elkington, my dear friend, whose enthusiasm and commitment to every - single - draft of this novel made this happen. Without you, both the novel and I would be much, much poorer. Thank you.

To my boys, Billy and Arthur, dreams really do come true! Billy, thank you for your gentle wisdom and abundant affection. Arthur, thank you for bursting into our lives like the sunshine you are. I love you both, just the way you are.

To my husband, Neville, together we are both strong and true. Thank you for everything. Love you always.

Printed in Great Britain
by Amazon